W9-AYE-021

Property of
THE HOTCHKISS LIBRARY
SHARON, CONNECTICUT

The Accidental Lawman

**Center Point
Large Print**

Also available from Center Point Large Print by Jill Marie Landis:

Heat Wave
Homecoming

This Large Print Book carries the Seal of Approval of N.A.V.H.

The
Accidental Lawman

JILL
Marie
LANDIS

CENTER POINT PUBLISHING
THORNDIKE, MAINE

This Center Point Large Print edition
is published in the year 2009
by arrangement with
Harlequin Books S.A.

Copyright © 2009 by Jill Marie Landis

This is a work of fiction. Names, characters,
places and incidents are either the product of the
author's imagination or are used fictitiously, and
any resemblance to actual persons, living or dead,
business establishments, events or locales
is entirely coincidental.

All rights reserved.

The text of this Large Print edition is unabridged.
In other aspects, this book may vary
from the original edition.
Printed in the United States of America.
Set in 16-point Times New Roman type.

ISBN: 978-1-60285-538-0

Library of Congress Cataloging-in-Publication Data

Landis, Jill Marie.
  The accidental lawman / Jill Marie Landis. — Center Point large print ed.
    p. cm.
  ISBN 978-1-60285-538-0 (lib. bdg. : alk. paper)
  1. Sheriffs—Fiction. 2. Texas—Fiction. 3. Large type books. I. Title.
  PS3562.A4769A64 2009
  813'.54—dc22
  2009016707

DEC 19 2009

NORTH E   BRARY

"For the Lord will not cast off for ever:
But though he cause grief,
yet will he have compassion according
to the multitude of his mercies.
For he doth not afflict willingly nor grieve
the children of men."
—*Lamentations* 3:31–33

To my dear family, friends and neighbors.
I love you all. Thank you for giving me
the time and space to write.
(You all know I'd much rather be playing.)

"A friend loveth at all times"
—*Proverbs* 17:17

Center Point Publishing
600 Brooks Road • PO Box 1
Thorndike ME 04986-0001 USA

(207) 568-3717

US & Canada:
1 800 929-9108
www.centerpointlargeprint.com

Chapter One

Spring 1874, Glory, Texas

An overly long dry spell baked the plains and prairies of Texas until the land was grit dry as coarse sand. Unseasonably hot, incessant winds whipped the hems of ladies' skirts, sent men's hats skittering along the boardwalk, picked up the dry earth and sent it billowing down Main Street.

As Amelia Hawthorne made her way down the boardwalk fronting the two blocks of shops and stores, she clamped her left hand atop her battered straw hat, squinted and blinked in an attempt to keep the dust out of her eyes. The wind had torn her braid apart by the time she reached her destination, the First Bank of Glory.

Any other woman would have scurried for cover but Amelia had never acquired the habit of worrying about her looks. She wasn't like some of her neighbors who lingered over the new E. Butterick & Co.'s catalogue at Harrison Barker's Mercantile and Dry Goods Store or waited breathlessly for every shipment of buttons, ribbons and yard goods. She hadn't the money nor the inclination to keep up with current fashion. Serviceable dresses of sturdy fabrics that lasted for years were good enough for her.

She'd worn her long russet hair in the same simple style all her life—pulled back and woven into a single thick braid that trailed to her waist. Her daddy always told her she was pretty, though not as beautiful as her mother. She took him at his word.

She decided that if a man ever took a shine to her again, he would have to like her just the way she was—a sensible, hardworking, God-fearing woman who'd been put on this earth to care more for others than she did her looks.

Now, as Amelia clung to her straw hat with one hand, she clutched a carefully wrapped paper packet of dried arnica blossoms in the other.

Despite the turn in the weather, she was intent upon delivering the packet to Mary Margaret Cutter in hopes that a strong dose of arnica tea would ease the woman's painful arthritis. Mrs. Cutter and her husband, Timothy, had founded the Bank of Glory shortly after the war and still worked there together every day.

Seen through the thick haze of dust, the handful of other folks on the street appeared as little more than blurred silhouettes. Amelia thought she could make out two tall men in wide-brimmed hats heading in her direction, but couldn't be sure. She reached the bank and fumbled for the door handle just as another strong gust hit her.

Eyes watering from the sifting grit, she cracked open one of the double doors, reeled into the bank and slammed into a man's chest.

She felt the scratch of wool against her cheek and heard him utter "Oof!" before she ricocheted back. Off balance, she tilted sideways. The next thing she knew, she was on the floor, eye level with the knees of a man's brown tweed trousers. She watched those knees bend as the man hunkered down beside her.

"I'm so sorry! Let me help you up, ma'am." His voice was deep and calm and instantly struck an unfamiliar chord in her. How, she wondered, could sound alone warm her from head to toe?

Amelia righted herself to a sitting position and realized her hat was missing. Her hand flew to her hair, which at this point surely resembled a rat's nest.

"Are you all right, dear?" Mary Margaret called from behind her teller's window.

Amelia's vision had cleared enough to reveal that she'd not only dropped the precious packet, but the dried petals were scattered over the wooden floor of the bank.

"Oh, no!" She rolled to her knees. With her legs tangled in the folds of her skirt, she could barely move but made a valiant attempt to crawl around and brush the arnica into a pile.

At least the man had the presence of mind to

shut the door, which kept the dried flowers from scattering farther.

"You all right, Amelia?" Mary Margaret called again.

Amelia glanced up at Mary Margaret's familiar face. In her late sixties, the woman had plump, rosy cheeks and a wreath of white curly hair gathered into a topknot. She reminded Amelia of a mischievous cherub.

"No harm done. I'll be right as rain as soon as I get this gathered up." Amelia frowned over her task. She knew how much trouble Mary Margaret's arthritic hands gave her and wanted to make sure the woman had at least a portion of her waning supply.

Movement caught the corner of her eye and Amelia realized the man who'd unwittingly caused the upset was on his knees beside her. His hands were large. His long, tapered fingers appeared to be stained with indigo ink. Just now those big hands were awkwardly cupping and brushing bits of arnica across the floorboards toward her.

Sneaking a glance at his face, she saw it was closely shaven. He had a rugged jaw, full lips and straight dark eyebrows. He was studiously intent on his task. His shoulders bunched beneath a suit jacket that appeared confining on such a big man. Beneath it peeked the brass buttons of a matching vest.

The newness of his clothes and the jaunty bowler atop his head confirmed he was a gent. Either he was a new emigrant from the East, or a traveler just passing through.

They were side by side on all fours. The pile of arnica had grown to a palmful. Amelia was fumbling with the paper packet, when the front door burst open and the fragile dried bits went swirling in all directions again. Heavy boot heels pounded across the threshold. Spurs clinked against the floorboards behind her.

Then a man shouted, "Hands in the air! This is a holdup!"

Amelia swung her head around and peered over her shoulder. A lanky man with a blue bandanna wrapped around the lower half of his face waved a gun as he charged farther into the room.

A half-second later he tripped over the gent in the tweed suit and bowler hat and hit the floor beside her. The robber's gun, much too close to her now, went off. As the shot reverberated, echoing in the small room, the acrid smell of gun smoke filled her lungs. Though her ears were ringing, she still heard the high-pitched ping as the ricocheting bullet hit something metal.

Mary Margaret squealed and a loud thud followed. Amelia covered her head with her arms. The man in the tweed suit lunged for the robber and they began to wrestle around like two pigs in mud, rolling back and forth across the floor.

Still on all fours, Amelia scrambled toward the open door. Through a fog of whirling sand, she *thought* she glimpsed a second male figure with a gun, hovering just outside the open door. Amelia caught her breath. The second man was leaner, but just as tall as the robber inside.

There was something haunting in the second man's stance, something in the way his hands dangled loosely at his sides that seemed familiar. Amelia held her breath, refusing to admit she might know his identity. It was too unthinkable.

She blinked and rubbed her eyes. When she looked up again, the second man—if he'd been there at all—had disappeared. After crawling across the floor, she slammed the door. Afterward, she realized she'd just shut them all inside with a gunman.

The bank was deathly silent. Crouched on the floor, she slowly turned, ready to dash toward the swinging half door and take refuge behind the low teller wall built to separate Mary Margaret and a cast-iron, black standing safe from the front half of the room.

She discovered, thankfully, there was no need to scramble anywhere. The gent with ink-stained hands had somehow wrestled the robber into submission. The villain was facedown on the floor with the man in tweed straddling him. With a death grip on the outlaw's wrists, the gent yanked the bandit's arms behind his back.

"Somebody get a rope!" the gent shouted. His bowler hat was missing.

"You can't hang him without a trial!" Amelia cried.

The man in tweed looked over his shoulder at her as if she'd taken leave of her senses. "I'm not going to hang him. I'm going to tie him up."

"Oh." Her face flamed, but her embarrassment quickly faded when a weak, pitiful moan issued from behind the teller's window.

"Mary Margaret?"

Amelia was on her feet in an instant. She ran around the low wall and found the woman sprawled on the floor. Blood seeped from a head wound near her temple.

A calmness took over as Amelia gathered the folds of her own serge skirt and pressed the hem against the older woman's head.

"Mr. Cutter?" She shouted loudly enough to raise the dead, hoping Mary Margaret's husband would hear her. "Mr. Cutter, are you in there?"

Timothy Cutter, seventy if he was a day, slowly opened the door to his office and peered around the edge. He squinted at her like a prairie dog just burrowing out of its hole into blinding sunlight.

"Amelia? Amelia, what's going on? I thought I heard a gunshot."

"You did, Mr. Cutter." That in itself was a small miracle. Timothy Cutter was nearly deaf as a

13

post. "Mary Margaret is hurt. I need some towels and hot water."

"I need a blasted rope!" The gent hollered from the other side of the wall.

"Who's that? Who needs a goat at a time like this?" Mr. Cutter's eyes were magnified to a startling roundness behind his thick glasses.

"Not a *goat,*" Amelia yelled back. "He needs a *rope.* There's a man out here who's captured a bank robber." She glanced down at Mary Margaret. The woman's eyes fluttered open. She stared at Amelia in confusion before she let out a weak moan and fainted again.

Amelia gingerly dabbed at Mrs. Cutter's temple and then tore off her own skirt hem for a bandage. The wound was merely a graze. It was nothing compared to the injuries she'd seen after her father had volunteered his services during the war.

Esra Hawthorne felt it was his duty to treat men no matter what side they fought for. Believing she had a natural talent for medicine, Doc Hawthorne thought nothing of teaching a fourteen-year-old to assist him in surgery as he struggled to put the battlefield-wounded back together again.

She had seen far worse than Mrs. Cutter's scratch, but the near miss was still nerve shattering. A fraction of an inch to the right and Mary Margaret would have been dead. As Amelia

14

continued to press the hem of her skirt against the cut, she primly folded her legs beneath her.

This, she decided, would take a while.

"Mr. Cutter," she shouted, "go next door and get Harrison Barker over at the mercantile."

Timothy blinked and nodded. The door closed again and he disappeared.

"Is she dead?" the gent inquired from the other side of the teller wall.

"Just grazed," Amelia informed him. "The bullet scraped her temple."

"You think he went for help? Is there a back door?"

"Yes," she answered to both questions. "At least I hope so."

She heard a moment of rough-and-tumble thumping, scrabbling and grunting on the other side of the divide and held her breath, hoping the robber wasn't going to break free. Suddenly, there was a soft thud very like that of a ripe melon hitting the floor, followed by a low groan.

She was afraid to ask what was happening and wished she'd picked up the robber's gun. Then the gent called, "It's all right. He's out for now."

Amelia whispered a prayer of thanks. Despite the near tragedy, the man in tweed had kept his wits about him. The Lord had given her the strength to keep her head, too. Now, if she could just forget about *maybe* seeing a second man outside, she'd feel much better.

"Mister? Who are you?" she asked the gent as she dabbed blood and checked Mary Margaret's wound. The bleeding had slowed to a trickle.

Before he could answer, the front door burst open. Shouts, animated voices and footsteps echoed around the room. It sounded as if everyone in Glory was filing into the bank.

As it was, just about everyone who had been in the mercantile next door rushed in first. Within seconds, nearly every shop and business in Glory emptied as word of the attempted robbery spread.

The first person Amelia saw peer over the teller wall was Reverend Brand McCormick. He and his sister, Charity, had arrived with the first wave of curiosity seekers. Charity volunteered to care for Mary Margaret.

Before she knew it, Amelia became the center of attention along with the man in tweed. They were jostled and prodded until they ended up shoulder to shoulder, surrounded by the curious and concerned.

Amelia blew a long strand of hair out of her eyes and wished she'd at least taken time to secure her braid and change from her oldest gardening skirt before she'd left home. She never imagined the simple task would land her smack in the middle of a crowd.

She clutched her fingers together to hide the

garden dirt under her nails. Mary Margaret's blood stained her skirt.

"What happened, Amelia?" Harrison Barker, owner of the mercantile and dry goods store, wanted to know. A pall of silence fell over the crowd.

"I came in to deliver some dried arnica to Mrs. Cutter and I—" She glanced over at the man in tweed. "I tripped . . . and then this gentleman . . ." She paused to let him supply his name.

"Hank Larson." He spoke in that warm, confident way again. "I'm new in town. I was here to see about a loan when—"

"He bumped into me," she concluded.

"Actually, I knocked her down. Accidentally. For which I apologize—"

"And we were both scraping up arnica when—"

The preacher interrupted. "How did you manage to apprehend the robber?" he asked Mr. Larson.

The man's face colored. He shrugged his wide shoulders.

"I don't know, exactly. I didn't stop to think about it. Somehow I managed to overpower him and just hung on."

Two cowpokes had the robber trussed up like a steer ready to be branded. A rope bound his heels, and his wrists were tied together behind his back.

17

Hank Larson glanced around the room. "Where's the sheriff?"

"Sheriff?" Harrison Barker laughed as did others around the room. "We haven't had a sheriff in this town since before the war."

"None?"

"No, sir. Never needed one. The army's been stationed in and out of here 'cause of the Comanche raids, so we never needed an official sheriff. Who'da thought this would happen?" Harrison gazed around as realization hit him. "Why, Mary Margaret coulda been kilt."

"Or worse," someone muttered. A somber hush fell over the crowd.

"Who's going to arrest and hold this man? Don't you have a mayor, either?" Hank Larson's brow knitted as he stared at the faces in the crowd.

Amelia noticed a quickly purpling spot on his left cheekbone beneath his eye and a small cut there, as well.

"Closest thing we've got to a mayor is the preacher. We haven't had a mayor since old Emmert Harroway, the town founder, kicked the bucket," Harrison said.

When he puffed out his chest, Amelia thought Harrison was about to volunteer to run the town when he surprised them all by announcing, "I move we make Mr. Larson here sheriff of Glory."

Resounding shouts of "Here, here!" and "Huzzah!" filled the bank.

18

As if she were his port in a storm, Hank Larson's gaze whipped to Amelia.

"Have they all lost their senses?" he asked softly.

"Some of them didn't have many to begin with." Amelia had leaned close so that only he could hear. She look around at the cowpunchers, bartender and patrons of the Silver Slipper, the one and only saloon in town.

Amelia sighed.

It's no wonder I'm still a spinster.

There were a few upright folks present, as well, she reminded herself—the preacher, business owners, married ranchers and their wives. Glory and the surrounding land had been settled by new immigrants and sturdy pioneer stock who had braved Indian attacks and killer storms the likes of which only the plains and prairies could whip up.

Right now, everyone in the room stared speculatively at Hank Larson.

At the mention of appointing a sheriff, Reverend Brand McCormick nodded in agreement.

"That's not a bad idea. Are you willing, Mr. Larson?"

The gent looked shocked. "Of course not. I'm a writer. I'm not a lawman."

"Not much to it," Harrison decided on the spot. "This is a small town. All you'd have to do is keep the peace. Kinda like what you did this morning."

"Keep the peace?" Hank Lawson blinked. Then turned to Amelia. "Keep the peace?"

"That's what he said." She shrugged.

With his dark hair flattened by his now missing bowler and his starched collar twisted to the left, he looked dumbfounded and completely incompetent. Certainly not prospective sheriff material. Amelia bit her lips together to hide a smile until her nagging suspicion about the armed figure she may have seen lingering outside in the sandstorm dispelled her lightheartedness. She was anxious to get home.

"He's a writer," she repeated to the crowd. "He doesn't want to be sheriff."

"He single-handedly captured our first armed robber," Harrison reminded, as if she hadn't been there on the floor when the outlaw walked in waving a loaded gun. As if she hadn't been there when the gun went off right beside her. Amelia shivered.

"Couldn't you agree to it temporarily, Mr. Larson?" Preacher McCormick asked.

"You'd be doing us all such a favor."

"I should really look at that cut on your cheek." Amelia wasn't actually addressing the man, but thinking aloud.

Hank Larson heard her, though, and turned. "Cut on my face?" He paled.

"It's really little more than a scratch." She noted he was quite handsome. His eyes were as blue as a clear morning sky and full of intelligence. It would be a shame if the cut left a scar.

He reached up and gently probed his cheek with his fingertips. She saw the ink again. A writer, he'd said. *That explains the stains.*

Why, Hank Larson wondered as he stared at the disheveled young woman beside him, *does nothing in my life turn out the way I plan?*

A month ago he'd spent nearly his last nickel on a used Hoe revolving printing press and made plans to travel west to set up a newspaper in a town that he hoped was hungry for news. He'd closed his eyes, stabbed his finger on a map of Texas and landed on Comanche County.

He asked around and narrowed his search to the town of Glory.

It had all seemed so simple once he'd made up his mind to act, but he should have known that the cards were stacked against him. For the past year, nothing in his life had gone right. He'd been a fool to think things were going to change overnight and that simply putting distance between himself and his past would make life worth living again.

He'd barely moved his last box into the small empty building he'd purchased sight unseen in the middle of Main Street. This morning he had kept an appointment regarding a loan with Mr. Cutter and now here he stood, surrounded by strangers, caught up in the middle of a scene worthy of the Wild West novel he'd planned to pen in his spare time.

The folks crowded around staring in admiration, completely unaware that his knees threatened to go weak if he allowed himself to think about what had just happened here. Somehow he'd actually jumped a gunman and pummeled him into submission. He reached up to scratch his head and realized again he had no idea where his hat had ended up.

To make matters worse, the young woman beside him with a mop of thick, auburn hair falling into her green eyes and a smattering of bright freckles across the bridge of her nose kept staring at what she claimed was "little more than a scratch" on his cheek.

He was inclined to sit down and lower his head between his knees, before he blacked out, but how could he with everyone in the room congratulating him on a job well-done?

For the life of him, Hank barely remembered the details of what had happened.

Not a very promising start for the town's only editor in chief.

"We don't have a badge." The storekeeper introduced himself as Harrison Barker and added, "But I'll order one."

"Badge?" Hank was fairly certain he'd just told them he had no interest in becoming the town sheriff. The young woman beside him was gently poking at the swelling on his cheek.

"We should have an official swearing in. Hold it at the church hall." This from a tall, clean-cut man of the cloth. If his white collar, black suit coat and radiant calm wasn't enough of a clue, he quickly introduced himself as Reverend Brand McCormick and warmly welcomed Hank to Glory.

"We're in your debt, Mr. Larson," the reverend said. "Why, if anything had happened to Mary Margaret or Timothy, the whole town would have been shattered."

"Not to mention broke. The contents of the safe would have been gone had you not intervened," Harrison added.

"You're our hero," a middle-aged woman in a simple poke bonnet said.

Hank shook his head. He was no one's hero. "It was all more of an accident than anything," he said.

"Why wait?" Harrison Barker surveyed the crowd. "Why not swear him in here and now? Never know what else might happen between now and the time it'll take to organize a fancy to-do over at the church hall. We could hold a town picnic in celebration later, but I'm all for swearing him in right now."

Shouts of approval went up all around. Hank felt as if he were mired in quicksand and sinking fast.

"Listen, I'm not . . ."

Apparently, no one cared what he was or wasn't. Timothy Cutter was summoned with a bellow. The frizzy-white-haired banker came blinking to the forefront of the group. His cheeks were ruddy, his eyes a faded blue behind his spectacles.

"Do you keep a Bible here, Mr. Cutter?" the minister asked.

"Why, nothing happened to anyone but Mary Margaret!" Timothy Cutter's eyes blinked faster as he scanned the crowd and shouted, "How can I be libel?"

The minister leaned close to the man's ear and shouted. "Not libel. Do you have a Bible here?"

Cutter visibly relaxed. "Of course. In the office. Like to browse through it after lunch." Muttering to himself, he hurried toward the back again.

Hank ran his finger around the edge of his suddenly too-tight collar. The young woman beside him didn't look any more comfortable than he.

"I really should get home," she said, thinking aloud.

"I really should have *stayed* home," Hank responded.

Life might have become unbearable in Missouri,

but at least folks there had learned to give him a wide berth. Now the good citizens of Glory, Texas, were intent upon railroading him into becoming the official sheriff.

"Have you seen my hat?" he whispered to the young woman, suddenly remembering someone had called her Amelia.

"Planning an escape?" she whispered back.

"One can always hope."

"Too late. Here comes Mr. Cutter."

Indeed, Timothy Cutter was back, moving with remarkable speed for someone of his age, a weather-beaten Bible clutched in his hands. "Here you go, Reverend."

Brand McCormick accepted the Bible and turned to Hank. For the first time, the preacher seemed to notice Hank was anything but pleased.

"You *are* willing to take an oath and help us out, aren't you, Mr. Larson?"

"Actually, I . . ." Hank met the man's eyes. There was a tranquility about Brand McCormick, a calm knowingness no doubt nourished by his faith. The man appeared to be in his late thirties —around Hank's age. He'd entered the bank with a woman.

Hank found himself wondering if Brand McCormick's faith had ever been tried? Had it ever faltered under an unbearable load of pain and sorrow?

"Mr. Larson?" The preacher's voice called him back.

"I can't do this," Hank said.

"Can't or won't?" the preacher asked softly.

"I'm not qualified."

"The outlaw tied up in the corner would beg to differ."

"I'm just a writer," Hank insisted.

"A very courageous one, I might add," McCormick said.

Hank looked into the expectant faces of those around him. He avoided looking at the woman beside him.

"I'm not your man. Sorry."

"Sometimes God has plans for us other than the ones we've chosen for ourselves. Why not agree to serve on a temporary basis? Today's event was an aberration. This is a nice town filled with nice people."

"Try it, just for a month or two." The store-keeper's head bobbed like a chicken's.

Hank knew all about how much God could forever alter a man's future. Hadn't God done enough to him in that regard already?

"What I still don't understand is, if this is such a safe town, why do you need a sheriff? And why me?"

"The Comanche were our major threat and they have settled down some over the past couple of years. We've never had an attempted bank robbery here before—so in that respect, this is a safe town. As far as why you? You've already proved yourself. Besides, it would be a good way for you to get to know everyone in Glory. There will be plenty of time to establish your newspaper," the good reverend finished.

"Why today? Why the rush?" Hank wanted to know.

The preacher looked thoughtful. "I believe God brought you here, to this spot, this very morning, to do what you did. And you served His purpose well. I believe you are the right man for the job."

Hank sighed. He turned to the woman beside him and found her watching him with a dubious expression. Only she knew that he wasn't the hero the crowd made him out to be. Only she knew the robber had tripped over them on his way into the bank. All Hank had to do was pin him to the floor and keep him there.

At the moment, the young woman was trying to finger comb the tangles out of her hair—without much success.

When their eyes met, she leaned close and whispered, "Why don't you just say yes and get it over with?"

"But . . ."

"Give it a week or two and then resign. Just do *something*. I need to get home."

He thought about what the preacher had just

said. He didn't for one minute believe he was brought here by some divine notion to save the day, but he did know how easily God could upset a man's plans. Glory was a one-horse town at best. Taking on the job of sheriff would, no doubt, be something he'd do in name only—unless the good reverend was trying to deceive him—which seemed highly unlikely.

Today's event was an aberration. This is a nice town filled with nice people.

As he looked into the guileless eyes of the preacher, he trusted that the man wasn't intentionally lying. Reverend Brand McCormick truly believed Glory was a peaceful place.

"All right," Hank said, ignoring the sinking feeling in the pit of his stomach.

"But only for a couple of weeks. Just until you find a replacement."

Chapter Two

The wind had died down by the time the crowd inside the bank broke up and Amelia walked back home. Surrounded by a split-rail fence, the small log-and-stone house set off by itself on the far end of town, was the first real home she had ever known.

Nine years had passed since she'd finally convinced her father to put down roots. They'd settled in, looking forward to living a good life, if not a wealthy one. The citizens of Glory were thrilled to have a doctor in their midst. Everyone sought out Doc Hawthorne for what ailed them.

Amelia planted a medicinal herb garden and honed her apothecary and homeopathic skills. Her knowledge of herbal remedies was a gift from God that she never took for granted. She assisted her father whenever he needed a nurse. They were not rich, but finally they were settled and life was good.

Two years later, shortly after her twentieth birthday, she'd lost her father to a bout of fever. Though she had no formal medical training, she knew far more than most newly turned-out physicians. She thought she would assume her father's place as Glory's unofficial doctor. Though the townsfolk turned to her for herbal remedies, nursing and midwifery skills, there were many, most of them men, who would never allow her to touch them, many who would never see her as qualified as a male.

The herb garden she carefully tended behind the house thrived, though it required hours devoted to toting water and pulling weeds. A mulberry sapling she planted had survived the elements and now shaded the front yard. In the dappled shade and full sun she planted her precious spring and summer garden. It wasn't large, but it was always beautiful.

She learned from tending plants and patients that only the strong survived and flourished on the Texas plains.

As she made her way toward the back of the house, she caught a glimpse of the sorrel mare tied up by the barn. It was Evan's horse.

All the anxiety she'd felt earlier instantly returned. She'd always done the best she could caring for her nineteen-year-old brother, Evan, but lately she seemed to have lost all influence over him.

She hadn't laid eyes on him for just over a week. Why, today of all days, had he shown up? Her relief was mingled with newfound dread. Was he the second man she'd seen outside the bank? The man who had disappeared into the dust?

She stopped where she stood, closed her eyes and whispered a hasty prayer.

"Lord, help me hold my temper. Give me the right words to say."

Forcing herself to be calm and confident in the Lord, she marched around the house. Sure enough, she spotted Evan stuffing a handful of shirts into his saddlebag.

"Evan?"

He turned, obviously startled, but relaxed when he saw it was her.

"Hey, Amy." His voice sounded calm, but his expression gave his impatience away. Tall and lean, he had their father's light brown hair and blue eyes.

"Where have you been? I haven't seen you in days." The words sounded accusatory and she immediately tried to make up for her tone. "I'm sorry, Evan. It's just that I worry when you disappear for days at a time without warning."

"I'm nineteen. A man grown. You don't have to mother me anymore."

Easy for him to say. She'd "mothered" him since the day he was born. He'd been *her* baby since she was eight years old and their mother died giving him birth. When her father lay dying it hadn't been hard to promise that she'd take care of Evan. It was second nature to her.

But watching out for him proved to be nigh impossible lately.

"I'm sorry that's how you see it. No matter how old you are, you'll always be my little brother."

"Don't try to make me feel guilty, either. I'm not like you, Amy. You're content to sit and relish being an old maid. I'm getting out of here while I'm still young."

An old maid? She might be twenty-seven and unmarried, but she'd come to think of herself as an independent woman, not an old maid. She'd been humiliated by a man once. *That* was never going to happen to her again.

31

Evan ignored her while he tied the latigo on his saddlebags and then tugged on the saddle cinch. Dropping his stirrup into place, he was ready to mount up.

"I'd hoped you'd be here for a while." Amelia's hope of convincing him to stay was fading fast. "I could sure use some help with repairs around the place."

The memory of the hazy figure in the bank doorway lay as heavily on her mind as the suspicions in her heart. His turning up unexpectedly this morning didn't bode well.

If she found out that he had, indeed, been a partner in crime with the robber the men had trussed and locked up in Harrison Barker's storeroom, how could she ever bring herself to turn him in?

Did she really want to know?

"I can't stay." Evan kept his back to her, staring at his saddle, his hands toying with the reins.

"Why not?"

He turned but didn't meet her eyes. "I hired on at a ranch in Johnson County."

"Johnson County? Why so far away? Why not go talk to Joe Ellenberg? I'm sure he'd have work for you at the Rocking e."

Joe was a good man, an honorable man who lived a few miles outside of town with his mother, Hattie, and his wife, Rebekah. Amelia had known the Ellenbergs for years and had delivered Joe's son. Joe had overcome his own troubles and recently found his faith again. He would set a fine example for Evan.

But Evan shook his head. "I'm making my own way, Amy. I don't need Joe Ellenberg looking out for me."

"When will you get back?"

He shrugged and turned to stare out over the open plain. "I'm not sure."

"How can I reach you? What if I need you?"

"You've never needed anyone but yourself and your Bible. Thanks to our father, you've always known who you are and where you're going."

"Oh, Evan." She'd never heard him sound so bitter, so jealous. Or so lost.

He turned to her at last. When his eyes met hers, she almost wished they hadn't. His gaze was raw with emotions that terrified her, and his face mirrored a hunger that bordered on desperation.

"Evan, what's *wrong?*"

She suddenly knew without his saying a word that he had been outside the bank that morning. If he had walked in as intended, things might not have played out the way they had. Now his accomplice had been caught. It might only be a matter of minutes before the man implicated Evan.

Tongue-tied with fear, she couldn't voice her

suspicions—not unless she was willing to face the raw truth.

"Look, Amy, leave it, will you? I'm not willing to sit in this one-horse town tied to your apron strings. You might be content wiping up sweat and blood and vomit, or doling out weeds for egg money and handouts, but I want more. I'm sick and tired of living hand to mouth. I have bigger plans."

He might as well have slapped her. She'd worked hard to provide for them both, just as her father always had. A hot rush of anger gave her false courage and she pushed him.

"What kind of *big* plans? Robbing banks?"

Deadly silence fell between them, thick as the dust that had filled the air earlier. An invisible wall went up between her and Evan, a wall that would take years to tear down again. Her heart was beating so hard she barely heard him when he said, "Why would you say that?" His voice was low, menacing.

"That *was* you, wasn't it? Outside the bank. That was you I saw."

He shrugged and turned around. She grabbed his sleeve.

"Answer me, Evan. At least tell me the truth."

And then what? Then what will you do with it?

Suddenly, she didn't want to know. She wished she could take it all back, the harsh words, the accusations. Wished she'd lingered with the crowd and hadn't come home to find him here. Watching the newspaperman squirm in his new role as sheriff would be far better than knowing the bitter truth about her little brother.

Without answering, Evan shook her off like a pesky gnat and mounted up in one smooth motion. He kicked his horse into a canter and headed out the gate in the back fence.

"Evan!" she shouted, staring after him, overwhelmed with hopelessness. "Evan Hawthorne, you come back here!"

He hadn't confirmed or denied her accusation. Hadn't tried to defend himself with an excuse or alibi, either. Helpless, worried sick, Amelia watched his horse kick up dust as Evan put more and more distance between them. Her brother was pushing the animal far harder than would an innocent man simply headed off to a new job.

Hank found Amelia standing at the split-rail fence behind the house, staring out at endless nothingness. He'd read accounts of settlers who had lost their minds after moving out onto the frontier and having to face the vast emptiness of the open sky and land that rolled on and on like a dry sea, the howling wind that came out of nowhere and lasted for days on end, the lack of neighbors and companionship.

The elements and loneliness took their toll on the weak in mind and heart.

Hank stared at the woman who was still unaware of his presence. He noted the rigid set of her shoulders, the way the breeze tugged at the loose strands that had escaped the thick, uneven braid trailing down her spine. She'd gathered the folds of her skirt in her hands and clung to the fabric as if hanging on for dear life. There was a determination in her stance, a telling pride in the rigid line of her spine. Hers was a spirit not easily broken.

He wished he could see her face. Wished he knew what she was thinking. Facing barren miles of nothingness, she presented a portrait of frontier courage, fortitude, steadfastness.

He watched her shoulders rise and fall on a long, slow sigh and found himself wondering what she might be thinking. Embarrassed at intruding on her solitude, he cleared his throat.

She turned quickly, her shamrock-green eyes wide and shiny as newly minted silver dollars. It wasn't until she tilted her freckle-dusted nose in the air and rapidly started blinking that he realized the radiance in her eyes was from unshed tears.

"Mr. Larson." She walked toward him quickly, her stride as efficient as he guessed she did everything. "What brings you here?"

He didn't know her well enough to be certain, but she appeared far more upset than she had been at the bank in the midst of all the chaos. Why? he wondered.

"Actually, the cut on my cheek. You mentioned infection. I thought maybe you would take a look at it." He shrugged. "I saw the way you cared for Mrs. Cutter when the crowd broke up and someone mentioned you had some healing skill —that you're an apothecary."

"I do what I can. My father was the town doctor."

He found himself wishing she'd smile.

"Well, I hear you're good at what you do."

She studied his cheek. "If you'll step up to the back porch, I'll wash that cut and put some salve on it for you."

"I'd be obliged."

"I see you found your hat." She nodded at the crumpled circle of felt in his hand.

He'd forgotten he was carrying it and stared at it mournfully. "Another casualty of the holdup." He held it out to her as they walked toward the porch. "You think you could save it?"

There was a glimmer of a smile around her lips now, but not enough.

"I'm afraid I'd have to pronounce it beyond help. You'd do better to buy a real hat now that you're sheriff."

"I'm already looking for my replacement."

"For the hat?" she asked.

"For the job," he said.

"Everybody seems perfectly happy with you."

"Everyone but me."

They had reached the porch and she motioned for him to have a seat at a small table near the back door.

"I don't mind stepping inside," he told her.

"That wouldn't be seemly."

"Seemly?"

She turned beet-red. "I'm a respectable woman, Mr. Larson. I never invite men into my house when I'm here alone."

He was too stunned to say anything for a moment but she lost no time.

"Have a seat," she said, pulling out a chair for him. "I'll get some water and the salve and be right out. Would you like a cup of coffee or some tea?"

There was no one waiting for him back at the storefront, nothing to look forward to but unpacking the press and cleaning up the second-floor room that was his living quarters. Amelia Hawthorne was an interesting character study, indeed, but he couldn't afford to linger.

"No, thank you. I've got a lot to do today," he told her.

He set the dented bowler on the table near his elbow. Watching the landscape was compelling, fascinating in a way. Much like his future, it could be viewed as either a blank slate where a man's destiny could be written, or an endless stretch of barren nothingness too depressing to contemplate.

Amelia appeared, balancing a washbowl that sloshed soapy water against her waist, a rag and a small round jar in her hands. He reached for the bowl and carefully lowered it to the tabletop.

She blew a wisp of hair out of her eyes and pulled an empty chair up close to his. Without preamble, she dipped the rag into the water and wrung it out. She paused for a moment and stared at the washrag. Her brow knit for a moment and then the frown was gone. She lifted the washrag to his cheek.

"This might sting." She leaned closer, intent upon his cheekbone.

"I can take it."

"That's right. You're the sheriff."

"What's that got to do with it? Ow!" He jerked back when she touched the warm water to the swollen spot beneath his eye.

"You're the new town hero and all."

"You know as well as I what really happened."

"I heard you try to explain." She gently patted and dabbed. He could tell she was trying to be as gentle as possible. Looking thoughtful, she paused for a moment and met his gaze. "Do you plan to take this seriously?"

He reared back. "You said it was just a scratch. Should I ask for a mirror?"

"It is a scratch. I was referring to your new

39

position as sheriff. Do you plan to take it seriously?" She seemed very interested in his answer.

"Everyone led me to believe there was nothing to do, that nothing ever happens here in Glory—nothing that requires a full-time sheriff."

"Until now."

"Until now."

They fell silent. She opened what proved to be a jar of salve.

"What is that? It smells awful."

"Sweet oil salve. Of all the towns in Texas, how did you choose Glory, Mr. Larson?"

"No newspaper."

"A wiser man might have realized that's because there's no news."

"There's always news, Miss Hawthorne. Life's unfolding drama can be most interesting. It's all in the telling. Life *is* news." His voice trailed off into silence.

She hesitated before applying the ointment to his cut. He stiffened and drew back when her fingers touched his cheek.

"Will your family be joining you?"

"My family?" The words lodged in his throat.

She nodded. "Do you have family?"

Tricia and their stillborn son. They'd been his life, his hope, his joy, until God saw fit to take them both.

"Mr. Larson? Are you all right?"

He didn't realize he'd closed his eyes. He snapped them open. "I'm fine."

"Hold still while I smear this on your cut. It may sting a little."

A *little* was an understatement. The minute the ointment hit his torn skin, he almost bit through his cheek trying not to yell for mercy.

"What's in there?"

"Linseed oil, sweet oil and a couple of secret ingredients."

She leaned close and blew gently on the stinging cut. He found himself staring at the crown of her head, at the crooked part in her glossy auburn hair. Tricia would have never gone out in public unless her hair was perfectly coiffed and she was dressed in style.

Amelia Hawthorne, on the other hand, looked like she'd thrown herself together without thought. Her hair was a disaster. The cuffs of her blouse were frayed. Her skirt, spattered with Mrs. Cutter's blood and missing a good portion of the hem, had seen better days long before this morning.

"There." She sat back, satisfied with her work. If she realized he hadn't answered her question about family, she deftly let it go.

"What do I owe you?" he asked.

"Owe me?" Her face went bright red. "Why, nothing."

"You must not make much of a living doctoring if you don't charge for your services."

"It's just a scratch. In a way, I feel responsible."

"I ran into you." They both said the same thing at once.

Hank chuckled for the first time in forever. Amelia didn't.

He stood up and dug a dollar from his vest pocket and set the coin on the table. "Is that enough?"

"More than," she said softly.

"Are you sure you're all right, Amelia?" Perhaps she'd been far more shaken than she'd let on earlier. After all, a gun had gone off right beside her. Perhaps she'd been thinking of the near miss when he caught her staring across the land a few minutes ago. For whatever reason, she was no longer acting like the plucky young woman he'd met in the bank. There were worry lines etched across her forehead and a distracted look in her eyes.

"I'm fine." She forced a smile. "Really."

"Then I'll be on my way. Thanks again." He started to walk away, to head back to his place, a former Chinese laundry turned newspaper publishing house.

"Mr. Larson!"

He was off the porch when she called to him. He turned and found her holding his flattened hat.

"You almost forgot this."

He walked back, reached for it. "Thanks, I think."

In that moment, as she stood there framed against the back porch looking bedraggled, worried and alone, he remembered that she hadn't badgered him about family—as if she'd understood that he couldn't bring himself to speak of them.

If there was one thing a reporter hated more than a dangling participle, it was an unanswered question. She'd asked. The least he could do was answer. He took a deep breath and steeled himself against the painful truth.

"My family won't be joining me, Miss Hawthorne." He forced himself to say the word he had avoided using for twelve long and achingly dark months. "I'm a widower."

Chapter Three

Amelia watched him walk away, punching his misshapen hat as he went.

She wasn't in the habit of being alone with a man and, yet, despite her worry, she'd been surprisingly comfortable talking with Hank Larson. He wasn't like most of the men in town. He was well-spoken, educated—

She stopped right there and reminded herself that she'd been embarrassed by a well-spoken stranger before. But Hank Larson wasn't just a handsome stranger passing through—he was here aiming to settle down and start a newspaper.

Even more reason to be on guard.

Newspapermen needed stories to tell and Hank Larson was easy to talk to. As the sheriff *and* a reporter, he was a double threat to her. She'd have to watch what she said around him— if she was ever around him again. She had to be cautious not to let anything slip about having seen someone who looked a lot like Evan outside the bank that morning.

She picked up the salve and the washcloth and stepped inside her small kitchen. She walked through to the front room that was both a parlor and her apothecary shop and replaced the salve on the shelf amid other potions and lotion bottles and jars. The interior of the house was still surprisingly cool. She raised the parlor shades now that the sun had moved high overhead.

As she passed the oval mirror on the hall tree near the front door, she paused to see her reflection, critical of what Hank Larson must have seen when he looked at her. Hair the color of rust pulled back in a messy braid. Her nose and cheeks were stained with freckles coaxed to life by too many sunny hours spent in the garden. Bloodstains marred the front of her ruined skirt.

It was long past saving even before this morning. The sight of the dark red stains called to mind the near calamity she'd witnessed.

She turned away and thought of another image, that of the tall, lanky man holding a gun outside the bank, an image she'd seen only through swirling dust.

Had anyone else seen the second man? If so, would they have noted his similarity to Evan?

There were a million and one things to do besides worry. Forcing herself to move, to think, she went into her room and changed into a navy serge skirt and fresh shirtwaist. As she balled up her ruined skirt in her hands, she felt a lump in the pocket she'd sewn inside the waistband. She removed her father's gold watch.

A shiver ran down her spine when she realized she might have been forced to hand the watch over to a thief. She might have lost it forever.

The watch was the one thing of value she owned, but even if it were worth nothing, she'd still have held it dear. She carried it every day and thought of her father whenever she felt the weight against the folds of her skirts. It ticked, slow and steady, an imitation of a beating heart. She set the watch on her bureau beside her mother's Bible and took up her hairbrush.

She unbound her braid, brushed her hair to a high shine and rebraided it, taking more care this time. After tying a grosgrain ribbon at the end, she walked back to the mirror near the front door and gave herself a curt nod of approval.

No sense in running around looking like something the cat dragged in.

She took a deep breath, closed her eyes and whispered, "Dear Lord, help me to begin this day anew. As always, I put my trust in You, knowing that whatever happens, You'll show me the way."

She prayed that no one else had seen Evan. She prayed for God to guide her brother onto the right path.

And she knew that if anyone asked her directly, if Evan had been outside the bank this morning, that there was only one thing she could tell them. The truth.

Two hours later, Hank was prying open a packing crate when the preacher walked into the narrow two-story building on Main Street. The false front over the entrance was supposed to make the place appear more impressive than it really was, but the space had originally housed a Chinese laundry and the acrid smell of lye with an overlay of incense and other exotic odors had seeped into the walls.

Hank hoped a fresh coat of whitewash would help, but he had no idea when he'd ever get to it. For now, he had to focus on making a living before what was left of his savings ran out.

"What can I do for you, Reverend?"

Brand McCormick took in the empty room, the Hoe press and cylinders, all the unopened crates and stacks of books and was polite enough not to mention the smell, though his eyes were watering a bit.

"Looks like you've got your work cut out for you," he said, blinking.

Hank nodded. "You can say that again."

The preacher hitched up his pant leg and sat on the corner of the desk. "Harrison Barker just reminded me that the fella who tried to rob the bank is still trussed up in his storeroom."

"Harrison?"

"The storekeeper."

"Ah." Hank pictured the talkative man who wore glasses and slicked his hair down, parted in the middle. "What's Barker going to do with him?"

"Well . . ." McCormick shrugged. "I'm afraid that's where you come in. As sheriff and all."

Hank rolled up his shirtsleeves. He'd already shed his jacket and vest and was thinking about unbuttoning his shirt collar. He looked around the crowded room.

"I don't have a storeroom, obviously. Even if I did, I wouldn't want some outlaw locked up in here."

"We were thinking that you could take him over to the county seat at Comanche. It's not far from here, as the crow files. I might even be able to scare up a couple of volunteers to go with you. You could hand him over to Oswald Caldwell, the sheriff over there, and Oz can hold him until the circuit judge comes through."

"You want me to escort a prisoner to the jail at the county seat?"

"You are the sheriff now, Mr. Larson."

"Call me Hank."

The good reverend nodded. "So, Hank, I was thinking if you left now, you'd be back before nightfall."

Hank set down the crowbar and forgot about the boxes. It was a little past noon. Outside, the temperature was rising.

"You know, I need to get this newspaper up and running, Reverend, if I'm going to support myself."

"I'm well aware of that," Brand told him. "Right now, I'm going to find a couple of men willing to ride over to Comanche with you." McCormick pulled a silver-backed watch from his vest pocket, checked the time and snapped it closed. "Could you be ready to leave in half an hour?"

Hank opened and closed his mouth before he said something he'd regret saying to a man of God. He mopped his brow with the back of his arm and ran his hand over his hair. Reverend McCormick was still smiling. Hank doubted anything ever flustered the man.

"I'll go if you can find someone to go with me. The *only* reason I'm doing this is because you somehow got me to swear an oath to uphold the law. Besides," Hank added, "I hate to think of anybody tied up and stashed in a storeroom for much longer. Last time I saw him he was trussed up like a stuffed pig."

"He's tied to a chair. Harrison's clerk gave him water and they're fixin' him some lunch. In regard to the robbery, I've heard that Laura Foster, a lady who owns a boardinghouse, claims to have seen *two* men hanging around outside the bank about the time of the robbery."

"Did she get a good look at them?"

Brand shook his head. "Her place is at the other end of the street, but she thinks she saw more than one man outside the bank before the robbery."

Hank massaged his temple with his thumb. "Well, that's something, isn't it? I'll have to talk to her later."

"You're probably used to interviewing folks. That'll be a real asset as sheriff."

When Hank ignored the comment, the reverend asked, "What are you going to name the newspaper?"

Hank frowned. "I have no idea. I thought once I got here and saw the place, I'd know what to call it. So far, nothing's come to me."

"Well, I'm sure folks will want to read your

eyewitness account of the robbery. That ought to sell a few papers."

"I doubt a sheriff ever published a newspaper before. You see any conflict of interest there, Reverend?"

"Not if you tell an honest tale, Hank. Not at all. Besides, this is Glory, not some big city. Where do you hail from, anyway?"

"Saint Joseph, Missouri. How about you? Were you born in Texas?"

"I'm originally from Illinois. I moved my children here, along with my sister, Charity, almost two years ago now. I'm a widower."

An ache, swift and searing, touched Hank's heart. McCormick seemed to say the word so easily. Hank wondered if it would ever be that way for him.

"Me, too," he said softly.

"Any children?"

The image of the stillborn baby boy wrapped in the small quilt Tricia had so lovingly made for him flashed into Hank's mind. He forced it away. He shifted, glanced out the grime-streaked front window at Main Street.

"No," he said, still avoiding McCormick's eyes. "No children."

"I have two. A boy and a girl. They're a handful. My sister is good with them, but she's a quiet soul by nature and by the end of the day, they've nearly run her ragged. You'll meet Charity and the children at church on Sunday."

"I'm not a church-going man, Reverend. Sorry."

"Well, the invitation is always open. It's the only church in town. Right there on the park at the far end of Main. You've seen it, I'm sure."

"Big white building with a steeple and cross on top? Hard to miss." Hank glanced around until he spotted his jacket amid the mess. He'd tossed it over the back of a chair. His dented bowler lay nearby. He couldn't help but remember Amelia's suggestion that if he didn't want to look like a rube he should buy himself a new hat.

That would have to wait, he supposed, until he was actually making some spending money. He gathered up his hat and jacket. McCormick took the hint.

"Well, I guess I should be going. I'll walk back to Harrison's store with you. Along the way we're sure to find someone to deliver the prisoner with you."

"My own little posse," Hank muttered.

"I guess so."

McCormick waited for Hank to lock the door. On the way down the street, the act of walking along the boardwalk in the fresh air revived Hank. They passed the bank and he remembered there was a mystery in the air and started thinking like a reporter.

"Has the prisoner said anything?" Hank asked. "Anyone know who he is?"

"He's not from around here and he's not talking."

"I ought to make certain he was acting alone." Hank figured if that were true, then the case was closed. "You mind standing in while I question him?"

"Not at all. Why?"

"Just so when I do write the story I won't be accused of embellishing it to make the 'sheriff' look more competent," Hank said.

"Just don't report it in a way that makes the 'sheriff' look inept, either. We both know how bad you want to shed the title."

"Does it show that much?"

"You might as well be wearing a sign."

Both men laughed. Hank liked McCormick, even if he didn't like the way the man had talked him into becoming sheriff. Good as his word, the preacher drummed up three volunteers to help Hank escort the prisoner to Comanche and waited while Hank questioned the man.

While Hank and the preacher were closeted in Harrison Barker's storeroom with the robber, the storekeeper fluttered back and forth between dry goods and sundries, straightening items on already straightened shelves.

Up close, Hank realized the holdup man was younger than he first thought, somewhere between twenty and twenty-five. The lower half of his face was covered with a couple days' growth of stubble. His eyes looked tired and wary. Hank had the feeling the man was just waiting for someone to slip up so he could make his escape.

"I'm Hank Larson." Hank had to clear his throat before he added, "Sheriff."

The robber's lip curled. His tone was surly. "Yeah. Wasn't for me you wouldn't *be* sheriff. I was there when they swore you in, remember?"

"I recall you tripped over me and fired off a round inside the bank. You nearly killed the teller."

"I wouldn't have fired off a round if you hadn't been on the floor nuzzling up to that redhead."

When Hank's face flamed, the cut on his cheek began to sting something fierce. He had to remind himself the man's hands were tied. He glanced over at Brand McCormick and caught the preacher eyeing him speculatively. He wasn't about to explain the remark. His actions had been perfectly innocent.

Hank walked around behind the holdup man, where he couldn't be seen. The young man strained at the rope that bound him to the chair.

"What's your name?" Hank asked.

"None of your business."

"I'm making it my business. We're taking you to Comanche and if I don't get it out of you, I'm sure there's a bona fide lawman there who has ways of finding out."

"Harvey. Harvey Ruggles."

"You dream up this robbery alone, Harvey?"

"Don't waste your breath, *Sheriff.* I've said all I want to say."

Hank decided not to waste any more of his time, either. This wasn't his job. He had a paper to publish, the sooner the better.

"I guess we'd better untie him so I can get him over to Comanche and be back before dark," Hank said to the Reverend.

"Don't forget to talk to Laura Foster," the minister reminded him.

Hank nodded. "Tomorrow will be soon enough for that."

Chapter Four

The next morning, Amelia found herself in the kitchen at Laura Foster's boardinghouse. Earlier Laura had sent her cook's son, Ricardo, to fetch her after the cook had nearly sliced his thumb off. The kitchen was larger than Amelia's parlor.

Amelia, like the rest of the townsfolk, had watched Foster's Boardinghouse take shape three years ago. The widow had spared no expense when it came to building her establishment, and since then Mrs. Foster had also built a reputation as a fine, upstanding woman with a good head for business. The boardinghouse was consistently occupied and guests raved about the food.

Thankfully, the bleeding had stopped by the time Amelia arrived. She found Laura hovering over the portly Mexican, Rodrigo, pouring the man a cup of coffee, speaking to him in Spanish.

Amelia immediately laid out her dressings, sticking plaster, needles and thread. The cut was deep but clean, so she decided to sew the edges of skin together rather than use plaster strips. The cook was silent and stoic as Amelia bent over his hand. She suspected, from the smell of whiskey in the air, that Laura had fortified the man with alcohol.

Amelia closed her eyes and whispered, " ' . . . and by his wounds are we healed,' " before she took a deep breath and slid the needle slowly into Rodrigo's flesh. As always, her hand was steady. She was confident in her healing skills for they were a gift from God, given through her father.

Laura stood at the cook's shoulder, watching. Amelia thought that a woman as genteel and polished as Mrs. Foster might blanch at the sight of blood or the process of stitching the wound closed, but the woman was not only attentive and helpful, she was cool and collected.

"I'm so thankful you were at home this morning, Amelia. I'm not sure what I'd have done outside of bandage the cut and wait for you to return." When a teakettle on the huge iron stove started whistling, Laura crossed the room and took it off the fire. She was back in an instant.

"I hope you'll stay for luncheon. In fact, I insist," Laura invited.

Amelia tied off the end of a semicircle of stitches and deftly cut the thread. Then she reached into her bag for a bottle of balsam. It was such a fine remedy for healing fresh wounds of horses or humans that she tended to make large batches at a time and leave some with patients to keep on hand.

She dabbed the strained mixture of gum benzoin and tolu powder, storax, frankincense, myrrh, aloe and alcohol on the wound, waited a moment and then dabbed on more.

"That's very kind of you," she said as she began to wrap a bandage around the cook's thumb, "but I really can't stay. I didn't get much accomplished at all yesterday." She refused to lose another day worrying about where Evan was, if he was safe, and whether or not he'd been involved in the robbery.

Easier said than done. Whenever she found her anxiety mounting, she closed her eyes, took a deep breath and reminded herself that God was looking out for Evan. That their lives were in *His* hands.

"But . . ." Laura's lips usually formed a perfect

bow. At Amelia's refusal of luncheon, her dimples disappeared and her smile began to droop, "I'd so very much like you to stay."

Amelia was flattered. She smiled up at Laura.

"Another day, if that's possible?" As far as Amelia could tell, the two of them had little in common—except for the fact that neither was wed—but she admired Laura Foster's independence and confidence.

Laura appeared to be in her early to mid thirties and was not merely lovely, she was stunning. Her golden hair curled around her perfect features. Her complexion was not marred by overexposure to the sun or freckles. Her hands were plump and smooth, her nails evenly trimmed and buffed. Her clothes were of the latest fashion.

Comparing herself to Laura was like comparing a battered straw hat to a fancy satin bonnet.

"Another day for lunch, then," Laura agreed. "I'll hold you to it." Her dimples were back.

Amelia gathered up her things and advised Rodrigo, "Try to keep the bandage dry for a few days. If the wound doesn't stop oozing, come to see me. It may need some additional balsam or powdered bloodroot."

"I'll see that he does," Laura assured her. "I'm sure his wife won't mind cooking this week, though she's not the talent he is."

"*Gracias, señora.*" Rodrigo nodded to Laura

Foster and then turned to Amelia and repeated, "*Gracias.*"

Laura reached into a biscuit tin on a low shelf before she walked Amelia back through the house to the entry hall where Amelia collected her hat.

"Thank you so much," Laura said, holding her hand out to Amelia. There were two shiny silver dollars in her palm.

Amelia shook her head in awe. She was used to being paid in vegetables, cuts of meat, loaves of bread and promises of payments that never came.

"Oh, no, please. That's too much." Embarrassed by the woman's generosity, Amelia had no idea what to say.

Laura grabbed her hand and pressed the coins into her palm. "Rodrigo's work is invaluable to me. I couldn't run this place without him. If you think that's too much, keep the rest as a down payment for future emergencies." Even Laura's laugh, a light, tinkling sound with an angelic lilt, was lovely.

Amelia tried to protest.

"I insist," Laura said. "No arguments."

"Well . . . thank you," Amelia said when she finally realized Laura was adamant.

Laura opened the door; Amelia took a step forward and found herself staring up at Hank Larson.

He looked as surprised to see her standing there

as she was to see him. Caught speechless, Amelia watched him doff his dented bowler hat and absently tap it against his thigh.

"Miss Hawthorne. Mrs. Foster." He nodded politely to them both

His manners were flawless. Amelia finally managed to acknowledge him with a nod of her own.

"I was just leaving," she mumbled. He'd come to see the lovely widow, after all, not her. She was surprised by a wave of disappointment.

She expected Laura to usher the man in, but the woman remained planted in the doorway.

"Mr. Larson, it's nice to see you again, but as I explained to you a few days ago, I have a policy of only renting to couples."

"I'm well aware of your policy, Mrs. Foster, but I've come for another reason entirely."

"I've *really* got to go," Amelia blurted, clutching her medical bag. "If you'll excuse me." She thanked Laura again and Hank stepped aside to let her move out onto the wide veranda.

Instead of asking Hank in, Laura joined him outside. Amelia bade them both farewell and was just about to step off the porch when she heard him say, "I was told that you may have seen not one, but two men loitering outside the bank around the time of the holdup. As you may have heard, I'm Glory's new sheriff and I'm here to see if you can help with a few details." He paused for a second and added, "If this is a good time."

"Of course," Laura replied.

Amelia turned away, her knees suddenly weak.

Laura Foster claimed to have seen two men loitering outside the bank yesterday and Hank Larson was here to find out more. Was one of the men Evan? Had Laura recognized him? Did she even know Evan? Amelia tried to recall if the widow had ever met her brother.

She paused before starting down the porch steps, hoping they wouldn't notice she was no longer in a hurry. She knelt, pretending to straighten her laces and tie her shoe. Her palms were sweating. She forced herself to focus on what Laura was saying.

"I really didn't get a look at them. I was sweeping off the porch until the wind came up and I decided that was fruitless. I was about to head back inside when I stopped to watch a whirlwind as it twisted down Main Street. Two men were standing outside the bank, as if about to walk in. They caught my eye because they lingered so long in the wind. After the whirlwind passed the bank, they were gone." She shrugged. "I assumed they both stepped inside."

Hank was silent. Amelia decided she couldn't pretend to be preoccupied with her shoe a moment longer and straightened. When she glanced over her shoulder, she caught Hank staring at her.

"Did you see anyone outside the door, Miss Hawthorne?" he asked.

She cleared her throat. "Me?"

She didn't like the way his brows knit as if she'd suddenly become a curiosity that needed further study.

"Did *you* see a second man outside the bank during the robbery?"

"I was on the floor," she reminded him. *The truth.*

He appeared to be waiting for a definitive yes or no.

"I . . ." She picked up her medical bag and clutched the handle tightly. She never lied. She wasn't about to start now. "I may have."

Suddenly, Hank's focus was entirely on her. "You *may* have seen a man *outside* the bank during the robbery? Why didn't you mention it before?"

"I wasn't sure. I'm still not sure," she admitted. "I . . . there was so much dust."

"There was an awful lot of dust," Laura agreed.

"But it could have been another man, a second holdup man." Hank left Laura's side and took a step toward Amelia. "What *did* you see, exactly?"

He watched her intently, as if *she* were suddenly a suspect. She forced herself to calm down, to take a deep breath. She had nothing to hide. She put her faith and trust in the Lord, tried to smile at Hank Larson, but failed miserably.

"I *think* I *may* have seen a man standing out-side the door when I was on the floor of the bank, but I wasn't really sure at the time. I certainly didn't get a good look at his face."

"Is there anything else you recall?" he asked.

No. Yes.

She bit her lips together. *God, help me and help Evan.*

"I'm not certain, mind you," she said, "but he may . . . he *may* have been holding a gun."

As Hank watched Amelia Hawthorne fidget and try to explain what she may or may not have seen outside the bank yesterday, he could tell she was upset. All the color had drained from her face. Her eyes were as big as bright green coat buttons.

"I . . . I *really* have to get home," Amelia said.

"Thanks for helping, Amelia," Laura said. "Take care."

Looking relieved, Amelia lifted the hem of her skirt and hurried down the stairs, heading home on foot.

Hank had wanted to pursue his line of ques-tioning, but he knew when to back down during an interview and when to take another tack. He didn't want to upset Amelia any further and found it odd that she was so riled now. Yester-day after the robbery, she hadn't seemed a bit nervous or distraught.

Many women would have run screaming from the bank or been felled by a fit of vapors under the same circumstances, but not Miss Amelia Hawthorne. She'd scrambled behind the teller wall to help Mrs. Cutter and had never even come close to tears as far as he could tell, let alone a fainting spell.

So why was Miss Hawthorne so jumpy now?

For a moment he was so preoccupied with Amelia that he almost forgot he'd come to interview Laura Foster. He had first met the widow when he arrived in Glory two days ago and had inquired about renting a room in the boardinghouse. Somehow he had missed seeing the sign posted on the front porch that read Couples and Women Only.

The widow politely informed him that at no time did she rent to single gentlemen.

He'd spent two miserable nights sleeping in a room above the bar in the Silver Slipper before he was able to acquire the former Chinese laundry building.

Laura Foster was a beautiful woman, no doubt about it, but aside from admiring her loveliness the way one might admire a fine work of art, she held no attraction. Tricia was the woman he'd loved and lost. Not even Mrs. Foster's beauty could overshadow his wife's memory.

"Did anyone else see an accomplice?" Laura asked.

"Not that I know of," he admitted.

"If you're finished, Mr. Larson, I've got plenty to do inside."

"I believe that's all for now. Thank you."

"I wish I could have been of more help," she said.

He turned away, distracted by the sight of Amelia hurrying down Main Street with a heavy black leather bag clutched in one hand. Head high, shoulders straight, she walked with purpose, her strides long and even.

As Hank returned to his office, he thought about what both women had told him. Dust was blowing down the street during the holdup. Laura thought she saw two men outside the bank, not just one—and then they were gone.

Amelia may or may not have seen someone who may or may not have been armed. Perhaps she'd been too shocked to mention it yesterday, but from what he recalled, he didn't think that was the case.

Had she purposely kept the information from him?

If so, for what reason?

Head down, hands clasped behind his back, he walked on. He always thought better on his feet. He listened to the hollow ring of his boot heels against the boardwalk, heard the springs on a buckboard creak as the wagon passed by. Lost in contemplation, he nearly tripped over a child who came careening out of the mercantile and then Hank crashed into a woman who ran out after the little boy.

"Sorry, ma'am."

The timid, fair-haired woman colored and mumbled an apology.

Hank moved on, reminding himself he really had to quit bowling into women this way. He remembered colliding with Amelia inside the bank, the way she'd frantically hit the floor and started to gather up bits of dried flowers. They must have looked like a pair, scrambling around on their hands and knees.

I think I may have seen a man standing outside the door when I was on the floor of the bank, but I wasn't really sure at the time. I certainly didn't get a good look at his face.

He walked a few more paces, pictured the way Amelia had lost color when he explained that he was there to question Mrs. Foster about what she'd seen the day of the robbery.

He stopped dead still in the middle of the boardwalk, reached beneath his hat to scratch his head and recalled the details of his encounter at the bank.

He had been about to leave when Amelia Hawthorne walked right into him. Had he really knocked her off balance, or had she feigned the fall?

Why had she chosen to enter the bank at that

moment? Was it by chance, or was there more to it than that? Why was she out running errands in the middle of a dust storm?

As much as he wanted to deny it, he suddenly couldn't help but wonder if she might have been involved in the holdup. Was she an accomplice? A distraction?

It was hard to believe those guileless green eyes could hide anything, but he'd be a fool to be distracted by a woman's eyes, no matter how innocent.

Hank stepped inside the hollow emptiness of the building still filled with crates, his printing press and his dreams. His eyes watered the minute he inhaled the remnants of strong lye soap and incense and he wondered if the smell left behind by the laundry was ever going to dissipate.

He wanted to start writing. He *needed* to start writing. He'd already planned the initial one-page edition that would be distributed free to everyone residing in and around Glory. An introductory edition with a full-page story of the robbery and a call for advertisers on the back.

He'd already decided on a headline: Lone Robber Attempts Bank Heist.

Now he wasn't so certain.

As editor in chief and sheriff, he had a duty to the townsfolk to ferret out the truth. Even if that meant discovering things he'd rather not know about Amelia Hawthorne.

Chapter Five

A loud knock on her door woke Amelia just as dawn's first light crept across the morning sky. Hoping it was Evan, she slipped into the old plaid robe that had been her father's and hurried through the house.

It wasn't Evan standing on her front porch, but Ready Bernard, a cowhand who worked on the Rocking e Ranch a few miles outside of town. Ready was a robust black man who was quick to smile but who said little. The minute she saw him, she knew why he was there.

Rebekah Ellenberg, Joe's wife, was expecting her second child any day. Amelia had successfully delivered their first, Orson, a little over a year ago.

"Mr. Ellenberg says you should come now. I'll wait and ride back with you," Ready offered.

She knew Joe Ellenberg would refuse to leave his wife's side and, rather than make him a man short, she suggested, "You head on back. I'll ride out to the ranch by myself. Tell them I'm on the way."

Ready lingered a moment, debating before he

tugged the brim of his hat. "Thank you, ma'am. I'll tell them."

She bade him farewell and closed the door. Ten minutes later she was dressed, her medical bag packed. When she led Sweet Pickle out of her stall, she discovered her mare was lame.

"Oh, Sweet Pickle, why now?"

There was no sign of Ready, no way to call him back. Amelia tied the ribbons of her straw hat beneath her chin and grabbed her medical bag.

Big Mick Robinson, blacksmith and owner of the livery stable, had loaned her a horse before, so she headed for his place. She kept up her pace, taking care not to trip on the uneven walk. A few yards down Main, a man crossed over to her side of the street. She recognized him in an instant. His bowler hat was a dead giveaway.

Since their brief encounter at Laura Foster's yesterday, she was bound and determined to keep her distance. Now here he was, hurrying down the boardwalk, walking directly toward her.

She knew a moment's panic and thought about heading home, but the Ellenbergs were depending on her. Besides the Lord must keep putting Hank Larson in her path for a reason. Perhaps it would be better to find out what, if anything, he'd discovered about a second holdup man.

He stopped when he reached her and doffed his hat. "Miss Hawthorne."

"Mr. Larson." She frowned. "Or should I call you Sheriff Larson?"

"Please. No." He centered his poor hat again. "What are you doing out this early?"

"I'm on my way to the livery stable to borrow a horse." She started walking again.

He did an about-face and fell into step beside her. "I'd be happy to loan you mine."

"That's very kind of you, but unnecessary." She reached up to brush a stray lock of hair away from her eyelashes. "I really need to hurry. I'm needed at a nearby ranch."

"An errand of mercy, no doubt. Then I insist on driving you. My carriage is already hitched up. It's right outside my office building."

"I'm sure you're far too busy. You have a paper to publish." *And outlaws to track down.*

"I can't very well put out a newspaper unless there's something to write about. As you so succinctly put it two days ago in the bank, a wiser man might have realized there was no news around here."

"Have you found out any more about the robbery? About the man Laura Foster and I *may* have seen outside the bank?" She tried to sound as if she were only making casual conversation.

"Not yet. I've been asking around, though."

She nearly tripped. He grabbed her arm just above the elbow to steady her. Amelia glanced over, met his blue eyes. She felt an immediate blush creep up her cheeks. Instantly, he let go.

"Thank you," she said.

"Sorry," he said.

She hurried on toward the livery. Time was of the essence. Anything could happen to Rebekah Ellenberg and her unborn child while she, Amelia, was trudging down the street with the "sheriff" trailing along beside her.

They reached the huge barn fronting Main Street, but the double doors were still closed.

"Mick!" she called out, expecting a response from inside. "Open up, Mick. It's Amelia."

Mick Robinson was usually up well before dawn, shoeing horses or tending to stock.

"Looks like you'll have to take me up on my offer," Hank Larson said.

Lord, I know You are never far from me.

She stared at the locked barn doors in frustration and then walked around to look over the fence bordering the lot. There was no sign of Mick anywhere.

Perhaps this was why God had sent Hank Larson to her this morning—the man appeared to be her only option.

"I take it this is an emergency . . ." Hank paused, waiting for an answer.

Finally she nodded. "It is. There's a baby on the way. I need to be there to deliver it."

His brow furrowed something fierce. His gaze became harsh and cold.

"You're a . . ." He appeared to be having trouble saying the word.

"Midwife." She nodded. Then she watched him go as still as a stone.

I should have known. Hank stared at Amelia. He'd heard she was an apothecary. He assumed people went to her to patch up minor scrapes and scratches.

She is a midwife.

But she wasn't a bona fide physician.

"What's wrong?" she asked.

Apparently he couldn't hide his disgust. "Nothing. We'd best get moving."

As they walked back up the street toward his office, he struggled with the bleak nightmare of a childbirth gone terribly wrong. The memory was as vibrant and alive as when it happened a year ago.

"There's no surgeon nearby? No *real* doctor?"

She broke stride and turned to meet his eyes. "*Real* doctor?"

"Yes."

"My father was a *real* doctor, if by that you mean a *man* with a medical degree. He taught me everything he knew." She recalled sitting beside her father as he quizzed her on anything and everything that would come to mind.

They'd reached the compact black buggy outside his newspaper office. A black gelding was harnessed between the traces.

"If you care to loan me your rig, I'm perfectly capable of driving myself out to the Rocking e."

"I'm certain you are, but I'd prefer taking you."

He'd spent the remainder of yesterday introducing himself around and getting to know the store owners along Main Street. Late in the day he had finally wandered into the Silver Slipper Saloon. In deference to his new position as sheriff, he asked for a sarsaparilla.

After a few minutes of conversation, Denton Fairchild, the barkeep, mentioned a group of young hotheads had been in and out of town the past month.

"They're a bad lot," Denton told him. "As a matter of fact, I know one kid who's been in here with them more than once. Everybody knows Evan Hawthorne's a troublemaker."

It struck Hank as odd that if *everyone* in town knew Amelia's brother was a troublemaker, not a soul except the bartender had mentioned it.

Truth be told, he'd rather do anything than drive her out to some ranch to practice her trade on some innocent woman and her unborn babe, but the journey would give him the perfect opportunity to ask about her brother. There was always the chance she might let something slip. After hearing about her brother, his suspicion that she might somehow be involved had only deepened.

72

•••

Amelia paused beside the rig for no more than a heartbeat before Hank reached for her heavy medical bag and tossed it into the buggy as if it weighed no more than a feather.

She reached for the side of the carriage, put her foot on the small iron step and pulled herself up. She was in the act of tucking her skirt neatly around her when she glanced over and realized he was staring. His expressive eyes were shuttered, hiding his thoughts. He hurried round the buggy and climbed in on the opposite side.

"I've upset you somehow," she said as they headed out of town.

He glanced over. She watched him closely from beneath the wide brim of her straw bonnet.

"It's nothing. Let's just enjoy the ride, shall we?" He kept his hands steady on the reins and followed her directions. They turned onto what appeared to be a well-traveled road leading out of town. Beyond them, the land opened up and the horizon rolled away beneath the sky for as far as the eye could see.

She thought back over their conversation as they'd hurried down the street.

"Am I to understand you think male physicians are better skilled at delivering babies than midwives?" she asked.

He remained silent, staring down the road. His expression had grown so dark, so closed, that she

73

wondered if she really wanted to hear what he was thinking.

Her father had warned her of the prejudice against women doctors. Ninety percent of his class at the university were against having women students among their number. But he was convinced she had a God-given talent for medicine and could do as much good as someone whose only qualification was a piece of paper.

She thought of all the babies she'd delivered in the years since her father had passed away. Remembered how hard she had prayed over mothers struggling to bring forth healthy children and how thankful she was for God's help and blessing each and every time she heard a newborn's first cry.

"I may not be a physician, but I know a woman's body better than any male doctor. What's more, I know a woman's heart. And I never forget that I am but an instrument of God's will. He's the one who guides my hands."

"What happens when there are complications? What happens when it's too late to call a doctor?"

She thought of all the things that could and sometimes did go wrong during childbirth. Her father taught her to recognize the four orders of labor: natural, tedious, preternatural and complex. Most babies presented naturally, but there were those occasions where she knew she would need all the knowledge her father had drilled into her, along with all the confidence and faith she could muster.

"There is no *doctor* to call, Mr. Larson. We are out here on our own."

He shocked her by abruptly changing the subject.

"I hear your brother runs with a wild crowd," he said.

Suddenly her insides were reeling. She hadn't once mentioned Evan to him. She was sure of it.

She knew so little about Evan, so little about his friends, she didn't know what to say.

"Where did you hear that?"

"I have my sources. I was asking folks if they knew anything about the robbery. Someone mentioned that he keeps company with unsavory characters."

"Were you asking as a newspaperman, or as sheriff?"

He paused, adjusted the reins. "Both."

She fell silent.

"You never mentioned you had a brother," he said.

"I . . . why would I? When would I have had the opportunity?"

"When I was at your house after the holdup, when you put ointment on my cut—which by the way is already healing nicely—"

"I noticed."

"You could have said something about having

a brother who lived there, as well."

"There was really no reason to mention my brother." She tried not to sound defensive.

"When did you see him last?"

"Who?" She stalled, knowing very well what he meant.

"Your brother, Amelia."

"Not long ago." *Please, please don't ask for more details*. "Turn here," she said, indicating the entrance to the ranch. "I hope we're in time."

"Have you delivered many children?" Again, he deftly caught her off guard by changing the subject. She detected a chill in his tone.

"More than I can count. You sound very harsh. Why is that?"

This was far safer ground than talk of Evan, or so she thought until he replied, "My wife and child died at the hands of an incompetent midwife."

Hank knew he'd shocked her. Amelia seemed to be gathering her thoughts as she stared at her hands, fingers knotted together in her lap. It was a good mile from the border of the ranch to the house. They rode in silence for a few minutes.

"How did you know she was incompetent?" Amelia finally asked.

Hank took his eyes off the road long enough to glance in her direction.

"I had no idea until it was too late that the

woman was inebriated that night. She locked me out of the room. My son was stillborn. My wife bled to death." He took a shuddering breath, wished the words hadn't conjured the images. "I didn't get to tell her goodbye."

They were closing the last few yards to the front of Joe Ellenberg's ranch house when Amelia said, "Sometimes, God—"

Hank cut her off. "I don't want to hear anything about God." He'd heard every platitude. *It's God's will. Trust in the Lord. The Lord giveth. They are in a better place.* He didn't care what God wanted. How was he supposed to trust a God who took His wrath out on helpless women and unborn babies?

"I can assure you I never drink spirits," she said softly.

Plummeted into despair, he ignored her and forced himself to concentrate on the scene unfolding before him. He saw things through a writer's eye, a writer's mind.

He saw not only the long, log home that appeared on the other side of a knoll, but also the smoke curling out of a chimney in a detached building at the end of a covered dogtrot. He saw a woman who looked to be in her late forties watching from the overhang of a covered porch. She appeared to be waiting anxiously to greet them.

She waved with one hand and clung to the

hand of the toddler beside her with the other. A little boy, a little over a year old. Hank even imagined what the woman must be thinking.

Where have you been, Amelia. Hurry. Hurry. We need you.

So dependent. So trusting of the local midwife.

Amelia Hawthorne seemed no more than a girl herself. As the buggy neared the house, he saw the woman on the porch had clear, bright eyes. Her plain hair was pulled straight back into a knot at her nape. The skin around her eyes was deeply etched with lines, as was her brow. She was rail thin beneath a serviceable skirt and calico blouse. Her eyes were shadowed with all the fears and concern she could not hide.

Her back was straight, unbowed. She wore her courage as easily as she donned her clothes. She was a product of the rolling plains and prairie, the harsh winters, the rain-soaked springs, the unbearably hot summers.

She would make a perfect character for his novel.

The woman scooped the little boy onto her hip, stepped off the porch and headed toward the buggy. Hank tugged on the reins. When they stopped, Amelia hopped out before he set the brake.

The older woman embraced her, but only for a second. Amelia took the time to ruffle the toddler's hair. She spoke to him só softly that

Hank couldn't hear what she said. The little boy laughed and then Amelia was all business again.

It was a touching scene. One he would remember—for the sake of the novel—he told himself. Nothing more.

Amelia was headed toward the house when, as an afterthought, she called back, "Hattie, this is Hank Larson. He's Glory's new sheriff. Thank you for the ride, Mr. Larson. I'm sure the Ellenbergs will see that I get home."

He watched her hike up her skirt, saw a flash of petticoat around the high tops of her black shoes as she dashed inside. He hadn't thought about merely dropping her off and leaving. He hadn't thought past delivering her here and questioning her along the way.

Now there was more he wanted to ask. More he needed to know. He'd like to believe she'd had no part in the robbery, that mere circumstance was how she ended up in the bank two days ago. Her talk of her belief in God might be genuine, or it might only be a cover.

Could Amelia be living an outwardly exemplary life, but in reality be a member of a roughshod gang of outlaws?

He reminded himself not to let his writer's imagination run away with him.

"I'm Hattie Ellenberg." The woman had remained near the buggy. She added, "This is my grandson, Orson Wolf Ellenberg."

The love, the joy she took in introducing her grandson shone on her face. For a heartbeat, she appeared years younger. He could see she had once been a fine-looking young woman.

He had a thousand and one questions for her. How did she come to be here living in a house of rough-hewn logs in the middle of the Texas plains? How long had she been here? Where was she from?

He'd been so focused on her face, on her expression, that it was another moment before he noticed that a puckered scar cut a wide swath across her head along her hairline. The scar set her hairline back a good three inches.

"Scalping," she said matter-of-factly. Obviously she'd caught him staring.

"Pardon me?" He thought she'd said *scalping*.

"I was nearly scalped. Luckily I lived to see my son married and my grandbaby here. With God's blessings I'll be holding his little brother or sister in my arms by nightfall."

"Nearly *scalped?*" Hank tried not to stare.

"By Comanche. I used to try to hide the scar, but a couple years ago my daughter-in-law convinced me it was a badge of honor and a sign of bravery. Now I only cover it up when we go into town. Puts folks at ease."

"I . . ." Hank rarely found himself speechless. Hattie Ellenberg was definitely someone he had to talk to at length.

"How about we go set on the porch and get out of the sun? I've got some coffee on." She started toward the house.

Amelia had dismissed him. There was no reason for him to wait, but he was intrigued by Hattie and unwilling to leave yet.

"Coffee sounds fine, but I don't want to take up much of your time, ma'am. Surely you've got your hands full. I'll just have one cup and be on my way." He purposely avoided looking at the toddler. What sane man intentionally poured salt in open wounds?

"Nonsense." Hattie motioned him to follow her inside. "Set a spell."

At just that moment, a tall, dark-eyed, dark-haired man strode into the kitchen. There was urgency in his tone and movements. He barely glanced at Hank.

"Ma, Amelia needs you." His worry was more than evident.

"What is it, Joe?"

"Amelia didn't say, but something's not right." Joe Ellenberg's gaze touched on things around the room. Hank knew the man wasn't seeing anything, that he was on the verge of panic.

"Amelia knows what she's doing. Don't you worry." Hattie handed Joe the boy, Orson. Then she flew over to the cupboard, grabbed a mug, filled a cup of coffee for Hank and set it on the table in the middle of the room. "You two set

81

and jaw and I'll see what Amelia needs. Keep that water boiling."

Joe sat in complete silence. Hank stood by awkwardly, then walked over to the other side of the table and sat down. The rancher seemed completely unaware of the child in his arms. The little boy picked at a button on Ellenberg's shirt.

"I'm Hank Larson," Hank introduced himself. He added, "I drove Amelia out." He lifted the coffee mug to his lips. It was too hot to drink. "Her horse needs a new shoe."

"Thanks. Much obliged." Joe jiggled his knee and the child perched there laughed.

"Amelia threw you out?" Hank didn't try to disguise his bitterness.

Joe shook his head no. "Rebekah asked for Ma. Amelia doesn't believe in keeping fathers away from the birthing."

"You don't say." Hank had never heard of such a thing and said so.

"It was her father's way, I guess. Some folks disagree with the notion, but Amelia's not one to run from a good head butting. Rebekah likes having me there."

If that were the case, Hank wondered how long Joe would sit and jaw.

Just as Hank lifted the mug again, a horrific scream cut the air. His own hands began trembling. When hot coffee splashed on the skin between his thumb and forefinger, he quickly set the cup down and willed himself not to think. Not to remember.

"I've got to go," Hank mumbled.

Joe Ellenberg's face went ashen. "Last time it was easier." He ran his hand over his son's dark hair, smoothing it against the boy's crown. "Didn't take more than a couple hours."

Hank was mute. His Tricia had suffered for what seemed like days.

"Amelia's here. She'll know what to do," Joe reassured himself aloud.

For this family's sake, Hank hoped it was true. He sincerely hoped Amelia was as skilled and confident as she had tried to lead him to believe. He still doubted she was as knowledgeable as any male physician.

Hank pushed out of the chair. He had to get away from this house, away from the nightmares the birthing conjured. He would head back to town without Miss Amelia Hawthorne and save his questions for another day.

Just then, another long, terrible scream rent the air and Joe Ellenberg stood so abruptly little Orson almost rolled off his knee and onto the floor. Joe caught him in time, hauled him up.

"I'm going back in." Joe headed for the door, turned around and shoved the toddler at Hank.

There was nothing to do but hang on as Ellenberg rushed out of the kitchen. Hank held Orson at arm's length and looked him over. The boy gurgled, laughed and waved his arms. He was chubby, pink cheeked and strong. Hank had to tighten his grip to keep the boy from squirming out of his hold.

Hank sat down heavily and moved the steaming cup of coffee beyond the child's reach. As the boy made himself comfortable on his lap, an ache the size of a boulder grew in Hank's heart.

His son would have been about this child's age. Is this how it would feel to hold his own flesh and blood on his lap? To feel the touch of his little hands as they explored the cuff of his sleeve? To hear his son babble nonsense noises and giggle?

By now, would he have been taking this sweet baby smell for granted?

If it wasn't for Miss Amelia Hawthorne, Hank could have remained numb to the pain searing his heart like a hot iron. He wouldn't have been forced to face all he had lost, to touch and feel all the joy he would never know.

And if it wasn't for *her,* he probably wouldn't be sheriff of Glory, Texas, either.

He had to get out of this house. Now.

Chapter Six

Upon entering the bedroom Rebekah shared with her husband, Amelia found the young woman lying on a pallet on the floor. Rebekah Ellenberg insisted on giving birth as she'd seen Comanche women do during her years in captivity. At least Hattie had successfully talked the young woman out of delivering her child on the ground outside.

Amelia had known the Ellenbergs for years. She'd nursed Hattie back to health after a Comanche attack on the Rocking e Ranch. She knew all the heartbreak Joe and Hattie had suffered. But time and prayer heals all wounds and when Rebekah came into their lives, Joe found his faith again.

Amelia prayed that one day, her brother Evan might find the peace of mind and of heart that Joe had finally found.

She knelt on the floor beside Rebekah and comforted the young woman in the last stages of delivery. Little Orson Wolf, named after his grandfathers, had come so swiftly Amelia had barely arrived in time to usher him into the world. But it appeared his sibling was not going to follow his lead.

Rebekah was in great pain, clinging to Joe's hand, pushing with all her might but nothing was happening. Afraid this might be a breech birth, Amelia sent Joe after Hattie and did a quick examination. The baby was well positioned, so Amelia suggested Rebekah scream as loud and long as she wanted. A few moments later, the child began to move.

Hattie knelt on the opposite side of the pallet and supported Rebekah's back. Amelia encouraged the young mother to push. The birth process was too far along for Amelia to give Rebekah a concoction of sweet nitre and syrup of saffron, or laudanum, or acetate of morphia.

The time for rest was over. There was nothing to do at this stage but encourage her to try to push her baby into the world.

When Rebekah screamed again, Joe came running. His dark eyes were shadowed with worry. Sweat beaded his brow.

"Where's Orson?" Hattie was about to leave, but Rebekah clung to her hand with a strength that belied her pain.

"I handed him to the gent that drove Amelia out here. I forget his name." Joe looked lost as he stared at his wife. As he smoothed back her hair, his hand shook. He pressed a wet towel against Rebekah's brow.

As if he sensed her gaze, Joe's eyes found Amelia's. She forced a smile.

"This isn't unusual, Joe. It's just not what you all expected after Orson's easy arrival. You let her hang on to you and everything will be fine."

"Dear God," she whispered. "Let this child come into the world to love and serve You. Let Rebekah and Joe continue to live out their lives as witness to Your goodness and the blessings You bestow upon us."

Joe and Hattie added, "Amen."

Rebekah screamed. And pushed. And screamed.

Twenty minutes later, Orson Wolf's sister entered the world with a lusty cry.

Amelia had two equal lengths of string ready. She tied off and cut the cord and handed the infant to Hattie, who carried her over to a wash table where a bowl of warm water waited. Rebekah's gaze followed the woman's every move until her mother-in-law brought the baby back and laid her in Rebekah's waiting arms.

As Joe and Rebekah stared in wonder at their perfect little girl, Amelia monitored Rebekah, expecting the womb to contract and expel the afterbirth. She wiped her hands on a clean cloth, slipped her father's gold watch out of the pouch pocket dangling at her waist and checked the time.

Ten minutes later, when nothing had happened, she lay her hand on Rebekah's abdomen, employing both friction and pressure to stimulate the contraction of the womb.

She glanced up and found Hattie watching her closely. The woman's eyes conveyed unspoken concern. Amelia gave a slight shake of her head. Nothing to worry about yet. She waited five more minutes. Time was of the essence now.

Rebekah appeared to be growing weaker. She lay back and closed her eyes. Joe and Hattie's expressions reflected their anxiety, but they didn't say anything. They watched Amelia expectantly.

As if she could hear her father voicing directions in her ear, she took the end of the umbilical cord in her left hand and used it to guide her right hand slowly upward until she could cup the placenta in her hand.

Once it was brought away from Rebekah, Amelia bundled the rags and washed her hands. She directed Hattie to fashion a broad binder or girth around Rebekah's body and tie it into place. This done, Amelia waited for the womb to contract on its own and was finally rewarded.

Not until she was certain Rebekah was in good health did she breathe a sigh of relief and whisper a prayer of thanks.

There was nothing left to be done. Unlike other mothers who relished a lying-in period of at least four days, Rebekah would be on her feet within the hour. This, she told Amelia, was the Comanche way. She had seen women give birth and within the hour disassemble a tipi, pack up their worldly possessions and be on the move.

Amelia left Joe and Rebekah to coo over their little girl and followed Hattie outside to dispose of the soiled rags. Then the women made their way along the dogtrot to the smaller log structure that housed the kitchen.

Amelia had all but forgotten Hank was there. The minute she laid eyes on him, she reminded herself not to let down her guard.

He was seated on a chair drawn up to the kitchen table. Orson Wolf was awake but his eyelids had grown heavy. His chubby cheek was pressed against Hank's vest, his fingers curled around a handful of Hank's shirtsleeve. The scene would have warmed the coldest heart if Hank's expression hadn't been as hard as stone.

Hattie hurried across the kitchen and gingerly lifted Orson to her shoulder without waking him.

"I can't thank you enough, Mr. Larson," she said. "We surely didn't mean to dump this child on you." Hattie patted Orson's bottom and instantly frowned. "Oh, no."

"Oh, yes." Hank shook his head and stared at the damp spot on the thigh of his wool trousers.

As Hattie hurried Orson away, Amelia covered a smile that threatened to bloom—until Hank's eyes met hers and she saw a fathoms-deep bleakness. It gave her the urge to comfort him, to lighten his burden somehow.

My wife and child died at the hands of an incompetent midwife.

She watched him swallow, heard him clear his throat.

He looked away. "Mrs. Ellenberg. Is she . . ."

Again, Amelia remembered Hank's own words. *I didn't get to tell her goodbye.*

"She's fine," she told him. "The baby, too. A healthy little girl named Melody Rain."

"Orson *Wolf* and Melody *Rain?*"

"Orson was Joe's father's name. Running Wolf was Rebekah's father's. Melody was Joe's sister's name. Gentle Rain was Rebekah's mother's."

Curiosity immediately replaced the sadness in Hank Larson's eyes.

"Rebekah is an Indian?"

"No, but Rebekah was raised by Comanche. She was a captive most of her life. But that's another story."

"One I'd love to hear someday," he said.

Suddenly exhausted, Amelia settled on a nearby chair. "I'm sorry to have taken up your day like this. I know you have work to do."

He got up and walked toward the dry sink, opened a cupboard and took down a coffee mug. She watched as he poured a cup of coffee and brought it to her without her having to ask.

"I'm not the happiest man alive right now, but I'm glad I could be of help."

She took a sip of the strong, black coffee. For a moment he appeared so thoughtful, she thought he was going to apologize for doubting her skill.

Instead he said, "If you plan on leaving soon, I'll wait a few minutes longer. You may as well ride back to town with me."

She knew Joe Ellenberg had plenty to do without worrying about how she was going to get back to Glory. He needn't spare a man to drive her back now that Hank was still here and offering. She stared down at her coffee cup before looking up at Hank's gaze again.

"If you're going to continue to badger me about Evan, I'll have to decline. I truly don't know where my brother was the morning of the robbery."

Hank suspected Amelia might not know exactly where her brother was the morning of the holdup, but he had the feeling she may have an inkling.

He also knew the truth often had a way of revealing itself on its own. "I won't badger you," he promised.

She looked relieved but completely exhausted. "Then I accept."

With a glimmer of a smile, her entire countenance changed. Arrested by the hint of a sparkle in her green eyes, he found himself wondering why such a well-spoken, dedicated young woman had never married.

Perhaps it was that dedication to her work that got in the way.

"I insist you let me help you make up lost time," she said. "When I walked down Main Street yesterday I happened to notice your storefront window was too filthy to see through. I'd be happy to bring over some vinegar and clean it for you. Do you have a ladder?"

"That's not necessary." He found himself picturing what she might look like perched atop a ladder. "But if you insist—"

"I surely do. I insist."

She was as good as her word.

The next day, as Hank was downstairs in his combination newspaper publishing house, print shop and sheriff's office assembling his Hoe revolving press, he heard determined footsteps outside the front door. He looked up in time to see Amelia come breezing in carrying a bucket and a crock of vinegar. She'd tucked a bundle of rags under her arm and had a long, navy-blue work apron tied over her dress.

The woman was ready for business. He wished he'd made as much progress.

"So, Mr. Larson," she began, "I'm here to wash your window." She surveyed the long narrow room and sniffed. "Could this lye smell be any stronger?"

"I'm hoping by the time I get some lamps in

here and the windows are all open every day that it'll air out."

"My father always suspected there was an opium den upstairs."

"That might explain the cloying smell of incense up there." He was beginning to suspect he knew why the previous owner had been so anxious to sell the place.

"Do you have a ladder?" Amelia set down her bucket, rags and crock and folded her arms. "Where is your water pump?"

"Harrison Barker said I could use his ladder. The pump's out back, but I'll get the water for you—"

"Don't bother," she called out over her shoulder as she grabbed the bucket and bustled out the door. He watched her long, rust-colored braid sway against her back, sighed as he looked at the press, and hurried out to borrow the ladder.

By noon she was still wiping down the wall around the window and waging a war on cob-webs. Pieces of the press were laid out around him and lined up across the top of his desk.

"Don't let me disturb you," she'd said when she first started. She hadn't stopped talking since.

He still wasn't much further along than he'd been the day before and if Amelia kept waylaying him, she was going to single-handedly sink his newspaper venture before he even got it off the ground.

"If I were you, I'd come up with another lead story. The robbery is old news." She paused to scuttle down the ladder to rinse out her rag. She'd been trying to talk him out of covering the robbery for the past forty minutes. "Nobody will be interested in reading about that now."

"It just happened three days ago. Everyone is still talking about it," he assured her.

She glanced over her shoulder, her eyes wide for a moment before she looked away again. He found himself staring at the braid trailing down her back, knowing without even touching it that her hair would be as soft as silk.

He watched her climb back up the ladder.

Hank turned back to the press pieces and tried to ignore her. He took a sniff and wrinkled his nose. The lye and incense smells now mingled with the odor of vinegar.

Twenty minutes later, she was polishing away at the window glass, but Hank wasn't doing much of anything except watching her. He reckoned that being so long without a woman's company, he was bound to begin to notice all the things he'd taken for granted when he was married; the turn of a woman's ankle, the merest flash of a petticoat beneath the hem of a full skirt, the softness of cottons, flyaway wisps of fine hair that refused to be tamed by pins or combs.

Shocked by the direction of his thoughts, Hank forced himself to concentrate on the bolts and screws and nuts lined up like metal soldiers on his desk. He wondered about this fascination with her and reminded himself how very different Amelia Hawthorne was from Tricia.

Headstrong and *determined* weren't words he would have used to describe his late wife. Tricia was cultured, soft-spoken, genteel. Her hands were manicured, her hair always perfectly coiffed. She was never in the sun without a wide-brimmed hat or an umbrella. Not a single freckle marred her perfect ivory skin.

No, Tricia was nothing like Amelia Hawthorne. It was impossible to imagine that he'd ever take a second glance at a woman like Amelia.

After Tricia's death, an old friend in Missouri tried to convince him that life goes on. He said that Hank would never forget Tricia, nor would he ever replace her in his heart, but Hank would surely find love again.

His friend said people's hearts healed over time, just like wounded flesh. Scars were left behind but you eventually healed. Hank didn't believe it.

Hank picked up a gear that worked the tumbler and found himself wandering closer to the ladder in search of a screwdriver. He shuffled through boxes of books, pausing to look over things in open crates—books he wouldn't need until everything else was set up.

He was backing up with a box full of stationery

in his arms when he accidentally bumped into the ladder. The thing began to weave, and Amelia gasped and let go of the wet rag. Hank dropped the box, turned to grab the ladder and the rag fell on his face.

He had overestimated his steps and bashed his shin against the lower rungs. The rag slid off his face. Amelia let out a squeak and Hank glanced up as she came tumbling down.

He held out his arms and caught her before she hit the ground. She grabbed hold of his shirtfront with one arm and hooked the other around his shoulder.

In less than an instant she'd gone from wiping down the front window to being cradled in his arms.

Dazed and amazed, Amelia found her face inches from Hank Larson's. She was so close she could see the small flecks of silver in his blue eyes. She watched those eyes of his widen in the same shock she was feeling.

"The ladder wobbled." For some reason she felt the need to explain. She wasn't in the habit of catapulting into men's arms.

"I bumped into it," he confessed. "I'm sorry."

"I think," she began, "you should put me down now."

"Of course, I—"

Just then, Mary Margaret Cutter came breezing

through the open door carrying a covered dish and calling, "Woo-hoo! Mr. Larson!"

She stopped dead in her tracks the minute she saw Amelia in Hank Larson's arms.

"Oh, my." The woman quickly glanced away, but her gaze ricocheted back.

Amelia landed on her feet when Hank unexpectedly let her go. She ducked her head, pretending to brush off her apron and her skirt, located her cleaning rag on the floor and retrieved it before she had the nerve to look Mary Margaret in the eye.

The banker's wife sported a thick, wide bandage across her temple. Far bigger, Amelia estimated, than the small wound beneath it. It would be hard for anyone not to notice it.

"I'm sorry I barged in like that," Mrs. Cutter said. "The door was *wide* open and I thought . . . well, I'm just here to deliver this layered beef and potato dish, since Mr. Larson saved our lives and all, it's the least I could do. I never expected to find you, Amelia, in the man's arms."

Amelia glanced up at Hank Larson. His face was as red as a radish. It appeared he was suddenly a writer without words. Apparently, it was up to her to explain.

"Mr. Larson gave me a ride out to the Ellenbergs' yesterday and—"

"Did Rebekah have her baby?" Mary Margaret asked.

"She did. A little girl. Anyway, in exchange for the ride—"

"Why, Amelia Hawthorne, I never—"

"This is *not* what you are thinking, Mrs. Cutter. In exchange for the ride I offered to *clean the front window* for him. I was on the ladder just now when he accidentally bumped into it—"

Hank interrupted. "I was carrying a box and not looking where I was going—"

"And I fell off the ladder," Amelia finished.

Mary Margaret looked them both over and winked. "Oh, well. If *that's* all there is to it. I'm glad you weren't hurt, Amelia." She looked puzzled for a second and then said, "Didn't the two of you run into each other in the bank the morning of the robbery?"

Amelia twisted the cleaning rag. "Mrs. Cutter, this is all perfectly innocent. This isn't Mr. Larson's *home,* it's his place of business. The front door was wide open. Why, I was right there in the window for all the world to see," Amelia reminded her.

Of all people to walk in and see her in Hank's arms, why did it have to be Mary Margaret Cutter? Word would be all over town in less time than it takes to melt sugar.

That morning, Amelia convinced herself she was really going to the newspaper office to talk Hank out of writing a detailed account of the robbery. The less said about the event, the less likely anyone was to tell him anything about Evan.

There was no way she'd have ever thought of using womanly wiles on him. Why, she didn't even have any to begin with. She was a God-fearing woman. Besides, Hank wasn't interested in her in the least. Especially not now that he knew she was a midwife. He'd been peevish and silent all the way back from the Ellenbergs', which had suited her fine.

"I'll just leave this here." Mary Margaret set the covered dish atop a box and started backing away toward the door.

Amelia elbowed Hank in the ribs. He actually jumped, but the nudge helped to shock him out of his stupor.

"Th-thank you, Mrs. Cutter." He started across the room to see her out the door. "I'll see that you get your dish back."

"You do that, young man. Don't forget we're all waiting for the first edition of the paper. If I were you, I'd tend to business around here." She paused in the doorway and gave Amelia a wave of her fingers. "Bye-bye, Amelia. You take care. A pretty young woman can't be too careful these days." With a sly wink, she was out the door.

When Hank turned around, he looked as if he wanted to crawl into a hole and pull it in after him.

"I certainly hope you don't think I initiated that," he told her.

"I certainly hope you don't think I threw myself off that ladder into your arms."

He remained planted near the front door.

She watched him from across the room but didn't budge.

Suddenly they both moved at once.

"I'll be going now. The window is clean," she said.

"I'd better get this press put together," he said at the same time.

Amelia grabbed her bucket, rags and vinegar. As she headed out the door, she vowed that from now on, she'd do her level best to avoid Hank Larson.

Hank stepped aside as she breezed past with barely a nod. Her cheeks shone with splotches of embarrassment as red as firebrands.

He watched her walk away.

She had felt softer than he expected. Warm and far more vulnerable than she let show.

The direction his thoughts had taken shocked him. How long would he have stood there mute, making a fool of himself, if Mary Margaret Cutter hadn't walked in?

After only three days in town, he'd been turned inside out by prim and proper Amelia Hawthorne.

From now on, he decided, he was giving her a wide berth.

Chapter Seven

"So nice of you to come, Sheriff Larson."

"It was nice of you to invite me, Miss McCormick." Hank gave his hostess a slight bow and handed her his hat. He waited uncomfortably while she hung it on a bentwood hat rack.

Charity McCormick was rail thin. She had light blue eyes, much like her brother, the reverend, and a ready smile. Unlike the preacher, who always appeared calm and confident, Charity had a worried look about her, as if she never quite relaxed.

As she was ushering him into the front parlor, there came a knock at the front door.

"I'll just be a moment." Charity appeared hesitant to leave him alone.

Hank glanced into the parlor. "I'll be fine."

She turned away and he stepped over the threshold. There was no one else in the room, or so he thought until he heard a giggle coming from behind the settee.

He bent over to look beneath the settee when suddenly, someone bowled into him from behind. His knees buckled and he fell forward.

Before he knew what hit him, a child climbed onto his back. The boy straddled him and then tried to slip a gag around Hank's mouth.

Almost immediately, two shiny black shoes appeared in front of his face. He craned his neck. A little girl with a white pinafore over a pink dress was standing over him with her hands planted on her hips.

"Better not hurt him, Sam," she warned.

"I'm gonna scalp him!" the boy assured her.

Having already lost a hat to this town, Hank was in no mood to lose any hair. He flattened his palms on the floor and pushed up, easily dislodging the boy who fell to the floor with an "Oof!"

Hank was dusting off his hands and straightening his jacket when he heard a gasp from the doorway.

"Sam McCormick! What have you done?" Charity rushed into the room and grabbed her nephew by the sleeve. She hauled him over to a side chair.

"Sit!" she commanded.

"You can't make me," the boy chided.

Charity looked as if she were about to burst into tears.

"He was going to scalp the sheriff, Aunt Charity," the little girl said. "I had nothing to do with it."

"You did, too!" Sam yelled. "You were the decoy."

Charity stumbled back, made it to the edge of the settee and swooned.

Hank was certain things couldn't get any worse, but then Amelia Hawthorne walked into the room. She hurried to Charity's side, reached for the woman's wrist and felt her pulse.

Hank was dumbfounded. When the preacher had asked him to dinner, he suspected he was being invited because he was new to town and Brand McCormick was a hospitable man looking to increase his flock. Then he'd heard from Harrison Barker that Charity McCormick was a spinster in need of a husband, so the last person on earth Hank expected to see tonight was Amelia Hawthorne.

"What are you doing here?" he wanted to know.

"I might ask the same thing of you, Mr. Larson." She pulled a handkerchief from a reticule dangling from her wrist and began to fan Charity's face. Then she turned to the little girl, who looked to be about seven years old.

"Janie, run and get your aunt a glass of water, will you please?"

Janie didn't budge. "How's she gonna drink it? She's just having a fit of the vapors. She'll be all right."

"Go, Janie." Amelia's tone brooked no argument. The girl stomped out of the room.

Hank glanced at Sam. The boy was still on the chair, but his arms were folded and his eyes narrowed to slits. He glowered at Hank and stuck out his tongue.

On the settee, Amelia fussed over Charity. The woman's eyes were still closed, but she was mumbling under her breath.

Hank was wondering if the promise of a home-cooked meal was worth all the drama when Brand McCormick walked in. As if his sister passed out every day, Brand made a bee-line to Hank and patted him on the shoulder.

"Glad you could make it, Hank. We're happy to have you here in our humble home."

Amelia simply couldn't fathom why the Lord kept throwing Hank Larson in her path. Three days had passed since Mary Margaret had walked in on that embarrassing scene in Hank's newspaper office and for three days she'd endured knowing smiles and innuendos wherever she went.

She'd so looked forward to coming to dinner tonight and sharing a meal and conversation with the McCormicks, and when the Reverend stopped by the house to invite her to dinner, she'd been happy to accept. Despite nine-year-old Sam's mischievous ways and his sister Janie's constant tattling, a dinner at the McCormick home was always pleasant.

Until now. She'd be forced to endure an entire evening in the presence of Hank Larson who, according to Harrison Barker, was still vigilantly questioning folks about the possibility of a second gunman outside the bank the day of the holdup.

She sighed and tried to avoid Hank's gaze. She simply didn't have the strength to guard every word she said tonight. As soon as Charity recovered, Amelia planned to make an excuse and leave.

A second later, Charity let out a long-suffering sigh. Her lashes fluttered, her eyes opened and Amelia helped her to sit up. She offered her some water, but Charity refused.

"Should I get her tonic?" Janie offered.

"I think she'll be fine now." Amelia watched Charity carefully for any sign that she might be suffering something other than nerves.

"I'm glad you could join us tonight, Amelia." Brand's smile could light up a room.

She glanced over at Charity, who still appeared to be dazed, but coming around. She was certain Charity's swooning episodes stemmed from the fact that the woman was overwhelmed caring for her boisterous young charges and nothing more.

Everyone knew, more often than not, the children ran her ragged.

"Thank you for inviting me, Reverend." Amelia purposely avoided looking at Hank. "I'm sorry to say that I just walked over to tell you I must decline."

"Is Evan home?" the reverend asked.

Amelia quickly shook her head. "No. No, I haven't seen him recently. I just . . . I can't stay."

Even without looking Hank's way, she felt him watching her from across the room. She shoved her hankie back into her reticule and pulled the strings shut. Then she got to her feet.

The relief on Hank Larson's face was almost comical. He didn't wish to be in her company any more than she wanted to be with him.

For some reason the notion bothered Amelia —far more than she wanted to admit.

Lord, why am I being tested like this?

If she knew the absolute truth of what happened the other morning at the bank, would it be any easier to be in Hank Larson's company?

Mr. Larson stepped closer to the settee and offered Charity a hand. Once she was on her feet and hurrying off to the kitchen, he turned to Amelia. Her eyes met his and, in that instant, her heart stumbled.

"I'm sorry you can't stay, Amelia," he told her. He didn't sound sorry.

She forced herself to breathe slowly. "Thank you, Mr. Larson."

"Hank, I'm sure you won't mind walking Amelia home," Reverend McCormick said. "The days are growing longer but dusk is nearly upon us tonight. I would accompany her myself, but I believe I'd best tend to these rascals of mine while Charity puts the final touches on the meal."

When Hank failed to respond, Amelia said, "There's no need for that, Reverend." She started toward the parlor door. "I can find my way home."

"I won't hear of it. Not when our able-bodied sheriff is right here. He's happy to walk you home, aren't you, Hank?"

"Well, I—"

Couldn't the reverend see that Hank was definitely *not* happy about the idea?

"I wouldn't send you two off alone if it were dark, not with Amelia's fine reputation to consider—but there's plenty of light left."

Amelia's cheeks began to flame. Had Reverend McCormick heard the gossip? Surely he put no stock in it or he wouldn't be suggesting they go anywhere alone together, even in broad daylight. Or would he?

"I've done nothing to soil my reputation," Amelia blurted. "Nor will I."

"Of course not," the reverend agreed.

"Reverend, I—" Hank ran his finger around the top of his collar as if it was suddenly two sizes too small.

Amelia quickly said goodbye to no one in particular and headed for the entry hall. She was out the front door and certain she'd made her escape until she heard the front door open and close behind her. Heavy footsteps echoed across the porch and within seconds, Hank Larson joined her on the street.

They fumed in silence for a moment before Amelia started off alone. There was no board-walk this far from the shops and stores of Main Street.

Hank was a few steps behind, but his long stride quickly brought him to her side.

"The preacher insisted I walk you home."

She didn't look at him. Couldn't look at him.

"I didn't want to do this any more than you wanted me to," he confessed.

"I know." She'd clearly seen his reluctance, his aversion to her earlier. It was hard to miss.

"Everywhere I go lately, I hear the story of how Mary Margaret walked in and saw you in my embrace," he added.

Amelia stopped walking. "It certainly wasn't an *embrace!*"

"I know that, you know that, but Mary Margaret is telling everyone that's what she saw."

"Then you need to tell them the truth. Write about it in your paper." Better to have herself as front-page news than the robbery.

"You want me to feed the flames?"

"I want you to put them out!"

They'd reached the edge of her yard. She paused by the gate in her picket fence.

"Thank you." She didn't sound grateful at all. It was impossible to hide her irritation.

"Listen, Miss Hawthorne, I'm not the one who insisted on you barging in and cleaning my front window the other day. If you hadn't been there in the first place, we wouldn't be a topic of gossip."

"*Barging* in? As you recall, I was there to repay a favor."

That, she decided, was stretching the truth. Mainly she'd wanted to try to talk him out of writing about the robbery. She wanted him to stop questioning people all over town.

"If *you* had never barged into *my* life, never moved to Glory to start your silly newspaper, wearing your silly bowler hat and that houndstooth suit of yours, if you hadn't run me down at the bank, then none of this would have happened and I wouldn't be walking around on eggshel—"

Suddenly, Hank Larson took hold of her shoulders, pulled her close enough for their lips to meet and kissed her square on the mouth. It was a second or two before Amelia realized what was happening, but when she did, she lay her hands flat against the front of his coat and shoved.

"What in the world are you *thinking?*" She reeled back and fought to catch her breath.

"I—" Hank looked as stunned as she felt. "I really have no idea why I did that."

"I would suggest, Mr. Larson, that you hurry

back to Reverend McCormick's. Perhaps he will enlighten you about honor and a pure heart."

She pushed the gate open and started up the walk. Halfway to the porch, she stopped. He was still outside her gate, staring after her with a bewildered look on his face.

"From now on, Hank Larson, keep your hands and your lips to yourself!"

Hank watched Amelia storm into the house and slam the door behind her. Remembering where he was, he glanced around, immediately thankful the street was empty.

The sun was just sinking below the horizon. Rays of pink and orange fanned out across a violet Texas sky.

He had no idea why he'd kissed Amelia just now. He hadn't thought before it happened, but suddenly in the middle of her tirade, he'd pulled her close and kissed her.

It was a chaste kiss, as kisses go. There was nothing seductive about it.

Nor had she kissed him back. But it had the desired effect. He'd managed to shut her up.

Now he'd forever have the memory of her lips against his. Each time he got a whiff of lavender and sage, he'd think of Amelia and the color of the Texas sky at twilight.

He didn't want his mind occupied with thoughts of Amelia Hawthorne. He wanted only memories of what had been—memories of his life with Tricia.

Now what? he wondered. *Now what? What does this mean?*

What if he eventually did learn that her brother was in on the attempted bank heist? What then?

What if he discovered Amelia herself had been in on it?

He seriously doubted that. She had a cadre of friends to vouch for her character. But Evan didn't. Though no one openly admitted her brother might be an outlaw, folks went silent whenever he brought up Evan Hawthorne's name.

Hank lingered near the gate for a moment or two longer. Amelia had yet to light a lamp inside, though night was swiftly falling.

He owed her an apology for that kiss. It would be a hard debt to pay.

And not only did he owe Amelia an apology.

Hank closed his eyes. *I'm sorry, Tricia.*

It broke his heart when he realized his wife's face was not as clear in his memory as it was before.

Inside the house, Amelia leaned back against the front door and pressed her fingertips against her lips. Her mouth tingled. Her stomach was so jumpy that she thought she might heave.

Chamomile tea was in order. Maybe a dose of her father's nerve potion would help.

What was Hank Larson feeling right now? He'd looked as shocked as she felt after he kissed her.

It was over before it even started and yet the kiss left her light-headed and trembling. She certainly hoped she hadn't just sinned or disgraced herself, but how could she be at fault? She hadn't even seen it coming.

Had she?

She thought back over the events preceding the kiss. Hank had appeared to want nothing to do with her. She'd barely made eye contact with him at the McCormicks'. She excused herself from dinner the minute she could. But outside her house, she'd lost her temper. She'd berated his move to Glory, blamed him for everything. She'd criticized his hat, his clothing.

Then he'd kissed her.

Let him kiss me with the kisses of his mouth—

She'd read and reread Solomon's Songs once when she was young, in love, and foolish. She'd fallen in love with a scoundrel. She'd believed his lies and he broke her heart. Not long afterward, she lost her father. She had Evan to provide for. Thankfully, with no one else able to supply medical care, many of the townsfolk turned to her for their medical needs just as they had her father. She had no time for herself, no time for anything but her work, her garden, her neighbors, her brother. She'd tucked away her dreams of ever finding romantic love.

And now, out of the blue, a man had kissed her. *I really have no idea why I did that.*

Amelia kept her fingertips pressed against her lips as she turned to the mirror framed in the hall tree. Slowly, she pulled her hand away. There was no outward sign that she'd been kissed except that her cheeks were flushed and her eyes were shining as bright as if she were feverish.

Her heart was racing.

"Dear Lord, help me," she prayed. "I don't understand what's going on. I have no notion why You've sent Hank Larson into my life."

She hung her reticule on the hall tree and hurried out to the kitchen pantry where she kept her supply of dried herbs, potions and elixirs.

She needed something to calm her erratic heartbeat. Surely some chamomile tea and an hour of prayer would restore her sense of calm and purpose.

Chapter Eight

For two weeks, Amelia avoided Hank Larson by visiting outlying ranches and homesteads. Making home visits was something her father had done every spring and fall as the weather began to turn. Each year since she'd taken over his practice, Amelia put her trust in the Lord for protection and off she went.

Folks thought she was crazy, traveling alone between stops. Anything could happen to her, they said. She could get thrown from her horse. She could get attacked by roving Comanche. She could get caught in a storm. Most of the time she ended up being escorted from one home to another, passed along from neighbor to neighbor. It was the best way she knew to raise her own spirits, especially when the folks she helped were happy to see her come and sorry to see her go.

Though the home visits kept her away from Hank Larson, they did little to help shed her ever-present worry over Evan. At the end of her travels, she returned home to find her garden beginning to show the first signs of a chaotic riot of summer color. Thankfully, there had been enough spring rain to keep them watered while she was gone.

Ignoring the weeds for now, she unsaddled Sweet Pickle and went inside. She set her medical bag down and hung her reticule on the hat rack near the back door before she wandered through the house, raising the shades and opening the windows.

Outside the front door, she found a single-page newspaper neatly folded and tucked beneath a stone. Beyond her small covered porch, the street was quiet. She carried the paper inside.

The free introductory edition had news stories on the front page and advertisements on the back. Harrison Barker's Mercantile, Patrick O'Toole's Butcher Shoppe and Foster's Boardinghouse shared the advertisement page along with columns of empty boxes that read: Your Advertisement Here.

Hank Larson was listed as owner, publisher and editor in chief of the *Glory Gazette*. There was a one-paragraph biography listing Hank's writing credits and telling of his recent move to Glory from Saint Joseph, Missouri.

The front-page article was an account of the First Bank of Glory holdup. It was written with detail that brought the event alive all over again for Amelia.

Mary Margaret and Timothy Cutter were quoted; so was Laura Foster, who stated she thought she saw two men outside the bank before the holdup.

No one else in town admitted witnessing anything of note. Denton Fairchild, the bartender at the Silver Slipper, claimed there had been some unsavory characters hanging around in his establishment, but it appeared they'd moved on.

There was a paragraph about Harvey Ruggles, who was still in jail in Comanche. He would be tried by the circuit court as soon as the judge rode through the county seat. If he had named an accomplice, there was no mention of it.

The article ended by saying anyone with any information regarding the robbery should contact Hank Larson, editor in chief and temporary sheriff.

Amelia sat down heavily on a hassock in the parlor with the paper resting on her lap. She stared out the window thinking. Hank hadn't mentioned her saying she *may* have seen someone outside the bank. He'd barely mentioned her at all—except to say she'd been inside the bank when the robbery occurred and that if it weren't for her, the holdup might have been successful.

Eventually, she turned to the paper again. There was an announcement that a future column would be entitled *Know Your Neighbors* and a call for suggestions for the first profile. Amelia wondered what Hank Larson would do for news when the robbery story had played itself out.

Amelia carefully folded the paper, carried it into the kitchen and laid it on the table. The *Glory Gazette*'s first edition, with its story about the robbery, brought an ache to her heart and a nervous uproar in her stomach. Her two weeks on the road had been a fine reprieve, but now she faced the same challenges she'd tried to escape.

How long before I run into Hank Larson somewhere?

What in the world was she supposed to say or do when she saw him? Why had he kissed her?

And what of Evan?

She pressed her palms against the surface of the kitchen table, closed her eyes and whispered, "Dear Lord, keep me strong. Help me to follow Your lead, to trust You to show me the way and the truth. Keep Evan safe. Help him to follow Your lead, to hear Your voice."

One look out the back window and her tasks for the day were clear. Before she could tackle the weeds in the garden, there were dried herbs to be ground and sifted into packets to replace those she'd used on her journey. She donned her apron, took a pestle and mortar off the shelf near the window, and then went into the small pantry between the kitchen and the back porch.

She was on a short ladder, unhooking a bunch of yarrow she had hung from a nail in a low beam, when she heard boot heels echoing against the back porch.

Her heart quickened its pace and for a moment she envisioned Hank Larson about to knock on the door, until she remembered only one person used the back door—Evan.

Her toe caught in the hem of her dress and she nearly fell off the ladder in her haste to climb down. She tossed the yarrow on the dry sink and was turning around when her brother walked in.

"Evan—"

A greeting died on her lips the moment she saw him. Above a dark growth of stubble, his eyes were weary. He looked as if he'd aged ten years. He was covered in trail dust, his clothes filthy. He took off his hat, ran his fingers through his hair and looked around.

"Let me get a fire going in the stove. Are you hungry?" She bustled over to the wood box. "I just walked in myself. I was out doing home visits." She avoided looking at him, afraid to discover he looked even worse than she thought at first sight. "I should have gotten the fire going first thing, but I had a big breakfast at the Ellenbergs' and was putting off cooking."

He didn't offer to light the stove for her. As she lit the kindling, she heard him walk to the table, pull out a chair. When she turned around, she saw him reach for the newspaper.

"How—" she balked, afraid to ask "—how is your new job?" She steeled herself against a lie.

"Fine." He glanced at the *Gazette*. Amelia clasped her hands at her waist. It had always been a struggle to get him to read anything. His hands tightened on the paper as he read the headline, Bandit Hits Local Bank. He bent over the sheet, slowly reading every word.

When he finally looked up, her heart sank to her toes. The truth was plain as day on his face.

He was *there that day*.

"Your name is mentioned," he told her. "Looks

like you were as much a part of foiling the holdup as the new *sheriff*." His eyes were hard, unforgiving.

"The gunman tripped over us." She took a deep breath. Shuddered. "You know very well what happened that day. I saw you outside the door."

There was no shock, no protest. He leaned back and casually hooked one arm over the chair. "Says here no one else saw anything, except maybe that lady with a boardinghouse. I know you, sis. If you were sure about seeing me, you'da turned me in. Your goody-goody conscience must be worrying you something fierce. Why didn't you tell anybody?"

"I . . . wasn't positive. You never really admitted . . ."

"But you suspected."

"I didn't want to believe it of you. The barkeep says you keep company with a bad lot."

"I suppose everyone's been talking about me."

She couldn't tell if that upset him or if he was bragging.

"We're known by the friends we keep," she said.

He stood up, shoved the chair back. "I can't stay here now." He looked as if he were about to leave, then surveyed the room as if he had no idea where to go.

"Why did you come back?" She glanced outside the window. "Where's Bucket Head?" His horse wasn't tied to the hitching post out back.

"In the barn."

He'd hidden his mount before he came in.

"What have you done, Evan?" Her hands were shaking. She clasped them together behind her back.

"None of your business." He shifted, scratched the stubble on his chin and glanced toward her pantry. "You got any money? If you're just back from your home visits, you musta got paid something."

She held out her hands and shrugged. "You know the folks around here don't have much. I got paid in ham and eggs. I got a sack of carrots from the Mitchells. Inge Martin gave me some almond cookies." She still had the two dollars Laura Foster had given her hidden in the pantry. She'd put the money away to help pay the taxes on the house when they came due.

"You're welcome to the food, Evan, but I really think you should stay and . . . and turn yourself in."

"Turn myself in? There's no law against standing outside a bank while a robbery is going on."

"You had your gun drawn."

"You sure about that? You told the sheriff you don't know what you saw."

"Memories often get clearer with time."

"And sometimes they fade."

He hovered in the center of the kitchen, filling the space with the heat and darkness that come before a summer thunderstorm. She knew she didn't have long to try to convince him to do the right thing.

"Get me a clean shirt, will ya, sis?"

His request threw her off guard. "A clean shirt?"

There was a pile of them in his room. Clean, pressed and folded, waiting for his return. She walked to his side, laid her hand on his sleeve.

"Evan, you don't have to turn yourself in to the sheriff, though I think he's a fair man. He'd hear you out. Why don't we walk over to the McCormick house? You can talk to the reverend and maybe after some prayer and counseling, you'll realize that staying on this path will only lead to destruction. I can't lose you, Evan. You're all I have."

He shook off her hand. "You still think the Bible can fix everything, don't you, sis? You think all there is to life is doing the right thing and everything will be fine. I'm here to tell you it's a waste of time for a man like me. We've never had anything and I'm sick of it."

"There are ways to make an honest living, Evan. Anyone in this town would take you in as an apprentice. Mick at the livery would be happy to have you. Why, Mr. Larson might even need someone to set the type on his printing press. You could—"

"I could end up with a noose around my neck if I don't get out of here."

"A noose? Have you killed someone? Are you a low-life horse thief now?"

"It's none of your business what I am."

"It is my business. I'm your sister—"

"Go get me a clean shirt. Please." He turned his back on her and walked over to pour himself a glass of water from a tall crockery pitcher on the dry sink.

Fuming, she decided it best to put distance between them. She'd gain nothing by arguing.

She prayed as she walked into his room, forcing herself to slow down, to take her time. His shirts were folded in the top bureau drawer. She stalled, prayed, opened the drawer and chose one with ticking stripes.

She heard him pacing the kitchen. Heard his footsteps in the parlor. Maybe he was going to sit down, to think about what she'd said. She took a deep breath, hugged his shirt and gave him a few seconds more alone.

Then the back door slammed.

She tossed the shirt on his bed, ran into the kitchen. He was already headed into the barn.

"Evan!" She ran across the back porch and started after him. She'd barely reached the bottom step when Evan rode out of the barn on horseback, trampled her herb garden, jumped the low back fence, and headed east.

Shaken to the core, Amelia stumbled back. She watched the distance widen between them. Her eyes filled with tears. His image wavered and shimmered against the sky. She clenched her fists, pressed them against her thighs. She wanted to scream she was so angry, but that wouldn't bring him back.

She could no longer ignore what was happening. She could no longer hide from the truth and still hold her head up before God and the good citizens of Glory.

Hank Larson had to be told that Evan was involved in the holdup.

She raised her fist to her lips. She couldn't face Hank after what had happened the last time they were together.

She decided she would go to Brand McCormick instead. The minister would listen without judgment. He could tell Hank about Evan. Brand McCormick would understand. He'd be more than happy to help her. Together, they would pray for Evan.

She went back inside, intent upon collecting herself enough to walk to the McCormicks' house. The moment she stepped over the threshold, she saw her father's mustache cup lying on its side on the table. She'd kept her savings stashed in the chipped cup for as long as she could remember. Her hand shook as she picked it up. The sound of coins was absent. She looked inside, knowing what she'd find.

The cup was empty. The two silver dollars Laura Foster had paid her were gone.

Evan had stolen from her. He'd been so desperate, so selfish, that he'd taken her savings. Taken the money that she'd set aside for taxes. Her tears overflowed. The room began to whirl. She quickly sat down on a chair, hung her head between her knees and waited for her head to clear.

She got up slowly and started toward the parlor until she remembered her reticule wasn't on the hall tree. She found it beside her medical bag near the kitchen door, but when she picked it up, it felt suspiciously light and her heart sank like a stone.

Her fingers fumbled and caught on the strings. Reaching inside, she searched for her father's gold watch, but her hand came away empty. She turned the small silk bag upside down and shook it. All that fell out was her yellowed ivory comb and three bent hairpins.

This morning at the Ellenbergs' she'd felt a hole at the bottom of the makeshift pocket she'd pinned to her waistband. A small niggling voice inside her told her to mend the pocket. Instead, she'd slipped her father's gold watch into her reticule.

Now, as much as she wanted to deny it, Evan had stolen the watch. It was like losing her father all over again.

Staring at the meager items in the palm of her hand, she slowly sank to the floor and began to sob, mourning the loss of the watch. Mourning the loss of Evan's innocence.

Chapter Nine

Hank walked down Main Street with a spring in his step that belied his inner turmoil. It was good to be outside, away from his desk for a change. He'd been to Amelia Hawthorne's house twice a week for the past two weeks and had yet to find her at home.

At first he had convinced himself she was hiding from him, that she had isolated herself behind drawn shades and locked doors. Then Harrison mentioned she was most likely doing spring home visits to outlying ranches and his guilt eased a bit.

He owed her an apology for what he'd done, and he meant to deliver it today if she had returned. Maybe then he could stop thinking about the spontaneous kiss. Maybe once he'd apologized, he could stop thinking about her altogether.

When he noticed some blue wildflowers blooming at the edge of the town square, he decided to make her a peace offering. He picked a few stalks and bunched them together, then kept walking.

When he reached her gate and pushed it open, he noticed that spring had come to Amelia's yard. It was filling up with flowers in every color of the rainbow.

Hank stared at the scraggly bunch of wildflowers in his hand and when he reached the porch, he set them down near the top step. Amelia had all the flowers she needed. His pitiful bouquet would make a paltry peace offering.

He noticed the shades were up. He glanced inside the front window but didn't see her in the parlor. He saw his own image and pulled off his hat. Then he finger combed his hair and tugged on his lapels.

He took a deep breath, knocked on the door and waited for a response.

And waited.

He knocked again and was about to leave when the door slowly opened and Amelia peered around it. She looked worn-out. Her eyes were red rimmed and swollen, her skin pale and blotchy.

"Are you all right? You look terrible." Concern replaced his nerves. The apology was forgotten.

"Why, thank you," she sniffed.

126

"Are you ill? After all, you've been out galli-vanting around the countryside for two weeks. It's no wonder you look like something the dog dragged in."

"What?"

He realized he might as well go all the way and jam his other foot into his mouth, too.

"Your hair is sticking out worse than usual and your eyes are all bloodshot and swollen. It looks as if you've been—" He stopped abruptly, stared at her a second longer as realization hit him. "It looks as if you've been crying."

She stuck her head out a bit farther and peered down both sides of the street. There wasn't a soul in sight. She stepped outside. She gathered her skirt in her hands, clutching it for dear life.

Suddenly he remembered why he was here. "Amelia, I'm so sorry for what happened the other night. I didn't realize I'd cause you this much distress. I don't know what came over me. I have no idea why—"

"You have nothing to do with my tears," she said flatly.

"I don't?" Relieved, he watched her walk over to the edge of the porch and sit down. She moved like a woman four times her age.

"In fact, I need to talk to you about some-thing," she said.

"You do?" He decided he sounded like a nitwit.

Not knowing how to deal with her strange mood, he sat on the step beside her. No harm in that. They were out in plain sight. In broad daylight. She was troubled, no doubt about it, and apparently her problem had nothing to do with him.

"My brother Evan . . . came home a while ago."

Hank glanced around at the open door behind them, half expecting to see the mysterious Evan Hawthorne standing there. "He's here? Now?"

She shook her head, propped her arms across her knees and then pressed her face against them.

Hank froze. "Did he hurt you, Amelia?"

She shook her head no again and mumbled something.

"Pardon?"

She raised her head, her eyes brimming with tears. He watched one slip over the edge of her spiked lower lashes and slide down her cheek.

"He hurt me deeply, but not in the way you think. He—" she swallowed a sob "—he stole our father's gold watch from me."

"He stole it?"

"Yes. And he . . . he was involved in . . ." Her voice went up an octave as she said, "He was involved in the bank robbery."

"He confessed?"

"He saw the newspaper you left here. He . . . yes. He finally admitted it. I tried . . . I tried to

128

talk him into turning himself in. I told him you'd be fair. When he refused, I suggested he see Reverend McCormick. He asked me to get him a clean shirt. I thought for a minute he was willing to get help, to throw himself on the mercy of the townsfolk—"

"And vow not to sin again."

"Something like that."

"Then what happened?"

"I heard him walking around and then he left. I discovered he'd stolen the watch."

"Is that all he took?"

"No."

"There's more?"

She wiped her eyes on the back of her sleeve. "He stole two dollars. That was my whole savings."

Two dollars was all the savings she had to her name? Hank stared down at the uneven part in her russet hair and squelched an urge to pull her into his arms and comfort her. She looked so small and vulnerable. So alone. So betrayed.

"What will you do now?" She turned huge green eyes his way.

He had no idea what to do with the information. He began to think aloud. "Well, I guess I should put a notice in the paper. Tell folks to be on the lookout for him."

"Oh, no," she moaned.

"And I should ride back over to the county

seat, talk to the sheriff there. Rangers might be able to track him down. I really wouldn't know how to go about tracking him myself."

She hid her eyes in the crook of her arm again.

"Did he say where he'd been? Where he was going?" Hank asked.

"No." Her shoulders rose and fell with barely audible sobs.

He reached out to pat her shoulder, then pulled his hand back.

"I'm sorry," he said. "I know this must be hard on you."

She raised her haunted eyes to him again. "You have no idea."

He didn't know much, but he knew he couldn't possibly leave her alone in this condition.

"Let me walk you over to the McCormicks' house."

She shook her head so vehemently he offered another suggestion, "How about Laura Foster's, then?"

Again, a definite no. "I'm used to taking care of myself."

She didn't sound as if she were soliciting his sympathy, but rather as if she were simply stating a fact of life. She was alone in the world. She had to fend for herself. He found himself wishing he could change things for her. He was convinced she shouldn't be alone now.

Life shouldn't have to be this way, he thought. An endless round of lonely days and lonely nights. He spent his own long empty hours throwing himself into his work. He imagined she did, too. He glanced at the small sign on her front door. Apothecary.

"Come on, Amelia. I'm taking you to the reverend's house." Seeing her ravaged expression, her sorrow, he let go all notion that she might have had anything to do with the robbery.

Slowly she got to her feet. "I'm too embarrassed to see anyone right now."

"Everyone here respects and admires you. There's no need to worry about them blaming you or talking behind your back. I have a feeling if Evan would have been anyone else, I'd have gotten a lot more information out of folks around here. As it was, I suspect the whole town clammed up to protect you, not your brother."

She pushed her hair back off her damp temple. "I wish I could say that makes me feel better, but somehow it makes me feel even worse. They trust in me. I should have told you what I suspected after the robbery."

"You didn't know for certain that Evan was involved, did you?"

"Not until today."

"He's your brother, Amelia. No one will fault you for waiting to find out for sure."

"When I think about what might have happened to Mary Margaret, or to you, or anyone else who might have happened by—"

She covered her mouth with her hand and for a second he was afraid she was going to vomit, but she recovered and closed her eyes.

"I guess the Hawthornes are single-handedly keeping your paper alive," she said. "I can just see your next headline—Robber's Sister Upchucks On Sheriff."

He was glad she could still attempt humor in a humorless situation. He thought for a second then said, "Or how about, Appalling Apothecary Spills Truth And More On Editor in Chief?"

She gave him the barest hint of a smile, but it was far better than more tears.

"Come on. Get whatever you might need. I'm walking you over to the McCormicks' house."

She didn't argue. This time she let him help her to her feet and went inside with a promise to be right back.

She returned in no time. She had toweled off her face, but hadn't taken time to change clothes or comb her hair.

As Hank walked Amelia down the street, neither of them mentioned what had happened the last time they were together. Right now, Hank's kiss was the furthest thing from both their minds.

Thirty minutes later, Amelia was seated on Brand McCormick's front porch, a cup of tea growing cold in her hands. Charity perched on a nearby rocker pretending not to listen, but she was concerned enough not to leave Amelia's side. Her incorrigible niece and nephew were in the front yard, trying to hack down an old mulberry tree with butter knives.

Amelia was glad Hank had talked her into coming. She wasn't able to stop worrying about Evan, but at least she wasn't sitting at home alone. Hank had just walked out from speaking with Brand in the reverend's office. Now he appeared to be ready to leave but hesitant to say goodbye.

She set the teacup on a small wicker table beside her chair, stood and stretched.

"I'll walk with you to the corner," she told him, ignoring Charity's curious glance as well as Hank's obvious surprise.

As soon as they were out of earshot of the house, she turned to Hank. "Promise me that if you find Evan, you'll come tell me first. Tell me before I have to read about it in the paper."

She thought it a simple request and wondered why he took so long to answer.

"Of course. That's an easy promise to make. Far easier to agree to that than make an apology."

"Apology?"

"For . . ." He finally met her gaze. "For kissing you."

In the disaster of the morning she'd forgotten

about all of it. Now, remembering brought instant color to her cheeks. She lowered her eyes.

"Apology accepted," she said softly.

When she looked up again, Hank was still there.

"You'd better be going," she urged.

"Will you be all right?"

"Of course. Life goes on, doesn't it? I'll head home right after luncheon." Charity had invited her to share a meal. "I have a lot to do, plenty of chores to catch up on now that I'm back. You have . . . things to do also."

He was aware that Evan Hawthorne's trail was growing cold. "You're right. I'd best go."

"Take care, Hank."

He started to walk away, paused. "Amelia, I wish I didn't have to do this."

"Thank you," she said. "I wish you didn't, either."

As Amelia dragged up the front steps of the McCormicks' porch, her feet felt as if they weighed a thousand pounds each.

"Would you like more tea?" Charity held the teacup Amelia had set down. The young woman's eyes were shadowed with worry. "I don't know what I'd do in your place, Amelia. This must be simply awful for you."

Amelia tried smiling but it didn't work. "It's not the worst thing in the world, Charity." The

134

worst thing would be losing Evan. Amelia was confident God was not going to let that happen. She put her trust in Him as always.

"Well, I certainly don't know how you're managing to hold up."

"One does what one has to do."

That's what her father had taught her anyway. She'd learned that lesson well as she'd served as his apprentice and nurse. She'd assisted with amputations, dug out bullets, cauterized wounds and stitched them up. She'd heard boys scream for their mothers, watched grown men cry buckets of tears. She'd prayed over the unmarked graves of unnamed soldiers from both sides. She'd grown up during the war years and by the time her father finally agreed they'd had enough she was barely eighteen but convinced she'd already grown old.

"War," her father said once, "is mankind's great folly. It serves no purpose but to set the stage for more of the same." He wasn't an outwardly religious man, but that day, he had quoted Isaiah. "It says in the Bible, 'They will beat their swords into plowshares and their spears into pruning hooks. Nation will not take up sword against nation, nor will they train for war anymore.'"

Looking around the rows of dead and dying soldiers on the blood-soaked ground after the Battle of Cold Harbor—where twelve thousand Union soldiers perished in one day—he had added, "Unfortunately, even after this carnage, I'm afraid I won't see any swords beaten into plowshares in my lifetime."

Yes, Amelia decided, there were many things worse than worrying about Evan.

She tried to change the subject. Not far from the porch, Sam and Janie were still hacking away at the mulberry trunk. "You'd think those children would realize they're not going to fell that tree with butter knives."

"I'm certainly not going to tell them," Charity decided. "It's the quietest they've been in hours." Before Amelia could comment, she asked, "Are you . . . do you have any designs on Mr. Larson?"

"Designs?"

Charity nodded. "Are you sweet on him? Mary Margaret said—"

"Me? Sweet on Hank?" She thought about Hank Larson, about how kind he'd been to her earlier, given the circumstances. He could have berated her for not being completely open about Evan, could have been angry that she hadn't voiced her suspicions. She thought about the kiss he'd given her and how, by his own admission, he had no idea why he'd done it.

"Mary Margaret was wrong."

Charity was watching her closely. She was blushing, obviously embarrassed.

"Why, Charity, are you sweet on Hank Larson?"

"Maybe. I . . . I'm not certain. I haven't had many opportunities to meet anyone like him since we moved to Texas. Someone refined. Cultured. Educated."

"Like yourself."

Now that she thought about it, Amelia realized Hank and Charity were well suited. Charity was a bit gawky, but she was young and pretty, though painfully shy.

"He's not a man of faith," Amelia warned.

"He hasn't attended church yet, but how do you know he's not a believer?" Charity glanced out at the children. They'd apparently given up sawing down the mulberry and now Sam was using a lariat to tie Janie to the tree trunk.

Amelia nodded. "His wife and unborn child died and I believe he blames God."

"Perhaps Brand could speak to him," Charity mused aloud.

"About your feelings?"

"No, about attending Sunday services, about the sustenance one receives from an unwavering faith."

"Perhaps." Amelia wondered why she suddenly felt more exhausted than before. She stared down the street in the direction Hank had taken.

Hank and Charity. She should have seen it before. Was Hank aware of Charity's feelings?

She realized she had absolutely no appetite. "I really can't stay for luncheon, Charity. I'm so sorry. I hope you understand," she said.

"Oh, dear," Charity's hands fluttered to her throat. "I hope it's not something I said."

Amelia shook her head. "Of course not. It's just all this trouble with Evan. I really . . . I would feel much better at home."

A few minutes later, Amelia was headed down the street, looking forward to being alone.

Charity McCormick and Hank Larson.

Be happy for Charity.

The young woman deserved a family of her own. Hank was a widower, eligible, handsome. He was still under forty. Surely he'd be ready to start a new life one day. Take a new wife.

Amelia paused outside her gate, surveyed the little house, her flower and herb gardens. Someday Evan would come to his senses. He could marry, settle down here. She could help raise his children.

This is enough for me. My life is here. This is enough.

Incredibly, her footsteps seemed to have grown even heavier between the McCormicks' house and home. She was about to go up the front steps when she noticed a bunch of bluebonnets lying on the porch. She picked them up, stared at the drooping stems. The flowers were slightly wilted, obviously having been picked much earlier.

She looked around, wondering who might have left them and when.

Chapter Ten

Harrison Barker introduced Hank to Charlie Scout, a Tonkawa who served as a tracker for the U.S. Army. Ever since the closest regiment had been transferred to Fort Griffin, Charlie spent most of his time hanging around in front of the mercantile.

One look at the bowie knife strapped to the scout's thigh and the two cartridge belts crisscrossed over his chest and Hank was convinced he didn't relish being on the trail alone with Charlie. But, since no one else stepped forward to help track Evan, Charlie was Hank's only alternative.

They set out following tracks that led away from Amelia's house, but the Tonkawa lost Evan's trail at a nearby creek bed. Together they rode on to Comanche County to report to Oz Caldwell again.

The sheriff's office was smaller than the row of jail cells strung out down a narrow hallway behind it. He took one look at Charlie Scout and told him to wait for Hank out front. If Charlie was offended, he didn't show it.

"What can I do for you, Sheriff Larson?" Caldwell asked.

Caldwell was a huge man by anyone's standards. Not only did he stand a good six foot five in his boots, but he was nearly as wide as a door. "You here to talk to Ruggles again?"

Hank was by no means short, but he had to crane his neck to look up at Oswald. *This* is what a lawman should look like, he thought. A lawman shouldn't have ink stains on his fingers and a busted-up hat. He rested those ink-stained fingers on the handle of a borrowed six-shooter in a holster riding his hip.

A lawman should at least own his own gun, Hank reckoned.

The trouble was, he barely knew what to do with one and had spent most of the ride over hoping he didn't blow off his toes with the Peacemaker.

"I'd like to talk to Ruggles again. I've got the name of another suspect in the robbery. A man named Evan Hawthorne, from Glory."

"Funny you should mention him." Caldwell swung his feet off the desk, stood up and stretched. He walked over to a small table near the front door and ripped open a brown paper parcel. "I was going to send you a stack of these."

He pulled what appeared to be a poster off the top of a stack and handed it to Hank.

Wanted!
For Robbery, Attempted Robbery,
And General Mayhem
Ned Perkins, Terrence Perkins, Silas Jones And
Evan Hawthorne
Also Known As "The Perkins Gang

"With a little encouragement from a couple of my deputies, Ruggles implicated all his friends. Seems like this bunch of young rowdies fancies themselves a gang. Shot up a saloon over in Dublin. Ruggles was dumb enough to do what the Perkins boys told him to do and got caught."

Hank knew what seeing her brother's name there would do Amelia.

"Ruggles say where they hide out?"

"If he did, I'd have them all in custody." Oz Caldwell turned around and walked back to his desk. "Take a few of those back to Glory and post 'em, would ya?"

Hank nodded.

Oz looked him over. "You still want to talk to Ruggles?"

"Sure," Hank decided. "He give you any other particulars?"

"Believe me, after we were done with him, if he'd a known anything else, he'd a told it."

"I'd still like to ask a few questions."

Oz walked Hank to Ruggles's cell personally but didn't leave. He leaned back against the bars of the empty cell behind him.

Ruggles was stretched out with his back to the door. "Sit up, Harvey. Someone here to see you."

When Ruggles turned around, Hank winced at the sight of his battered face. It was obvious how Caldwell had come by his information. More than obvious.

If Hank hadn't been lying on the floor of the bank the day of the robbery, and if Miss Cutter hadn't been wounded, and if Amelia's life hadn't been in jeopardy, he might have felt sorry for Harvey Ruggles.

But he didn't. Not now.

"I'm here to ask *you* about Evan Hawthorne, Ruggles. We know he was with you the day of the robbery."

"Who says?"

"Evan."

"Then talk to him, not me."

"I'm here to talk to you. I want to be real clear about his part in the holdup."

"He had as big a hand in it as I did. We were told to rob the bank in Glory. I tried. If Evan hadn't turned tail and run, we'd a done it."

"How do you know Hawthorne ran?"

"He weren't in the bank, were he? If he'd a been there, we'd a got away with it."

"So as you see it, he didn't go through with the robbery?"

"As I see it he sure didn't."

142

"Thanks." Hank walked out. Oswald closed the door to the cell area behind them.

"You heard him," Hank said, turning to the sheriff. "Evans wasn't in on the robbery."

"He was in on the planning stages."

"Still, I want you to consider that if you find him before I do."

Caldwell looked Hank over. "Oh, I'm restin' pretty well assured I'll find him before you do. How long you been a sheriff, anyway?"

"A handful of days. In fact, I'm just a temporary solution and looking for a replacement." Hank paused, hoped he was getting through to the man. "Just remember, Evan is from Glory. He's got family that wants to see him get a fair chance at a trial."

"I'll try and keep that in mind," Oz Caldwell said, "but when things get fast and furious, no telling what might happen."

Amelia loved Glory's white clapboard church. Back when they'd first moved to town, services were held in a log structure with a leaking roof. Her father had been on the church board then and she remembered the board members meeting at their house, poring over architectural plans.

The bell tower boasted a steeple and there were double doors that opened directly into the church proper. The funds saved by using a simpler design and expanding on it were allocated for the stained-glass window behind the altar. Tinted light streamed through the panes of colored glass depicting the Good Shepherd with His staff in His right hand, a lamb draped over His shoulders and His left hand resting upon a ewe's head.

As she waited for Reverend McCormick to appear, Amelia's gaze drifted from the window to Charity. The young woman was seated in the front pew between the pastor's children. There wasn't anywhere within a three-hundred-mile radius where a woman could buy a pink day dress the likes of which Charity was wearing. Charity's fancy bonnet sported a long pink feather dyed to match. Whenever Sam disappeared the feather bobbed each time Charity reached beneath the pew to snag him.

Amelia smoothed her hands over her own brown serge skirt. Times were always lean for a doctor whose patients lived hand to mouth. Someday, perhaps, Glory would flourish, but those times were in the distant future. Of the folks who settled on outlying ranches after the war, only the stalwart remained.

As the congregation began to sing "Shall We Gather At the River," Amelia found herself thinking about Hank Larson. He'd been gone for two days, and he still hadn't come to tell her that he'd found Evan. She believed him when he promised she'd be the first to hear if he did.

Hank and Charity.

She stared at the pink feather bobbing on Charity's hat and experienced something she'd never felt before—an intense wave of jealousy.

I, the Lord your God, am a jealous God.

One thing for God to be a jealous God, to want His followers to love only Him, but Amelia knew that jealousy was a sin. She truly did not covet Charity's fine clothes or her shining blond hair. The young woman was as shy and kind and well-meaning as anyone Amelia had ever known.

But when she pictured Charity and Hank together, a niggling, worrisome sensation in the center of her being clenched up and refused to let go.

Stop it! Amelia warned herself.

Jealousy, she decided, was an utterly ridiculous feeling to entertain, especially when Hank Larson meant absolutely nothing to her, nor she to him.

The only other time she'd ever even entertained the notion of falling in love, she'd been abandoned without so much as a by-your-leave. Since then, she'd wasted very little of her precious time worrying about love. This was certainly no time to start, what with Charity setting her sights on Hank and Hank out tracking down Evan.

The light shifted and a ray of sun streaming through topaz glass fell across her. Amelia stared up at the stained-glass window and turned her thoughts to Evan. She took comfort in remembering that no matter where he was, no matter what he was doing or what he might have done, the Lord continued to watch over her brother as He did all His sheep.

From behind the lectern, Brand McCormick began his sermon.

"No one shall enter the Kingdom, save through the Lord, for as Jesus himself told us, "I am the way, the truth and the life. No one comes to the Father except through me.""

Amelia sighed and closed her eyes. Through repentance and acceptance of Christ, Evan would be saved. There was no reason to give up on her brother yet, for the Lord would never give up on him. She vowed to remember that, and to believe that Evan would come to his senses and see the light. The good Lord would show him the way.

When services ended, Amelia walked outside with the others.

Reverend McCormick had just announced the church would be holding its first masquerade party at the end of the month in an effort to raise funds for choir robes. Everyone in town was invited and the congregation was to spread the word.

"So are you going?"

Amelia recognized Hank's voice before she

turned around and looked up into his eyes. For a split second she forgot all about Evan, about Charity. She forgot that there was anyone else in the whole world except him.

"Going to what?"

"To the social. I heard Mary Margaret yelling something about it into her husband's ear."

"The church fund-raising committee is holding a masquerade party. At the end of the month."

"That should be interesting."

"Would you actually attend?" She spotted Charity beneath the trees in the park in front of the church hall next door and experienced a wave of guilt.

"There aren't many sources for news around here, as you so kindly pointed out to me the day we met."

His words forced her to recall the robbery. Suddenly she wished all she had to think about was the upcoming church social.

"Did you . . . find Evan?"

He reached inside his coat and drew out a folded piece of paper. He glanced over his shoulder. People were milling all around the front of the church, some making their way over to long trestle tables where a potluck supper was set up beneath the trees in the square.

"Can we go somewhere alone?" he asked.

"That's not seemly."

"How about we just walk around the corner of

the church? Or we could step inside. I don't want anyone else to see this."

"But—"

"I made you a promise, Amelia. I intend to keep it."

I made you a promise.

Her heart sank. It ached so badly that she was afraid if she looked down, she'd discover she was standing on it. She turned and began to walk away. She didn't want to hear what he had to say, but there was no avoiding it.

In two strides Hank caught up. Did she feel folks watching them, or was she just imagining it?

Once they reached the corner of the church, she looked over her shoulder and saw that Charity was watching them from beneath the brim of her fine pink hat. Amelia reminded herself she wasn't betraying her friend. She had to know what Hank had found out about Evan.

Oblivious to her thoughts, Hank handed over the paper.

"What is this?" She wasn't afraid to stitch a man's wounds together, but she was afraid to unfold the page.

"It's a poster. I brought a pile of them back from Comanche."

Her hands nearly failed her as she opened the poster and saw the names of the Perkins Gang listed there. Evan's name was among them.

"I wanted you to see this before I post them

around town," Hank said. "I thought I'd go around, talk to folks first. Ask if anyone has seen Evan. I wish I had better news, Amelia."

"How did you find out? How did my brother's name end up here?"

"Harvey Ruggles sang like a songbird," Hank said. "He says your brother was in on the robbery, but he got cold feet and disappeared."

"Has Evan done anything else? Harmed anyone? Robbed another bank?"

Hank shook his head. "Not that I know of. He and his friends shot up a saloon in Dublin, though."

Amelia dropped her arm to her side. Forgotten, the poster drifted to the ground.

She turned on her heel and headed into the church.

Hank watched her go pale and drop the poster. He wanted nothing more than to take her in his arms and tell her that everything would be all right. But there were things beyond his power to make right, things well beyond his control. He'd found that out when Tricia died.

He watched Amelia slip inside the deserted church. Her feet nearly faltered but she held her head and shoulders high and didn't bow under the weight of her pain. He wanted to follow her in, to sit beside her in silence until she could face the world again.

But she hadn't asked for his company and she'd made it perfectly clear that she didn't need it. The best he could do was park himself on the steps and wait for her to come out again.

A few minutes later, Amelia dried her eyes and pulled herself together. Once she was outside, she nearly fell over Hank Larson seated on the church steps.

"What are you still doing here?" Wasn't it bad enough that he'd brought her such horrendous news?

"Waiting for you."

"I don't want you waiting for me." He was the man charged with bringing Evan in. He was the man Charity had set her cap for. She didn't dare let herself care about him.

He shrugged. "I'm worried about you."

"As I've told you before, Mr. Larson, I'm more than capable of taking care of myself."

"Do you want to?"

"Do I want to *what*?"

"Take care of yourself. All the time, that is? Wouldn't you like to have someone else take care of you once in a while?"

She'd taken care of her father and her brother since she was eight years old. She'd taken care of the house and the gardens, and for the past seven years, nearly everyone living in and outside of Glory.

Now Hank was asking if she wouldn't like to have someone else take care of her once in a while.

She'd never dared to even let herself dream of it.

His face suddenly wavered before her eyes as they filled with tears.

He reached into his coat pocket and whipped out a linen handkerchief and handed it to her.

"You seem to be leaking, Amelia."

She swiped her tears away. "You are quite simply the most irritating man I've ever met."

"I'm not all bad."

"Did you bring me flowers?"

He looked away. "I brought you a poster."

"No, I mean the other day. Did you leave some bluebonnets on my porch?"

She watched him shift his stance, give his collar a tug. "Those were just weeds. I never realized you'd have so many flowers in your garden. Real flowers."

"It was . . ." She didn't know what to say. "It was a kind gesture. Thank you."

He nodded. "You ready to join the crowd?"

"I'm heading home."

"There's a potluck supper laid out."

She could see folks gathered around trestle tables. She'd brought a crock of baked beans smothered in bacon.

"Come on, Amelia. You have to eat."

Charity was sure to be watching.

When he looked as if he were about to take her arm and lead her to the table, she started walking in that direction on her own. As they moved through the crowd gathered around the serving tables, she heard folks greet Hank warmly and realized he had gotten to know quite a few people in a very short time. Everyone seemed comfortable chatting with him.

What would they say tomorrow when he walked into shops and businesses with his posters? What would they say about Evan? About her?

She ladled a few beans and a slice of beef onto a plate. She didn't care if she never ate another bite in her life.

He must have felt sorry for her because Hank seemed intent on sticking to her like glue. She glanced around the tables set up in shady spots and blankets spread out on the ground and finally located Charity beside Brand. There was one extra chair at their table. Mary Margaret and Timothy Cutter were on a blanket yards away from the McCormicks.

"I'm going to go sit with the Cutters," Amelia announced, hoping Hank would take the hint and walk away.

Hank followed her gaze and said, "There's only one place left beside them."

"Yes. But there's a seat open beside Charity and Brand. You should join them."

Hank paused, nodded at the McCormicks and turned to Amelia. "I don't want to leave you alone."

"Look around, Mr. Larson. We're hardly alone."

He'd kept his word. Despite their odd beginning, despite the fact that he was sheriff for now, Hank Larson was a kind man. He and Charity would make a fine pair. She certainly wasn't about to stand in her friend's way.

He left flowers on your porch.

His way of apologizing for something he should have never done.

He kissed you.

Spontaneously. And, according to him, for no apparent reason.

She reminded herself that he was the man charged with bringing Evan in for attempted robbery.

There was no reason to think he was attracted to her in any way. She'd read a man wrong once. She wasn't about to be fooled again.

Most of all there was Charity to think of, Charity's feelings.

Hank and Charity were far more suited. Perhaps all she needed to do was point that out to him, to give him a shove in the right direction.

If they are so suited for each other, why does it bother you so much?

Amelia stilled the voice inside her, forced a smile and met his gaze.

"Thank you for your concern, Mr. Larson, but I'm fine. I suggest you go and sit with the McCormicks. I know for a fact that Charity would appreciate your company."

His jaw gaped like a widemouth bass before he snapped it shut again.

Amelia turned to walk away, but not before she heard him say, "Miss Hawthorne, you are quite simply the most irritating woman I've ever met."

Chapter Eleven

Just then, Reverend Brand McCormick called to Hank and Amelia both, inviting them to the table. Amelia motioned that she was going to join the Cutters. There was nothing Hank could do but smile and head toward the preacher's group.

As he slid into the only empty chair at the makeshift table of boards resting on sawhorses, Hank couldn't help but notice the rosy blush staining Charity's cheeks and the way she batted her lashes and then coyly looked away.

He hadn't been in her company more than twice, hadn't any idea that Charity would be, as Amelia had put it, *appreciative* of his company.

From the moment he sat down, Charity remained silent except to correct one of the children. She sat with her hands folded in her lap, staring intently at his profile as he spoke with her brother.

"Any luck in Comanche?" the reverend asked.

Hank tried to ignore Charity's intense stare. "Ruggles, our holdup man, was encouraged to talk—"

"Knowing Oz Caldwell, I can imagine he had little choice. You realize I can't condone that kind of treatment of prisoners." Brand paused in the midst of slicing a piece of ham and looked over at Hank.

"Nor do I. Besides, I don't intend on holding anyone here in Glory. There is no jail and, as far as I'm concerned, you folks haven't much of a sheriff, either."

Brand smiled around the piece of meat he forked into his mouth.

"Anyone stepped forward to volunteer to take my place while I was gone?" Hank wanted to know.

"Not a soul."

"I'm going to run an advertisement for a new lawman in the *Glory Gazette* until I find someone." He dug into a pile of creamed corn, well aware that Charity's stare was nearly burning a hole through his cheek. He glanced at her, watched her lashes flutter. He felt obliged to smile at her around a mouthful of corn before he returned his attention to Brand.

Thankfully, Reverend McCormick was an orator. As he continued to chat, pausing now and then to take a bite, chew it and then go on, Hank pretended to listen. He caught only fragments of the preacher's conversation. ". . . think the masquerade party will be well attended . . . fund-raiser for the choir robes . . . never had them . . . really hope someday you'll join us for services . . ."

While the preacher chatted on in one ear, Hank felt Charity staring, and debated what to do. He wasn't looking for a wife and even if his battered, broken heart would allow it, Charity would definitely not be the woman he'd choose. Some might consider her quite lovely. She was obviously a pious, modest young woman. He found her too shy, too thin, and she had no backbone. Brand's two children ran all over her.

He lowered his head and his attention drifted over to Amelia and the Cutters. She was seated on a blanket in the dappled shade beneath a tree, her supper plate forgotten on her lap, her legs crossed at her ankles. She leaned close to Timothy Cutter and spoke directly into his ear. Her bonnet was years out of style. It had slid to the back of her head, exposing her already freckled complexion to the sun.

As he watched, she threw back her head to laugh at something Timothy Cutter said. Her hat slipped farther but was caught by the wide blue ribbons around her slender throat. Hank's heart stuttered, as if trying to chug to life like a steam engine long out of use. He was too far away to hear Amelia's laugh and he realized he'd never heard it before.

Suddenly, more than anything in the world, he wanted to hear what that laugh sounded like. Arrested, he couldn't take his eyes off of her. Charity was forgotten. As he watched Amelia, he saw her quickly sober and knew that her laughter had, no doubt, been silenced when she remembered the news he'd brought her today.

The reverend's voice drifted to him again. ". . . certainly hope you'll join us for services next week."

He turned to Brand, who was waiting expectantly for a reaction to his last remark. Hank sifted through his thoughts, fumbled for an answer.

"I . . . it's certainly something to consider."

Brand pounded him on the shoulder. "Good. That's wonderful. We'll look forward to seeing you."

He had no idea what he'd just agreed to think about.

Charity touched his sleeve, drawing his attention away from her brother. "Would you care for some cake? I'll bring you a piece."

Across the open square, women were replacing

crocks and pots of food with pie plates and cake stands full of delicacies. Sam McCormick was at one end of the table, unabashedly stuffing his vest pockets with cookies. His sister was covertly walking along the length of the table dragging her finger through the frosting on every single cake. There was a multicolored lump of frosting the size of an apple on the end of her index finger.

Hank looked into Charity McCormick's wide eyes, took in her somewhat dazed expression and lost his appetite. "I'm full as a tick," he told her. "I think I'll forgo the dessert."

She appeared at a loss until Brand said, "I'd love some cake. And a piece of pie if there's extra."

Hank decided that Brand was completely unaware that his sister was smitten. No one could be that adept at acting oblivious.

While Charity went to fetch her brother's dessert, Hank made up his mind to put a halt to any infatuation she might be nurturing. Better to put an end to it now. *Nip it in the bud, son.* It's what his father would have advised.

She returned to the table and handed Brand a plate piled high with desserts.

"My brother has a sweet tooth," Charity spoke without actually looking at Hank. Her face was aflame. "It's his one vice."

"As far as I know, and I've studied the Bible

extensively for years, sis, there is no sin in eating sugar."

"How about gluttony?" She turned to Hank and winked.

He hoped the wink was only to let him know she was teasing. He pushed his chair back.

"Miss McCormick, I was wondering if you'd like to take a stroll with me? Reverend, with your permission?"

Brand nodded, mumbled his approval around a mouthful of chocolate cake. "Certainly, Mr. Larson."

Charity wasted no time getting to her feet.

Hank felt he was about to cancel Christmas when he took one look at her face, but a man had to do what a man had to do. He didn't risk looking over at Amelia as he offered Charity his arm. He was flustered enough.

Amelia gave up on eating the minute she joined Mary Margaret and Timothy on their blanket in the shade and pretended to be interested in Mary Margaret's endless stream of conversation.

"The arnica tea isn't helping my arthritis, Amelia. Is there anything else we might try? Your father's elixir, perhaps? It settles my nerves and, to my mind, I think my nerves might be half the problem."

"I've a few bottles of tonic left," she told Mrs. Cutter. "I'll bring one by."

Timothy ate in silence, smiling and nodding as if he heard every word. His cheeks were full, and his jowls bounced with every bite.

Amelia found her eyes had a will of their own. No matter how often she forced herself not to look across the square at Hank, her focus returned to him again and again. He was, indeed, seated beside Charity, who never took her eyes off of him.

". . . lying there on the floor of the bank, when I realized I wasn't going to die," Mary Margaret was saying, "I told myself it was because the Lord was saving me for something else."

Timothy leaned closer and yelled, "I'm not putting up another shelf!"

Mary Margaret yelled back, "Not another *shelf.* Something *else!*"

"You've already stuffed that pantry full of dishes and folderol. If I put up another shelf, you'll just buy more."

Happy for the reprieve, Amelia laughed. But her laughter was short-lived when she remembered the poster with Evan's name on it.

Where was Evan now? Hiding out like some hunted animal on the run? He'd been desperate enough to come home and steal their father's watch from her. How desperate was he? What other sinful acts was he capable of?

Across the way, Charity watched Hank concentrate on his plate. They made a striking

160

couple: Hank, in his suit, Charity in her stylish hat and dress.

A few minutes later, Amelia's gaze drifted away from the children gathered around a pony cart across the square and unerringly fell upon Hank and Charity once more. Hank was standing now, waiting while Charity rose to her feet.

He offered her his arm, as if it were the most natural thing in the world, and together, the two of them began to stroll across the grass.

Amelia took a deep breath and said a silent prayer. *Thank You, Lord, for knowing what's in our hearts and making all things right. Thank You for forgiving Evan, for helping him find his way back, as I know You will.* Then she added, *And thank You for bringing Hank and Charity together.* As she spoke the words, she truly meant them. Hank Larson was not for her.

A calmness, a gentle peace came over her and she knew the Lord was listening, that He was there.

They were on their second pass around the edge of the square when Hank finally worked up the courage to say, "Miss McCormick, I . . . you must know I find you charming—"

A sound escaped her, a small gasp of surprise and the instant he heard it, Hank knew he'd taken a dive into muddy waters. He slid a sideways glance at Charity and his steps faltered.

She stopped, waiting breathlessly for more. Her eyes were huge blue orbs filled with gratitude and excitement. He'd never seen anyone actually jump for joy, but he had the feeling she was about to do just that.

He rushed on before things went from terrible to worse.

"—but I would certainly be remiss if I led you to believe that I harbored any feelings besides admiration for your character, your manners and your comportment." Sometimes being a writer paid off.

He chanced another glance and found Charity looking quite confused.

"In other words, Miss McCormick, I don't harbor any affection for you—at least none of a romantic nature. Nor do I foresee myself nurturing any in the future."

He heard that little gasp again and was forced to face her. She'd gone pale as a hothouse lily. "What . . . what are you saying, Mr. Larson?"

He thought he'd made himself perfectly understandable.

Hank cleared his throat. "I'm not attracted to you in a romantic way, Charity. I'm sure there is a much better man out there for you."

She began to fan her face with both hands and press her lips together. He was afraid she might faint dead away.

"Amelia?" Charity whispered. "Amelia told you

I was sweet on you? Oh, how embarrassing! How *could* she?"

"She was trying to help, I think."

Charity shook her head. "Amelia wants you for herself."

Hank laughed. "I very much doubt that, Miss McCormick. Amelia and I barely tolerate each other."

He watched her take her time smoothing her hands over her cheeks, her hair. She fluffed the lace trim on the cuff of her sleeve and took a deep breath. Hank was amazed at the way she calmly pulled herself together until her placid smile was once more in place.

"Thank you for being so completely honest, Mr. Larson."

"You're welcome, Miss McCormick. Let me walk you back to your family."

"No, thank you. I'm fine."

"It's no trouble, I—"

"Really, I'd relish a moment alone, believe me." She nodded and then smiled. This time it was genuine. "I'm certain the Lord has someone else in mind for me. Thank you again for your honesty."

He marveled at her certainty as he bade her good-day. Hank watched Charity walk away, head high, shoulders straight.

Then his gaze unerringly found the Cutters seated on their blanket beneath the trees, but Amelia was gone.

Chapter Twelve

The following Saturday, Amelia found herself at home mixing a pint of rheumatism liniment for Hattie Ellenberg while Rebekah nursed the baby and little Orson amused himself exploring the parlor floor.

"What's in it?" Hattie eyed the amber bottle on the counter that ran along the back wall of the room.

Amelia was carefully writing on a label to glue on the bottle.

"Laudanum, oils of sassafras, cedar, some turpentine and some camphor gum. I also added tincture of capsicum." She shoved a cork in the top of the bottle and shook it. "All in an alcohol base. Rub it on your feet whenever they get to bothering you."

"Mind if I use some right now?" Hattie's eyes were shadowed with pain. "My ankles hurt like the dickens."

"Of course. When you get back to the ranch, apply some more and stay off your feet for a while."

Across the room, Rebekah shook her head, fastened the bodice on her gown and lifted the baby to her shoulder to burp her. "Hattie doesn't like to sit down."

Amelia smiled. "Your English is nigh onto perfect now."

After spending most of her life among the Comanche, Rebekah Ellenberg had to relearn everything she'd known in her former life, including English.

Hattie sat down on the old overstuffed chair that Amelia's father used to favor most and began to unlace her worn shoes. Orson toddled over to watch and clung to the folds of Hattie's skirt. Once his grandmother had her shoes and socks off, Orson tried to grab for the liniment bottle.

With Rebekah's hands full, it was up to Amelia to rescue him. She crossed the room and swung him onto her hip.

"No wonder you have rheumatism, Hattie, if you're hefting this little one around all the time. This child is heavy as a boulder."

While Amelia jiggled Orson up and down, Hattie massaged liniment onto her ankles and feet. Once she was finished, she began to pull on her socks again.

"Feels better already," she said.

"Good. I've been experimenting with the formula a bit," Amelia told her. "If it stops working, let me know. I've got another recipe with camphor and skunk oil—pretty drastic measures, though."

"Skunk?" Rebekah shrugged, a puzzled expression on her face.

"Black-and-white animal. Size of a cat." Hattie held her nose and said, "Pee-ewe!"

"Yes, I know skunk." Rebekah laughed, the sound filling the empty corners of the small room.

As Orson reached up and began to dislodge her braid, Amelia wondered what it would be like to share her days with family within these walls. Evan had been making himself scarce since he was fifteen. Folks would drop by or send someone for her, but when she wasn't treating someone, she spent hour upon hour alone with her oils and dried herbs, her volumes of handwritten recipes or working in her garden.

Hattie paused and asked Amelia if she had a button hook. Rather than put Orson down, Amelia carried him into her room and back again. She handed the metal hook to Hattie.

"How are you holdin' up, Amelia?" Hattie asked, her head bent over her high black shoes, and deftly worked the hook. "We saw the posters all over town," she added. "It can't be easy, worrying about Evan."

True to his word, Hank had spoken to many of the townsfolk before hanging Wanted posters around Glory. Though she hadn't seen him since the church potluck, answering sick calls forced her out of the house. Everywhere she went, people were caring and solicitous, still, it was hard to hide her embarrassment.

She was constantly plagued by the notion that she had not only failed Evan, but in so doing, she'd failed to keep her promise to her father.

"It's difficult," Amelia admitted. She looked at Hattie, a woman who had borne terrible pain and loss in her life—the death of her husband and daughter at the hands of Comanche raiders, her own near scalping and unspeakable crimes against her person—and yet Hattie had found the strength to persevere.

"I put my trust in the Lord," Amelia added.

"That's all any of us can do," Hattie agreed with a nod. "'Though He brings grief, He will show compassion.' The Lord has seen me through impossible times."

She finished hooking her shoes and reached for Orson. "Now look at everything I have to be thankful for . . . not only is Joe content working the ranch his father and I started, but he's got a fine wife in Rebekah here. And I've got these two healthy grandbabies. There's not a luckier woman in all of Texas. You just hang on, Amelia, you hear?"

Amelia promised she would.

"We saw that Silas Jones is part of this Perkins Gang," Hattie said. "He worked roundup for us a couple of times. Always seemed like a bad apple to me."

"Not a good man," Rebekah agreed. "He has a dark heart."

It was hard to imagine Evan hanging out with dark-hearted men. Amelia watched Rebekah gather up baby Mellie. Hattie set Orson on the floor, then fished around in her reticule. Coins jingled against one another.

"Here's two bits." She handed the quarters over to Amelia. "I'd pay double if you'd let me. My ankles feel better already."

"I'm glad to be of help." Amelia took the coins and set them on the makeshift counter beside a brass balance scale she used for measuring herbs.

Hattie noticed folded copies of the *Glory Gazette* on a hassock nearby. "We've sure been enjoying the newspaper. One of the neighbors dropped the first issue by a few weeks ago. That Hank Larson seems like a real nice man. Ran into him at the mercantile this morning and he asked if he could interview me. Wants to tell my story. What story have I got to tell? I'd like to know. He says I should tell how I survived the attack. Said that folks back East would be real interested. I told him I did what I had to do— with the Lord's help."

"What about Rebekah?" Amelia suggested. She turned to the lovely young woman with startlingly blue eyes and rich dark hair and watched Rebekah's cheeks darken. "She has quite a story to tell, too."

Amelia doubted Hank could find a more interesting subject than Rebekah Ellenberg, former Comanche captive.

"That would depend on Rebekah, wouldn't it?" Hattie and Amelia turned to Rebekah. The young mother watched them with interest.

Rebekah began slowly, "Would the newspaperman tell the story of the Nermernuh? Of my life with them?"

"The what?" Amelia asked.

"The Comanche," Hattie explained, scooping up Orson as he was reaching for a doily hanging off a nearby spindle table.

Amelia thought for a moment, then nodded. "I think everyone would be interested in knowing how you survived for so long."

Just then, there was a quick knock at the door and Joe walked in.

"Hello, Amelia." He pulled off his hat, his attention going straight to his wife and newborn infant, and a smile lit up his face. "I came to collect my family."

"They're all ready," Amelia said, thrilled to see Joe so happy.

Hattie reached for Amelia and gave her a mighty hug. "Thank you so much for the liniment. I'll remember Evan in my prayers."

"Thank you, Hattie." Then Amelia turned to Joe, "Since she won't listen to me, I'd like you to see that she stays off her feet for a few days.

Give that liniment a chance to work." She watched him reach for Orson.

"I'll try, but you know Ma."

"I'm proud to say I do," Amelia told him.

Hattie and Joe were out the door, headed for the wagon parked out front, but Rebekah lingered behind.

"Is everything all right?" Amelia feared there might be something wrong with Rebekah or the baby that the young mother wanted to speak of in private.

"I hope maybe you will do something for me," Rebekah said, glancing outside where Joe helped Hattie up onto the seat of the buckboard.

"Of course." Amelia agreed without hesitation.

"Tell the newspaperman that I would like to talk to him. I will tell him the truth about the Nermernuh."

Rebekah was off the porch and heading toward the front gate before Amelia could tell her that talking to Hank Larson was the last thing in the world she wanted to do.

It was late afternoon but there were still plenty of hours of summer sunlight left in the day as Hank stepped out onto the street in front of the newspaper office and joined other costumed revelers heading down Main Street toward the church.

He fell into step behind a pirate, a woman

dressed as a cowhand in a split skirt, and a little butterfly in a fluffy pink gown with droopy organza wings. The family in front of him laughed together as the little girl ran ahead a few yards and then back to urge her parents to hurry.

Hank's costume—hastily put together from an assortment of bean tins and bottles he had dug out of the trash and strung together with twine —clinked and clanked with every step. Earlier in the week, when Brand McCormick showed up at the newspaper office to encourage him to attend the masquerade, Hank convinced himself the only reason he was going was to report on the event and hopefully find a replacement sheriff.

Desperate times called for desperate measures.

Tonight, as the sky painted itself with the pastel tints of twilight, he walked the boardwalk chiding himself for being such a fool with every step he took. With every clink and clank he warned himself that he was not only going to run into Charity, but possibly Amelia, though he couldn't imagine her showing up at the masquerade with her brother's name on Wanted posters plastered around the county.

No matter how hard he tried to dismiss her from his mind—and sometimes he actually succeeded for an entire hour—thoughts of Amelia kept coming back to haunt him. Once in a while he would catch a glimpse of her walking down

Main Street and suddenly he recalled the scent of lavender that lingered about her, the sound of her voice, the warmth of her presence. He tried to ignore his feelings. Finally, feeling guilty because he was betraying Tricia's memory, he had faced the fact that he would be a fool to deny his attraction to Miss Amelia Hawthorne.

Angry at himself for his weakness, he kicked a pebble off the boardwalk and kept walking.

Avoiding Amelia only seemed to make matters worse. He'd heard from others that she seemed to be "holding up well." Mary Margaret Cutter informed him that Amelia looked a bit "peaked" and Harrison Barker added that she appeared to have lost some weight. Hank spent time alternately worrying about her and hoping that her brother would be apprehended in another county by another sheriff and that he'd soon be rid of his duties—which so far had only amounted to nothing but hauling Harvey Ruggles to Comanche and hanging Wanted posters around town.

The closer he got to the church hall, the more he became convinced he should head back home. He noticed an assortment of people dressed as circus clowns congregated beside the open double doors.

Just inside, Reverend McCormick wore street clothes beneath a red cotton cloak tied over one shoulder. A Roman gladiator's helmet covered his blond head. Brand stood in the doorway, greeting folks as they entered the hall. When he spotted Hank lingering outside, the preacher called to him. It was too late to turn back.

Hank moved forward with the crowd, shook Reverend McCormick's hand as he entered.

"Welcome, Sheriff!" Brand pounded Hank on the shoulder, which sent up a chorus of clanks and clunks. "What are you supposed to be? A rubbish heap? Glad you could make it!"

Before Hank could answer, Brand was already greeting the family behind him. Hank stepped into the hall and immediately spotted Charity across the room near the small platform stage. She was dressed as a baker with a high white hat and white apron.

Beside her, young Sam was standing over a huge bass drum, threatening to beat it to death with a serving spoon. The boy was wearing a bowler hat that was so big it had slipped down to his eyebrows. Sam's false mustache kept twitching and drooping to one side. His sister was nowhere to be seen.

Charity's attention was focused on her charge, so Hank slipped into the room unnoticed. As a king and queen in paper crowns with broom handle scepters strolled by arm in arm, Hank gazed around the room, reminding himself to ask the preacher to let him make an announcement, a plea actually, for someone to volunteer to take over as sheriff.

A cowboy sauntered past in a court jester's hat complete with bells. Hank looked around for the Ellenbergs, but didn't see them anywhere.

And then he saw her.

Amelia was off to one side of the stage all alone. She'd dressed as Bo Peep with a ruffled, lemon-yellow pinafore over one of her plain black skirts and white shirtwaist blouses. Her hair was parted into two thick braids and a huge floppy white bow was pinned atop her head. She had both hands wrapped around a tall wooden staff —also tied with a bow. She'd be mortified if she knew how vulnerable she appeared tonight—as if Miss Peep had lost her last lamb.

Amelia watched the room fill with not only excited church members, but other townsfolk, as well. Everyone from near and far was welcome, even encouraged to attend. She thought the masquerade gala and bake sale one of Reverend McCormick's finest fund-raising ideas. The costumes folks had created on such short notice were amazing. There was a couple dressed as Shakespeare's Romeo and Juliet, as well as Lord and Lady Macbeth. One of the ranchers wore a coat of many colors.

What she did notice—possibly because of her mood—was that nearly every single person who had entered the church hall was with someone. Not only were there families present, but clusters of cowhands from nearby ranches. She even recognized a pair of Indian scouts who had worked for the army. They hadn't bothered to wear costumes, but in their usual regalia—a mix of traditional Indian loincloths over army trousers and pieces of uniform jackets—they fit right in.

She'd never been more amazed at her friends and fellow townsfolk than she was tonight. And she'd never felt more alone.

It had taken all the mettle she could muster to attend, but everyone she'd ministered to this past week, as well as people she ran into on the street, insisted that she not let the fact that Evan was in trouble keep her at home. Though everyone assured her over and over that his actions had nothing to do with her, she wondered how she had missed the signs of his deep discontent. Why hadn't she been able to help him before it was too late?

She scanned the room, certain no one would notice if she slipped out the side door. She was about to make her move when she saw Hank Larson heading for her with a determined stride. His every step set off a terrible ruckus.

He stopped when he reached her, but the cans and bottles dangling from pieces of twine attached to his person continued to sway and rattle a moment longer.

"Miss Peep," he said in all seriousness.

"Mr. Larson." She found herself unable to look away from his intense eyes.

He seemed at a loss for words and said absolutely nothing for so long she wondered if he'd been rendered mute. She wasn't in much better form.

Finally, she forced herself to ask, "Who are you supposed to be, Mr. Larson?"

He mumbled something she couldn't hear. Amelia leaned closer.

"I beg your pardon. What did you say?"

"Not who. What," he said.

"Oh. *What* are you supposed to be, then?"

"A wind chime."

For the first time in days, she found herself laughing. She drew back a step, looked him up and down, took in all the hanging tin cans and bottles.

"A wind chime?"

"That's right," he said.

"That's ingenious."

"I was desperate. The reverend thought I was a rubbish heap."

"I hope you won't have to sneak up on anyone tonight."

She laughed, then quickly sobered. There still loomed the very great possibility Hank might be called upon to arrest Evan. She didn't know whether to hope that was the case—since he might show her brother some mercy out of courtesy to

176

her—or to pray that Evan turned himself in on his own and Hank would have no part in his arrest.

"I hope I don't, either. In fact, the only reason I came tonight was to try and talk someone else into taking over as sheriff."

He glanced around the room and then she found herself staring up into his eyes again.

"What do you think of Joe Ellenberg?" he asked.

"He'd make a wonderful sheriff." She couldn't imagine a better candidate. Especially since Joe had known Evan for years. "If he lived in town," she added.

"That's what I thought, too. Residing in Glory is certainly a requirement."

"Perhaps you should move out of town and disqualify yourself," she suggested.

"Don't think it hasn't crossed my mind, but I can't afford two places."

Though Evan was never far from her mind, while talking to Hank, Amelia found herself feeling lighter than she had in days.

"By the way," she began, "I was asked to tell you that Rebekah Ellenberg is interested in speaking with you. She would like to relate the story of her experience living with the Comanche."

She watched a transformation come over him, saw the curiosity and excitement that filled his eyes. His work meant a great deal to him, that much was evident.

"Is she here?"

"I haven't seen them."

They both gazed slowly around the room. Not far away, three cowhands without costumes ogled Laura Foster. The boardinghouse proprietress was decked out in a long white robe with flowing sleeves, a gilt cord belt that appeared to be a curtain swag, and white angel wings fashioned out of ostrich feathers. She'd piled her thick blond hair atop her head. One cowboy was particularly flushed, his eyes suspiciously bright. Amelia suspected it wasn't only from staring at Laura but from the bottle of spirits the cowboys made a poor attempt at hiding.

"When did you last see Rebekah?" Hank asked.

She answered honestly. "The beginning of last week. I . . . probably should have come by to tell you she was interested in talking with you but I . . . I've been very busy." She had been busy, she decided. Busy avoiding him.

"There's Charity." When Amelia saw her across the room, her heart sank of its own accord. The urge to slip out the side door and head home came over her again. She waited for Hank to excuse himself and join the preacher's sister.

But he didn't even look Charity's way. In fact, Amelia found herself growing heated with embarrassment at the way he continued to stare at her instead.

"May I be completely honest with you, Amelia?"

"Of course."

"I have no interest in being with Charity—not in a romantic way, that is. She is a nice enough person, a fine young woman, but I'm just not—" He stopped abruptly and tugged on the hem of his jacket. One of his cans hit the floor. He ignored it. "I don't harbor any romantic feeling for her. I told her as much." He added, "And as gently as I could."

"Oh, my."

"Yeah, well . . ."

"How did she take it?" Amelia suspected Charity had been so very smitten.

"Like a lady." Hank grabbed the tin off the floor. "Would you care for some punch, Amelia? Or should I call you Miss Peep?" He tried to smile, but his own embarrassment was evident.

"That would be nice," she said, then realized that perhaps he was looking for an excuse to walk away. She quickly added, "You really don't have to wait on me."

"No trouble at all. I'll be right back."

He'd no sooner stepped away than two of the cowhands who'd been staring at Laura came striding over. Their clothes were worn but clean. They were both tall and lean, their skin tanned the color of caramel hides.

"Looks like you lost your sheep, little lady," the tallest of the two said. He chucked her under the chin. "Maybe I can help you find them."

179

"I'd thank you to keep your hands to yourself." She rapped him on the hand with her staff, narrowed her eyes and glared, hoping he'd take the hint and leave.

"You look mighty tempting. Like a buttercup. My friend and I was wondering if you'd like to take a little walk outside." He was nothing if not persistent.

"I'm waiting for someone," she said.

"That gent what was here? The one you was talking to? He ain't worth waiting for."

The second cowhand spoke up. His boots were so worn at the heels that his ankles were bowed out. "I hear tell your brother's riding with the Perkins Gang."

Amelia nearly dropped her staff. She'd never seen these men in her life. For all she knew, they could be part of the Perkins Gang themselves.

"Do you . . ." She could barely whisper, so great was her shame. "Do you know my brother?"

"Seen his name on them posters around town. Heard some lady point you out earlier. We figured you prob'ly aren't as straitlaced as you look. In fact—" he reached for one of her braids and rubbed it between his thumb and forefinger "—I'm bettin' there's some real fire brewing under that yellow apron."

Amelia was so mortified she failed to hear the clank and clunk that accompanied Hank across the room. The cowhands weren't distracted by it, either, not until Hank nudged the taller man aside and handed Amelia two punch cups.

"May I help you two?" Hank turned on the men, taller than both of them.

Somehow he'd smoothly ended up between her and the cowboys.

"We're doing just fine," the shorter man said.

"I believe I smell whiskey, gentlemen. Which means you'll have to leave the premises immediately."

The taller cowhand spread his arms. "What whiskey? Prove it."

"This is a church social, mister. I'm asking you politely to take your friend out of here and leave."

"Who's doing the asking?"

"Hank Larson, sheriff." Hank didn't smile. "Now, are you going peaceably? Or am I going to have to throw you out?"

Amelia stared at Hank in awe. *Throw them out?* She peered around his shoulder at the two men. Neither of them looked interested in leaving. Hank was taller, sturdier of build than either of them, but the cowhands were whipcord thin and looked as tough as nails. They weren't threatened by him in the least.

"How come you ain't tossed her out if this here sociable is just for the goody-goods? Her brother runs with the Perkins Gang and she—"

Amelia didn't see who threw the first blow, but later on, folks claimed it was Hank. All she knew was that one minute the three men were standing in front of her, and the next fists were flying. A cup of punch flipped upward and stained her apron before she was nearly knocked to the ground in the melee. She kept her footing and tossed the second cup in the shorter cowhand's face as he reached for Hank's collar. Blinded, he reeled backward and Harrison Barker—dressed as George Washington with a tricorn hat atop his powdered hair—hit the man on the head with a chair.

The taller cowhand and Hank exchanged blows accompanied by the terrible smack of fists against flesh and the rattle and clank of tin and glass. The circle around them widened, apparently no one was willing to risk injury to break them up.

Amelia was pressed back against the edge of the stage.

Surprisingly, Hank Larson gave as good as he got. Finally he landed a punch to the cowhand's jaw and the man toppled backward like felled timber.

Hank ignored the man on the floor and immediately turned to Amelia. He grabbed her by the shoulders, searched her face.

"Are you all right, Miss Peep?" He was smiling, though his left eye was already purpling.

"I'm fine," she assured him. "But your nose is bleeding pretty bad."

He reached up to cup his nose, then pulled his hand away and stared down at his bloody fingers.

Without another word, he passed out cold.

Chapter Thirteen

Hank opened his eyes and found himself staring up at Amelia. Somehow he'd ended up on the floor with his head cradled in her lap and, for the life of him, couldn't recall how he'd gotten there. He quickly decided it wasn't a bad place to be.

He sighed and let his eyes drift closed.

For some reason she insisted on tapping his cheek.

"Hank? Hank. Open your eyes. Are you all right?" Her voice floated to him as if through cotton batting.

Slowly, he forced his eyes open, certain the dream would have faded, but Amelia was still there, her face hovering above him. Her long rust-colored braids trailed over her shoulders. The front of her apron was smeared with blood and punch.

He struggled to sit up, but she held him down.

"What happened? Are you all right?" He realized he wasn't dreaming, that this was real.

"I'm fine. You fainted at the sight of your own blood."

"I did not."

"You did, too. But you knocked out a cowhand first."

He blinked a couple of times and vaguely remembered arguing with two cowboys. The room finally came completely into focus. They were surrounded by an odd assortment of individuals from clowns to kings and queens, to wild Indians with knives strapped to their thighs. Even George Washington was staring down at him.

Hank's addled thoughts fell into place and he realized the esteemed first president was really Harrison Barker. Standing behind Amelia, Harrison raised his tricorn hat, exposing his white powdered hair.

"He's all right, folks," Harrison called out to the assembly "No need to worry. The sheriff's fine."

A round of applause filled the room and everything came back to Hank in a rush. The masquerade social, the cowhands smelling of whiskey, one of them insulting Amelia.

She was tenderly pressing a wet compress to the side of his face, dabbing at his nose. He would have been mortified if he didn't recall that one of the cowhands had hit the floor—thanks to a well-aimed punch he didn't know he had in him. That was about the last thing he remembered.

He ignored Harrison and the rest of the crowd and stared into Amelia's concerned eyes. "I'd like to stand up," he told her.

"Are you sure?"

He was certain if he stayed there any longer with his head resting in her lap, staring up at her huge green eyes and gold-tipped lashes, that he'd never, ever want to get up again.

"I'm sure." He made a feeble attempt to sound convincing.

"Please, help him up carefully, Harrison," she said.

The storekeeper and a clown helped him to his feet. Then Hank extended a hand to Amelia. She hesitated slightly before she accepted, but she did slip her hand into his.

Holding her hand gave him the oddest sensation—as if he were linked to the rest of the world again in a way he hadn't been since Tricia and the baby died. He'd been existing in the world, but not a part of it. He'd been an observer of life, not a participant.

Observation and the ability to step back from the world was a writer's gift, but without a heartfelt connection, the work often lacked passion and depth.

Through Amelia, through the warm and gentle touch of her hand, he suddenly had a glimmer of what life used to be, of what living used to feel like.

He pulled her to her feet. She let go and the connection was broken. His head started to throb.

"How is it we always end up on the floor together?" he asked.

He watched her close her eyes and give a slight shake of her head before she said, "I guess some folks just have more luck than others."

She opened her eyes. "Don't look down, Mr. Larson. Your nose is bleeding again." She quickly handed him the compress. "You need some packing."

"What I need is for somebody to cut all this rubbish off of me."

Before he would let her tend to his nose, he asked Harrison and a few of the other men to send the drunken cowhands packing. They were kind enough to oblige.

Just then, Charity stepped forward.

"Maybe I can be of some help." She'd grabbed a knife off the pie table and began to cut the strings of Hank's cans and bottles.

"Thank you, Miss McCormick," he mumbled from behind his compress.

"You're quite welcome, Mr. Larson."

Amelia turned aside, bent down to collect his bowler.

He lowered his voice and leaned closer to Charity. "No hard feelings?" he asked.

"Of course not. No hard feelings."

Charity quickly relieved him of his burdensome wind chime. Amelia handed him his hat. Hank went out to check on Harrison and the others.

"I'm sorry, Charity," Amelia said softly. "I didn't mean to embarrass you by telling Hank—"

Charity held up a hand to stop her. "Nothing to apologize for. Really. I don't know what I was thinking. I have Sam and Janie to worry about. My life is full. If and when the right man comes along, he won't need prodding."

Charity made an excuse to round up her charges. Near the dessert table, the preacher started the pie auction.

Hank returned to find Amelia and, together, they left the hall unnoticed and walked in silence to her house. Twilight was gathering, the sky purple as a bruise. A lone star rode the sky, or maybe it was Venus, Hank had no idea.

"Should I come in?"

"You know better than that." She entered alone, lit the lamps in the front room and left the shades up before she joined him on the porch.

"I can't very well patch you up out here in the dark," she said. He heard the indecision in her tone.

"Leave the front door open. With the shades all up and the lights on, folks can see inside."

She stepped aside, let him in.

"I'll just go put some water on to boil. Have a seat." She seemed nervous as a caged butterfly.

He smiled, hoping to put her at ease as he stepped into the front room, a combination parlor and apothecary shop. The entire back wall was lined with shelves. A counter fronted them. The room was impeccably neat. Bottles, jars and beakers filled the shelves. Neat labels separated them into categories. There were confections and electuaries, embrocations and liniments, ointments and cerates.

There were feminine touches here and there, doilies under the lamps, a fringed throw pillow. A century-old candlestick holder on a side table near a leather-bound family Bible. Like his own quarters above the newspaper office, her home was tidy but soaked with silence.

When Amelia came back into the room she'd shed her Bo Peep bow and bloody, ruffled pinafore. She stepped behind the counter. As always, she was no-nonsense and efficient as she gathered what she needed.

He adjusted the wet towel pressed to his nose, afraid to drip blood on her floor. His nosebleed appeared to have slowed to a trickle. He chose a straight-backed chair beside the table in the front window and sat down.

His focus drifted back to Amelia. She appeared lost in concentration as she reached for a small bottle. She unstopped the cork and tapped a few sprinkles onto a small dish. Then she deftly wrapped a plug of gauze. She used an eye dropper to take water from a small beaker, moistened the plug with a few drops of water and then dipped it into the powder.

"What is that?" He wanted to know. "Nothing that stings, I hope."

"It's powdered gum arabic," she said without looking up.

"I've seen the apothecary sign outside your door, but I had no idea you had the makings of a first-rate shop in here."

"We were in a small town in Kansas in our search for a place to live when my father met the widow of an apothecary. She was forced to sell the business and the time was right, so Papa bought everything he could afford, packed it all up in crates and boxes that we hauled all over Texas until we finally settled down here."

Her voice held a trace of sadness. "His dream was to do the doctoring while I ran an apothecary shop on Main Street. Unfortunately, he passed on before he could see his dream realized. So many dreams died with him," she said softly.

"You learned a lot from him, obviously."

She nodded toward a thick book on the end

of the counter. "And from *Dr. Chase's Recipes*. I've read it completely through twice already, and keep it handy for reference."

She crossed the room with a pair of long thin tweezers in one hand, the linen plug tipped with gum of arabic on a saucer in the other. She set the plate on the table beside him and pulled the lamp closer.

Amelia seemed hesitant to draw near. He watched her take a deep breath. He closed his eyes, thinking that might make it easier for her to treat him if he wasn't staring. Besides, closing his eyes might keep him from passing out at the sight of his own blood again.

"Tip your head back," she instructed softly.

He did. She took the rag from him.

Hank kept his eyes closed. He sensed her nearness, knew when she was leaning over him. Her hands were on his temples, his cheeks. She gingerly felt along the bridge of his nose. He caught the scent of lavender and sighed. At least the blow to his nose hadn't ruined his sense of smell.

He heard the clink of metal against china, pictured her using the long, slim tweezers to pick up the linen plug. Her hands were gentle, though her touch was firm and confident. He found himself remembering how hard he'd been on her the day he drove her out to the Ellenbergs' ranch. He'd disparaged her midwifery skills though he hadn't known a thing about her personally, put her in the same category as the shameless woman who had botched his wife's delivery.

"I'm sorry, Amelia." The apology slipped out of its own accord.

"For what?" She was standing much closer than he realized.

"For being so rude to you the day I drove you out to the Ellenberg place."

"It was nothing."

"It was rude and inconsiderate. I didn't know what I was talking about."

"A lot of men share your views about female doctors."

"Narrow-minded lot, eh?"

"Uneducated, perhaps."

"I didn't know you then." He was tempted to open his eyes, certain that she was leaning over him, close enough to kiss. All the more reason to keep his eyes closed, his mind on something else.

"Do you know me now?" she asked.

"I would like to know you better."

She fell silent. He was tempted to take a peek, gauge her expression. An awkward moment passed. He didn't look up.

"This might hurt a bit. Sit as still as you can." She cupped his cheek with her left hand. He felt the linen plug below his nostril and held his breath. He winced when pain shot through his nose, though it wasn't as bad as he expected. She was fast and proficient. With the plug in place, she stepped away, taking the scent of lavender with her.

He straightened, cautiously touched the side of his nose.

Amelia was already behind the counter, straightening, wiping off the tweezers, corking the arabic. Generally ignoring him.

Golden lamplight flickered against the walls around them. It was so quiet in the room that the slight sounds of Amelia's movements were magnified—her heels against the worn but polished floorboards, the hush of her skirt. In the kitchen, the teakettle was hissing.

She balled up the wet compresses and finally met his eyes. He saw the nervousness there. For a few moments he'd forgotten they were all alone.

"Would you care for a cup of tea? We could . . ." She looked away and then her gaze touched his again. "We could have tea out on the porch."

Out in the open where she would feel safe. Where they could keep things proper between them. Suddenly, he discovered he didn't want to do the right thing. The proper thing.

But he wouldn't hurt Amelia for the world. She'd been hurt and embarrassed enough by her brother.

"Some hot tea sounds good." Anything not to

have to leave and break the spell. "I'll wait for you out on the porch."

Relief banked the light in her eyes. "I'll be right out."

When she turned and went into the kitchen, he got up and walked across the room. He dug a silver dollar from his vest pocket and set it on the long counter without making a sound. Then he headed for the front door.

Amelia took her time in the kitchen, let the tea steep in the pot longer than necessary, using the extra few minutes to calm herself. Inviting Hank into the house, touching his face, standing close enough to him to be able to see each individual eyelash, listening to the rhythm of his breathing —the perfectly innocent situation took on a raw intimacy of its own.

Delight yourself in the Lord and He will give you the desires of your heart.

Desire.

She closed her eyes. She'd desired things before, certainly. She wanted Evan to walk on the side of the law, wanted him to trust and confide in her. She wanted to heal her friends and neighbors. She wanted to be able to make ends meet. To love and serve the Lord.

But even when she thought she was engaged to marry, she had never, ever felt this intense stirring inside.

I delight to sit in his shade.

She never fully understood those words before, but they came to her now. Just standing close to Hank had given her much delight.

Stop! She shook herself. Opened her eyes.

She took a deep breath. She poured rich, dark tea into two plain ceramic mugs and carried them out to the front porch.

Hank sat on the top step resting his arms across his knees. She handed him the tea with a warning that it was hot and then sat beside him. She smoothed her skirt over her knees and blew across the steaming surface of the tea in her mug.

"Have you ever been in love, Amelia?"

She nearly dropped the mug in her lap. It took her a moment to recover from the shock.

"I don't see how that's any of your business, Mr. Larson." The nerve of the man. She didn't know if she was angry because he'd asked, or because his question pierced the very heart of her wayward thoughts.

"I've been a reporter nearly half my life. I ask questions."

"Blunt questions."

"That's the only way to get to the truth."

"Are you interviewing me for your *Know Your Neighbors* column? If so, my love life is not anyone's concern."

"So, you do have a love life?"

"I most certainly do not."

194

"I'm sure there must be something about love and marriage in that Bible of yours, Miss Hawthorne. Why, even a heathen like me knows that marriage is a sacred covenant between a man and a woman. Preachers marry. Reverend McCormick was married. He's got the children to prove he—"

"Of *course* I don't believe love is a sin. I just don't think I've ever been *in* love." She thought she'd been in love once, but what she'd felt for a traveling drummer had been nothing more than admiration compared to the feelings Hank inspired in her.

And to think that all he'd done was close his eyes, tip his head back and let her plug his bloody nose!

"So you've never had a beau?"

"If nothing else, you're persistent."

"So I've been told."

"I had a beau once. A stranger passing through town. He came calling a few times. He talked about settling down, but then one day he left without so much as a by-your-leave." She shrugged, stared into the mug. He didn't need to know all the details. "I guess he wasn't the settling-down kind. Better I found out before it was too late."

"I've been sitting out here staring at that star up there, debating about just how honest I should be, Amelia."

She loved the sound of her given name on his

tongue, the way he drew out the sound with a mid-western twang, almost as if loath to let it go.

"Honesty is the best policy." She had no idea where the conversation was going until she remembered Evan. "You know something about Evan, don't you? Is he all right?"

"I don't know any more about your brother than I did before."

"Then what is it that you have to be honest about?"

She heard him take a deep breath, let it out. He set his empty cup down beside his hat.

"After I lost Tricia and the baby, I shut myself off from the world. I turned to my work, spent nearly all hours of the day and night writing. Finally, when I couldn't abide life in Saint Joe anymore, I bought the printing press, packed up and left, intent upon starting over. I chose to be alone. I chose to wall myself off from the rest of the world. I didn't want to feel anything. I didn't want to come close to falling in love again."

Falling in love again.

With her? Surely not.

He'd walled himself in and now he needed someone to talk to, that was all. She understood him completely. She'd felt the same way when her father died. She couldn't count on Evan for companionship. She'd been alone and had embraced that loneliness rather than let it defeat her.

"Friends told me it wasn't right, it wasn't healthy to shut out the world, but I didn't listen," he continued. "Tonight I realized they were right. Tonight, when you took my hand so that I could pull you to your feet, I felt a connection that shocked me, that awakened something inside me. Something I thought I'd lost and would never recover."

What did he mean? What was he really saying? She found herself staring into his eyes, searching his face for answers.

"Did you feel anything, Amelia?"

Did she *feel* anything? She'd been afraid to let herself think about her feelings for him. Afraid they were too overwhelming. Afraid of what might happen if she let herself go.

"I . . ." What in the world could she say?

"Tell me, Amelia. What do you feel when you're with me?"

"I can't say—"

"Because of Charity? Are you afraid to hurt her?"

Charity seemed genuinely fine around Hank at the masquerade. Apparently, she harbored no hard feelings toward him.

"No, I . . ." Never at a loss for words, she felt like a moron.

He reached for her tea mug, took it in his hands and set it down beside his. Then he took her hands in his and held them gently.

"I never thought I'd care for anyone again. I still have no idea how much of my heart I can give. Perhaps you hold no tender feelings for me, but if you do have any inkling—I guess what I'm asking is for your understanding and patience. But there is something here—"

Without any idea she was about to do it, she leaned close and kissed him much the way he had kissed her—without forethought, without finesse. She kissed him quick—cutting him off in mid-sentence. She had no idea what she was doing. It was fast, it was chaste—and it was still wonderful.

When she drew back she wanted to die of embarrassment.

"I don't know what just came over me," she said, pulling her hands out of his and jumping to her feet.

"Believe me, I completely understand." He stood a little too quickly and wavered on his feet.

She reached for his arm. "Are you all right?"

"That kiss made me light-headed."

"I think more likely it was the blow to your nose."

She glanced up and down the street. There was no one around. A few blocks away, light spilled out of the church hall. The distant sound of fiddle music danced on the air. Folks were still enjoying themselves on the warm summer's eve.

She bent down, grabbed his hat and shoved it at him.

"You'd best be going, Hank."

"I'll consider it progress that you didn't just call me Mr. Larson."

"Please go," she whispered, mortified at her behavior.

He didn't budge. Instead, he captured her hands in his again. She could have pulled them away, but she didn't want to. His hands were large and warm and covered hers completely.

"Will you think about what I've said, Amelia? I wouldn't hurt you for the world, I want you to believe that. All I ask is that you'll at least consider letting me call on you formally."

Hank wasn't promising love, he wasn't asking for her hand. He was merely asking to call on her. Asking her to be patient with him while he sorted out his feelings.

"I'll think about what you said," she promised.

"Good." He nodded, then centered his dented hat on his head. "Great. Thank you, Amelia." He tugged on his hat brim. "I'll see you soon."

Chapter Fourteen

The next morning, Amelia woke before dawn. The still, close air and cloudless sky marked the beginning of what was sure to be a stifling day when she started filling water buckets from the hand pump near the back step. Carrying water was backbreaking, but her garden was precious to her apothecary work, so letting the plants die was unthinkable.

Each time she emptied a bucket and straightened to stretch her back, she was tempted to look down the street to see if Hank might be on his way over. She reminded herself he was a busy man, that he had people to interview and advertisements to solicit.

What do you feel when you're with me?

She blushed just thinking of the things he had said last night.

I still have no idea how much of my heart I can give.

I guess what I'm asking is for your understanding and your patience.

If there was one thing she had in abundance, it was patience. She could sit for hours beside a feverish child, watching, waiting for any small sign that marked a turn toward recovery. Her life revolved around methodically having to wait and watch over her medicinal garden, to cut, trim, hang and dry the plants, to store the seeds and leaves, pulverize small amounts to mix into potions and elixirs, categorize and organize them.

She knew without a doubt that she could wait for Hank to sort out his feelings. She could wait for love to grow between them, just as she waited for her garden to produce lifesaving medicinals.

The same God that nourishes my garden will nourish our love if it is meant to be.

Someone finally arrived at her gate near noontime, but it wasn't Hank. It was a hired hand who worked for Lemuel Harroway, son of the town's founding father, Emmert Harroway.

She was on the porch, drying her hands, fingering a strand of hair back into her braid as Isaac Brown drove up in the fancy black Harroway rig and then walked up the path through the front garden.

"Howdy, Miss Amelia." The moonfaced hired man was in his late sixties. He smiled and tipped the brim of his hat. "I reckon you know why I'm here."

"Fanny?"

He nodded. "She's havin' a real bad spell. Been going on since yesterday. Miz Harroway needs you to come soon as you can."

Amelia knew that it wasn't a request. "As soon as you can" meant immediately. Among some of the wealthiest ranchers in Texas, the Harroways were used to people jumping when they said jump. They paid their help well, but that wasn't what sent Amelia flying to gather her medical bag and the compounds she would need.

Fanny Harroway, Emmert's only daughter, was prone to fits of hysteria and was in the care of her brother, Lemuel, and his wife, Sophronia. Most of the time Sophronia and the nurse assigned to watch over Fanny had no trouble tending to the young woman, but whenever Fanny had a particularly bad spell, Amelia was called in to help them.

Minutes later, Amelia climbed into the buggy and they left Glory behind in no time. Eight miles out, they crossed Cottonwood Creek. The day was heating up faster than Amelia imagined it would. Close heat, dry as if it rolled out of an oven, shimmered about them in waves by the time they finally reached the ranch.

Harroway House was, by anyone's standards, a grand mansion. The elder Harroways, with money and slaves in tow, left their cotton plantation in Louisiana a good ten years before the start of The Great Unpleasantness, as they called the War Between the States. They founded the town of Glory, bringing commerce and faith to the frontier.

Lemuel, the second generation Harroway, continued to prosper—though he had abandoned his father's faith. Neither Lemuel or Sophronia ever came into town, not even to attend church. Amelia saw them only in times of crisis.

Amelia's gaze drifted up the long columns that fronted the mansion. Her knock was answered by Sigrid, a recent immigrant from Sweden. The tall, strapping young woman had bright blue button eyes, fair skin and yellow hair. She nodded at Amelia and said something that sounded like, "Da missus say go up."

"Thank you, Sigrid. Would you bring up a cup of hot water, some cream, sugar and teacups?"

Sigrid had been in the Harroways' employ for nearly two years. She didn't hesitate to do as Amelia requested.

"De vater is already boiling." She bobbed what passed for a curtsy.

Bag in hand, Amelia stepped into an entry hall nearly as big as her entire house. A wide staircase cut the hall in half. She started up the stairs without having to be told where to find Fanny and Sophronia. Lemuel's sister's suite was isolated from the rest of the household at the far end of the hall on the second floor. On bad days, Sophronia kept her sister-in-law locked in. On good days, Fanny was allowed to roam the house in Sigrid's care.

From the high-pitched sounds of women's

voices raised in anger on the second floor, this was definitely *not* one of Fanny's good days.

Amelia paused in the hallway outside Fanny's door. A loud crash punctuated the sound of breaking glass and Sophronia shouted, "Keep away from me, Fanny, or I swear I'll shoot!"

Amelia whispered a fervent prayer. "Lord, help me, guide me, keep me safe. Protect these poor women from themselves and each other. Help me to do the right thing, to choose the right course of healing. I trust in You, Lord, and Your love and grace." Amelia said amen and tried the doorknob.

When she discovered it was locked, she banged on the wooden panels and the voices inside fell silent.

"Sophronia, let me in. It's Amelia."

She waited, held her breath until she heard hurried footsteps. The lock clicked. The door opened and Sophronia stood on the other side. She had a Colt trained on her sister-in-law. Fanny was crouched on the other side of the room with a long shard of glass in her hand. The remnants of a shattered light globe lay at her feet.

The room was large and yet crowded with books, clothes and furniture. There were bars on every window.

"Thank heavens!" Sophronia cried when she saw Amelia. "Do something with her, would you?"

Her usually flawless hair had escaped its coils

and pins. Half of her long black tresses drooped over her shoulder while the rest rode high on the crown of her head.

A swift glance assured Amelia that Sophronia was unharmed. The woman, somewhere in her late thirties, stepped close to Amelia and whispered, "I'm at the end of my rope."

Hattie Ellenberg always said, "When you get to the end of your rope, tie another knot and hang on." But Amelia had the feeling Sophronia wasn't in the mood for a dose of Hattie's wisdom just now.

She slipped silently into the room and heard the lock fall into place behind her.

Six months ago Fanny Harroway had turned thirty. She was prone to hysterics and a nervous disorder of the brain that led her to believe she heard voices. Voices that she could not silence of her own accord.

Amelia's father had treated Fanny before he died, so Amelia was not afraid of her. Doc Hawthorne had held the opinion that Fanny should not be locked away to live out her days in an asylum, so Lemuel Harroway refused to have his younger sister confined in a madhouse — much to his wife's chagrin.

As Sophronia hovered near the door with the Colt still trained on Fanny, Amelia set her medical bag down and began to inch forward, one cautious step at a time.

"Put the broken glass down, Fanny. You could hurt yourself. You don't want that, do you?" Amelia paused to observe. The young woman was crouched against the wall beneath the window, her hand wrapped so tightly around a long shard of glass that blood dripped out of her fist onto the highly polished floor.

Sophronia, tired of hearing Sigrid complain about having to comb the knots out of Fanny's tangled hair, had it cut off months ago. Now, Fanny's shorn brown locks stuck out all over her head. Despite the uneven crow's nest of hair, Fanny was beautiful. Her eyes were deep and soulful. Violet shadows smudged the hollows beneath them. Her skin was pale as milk, her arms painfully thin. There was a haunted, ethereal quality about the woman who, because of circumstance, was as innocent as a child.

Fanny stared up at Amelia, her head cocked to one side, distracted, as if listening to something in the distance.

"Amelia?"

"That's right. Fanny, put the glass down. You've hurt yourself and I'm here to help you."

"Are you going to make me drink the tincture?" Fanny was shaking, whispering hoarsely. She hated the taste of the valerian nerve tincture Amelia left for Sophronia to administer.

From the other side of the room, Sophronia informed Amelia, "We ran out of medicine a couple weeks ago. I should have sent for some but—"

It wasn't the first time Sophronia had let Fanny go without her nerve medicine. Thankfully Amelia had an extra bottle on hand.

"I brought you something new to try, as well," Amelia began.

"Does it taste good?"

"I've tasted it myself." Amelia sampled every concoction she mixed. "It's not half-bad."

"Is it *delightful?*" Fanny tipped her head the other way, suddenly focusing on Amelia.

Amelia smiled. "I wouldn't say it's delightful, but it won't make you wince. It tastes a bit like tea and is taken the same way." She inched forward again. "Will you give me that piece of glass and let me wrap that cut on your palm before we try some?"

At Amelia's words, Fanny stared down at her palm, saw the blood on her skirt and the floor and dropped the shard. She held her open palm out in front of her and watched the blood leak out.

"It's about time," Sophronia said behind them.

Seeing to Fanny's welfare was a task not many women would be up to. As a woman possessed of a cool, demanding temperament, Sophronia did the best she could and, thankfully, she had her husband's fortune at her disposal.

"Come over here, Fanny," Amelia instructed as

she walked over to a wing chair near the window. There was a reading table beside it. She set her bag down, opened it, and waited for Fanny to rise and cross the room.

The young woman did as she asked, moving as if in a trance, appearing to listen, always listen, to something otherworldly.

If only she heard the voice of the Lord.

Fanny stood beside Amelia and stared out the barred window. From her room, Fanny had a view of miles and miles of open ranch land.

"He isn't here now," Fanny whispered.

Amelia took her arm and encouraged her to sit in the wing chair. It was a moment before the young woman could tear her gaze away from the window.

"Who, Fanny?"

"The shadow man."

A chill ran down Amelia's spine. What darkness had Fanny's mind conjured up now?

"Look at this cut, Fanny. You really should be more careful with your things, you know. Glass can be very dangerous."

"I didn't know."

"Now you do." Amelia realized that on some level, Fanny knew glass was indeed dangerous, for she'd used the shard to keep Sophronia at bay. Amelia swabbed the cut with a piece of linen and then pulled the edges together. She applied strips cut from a stick of adhesive plaster she'd made of white resin, beeswax and mutton tallow to close the wound.

Fanny watched her closely. "Why, Amelia! You are sticking me back together," she said, amazed.

"You mustn't touch this after I bandage it. Your skin will grow back together nicely if you leave it alone."

There was movement behind them as Sigrid slipped into the room carrying a tray with a small pot of hot water, cream, sugar and three cups. She set it down near Amelia's medical bag.

"Thank you, Sigrid," Amelia said.

"Thank you, Sigrid," Fanny mimicked.

The maid curtsied. "Vill that be all, Doctor?" Though Amelia always protested, Sigrid never addressed Amelia as anything but doctor.

"Thank you, yes." Amelia turned to Fanny. "I have a new compound for you, Fanny. I think you're going to like it. I know you like tea."

"What did you say?" Fanny asked.

"I said I know you like tea."

"I wasn't talking to you, Amelia. I was talking to *them*."

Amelia paused. No matter how many times she saw Fanny, no matter how many times they'd had this conversation, the idea that Fanny heard imaginary voices she couldn't silence or ignore greatly disturbed Amelia.

"They don't trust him anymore, but I do," Fanny said.

"They?"

"My voices."

Amelia knew Sophronia was dead set against encouraging Fanny to discuss her hallucinations. Sophronia hovered across the room, listening, watching.

Fanny appeared so very sincere, so intent, that Amelia could not ignore her.

"Who don't they trust?"

"The shadow man. He doesn't want anyone to see him."

"Why not?"

Fanny leaned close to Amelia and whispered, "No one must know about his visits."

"Where does he come from?"

"He lives here."

"He lives here? In the house?" Amelia thought of the many ranch hands in Lemuel's employ. It wasn't impossible that one of them might have found a way to get to Fanny. She was as innocent as a lamb.

"Shh. I can't say anything else." Fanny looked around furtively. "He made me promise not to tell."

"Tell what?"

"He's talking to me *right now*," Fanny smiled with a far-off look. "I can still hear him."

Amelia relaxed a bit. The "shadow man" was another figment of Fanny's imagination. She drew a small cobalt bottle of pulverized skullcap, valerian, catnip, cayenne and coriander seeds from her bag and carefully measured out a teaspoonful and placed it in the bottom of a teacup. She poured in a dash of hot water, dissolved the powder and then added more water, cream and sugar.

She handed the cup to Fanny.

"You drink some," Fanny said, accepting the cup but lowering it to her lap.

Sophronia moved up beside Amelia and hovered at her shoulder. "What is that you're giving her? It will work better than the tincture, I hope."

"It tranquilizes irritable nerves without debilitating."

"Are you actually going to have some?" Sophronia watched Amelia measure out a half teaspoon more and drop it into an empty cup.

"Not only am I going to have some," Amelia smiled at Fanny, "but I think you'd do well trying a cup yourself, Sophronia. I know I could use some nerve strengthening myself right now."

"I have things to do." Sophronia straightened, smoothed her skirt, raised a hand to her hair and realized her pins had come undone. "Oh, my goodness!" She left the room in a flurry of sound and motion, calling for Sigrid the minute she hit the hallway.

"She doesn't like her hair to become mussed,

you know," Fanny said. When she saw that Amelia had made a cup of tea for herself, she raised her own cup to her lips, blew across the surface and then took a sip. "This isn't horrible."

"I'm glad." Amelia looked around and pulled up a smaller chair. "What happened today, Fanny? What upset you so? You have been doing quite well."

Fanny shrugged. A faraway look came into her eyes, and she leaned forward, straining to listen again. Then she sat back and a sly smile crossed her face.

"What are you thinking?" Amelia asked.

"Do you think I'm crazy, Amelia? Sophronia does. She told me so. She said I'm crazy as a loon, always have been, always will be. She said there's no hope for me."

"I don't think you're crazy, Fanny." Amelia stirred cream into her cup.

"Even *I* think I'm crazy." Fanny polished off the rest of her tea, turned the cup upside down and shook out the last drop. It landed on her skirt to mingle with the blood droplets. She set the cup down, ran both hands through her hair until it stood up like spines on a hedgehog.

Then she tapped her index finger against her temple, leaned close to Amelia and, in a tone that sent a chill down Amelia's spine, Fanny whispered, "Sometimes, I'm as crazy as a fox."

Amelia encouraged Fanny to change into a clean skirt, then prop herself up on a bank of pillows in bed and draw in her sketchbook. Once Fanny was settled and apparently calmer, Amelia bade her goodbye, locked the door and headed downstairs.

Sophronia had pulled herself together and was waiting for Amelia in the formal parlor. She'd changed into a bombazine day dress that to Amelia was as fancy as a ball gown. Not a hair was out of place. The only sign that she'd had a trying morning was the frown still creasing her brow.

"Thank you for coming to the rescue again, Amelia. I was at my wit's end."

"Is Lemuel away?" Lemuel Harroway had a far more calming effect on his sister, more than Sophronia, even though the majority of the young woman's caretaking fell to his wife.

"He's in Austin on business. Lately, he's always away on business." She looked around the elegantly appointed room and sighed. "I suppose having all of this is worth the time he sacrifices to traveling."

"I'm sure you miss him."

"Oh, yes. I can't wait for him to return so I can explain why I had to take all the lamps out of his sister's room." Then Sophronia said, "Tell me about this new nerve powder."

Amelia shrugged. "I found the recipe in Dr. Chase's volume of information. Fanny is right about the tincture. It really *is* foul tasting and I think perhaps her system has grown used to it." She reached into her bag. "I've brought you another bottle to keep on hand, as well as a packet of the nerve powder I tried today. It's mostly valerian and skullcap. Both soothe the nervous system. She seems calm enough now." Amelia set the items on the table between them.

"Tea?" Sophronia gestured toward the silver tea service on the mahogany butler's table. The silver was polished to a high shine.

Amelia declined, anxious to head back to town but unable to let herself think about the reason why. She was afraid to put much store in the words Hank had said to her last night as she was unwilling to admit how much they meant to her.

"What brought on Fanny's upset?" She settled back into the chair opposite Sophronia's.

"Sigrid unlocked the door this morning and found Fanny in a complete state of undress, parading before the mirror. After a game of cat and mouse, she finally agreed to let Sigrid help her dress. She was pulling at her hair, babbling on to one of her invisible 'friends' about escaping this 'prison' and I'm afraid I simply couldn't take it anymore, Amelia. I lost my temper and told her she was crazy as a loon."

"Why the gun, Sophronia?" Amelia wanted to know.

"I carry it every time I go into her room. Ever since she told me that her 'friend' wanted to kill me. She said the voice told her that once I was 'taken care of' she would be free." Sophronia shook her head and presented Amelia with her profile as she turned to stare out a nearby window.

"One of her invisible 'friends' wants to kill me. It terrified me so that I threatened to have her committed to the insane asylum in Austin as soon as Lemuel returned. I told her that he wouldn't mollycoddle her if he knew she wanted me dead. She insists it's not her but the shadow man who has plans for them both."

"She mentioned him to me."

Sophronia shrugged and traced the lace on her skirt with her fingertips. "I don't know what to do anymore, Amelia. Life is so unfair."

Amelia was tempted to remind Sophronia that aside from caring for Fanny, life had been far from unkind to her. Fanny was a trial, but when treated gently and watched over with care, she could be handled. Amelia suspected Sophronia would always feel lacking until she let the Lord into her life.

"The one thing I've always wanted has been denied me," Sophronia said softly. "Does your Dr. Chase's book contain anything that will help me conceive, Amelia?"

Amelia shook her head. "No suggestion other

than red raspberry leaf tea. If I hear of anything, you'll be the first to know." She paused for a moment before she said, "Have you ever tried prayer, Sophronia?"

Sophronia finally met her gaze square on. "Do you really believe, Amelia, that if there was a God in heaven, He would create someone like Fanny? What kind of a God would put me into a gilded cage filled with so many sacrifices—no children, an insane sister-in-law to care for, a husband who is never here?" She shook her head. "No, Amelia. I don't believe prayer is the answer. I refuse to believe in a God who doesn't play fair."

As Isaac drove her back to Glory, Amelia couldn't fathom how Sophronia or Hank could walk the road of life without knowing that God was beside them all the way. How did they exist in a world without God to turn to in times of not only sorrow, but delight?

From God all blessings flow. She truly believed, as sure as she was sitting here sweltering under the hot Texas sun, that God was with her. He was her strength. It seemed so clear to her, so simple; without Him, there was nothing.

She said a prayer for the women in the Harroway household. And then she said one for Hank. Perhaps with God's help, he would realize that his heart was capable of infinite love. Perhaps one day he would realize there was room enough in his heart for him to love her.

Chapter Fifteen

Hank felt more like a prowler than a sheriff as he closed Amelia's barn door and headed back through her garden toward the front of the house.

He'd walked up and down Main Street that morning, ostensibly to chat with folks and dig up any news fit to print. He had stopped by the church, by the hall, spoken to Reverend McCormick, all the while secretly hoping to run into Amelia. Eventually he gave up pretending to be interested in anything else and headed for her house.

She'd left all her windows open—it had grown suffocating out—and the doors were unlocked, as well. He'd tried the knobs and called out to her, peeked in all the windows, but couldn't figure out how she'd gotten very far with Sweet Pickle staked in the shade beside the barn.

The notion that she might be in danger entered his mind.

He tried to warn himself that his writer's mind was running away with itself, but he had nearly worked himself into a lather and was standing on Amelia's front porch with his hands on his hips and his hat shoved back when she came riding up in a spit-shined black rig that had set someone back a fortune.

He bounded off the porch, intent on helping her down as soon as the buggy stopped, and was rewarded with a smile the minute she laid eyes on him. Within seconds, that smiled faded into concern.

He took her hand. She stepped out of the buggy. He retrieved her heavy bag for her and she bade the driver thanks and farewell.

"What is it, Hank? Have you news of Evan?"

Her brother stood between them like a haunting shadow that was never really gone.

"No news at all. Where were you? I came to see you and when I found you weren't here, I worried." He paused, tugged at his collar.

"I was summoned to Harroway House," was her only explanation.

"Harroway House?" He pondered a second longer and added, "Any connection to Emmert Harroway, Glory's founder?"

"His son, Lemuel, lives there with his wife, Sophronia, and his sister."

"I haven't met them."

"They don't come to town."

"I guess I'm not the only one around here who doesn't go to Sunday church meeting."

"No. You're not."

"Are you upset with me?" Hank pulled off his

hat, dusted it with his shirtsleeve and then put it back on. "Are you upset about last night?"

Amelia shook her head. "I'm just tired. I think it's the heat. I was up at dawn watering the garden and the sun is already drying out my plants again."

"Have you had a midday meal?"

She shook her head no.

"Let's go see if Mrs. Foster is still serving."

She'd never dined at Foster's Boardinghouse. Walking in with Hank had been awkward to say the least. Before he had asked permission to court her, conversation with him—if not always cordial—was at least easy. On the way down Main Street she'd been hopelessly tongue-tied.

Hank, on the other hand, chatted all the way. He was excited about going out to the Ellenberg place to interview Rebekah. He was confident that within the week he'd find someone to take over as sheriff and, after last night's events at the masquerade, two more merchants had taken out advertisements in the *Gazette*. If he noticed her nervousness, he didn't let on.

Laura Foster was most gracious, welcoming them in for luncheon.

"There's always room at my table for you two, and if there wasn't I'd make room." Laura's laughter was infectious. Once seated at the table across from Hank and surrounded by

Laura and her boarders, Amelia relaxed.

"Amelia was telling me about the Harroways," Hank mentioned between tender bites of pot roast, carrots and potatoes. "I know Emmert Harroway was the town's founder, but didn't realize his descendants still lived in the area."

"I've been here almost four years now and I've never met them." Laura passed a boat of steaming gravy. "What are they like, Amelia? Why don't they come to town?"

Amelia declined gravy and passed the dish to a widow seated on her right. The war had taken the woman's husband. Now, ten years later, she'd decided to move to California to join her kin. The boardinghouse was a temporary stop.

Amelia thought about how much she could tell the gathering without revealing anything about Fanny's nervous condition.

"Lemuel Harroway's holdings are extensive. He's away much of the time on business. Sophronia, his wife, is of Spanish decent through her great-grandmother, I believe. They have a lovely home." She took a bite of carrot, looked up and caught Hank smiling at her across the table. His dark eyes studied her carefully. The heady warmth his expression radiated was so intense that she nearly choked when she tried to swallow.

Her heartbeat danced triple time and, as if he knew he had the power to make her pulse race, Hank winked at her across the table. Her cheeks instantly flamed. She could feel them burning something fierce. Suddenly unable to take another bite, she dropped her gaze, set down her fork.

The conversation flowed around her. Someone at the table had heard that Harroway House was a mansion.

"I remember now." Laura tossed her head, rolling her deep blue eyes toward the ceiling as she concentrated on a memory. "I overheard something at the mercantile one day—someone said they keep an insane Harroway woman locked upstairs in the attic."

"Locked in?" The war widow was suddenly quite interested.

"Is that true, Amelia?" Laura asked.

She decided it was better to squelch unfavorable gossip with a dose of truth than to deny anything.

"Fanny Harroway is Lemuel's sister. She has a nervous condition and she's *not* locked in the attic." Amelia couldn't help but picture Fanny crouched on the floor in the corner clutching the glass shard, blood dripping from her palm. It would be a while before she forgot the wild look in her eyes.

"How does this nervous condition manifest itself?" Hank wanted to know.

Amelia finally felt safe meeting his gaze again. The startling warmth was still there, but his innate curiosity was back. She concentrated on that.

"She often becomes agitated and upset," Amelia added.

Laura shrugged. "So do I. No one better dare lock me up."

Hank laughed.

The guest persisted. "Surely there must be more."

"Nothing I can relate," Amelia told her.

As if aware of Amelia's discomfort, Laura changed the subject to the weather, talking about how one day it was spring and the next they were suffering the sweltering heat of summer.

Though no one brought up Fanny's condition again, Amelia thought about her throughout the rest of the meal and as they enjoyed fresh sliced melon for dessert.

I wasn't talking to you, Amelia. I was talking to them.

Amelia considered herself a sensible woman. She wasn't taken to flights of fancy, nor did she often let her mind wander, but as the conversation flowed around her, she went over and over her conversation with Fanny. At times the girl seemed absolutely sane while speaking of the shadow man.

They don't trust him anymore, but I do.

He doesn't want anyone to see him.

He lives here.

There was something so covert about the way Fanny spoke, such a fanatical light in her eyes that Amelia couldn't help but wonder what, if anything, Fanny might have actually witnessed that affected her troubled mind in such a way that she'd twisted the truth into a figment of her imagination.

Fanny often talked of hearing voices in the past, but they were just that, disembodied voices that whispered to her, taunted her.

Either Fanny's condition was growing worse or—

Suddenly she realized Hank was thanking Laura for a fine meal and digging in his vest pocket for coins. Amelia laid her napkin alongside her plate and prepared to leave, bidding Laura good-afternoon and sending her compliments to Rodrigo in the kitchen. She was glad to hear from Laura that his thumb had healed nicely.

Hank walked Amelia home again.

"Surely you have business to attend to," she told him when they reached the newspaper office.

"I publish one page per week if I'm lucky, Amelia. That's hardly a pressing deadline."

"Are you working on your novel?" It was his dream, she recalled. His passion to write a fictional story of the West had brought him to Glory.

"I've been collecting my thoughts and making notes. Serious writing doesn't always involve the physical act of writing itself. Sometimes

I'm working when I'm just staring into space."

Amelia laughed. "I wonder if staring into space will get my garden watered tomorrow morning? Or my laundry done?"

"Staring at nothing and calling it work is a gift given only to writers."

"We all have different gifts, according to the grace that's given to us. At least that's what the Bible tells us."

They walked along in silence until Hank noted, "You seem preoccupied."

"You're an educated man. Are you familiar with mental infirmity?" she asked.

"You think I might be mentally infirm?"

"Of course not. I was just wondering if, as a writer, you've ever come across any research or written about someone who was. I'm confounded by Fanny Harroway's condition. She seems to be growing worse."

"In what way?"

"She is convinced that someone has been visiting her at night. She's not only spoken to him but seen him. He has asked her to keep the visits a secret. Before this, she always claimed the voices were only in her head."

"Did she describe this *someone?*"

Amelia shook her head. "No. She calls him the shadow man."

As they walked on, he matched his stride to her shorter one.

"Is it possible she might actually be talking to someone, a ranch hand perhaps?"

"I don't know how anyone could have gotten to her."

"So they do keep her locked up in the attic? This sounds like a Nathaniel Hawthorne tale. By the way, was he any relation to you?"

"No, he was not. Not that I know of. And no, they do not keep Fanny locked in the attic."

"But they do lock her in."

"In her room." She pictured the shattered lamp globe. "For her own safety. The door is locked and there are bars on all the windows. Only her family has access to her."

Something dark and forbidden about the situation had escaped her earlier and now that something was teasing the edges of her mind, a suspicion she either couldn't grasp—or refused to.

"What if she really is hearing voices?"

"Are you serious?"

"What's to say Fanny isn't telling the truth? At least as she sees it? Or maybe—" he reached around Amelia to open the gate for her "—maybe someone is actually visiting her at night and talking to her."

"In her head?"

"No, in person."

"Who?" Amelia wondered aloud. "No one has access to her save the maid and her family."

"We'll probably never know. Still, I'm very intrigued. What a story—"

Without thinking, Amelia caught hold of his coat sleeve. "Surely you wouldn't think of going to interview anyone at Harroway House, would you? I would never betray their trust—"

He reached for her and Amelia caught her breath. Was he going to kiss her again?

All he did was innocently tuck a wayward strand of her hair behind her ear. Still, it was enough to make her weak in the knees.

"I would never take advantage of anyone's heartache, Amelia. I hope you don't think I'm that kind of man." He placed her hand on his arm and covered it with his own.

"No, of course not." She couldn't deny that he'd been more than kind to her in regards to Evan. Even in the story of the holdup, he'd reported only the facts. There was no embellishment, no editorializing. She truly didn't think he would cash in on her or anyone else's heartbreak.

She only hoped that he wasn't the kind of man who would someday break her heart.

Chapter Sixteen

In the week that followed, Amelia treated more patients than usual. When Timothy Cutter came down with a bad case of heartburn, she prescribed baking soda dissolved in water followed by a cup of warm milk. She soothed a cowhand's sunburn with a paste of baking soda and vinegar, a grandmother's earache with three drops of warm paregoric, and when Harrison Barker's mother, Barbara, showed up complaining of a terrible pain in her leg, Amelia tied a string soaked in turpentine around the offending limb and sent her home to rest. The next morning Mrs. Barker returned and claimed she'd never felt better.

Though Mrs. Barker paid her with a package of needles and a new thimble, most everyone else had paid in coin. Though it broke her heart to do so, Amelia found a new hiding place for her growing savings—an old sock tucked into her bottom bureau drawer—in case Evan came back.

As the days passed, her brother was never far from her thoughts. She prayed for God to guide and protect him throughout the day, remembered him during her bedtime prayers. When she wasn't thinking of Evan her thoughts drifted to Hank. She wondered what he was doing, wondered if he was thinking of her.

He made arrangements to stop by and take her for a stroll after Sunday service and that afternoon, when she heard footsteps on the front porch, she forced herself to walk, not run, to answer. She paused before the small mirror on the hall tree and smoothed her hand over her hair. She'd taken the time to comb out her long braid and brush her hair to a high, glossy shine before she coiled it into a thick chignon at the nape of her neck.

She never wore jewelry—she had none to wear —but she'd picked a few sprigs of lavender and tucked them into the left side of her chignon and secured them with small tortoiseshell pins. Her gown was her newest, only three years old. The calico was a joyous pattern of miniature sprigs of pink and yellow daisies scattered over a white background and reflected her mood.

Amelia was smiling as she opened the door, but her smile quickly wilted when she discovered not Hank, but a huge man, well over six feet, standing on her front porch. He wore a leather vest over a chambray shirt, serge pants tucked into knee-high boots, and a weather-beaten ten-gallon hat that might have been bone-white once upon a time but was now the indiscriminate color of Texas trail dust.

"You Evan Hawthorne's sister?" he asked before she could voice a greeting.

"I am." She refused to let his size and scowl intimidate her.

She tried to see around him—he was nearly as wide as the door and almost as tall. She noticed there were three men waiting beside their horses beyond her fence.

Could this be the leader of the Perkins Gang? Had Evan sent him to her very door? A vision of the townsfolk of Glory, of Hank, Charity, the McCormicks, all the friends and neighbors who relied and trusted her. Had she brought this threat down upon them all?

Dear Lord, please help and protect me. Protect us all.

She was frightened but she stood her ground.

"I'm Amelia Hawthorne. And you?" She looked him up and down for good measure.

He brushed aside his vest where it had fallen over the bright brass star pinned on to the front of his shirt.

"I'm Oswald Caldwell, sheriff of Comanche County. The Perkins Gang robbed an army supply wagon up near Brownwood. We tracked them up to thirty miles from Glory. Have you seen your brother in the past two days?"

"I haven't seen him for nigh onto a month or more." She could tell by the skeptical look in his eye that he didn't believe her.

"So he's not here."

"No, sir, he is not."

"Then you won't mind my having a look around, will you?"

"Of course not." She didn't like the man—and not just because he was tracking Evan. He was overbearing, curt, and used not only the badge on his shirt but his height and strength to try to bully her into acquiescence.

The minute she granted permission, she realized if Evan was in the vicinity, he might very well have snuck home that morning while she was at church. Even now, he might be hiding in the barn or one of the outbuildings. He could have ridden into the barn, climbed up into the loft. There could be a host of outlaws with him.

Oswald Caldwell motioned to the men behind them. Within seconds, they searched her home with guns drawn. Their booted footfalls trod heavy, their spurs jangled metallically, scarring her floor with every step. They split up, each took a room.

Amelia followed behind, dashing into one and then the other bedroom. She watched them open armoires and peer under beds. One of the men jerked open her pantry door while another leaned over the apothecary counter as if Evan might have folded himself onto a shelf to hide.

When they were finished, they congregated in the kitchen. The county sheriff shoved aside the faded yellow curtain at the window above the dry sink.

"You three fan out, check the barn, the outhouse, the shed."

The men hurried to do his bidding. Amelia started after them. If they found Evan, if her brother put up a fight—

She wanted to be there, to try to talk sense into him before it was too late.

She'd taken but one step toward the back door when she felt Sheriff Caldwell's huge fingers close around her upper arm and draw her back.

"Hold on there, missy. Best you wait right here, outta the way."

She tried to wrest herself free but his grip was strong as iron. And then, from behind them, she recognized Hank's voice.

"Best you let her go, Caldwell."

His tone brooked no argument. Oswald released her, but shot her a warning glance when she started to head for the barn.

"Wait, Amelia. Please," Hank said. "What's going on?"

Amelia held her breath, thankful no gunfire had issued from the barn or the tool shed. One of Caldwell's men walked back out into the open and yelled, "All clear, Sheriff."

The air went out of Amelia and she feared she might fold up like a wilted buttercup. Suddenly, Hank's arm slipped around her shoulder. Despite her resolve not to let Caldwell know how badly he'd shaken her, Amelia found herself leaning against Hank for support.

"What's going on, Sheriff?" Hank demanded again.

"The Perkins Gang is on the move. They held up an army supply wagon headed for Fort Griffin. Didn't get much, but they got away. Silas Jones shot and killed a man near Brownwood when they holed up there last week. Yesterday afternoon someone thought they sighted them headed this direction. Since Hawthorne is from Glory, we rode over here on the off chance he came home."

He looked at Amelia for a second, took note of the way Hank had his arm protectively curled around her. "I hope you'll do the right thing, Larson, if and when Hawthorne shows up here again."

Amelia felt Hank stiffen at the insult. She tried to move away but his hold tightened.

"I swore an oath to protect this town, Caldwell. I don't take my promises lightly."

"You told me yourself you're looking to find a replacement."

"The fact that Evan Hawthorne is wanted has nothing to do with me stepping down. I never asked for this job, but as long as I have it, I'll do my duty."

Caldwell stared at Hank, taking his measure.

Finally satisfied, he turned away long enough to instruct his men to head back around front and wait for him there.

"I've got some new Wanted posters with me," Caldwell told Hank. "Now that Silas Jones is wanted for murder, there's a reward for him dead or alive. The others have all been implicated in the supply wagon robbery. Sooner or later, we'll find out where they go to ground."

Amelia was treated to his cool regard again as Caldwell added, "Mark my words, we'll bring them all down before too long."

She forced herself to stand tall and gently push away from Hank. This time he let her go.

"You get my drift, Miss Hawthorne? Your brother will be brought to justice," Caldwell promised.

Hank took a step toward the taller man. "You should be talking to me, Caldwell, not trying to intimidate Miss Hawthorne."

Oswald Caldwell looked them both over cooly. "I didn't realize you two were so close. You plan to run this new information in your paper, Larson, or keep it quiet as a special favor to your sweetheart?"

"I am *not* his sweetheart and Hank will report the news, Sheriff. All of it."

Avoiding Caldwell's stare, she smoothed down the front of her skirt, careful not to let her hem brush against the odious man's boots.

"Now if you are finished ransacking my home, I'd thank you to leave."

"I'll walk you out." Hank gave Caldwell no excuse to linger and insult them any longer.

Oswald Caldwell turned on his heel and headed back through the front room and out the door they'd left standing open in their haste. He signaled one of the men to join them, waited for him to bring Hank a roll of new Wanted posters.

"I'll be seeing you, Larson," Caldwell promised.

Hank nodded but said nothing. Amelia wished the man would get off her porch and leave but he lingered a moment longer.

"A word of advice?" he said.

"Go ahead," Hank muttered.

"I'm not telling you how to do your job, Larson, but if I was you I'd ride out to the surrounding ranches and alert them to the fact that the Perkins Gang was seen headed in this direction and to keep an eye out for them."

"Point taken."

Caldwell pinned him with a hard stare again. "Then I'll be on my way. You know where to find me. I'll expect to hear from you if you find out any of the Perkins bunch is around."

Caldwell rode off, taking the joy out of Amelia's day.

"What an odious man." She voiced her thoughts aloud as she stood beside Hank and watched the man and his deputies head down the street.

"I hope you don't mind my barging in like that, but when I saw those horses hitched up out front and your door standing wide open, worry got the best of me," Hank explained.

"I'm glad you were here. I don't know what I'd have done had that man found Evan in the barn. How could I have ever proved I hadn't known my brother was here? How could I have protected Evan?" She ignored the open door, walked over to the edge of the porch and grasped the wood railing.

She felt Hank move up behind her, felt his comforting presence though he didn't say a word. Finally, he touched the back of her hand. "Do you still feel like taking a walk?"

Tears threatened to fall. She blinked them away, turned to look up at him over her shoulder. "Not really. I'm sorry."

"I am, too. I know how much this hurts, Amelia."

She let go a long sigh. "You should probably go. You have a story to write."

"You know I'd do anything to spare you this but—"

"It's your duty, Hank. I'd rather you bring my brother in than have Caldwell do it."

"I know that. I'm sorry Caldwell insulted you with his insinuations. You've done nothing to be ashamed of."

235

Her face flamed. She dropped her gaze. "I kissed you," she whispered.

"I kissed you, too. There was nothing untoward in those two innocent kisses, Amelia. Nothing unchaste."

"Maybe you should go, Hank."

"I hate leaving you alone while you're upset."

"I'm fine." It wasn't the complete truth. She was far from fine, but she was made of sturdy stock. She wasn't going to fall apart now.

"I'm never alone, Hank. The Lord is always by my side."

"I'll stay a while longer if you don't mind."

Since it appeared he wasn't leaving, they sat together in the shade of the front porch, each trying to act as if Oswald Caldwell's news hadn't just turned her life upside down.

Hank leaned back against the porch rail and tipped his hat back onto the crown of his head. Amelia warmed from head to toe when Hank's smile almost made her forget about Evan. Almost. She glanced at the roll of posters he'd placed on the old rocker near the front door.

"You have work to do, Hank. And I have things to tend to."

"Surely you don't work on Sunday."

"No." She shook her head. "But I think I'd feel better if I spent some quiet time reading the Bible."

"I envy you your faith. It appears to be of great consolation to you."

A sense of peace came over her. "It is," she answered truthfully. "I don't know what I'd do without it."

"Then I'll leave you to your reading." He reached for the posters. "Would you like to see one of these before . . ."

He stopped so abruptly she knew exactly what he was going to say.

"Before I see one on the street? No, Hank. I don't want to see one yet."

He tucked the posters beneath his arm, then reached for her hands and stared deep into her eyes. She was warmed by his concern.

"I made you a promise, Amelia. I'll do the best I can for Evan. If I do run into him before Oswald does, I'll try to talk him into turning himself in peaceably. Maybe if I can convince him to testify against the others, his sentence will be lighter."

She never in all her life thought she'd be having a conversation like this about her own brother.

"Are you all right?" he asked.

She nodded but a lone tear slipped down her cheek, embarrassing her with the sheer rawness of the emotion it conveyed. She couldn't hold back her tears any more than she could protect Evan.

Hank reached up, cupped her cheek with his palm and thumbed away her tear.

"Evan will be all right, Amelia. I promise."

Long after he was gone, she prayed it was a promise he could keep.

On Monday, Hank hung four Wanted posters on Main Street, one at each end, one outside the Silver Slipper, and one on a tree near the land office. He figured one poster was enough for those living on the more respectable end of Main Street near the park, the church and the homes nearby. Most folks already knew to be on the lookout for Evan. They also knew Amelia well and Hank reckoned they'd appreciate him sparing her embarrassment whenever possible.

On Tuesday morning, he had just called upon Timothy Cutter at the bank when he walked out and saw Amelia on the boardwalk nearby. Her head was tipped back, her profile hidden behind her wide-brimmed straw hat. A basket dangled forgotten from her right hand. He started to call out a greeting, then realized she had stopped because she'd seen the new Wanted poster he'd tacked to the side of the butcher shop.

He watched her a moment longer, admired the cut of her neat white blouse and the way her fitted navy skirt showed off her slim waist—but when he noticed the way she was staring at the poster, he crossed the street and hurried to her side.

By the time he reached her, the basket hung perilously close to her fingertips. Shaded by her hat brim, her face was drained of color, her lips faded and set in a grim line. He expected tears, but there were none.

"Amelia?" He slipped his fingers beneath the handle of her basket and gently took it from her. She didn't even seem to notice—until she spoke without even looking at him.

"I can't really believe I'm seeing my brother's name listed alongside thieves and murderers," she said softly. When she finally turned to him, her green eyes were wide with disbelief and confusion. "How can this be?"

She glanced around, watched as a buggy rolled by. "Everything appears so normal, so ordinary. There's Harrison sweeping off the walk outside the mercantile. There's a rancher delivering a side of beef to the Butcher Shoppe. There are two cowboys riding down the street, probably headed for the Slipper."

She turned her huge eyes his way. "It's all so routine, and yet, my life will never be the same. Evan's life will never be the same."

He reached for her hand, held on tight, afraid for her. He knew the pain of loss, saw it in her eyes. Evan might not be dead, but life as both the Hawthornes had known it was surely over.

Witnessing Amelia's pain stoked Hank's temper. He hoped he would eventually have an opportunity to talk to Evan Hawthorne face-to-face. He'd tell the young man exactly how deeply his actions had hurt his sister.

Hank knew she was right. Her life would never be the same. Her brother would forever be labeled an outlaw. Amelia would be known as the sister of a wanted man.

Suddenly, he was a writer without words. He had no idea what to say to console her. He looked into her upturned face, into eyes that were so clear, so open and once so trusting. Then he remembered that, unlike him, she was a woman of faith.

"Surely there are some words of wisdom in the Bible. Something to help you carry on in times of adversity. Cling to them," he told her, even as he tightened his hand around hers. "And remember I'm here, Amelia. I'll help in any way I can."

She looked down at their clasped hands, then met his eyes again.

"Thank you, Hank, for your friendship."

"I hope someday I'll be able to offer you much more, Amelia."

In his heart he thanked her for her understanding.

"What's this?" He looked into the basket he was holding. Inside, she'd nestled six slim brown bottles in a dish towel. They were lined up like glass soldiers.

"I was delivering those to Harrison at the mercantile. They're bottles of walnut hair dye." He kept the basket and offered the crook of his arm. Together they headed toward the dry goods store.

"Walnut hair dye?"

"Walnut shells, rectified alcohol and cloves."

"Does it work?"

"Fairly well. It stains the skin longer than it dyes hair, though."

"I had no idea you had such far-reaching talents, Miss Hawthorne."

She shrugged. He wished she'd smile but figured that was too much to ask today.

"I concoct whatever people might need. I like experimenting."

"Ever had any real disasters?"

"What do you mean?"

"Elixirs gone bad. Hair dye that made someone's hair fall out?"

"You ask the oddest questions, Hank."

It was his turn to shrug. "There's a story in everything."

"I've never poisoned anyone, if that's what you mean. And no one's hair has ever fallen out."

He couldn't take his eyes off her. Her face had finally taken on some color. The corners of her lips twitched a bit as if she might even smile.

"Here we are," he said as they reached the mercantile. "I'll wait while you deliver these and then we'll be off."

"I didn't realize *we* were going somewhere, Mr. Larson." She took the basket and paused there in the doorway.

"We're heading out to the Ellenbergs'. I'm going to interview Rebekah and I want to talk to Joe, too. I figured you might want to see how the new baby's doing."

"You figured that, did you? I don't recall you asking if I'd like to go along. Or if I had anything else planned."

After the way she'd looked a few minutes ago, so worried, so lost, he was bound and determined to keep her spirits up and her mind occupied.

He immediately swept his misshapen hat off his head and gave a courtly bow from the waist.

"Miss Hawthorne, I'd be grateful if you'd do me the honor of accompanying me to the Rocking e Ranch today. That is, if you have no other plans."

He could tell by the way her cheeks flushed pink that she was well aware that a handful of shoppers were watching and listening to every word of their exchange.

"I'll go with you," she whispered, "if you promise never to make a scene like this again."

Chapter Seventeen

A melia was quiet on the way out to the Rocking e and Hank was content to let her dwell in silence. He knew that no matter where she was or what she'd be doing, worry wouldn't be far from her mind. At least this way, he could be with her and when shadows haunted her lovely eyes, he could try to chase them away for a while.

It felt natural to have her beside him on the narrow buggy seat. They were so close their shoulders touched with every dip and sway as he drove down the dry, dusty road toward the Ellenberg ranch.

As soon as they saw the house itself, Hank decided that if he was a rancher, this was exactly the kind of spread he'd like to call his own. The log structure, modest in appearance but not size, was nestled in a wide open valley. A gentle rise sloped upward behind the many corrals, barns and outbuildings.

Topped by a spreading oak, the low hill was home to two graves. Their white crosses, shining in the sunlight, were the opposite of a mournful sight. The grave site spoke of timelessness and blood ties to the soil, of commitment to the land and the memories, happy and sad, that were made here.

As before, Hattie greeted them as he pulled his buggy up near the hitching post. She stepped away from the low fence surrounding a hog pen and set down the empty slop bucket in her hands.

"When I saw you driving in, my heart jumped for joy," Hattie said as she hurried over to greet them. "What brings you out this way in the heat?"

"I came to interview your daughter-in-law, if she's still willing. I thought Amelia here could use a little time away from town." He turned to the buggy, offered Amelia his hand.

As her fingers touched his palm, Hank wondered if she felt the same rush of warmth that he did. She was smiling at Hattie now, but when she stepped out of the buggy, she held his hand a little longer than necessary before she let go.

"I thought that as long as Mr. Larson had invited me, I might as well come along and see how little Mellie is doing."

"She's eating more than a newborn shoat, that one." Hattie laughed as she started toward the house. "You're just in time for the noon meal so come along with me and I'll fatten you up with some of my corn bread, white beans and ham."

After they ate, Hattie asked Amelia to watch over the baby while she tended to a newborn colt and Hank interviewed Rebekah on a side porch overlooking a tall mulberry tree.

He found Rebekah as lovely a woman inside as she was out and marveled at the story of her life among the Comanche before the U.S. Army attacked and recovered her along with nearly a dozen other white captives.

He hadn't realized the vast numbers of settlers who had been taken by the various renegade tribes over the years, nor had he any idea before listening to Joe's wife, that many captives became assimilated into the tribe, took Comanche spouses and fought to the death beside their captors.

His mind was racing with possibilities for stories, so much so that he hadn't realized how much time had slipped by until Rebekah excused herself to relieve Hattie of the children. Hank walked back around the veranda to join Amelia.

He found her with little Mellie in her arms, staring out over the corrals and rolling prairie beyond. The infant was sound asleep on her shoulder.

As he watched Amelia place a kiss on Mellie's crown and smooth her hand gently down the baby's back, he felt a tug on his heartstrings. It was followed by a sensation that he could only liken to the way a frozen lake melts under the warm spring sun. Staring at Amelia with the baby in her arms, he was convinced he could actually feel his hardened heart begin to thaw.

She looked up, caught him staring and smiled across the space that separated them. He thought —he hoped—he saw a light in her eyes that reflected the warmth in his own heart.

"How does it feel," he wondered aloud as he joined her, "to hold a child in your arms that you helped bring into the world?"

She looked thoughtful for a moment and then said, "As if I'm holding a miracle."

"I hope you've forgiven me." He stared at the gingham tablecloth on Hattie's table.

"For what?" Her brow puckered.

"For the things I said to you when I found out that you were a midwife."

"You've already apologized and, yes, I've forgiven you. You were reacting to your loss, Hank. Dealing with your own heartache. People tend to lash out when that happens."

He leaned across the table until he could touch the back of her hand where it rested on Mellie's back. "Has anyone ever blamed you for their losses?"

The minute the words were out, he saw the light in her eyes dim. He pictured himself the night Tricia and the baby died. He'd nearly torn the house apart, so great was his anger, so deep his sorrow. If his father-in-law hadn't held him back, his own blind fury might have led him to strangle the life out of the drunken sot who had not known enough to send for a doctor when the delivery made a turn for the worse.

He was horrified to think that anyone in his right mind would blame Amelia for something outside the realm of her expertise. How could anyone want to harm this fine young woman who gave so much? Cared so much?

"Of course, some blame me." She said it so calmly, with such acceptance. "After the initial hurt subsides, most folks apologize for the things they've said when they were in pain and shock. Anger is a way to give grief a voice. It's easy to blame the person that you've pinned all your hopes on." She patted the baby's back, shifted her a bit higher on her shoulder. Then she smiled and her face took on a tranquil glow.

"When I walk into a house to help someone, I always say a prayer and ask for God's guidance. I know I'm not the one who will save a patient. I'm merely there to help ease their pain and suffering. God is the One in whom we must trust. It's His will that is played out."

"Sometimes I wish I had your faith, Amelia."

Their eyes met across the child in her arms. "All you have to do is trust in the Lord and know that He is there for you whenever you are ready to accept Him into your life and into your heart."

Just then Rebekah came around the corner of

the house. Joe walked beside her beating trail dust off his clothes with his hat. "Good to see you, Amelia," he called out to them. "You, too, Mr. Larson. My wife says you're a good listener. She claims that's the sign of a good storyteller."

Hank stood up as the couple joined them. "Thank you, Rebekah." He nodded toward Joe's wife, then he turned to Joe. "Mind if we take a walk? I'd like to see that new colt your mother mentioned." He hoped the look he shot Joe said more than his words conveyed.

The rancher picked up on his meaning immediately. Hank was relieved as they left the women at the table and Joe led the way toward the barn.

"Thanks," Hank told him when they were out of earshot. "I wanted to talk to you in private."

"What's going on?" Joe shoved his hat to the back of his head. His forehead, rarely exposed to the sun, was paler than the rest of his face.

"I didn't want to say anything in front of Amelia, although she already knows, but there's now a price on her brother's head."

He slipped a folded poster out of his vest pocket and handed it to Joe. The man didn't open it, merely shoved it into the back pocket of his denim pants. He walked a few paces away from the barn and Hank followed.

He told Joe what he knew about the Perkins Gang to date and added, "Oz Caldwell trailed them this way but lost the sign. I'd like word to get out to the surrounding ranches and home-steads to be on the lookout."

"I'll help pass the word."

"Much appreciated. By the way, I hear Silas Jones worked for you."

"He did. A couple years back. I had to fire him."

"Mind telling me why?"

"He has a bad habit of running off at the mouth. He insulted Rebekah."

Hank knew that's all it would take for him to fire a man, too. "Can't say as I blame you. You should probably keep an eye out for him and the others."

"Don't worry."

Hank hadn't failed to notice Joe wore a gun. "Why is it a rancher feels the need to walk around armed?"

Joe shrugged. "Snakes, wolves, injured animals that have to be put down."

"I guess I should have thought of that," Hank said.

"There are two-footed varmints around, too," Joe added. "You're not comfortable around guns, are you?"

"Not really."

"Funny quality for a sheriff."

"I'm still trying to find my replacement. Any suggestions?"

"Nope. Good luck." Joe leaned against the rails of the corral, his brow creased. "I doubt the Perkins Gang ever stays in one place very long, or they'd have been caught by now. I just hope Evan stays clear of Amelia."

Hank nodded. "I hope so, too." He pictured Amelia standing in front of the Wanted poster that morning. Remembered the lone tear streaking down her cheek. He let his emotions do the talking. "I hate him for hurting her the way he has. She doesn't deserve it."

"Next to my ma, Amelia's one of the strongest women I know," Joe said. "But when it comes to Evan, she's the most vulnerable. She raised him and thinks of him more as a son than a brother."

"I got as much from talking to folks around town."

"You sweet on our Amelia, Mr. Larson?"

"Call me Hank." He thought for a minute before he committed. "I am, Joe. I'm sweet on Amelia and it's getting worse by the day."

Hank watched Joe's expression harden and was shocked at the change in the man's disposition. This was a hard-edged, no-nonsense side of Joe Ellenberg that Hank had never seen.

"Amelia's got no family to speak for her, so seeing as how I've known her for a long, long time, I feel it's my duty. She was hurt once before. Left at the altar you might say, so you take care, Mr. Larson. Do not toy with her feelings or break her heart, or you'll have me to answer to, understand?"

"Completely." Hank was shocked to hear there was more to the story of Amelia's love life than she had already told him. After hearing what Joe said, he was determined to take even greater care with her feelings.

Having seen this other side of Joe, Hank had to ask, "You sure you don't want to be sheriff?"

Joe laughed. "Fat chance. I've got enough to do right here. There's no way you're going to find a rancher worth his salt who can sit around waiting for trouble to find him."

"So far, trouble hasn't managed to find me," Hank said. "Not since that first day at the bank."

"It's just a matter of time. Trouble has a way of finding us all. Hopefully, I've put my hard times behind me for a while." Joe pushed off the fence rail and headed for the barn door. "Guess we ought to go see that colt, just so you can say you did."

"You know anything about the Harroways?" Hank asked as they stepped into the shaded interior of the horse barn.

Joe led the way to a stall where a newborn colt stood on wobbly legs before he answered.

"I know some, but not much. Old man Harroway founded the town in the early fifties. Came to Texas from Louisiana with most of his family. Lost his two brothers and their families to Comanche and Kiowa raiders early on. He was a determined old buzzard and stuck it out. Had two children, a boy and a girl. Built the first church in Glory and ran through a passel of preachers before one took. My ma would know more than I do."

"You know anything about the son, the one who lives in Harroway House now?"

"Lemuel. He built the mansion. The house his pa had in town wasn't grand enough for him. He's rich and handsome. Looks younger than his years. Got him a beautiful wife from San Antonio, the granddaughter of some Spanish landowner down there. Doesn't matter how beautiful she is, though."

"What do you mean?"

"Lemuel is a womanizer. Always has been. Leaves her to run the place."

"Amelia said he has a sister—"

"Fanny. Haven't seen her for years. Not that I've seen either of them for years. They stick to themselves. Old man Harroway might have founded Glory, but Lemuel's always thought the town and the folks in it were beneath him." He paused to study Hank for a moment. "Why all the questions?"

"Just curious," Hank admitted. "Amelia was called out there last week. Before that, I had no idea any of Emmert's descendants lived nearby."

"If you're thinking of talking to them about a story, they won't oblige."

"I thought I should go by and at least warn them about the Perkins Gang sighting, but it sounds like I might not get a very good reception."

Joe gave the mare a carrot as Hank marveled at the size of the colt. Within minutes they were headed toward the house again. Even from a distance, Hank could tell Amelia was laughing and smiling as she spoke to Hattie and Rebekah. He was glad he'd brought her along.

Just then, a rider appeared on the road leading to the ranch house.

"Looks like somebody's in a hurry," Hank commented as Joe watched the rider approach at breakneck speed.

"That's not one of my men." Joe rested his palm on his gun handle.

Hank waited with Joe as the rider reined in and dismounted right in front of them.

The man couldn't have been a day younger than sixty-five. The old cowhand tipped his hat. "I'm Isaac Brown. I work over to the Harroway place. I'm looking for Miss Amelia. They told me in town she might be here."

"She's here." Joe nodded toward the house. "You'd best walk that horse and cool him down."

"Miss Amelia's needed over at the Harroway's. Pronto," Isaac said.

Joe turned to Hank. "Well, it looks like you're going to find out about what kind of a reception they'll give you a lot sooner than you planned."

Amelia asked Joe to lend her a horse but Hank insisted on driving her to Harroway House.

"This is no time for you to be gallivanting around the countryside alone," Hank reminded her. "Not with the Perkins Gang at large."

Joe concurred. Amelia began to protest until Hattie chimed in.

"Being independent is a fine quality unless it borders on stupidity, Amelia. This is no time to be stubborn. You let Hank drive you over to the Harroways'."

Amelia grudgingly agreed.

As they headed away from the Rocking e and turned onto a well-traveled road that led north-east, Hank said, "I'm glad I'll be getting a look at Harroway House."

"The Harroways have always been able to trust me to keep their troubles private," she began.

"Are you afraid I'm going to make them front-page news?"

"If it wasn't for my brother, you'd have nothing scandalous at all to write about."

"Do the Harroways have something of a scandal brewing?"

She grabbed her medical bag from the floor of

the buggy and plopped it in her lap. "Stop the buggy. I'll walk."

Hank looked around and made the mistake of laughing. "Settle down, Amelia. We're miles from anywhere."

"I can go back to the Ellenbergs' and get a horse. It's not that far."

"I'm sorry, Amelia. I was just teasing."

"It wasn't funny." Nothing seemed funny anymore. Except for a few blissful moments now and then, when Hank smiled at her in his warm, special way, or back at the Ellenbergs' when she'd held the peacefully sleeping child or had laughed at something Hattie told her—except for those respites, there was only torment over Evan.

Suddenly she realized Hank was pulling back on the reins. His horse stopped in the middle of the road. She looked out over the prairie. The minute the buggy came to a standstill, the sun's heat seemed to intensify.

Was he really going to let her get out and walk?

"I'm sorry, Amelia," he said softly.

With her hands fisted around the handles of the medicine bag, she turned to Hank. He draped his arm across the back of the buggy seat, not touching her, but it was a move that reminded her of the day he'd held her in the shelter of his arm when he stood up to Oz Caldwell for her.

That day she'd felt cared for, protected. Usually she was the caregiver, not the other way around.

She stared at her hands, afraid to look into his face, into his eyes.

Afraid she might shock them both by kissing him again.

"I shouldn't have teased you, Amelia. I know how much your reputation as a healer means to you. I would never jeopardize that by printing a story that should remain confidential."

She swallowed. "Thank you."

She shifted her gaze out to the horizon and listened to the erratic beat of her heart.

"Have you ever thought of going to medical school?"

"Pardon?" Caution flew as she turned to meet his gaze.

"Medical school. From what you've told me of your work with your father during the war, you've had more experience than many bona fide doctors."

"I'm—I'm too old," she mumbled.

"You're what? Twenty-three?"

"Twenty-seven," she whispered. He thought her younger? She was nearly thirty. Nearly at an age when most women lost any hope of marrying or having children of their own. Would he think differently of her now?

"You say that as if twenty-seven were a hundred."

He was doing it again. Staring in a way that made her want to lose herself in his eyes. She wished she could distill and bottle whatever magic was in his gaze as easily as she bottled one of her elixirs.

"Amelia?"

"We should be going," she whispered.

Hattie was right. It wasn't safe out here on the prairie alone and she certainly wasn't safe with Hank while having such wayward thoughts. She reminded herself of who she was and where they were going.

"I'm needed at Harroway House," she said.

His smile was nearly her undoing.

"I'm beginning to realize how very much I need you in my life, Amelia."

She could barely concentrate when they arrived at Harroway House. Sigrid came flying off the porch to meet the buggy when it pulled up. The lovely young woman with her plaited hair bound up atop her head like a crown barely gave Hank a second glance as she waited for Amelia to climb down.

"Missus is havin' a bad time vit Miz Fanny."

Amelia grabbed her arm before she could say more in front of Hank. She turned to him and called over her shoulder, "Wait here for me. I'll send Sigrid back out to let you know how long I might be."

"Don't worry about me," he called.

Seeing the maid's distress, Amelia realized

257

that in that moment Hank was the least of her worries.

Amelia lowered her voice as they hurried toward the wide veranda framed by huge white columns. "How bad is she? What's happening?"

"Miz Fanny has been tro'in up all her meals. She stood up dis morning and she . . . she . . ." Sigrid put her hand to her forehead and pretended to swoon. "She hit her head on da edge of da table."

"Fainted?"

The maid nodded. "Ya. Fainted. She's been sick as a mule."

"Dog. Sick as a dog," Amelia corrected absently.

"Ya. Dat, too."

They hurried up the stairs and found Sophronia pacing outside Fanny's door. She ran to Amelia, grabbed her free hand and dragged her away from the locked door.

"It's about time, Amelia," she said in a rough whisper. "Where *were* you?"

Amelia ignored her rudeness. "Sigrid said Fanny hasn't been eating?"

Sophronia nodded. "She can't keep anything down, not even water. She's worse than ever. Ranting, talking to herself. Bouts of hysteria, yelling, sobbing. She's sure she has a tumor and that she's dying of it."

"She didn't mention a tumor when I was here last week."

"This is a brand-new obsession." Sophronia glanced down the hall and then shook her head. "Before long I'll be as insane as she is."

The woman was so angry, so upset, that Amelia didn't want her around Fanny.

"Why don't you unlock the door and then go downstairs and have a cup of tea. I can handle Fanny."

Sophronia appeared doubtful. "I've never seen her like this. Do you think you might have made a mistake when you concocted that latest tea mixture? She's gotten worse."

Amelia thought back, realized this was no time to doubt herself. She wrote down every formula in her notebook, checked and rechecked every measurement just to make certain no patient ever received the wrong dosage of any curative agents.

She put her hand on the woman's shoulder. "There was nothing wrong with the tea. Unlock the door and I'll try to find out what's ailing her. You try to relax. I know how taxing this must be for you."

There were deep shadows beneath Sophronia's exotic dark eyes. She seemed embarrassed by Amelia's concern. As if aware that she'd let down her guard, she turned her attention to the ring of keys dangling from her waistband and led Amelia back to Fanny's door.

Sophronia slipped the key off the ring and handed it to Amelia.

"Be sure to lock the door after you. She's slippery as an eel when she wants to be."

Amelia nodded. She paused with her hand on the knob and offered up a silent prayer. Then she waited until Sophronia walked away before she knocked softly on the door and called out, "Fanny? It's Amelia. I'm here to see you, to find out what's wrong. May I come in?"

There was no answer so Amelia knocked again. "Fanny? I need to examine you."

"I'm dying. There's nothing you can do," Fanny called back. She sounded weak and forlorn.

"Why don't I take a look and we'll see about that?"

"It's no use."

Have you ever thought of going to medical school?

She tightened her hand on her bag, straightened her spine.

"I'm a very good doctor, Fanny. Let me take a look at you."

"The door is locked, of course."

Amelia unlocked the door, opened it a crack and poked her head into the room. Fanny, dressed in a long white nightgown, was reclining on the bed. The covers were rumpled and askew, pillows tossed around. There were books scattered all over the floor, the table, the window seat.

"May I come in?" Amelia could tell by the look on Fanny's face that no one ever asked permission to enter her room, they simply unlocked the door and breezed in.

"Of course." Fanny grabbed a pillow and tried to prop herself up, but a greenish pallor tinted her face and she lay flat again and moaned. "Every time I sit up, I vomit."

Amelia crossed the room. When she reached Fanny's bedside, she felt the young woman's forehead and found it cool to the touch.

"Stick your tongue out, Fanny."

Fanny did. Amelia nodded.

"Looks fine to me," she said. She pulled a chair up beside the bed and held Fanny's wrist. "Your pulse is steady."

"I'm dying," she moaned. "I have a tumor."

Amelia sat back. "Where exactly do you think this tumor might be?"

Fanny placed her palm on her lower abdomen. "Right here. I can feel it growing inside me."

"May I feel it?" Amelia stood and leaned over Fanny.

"Go ahead. You'll see."

Amelia opened both her palms and pressed them gently against Fanny's abdomen. She moved her hands over the top and sides of Fanny's flat belly and then a bit lower. There

261

was no evidence of any growth large enough to feel.

"Well?"

"I don't feel anything."

"That doesn't mean it isn't there." Fanny's eyes widened and she grabbed Amelia's wrist hard. "I *know* it is. I know it is. I know it is."

Amelia gently wrested her wrist back from Fanny and sat down again. "How do you know?"

"They told me! That's how I know. They never lie to me. They told me I have a tumor and it's all my fault. Sinners must be punished, you know, Amelia. My papa always said sinners are always punished. That's what they say, too." She always referred to the voices in her head as "they."

Amelia looked around the room. "How do you feel you have sinned, Fanny?"

"It's a secret I can't tell. I'm not to ever tell anyone. Ever."

Amelia reckoned Fanny feared death more than the voices in her head.

"I'm sure that if they knew telling might save your life, then it would be permissible, don't you think?"

Fanny reached up and grabbed handfuls of her butchered hair and tugged.

"I don't know. I don't know," she groaned. "You have to help me."

Amelia studied the lovely floral pattern of the

Persian carpet beneath her feet, trying to come up with a way to help the tortured soul.

Fanny began to thrash and roll from side to side mumbling, "I hate waking up. I can't even put my feet on the floor anymore. I can't stand the smell of that tea you gave me. I don't know what's to become of me. They whisper to me that I'm doomed. I should have never listened to the others. Never, ever, ever, ever, ever, ever—"

"Fanny, stop!" Amelia's sharp command halted the tirade. "I need silence."

"Are they talking to you, too?"

"No," Amelia assured her, closing her eyes. The sight of Fanny stretched out on the bed tearing at her hair was too distracting. "They aren't. I'm just thinking."

Smells bother her. She feels faint upon standing.

Nausea. Loss of appetite.

Sinners must be punished, you know.

Suddenly Amelia opened her eyes and stared at Fanny. She reached for her bag, unwilling to leave it with the girl, and stood.

"Where are you going, Amelia? You're giving up, aren't you? I'm going to die, aren't I? I knew it." Then Fanny paused, cocked her head to one side as if listening and then began nodding yes vigorously. "I know. I know."

"What are they saying, Fanny?"

"They are reminding me that you can't help

me." She dissolved into hysterics. Shrieking and sobbing, she rolled across the bed and began to rip the sheets away from the mattress. "No one can help me! I'm doomed! I'm dooooomed!"

The door flew open and Sophronia came charging in.

"What have you done, Amelia? She's worse than before. At least I'd had her calmed down a bit." Sophronia stared down at her charge, her hands clasped.

Amelia signaled Sophronia and they crossed the room to stand before the window seat.

"When was her last menses?" Amelia whispered, not wanting Fanny to hear.

"Her last menses?" Sophronia's lips pursed. "Why? Surely you aren't thinking—"

"I'm thinking that if there's some blockage, if there is some reason why she hasn't had her monthly, then that would account for these hysterics—"

Sophronia turned her sharp gaze Fanny's way. "You mean she may actually have a tumor?"

Fanny let out a shriek.

Amelia leaned close and whispered, "Is there any possible chance that she may be . . . that she could be . . . expecting?"

Sophronia blanched white. Her severe hairstyle accentuated her high cheekbones and her arching raven brows.

"Expecting? A child?" She could barely utter

the words. "Preposterous. How dare you insult me like this? I have given up my own life to care for her as if she were my own blood relation and not Lemuel's. How on earth could she be expecting? No one goes in or out of this room without my knowledge—only Sigrid and Lemuel."

Amelia stared at the stables and the corrals beyond the window bars. There were at least five cowhands within view at this very moment. It wasn't impossible that one of them might have found a way into the house—

"Amelia?"

"I'm sorry . . . I was just thinking."

Across the room, Fanny's shrieks had subsided to loud, heart-wrenching sobs.

Sophronia was still ranting. "Why, it's preposterous. Ridiculous. As if any man would find *her* attractive—"

"Someone could have taken advantage of her—"

"Stop!" Sophronia held up her hand. "I refuse to hear more."

We'll know in time, Amelia thought, as she stared over at Fanny. Until then, the poor wretched creature needed help.

"Should we restrain her? Tie her hands and feet?" Sophronia suggested.

"Absolutely not. I'm going to give her some laudanum. That should calm her down quickly

—unless her body has built up a tolerance to it."

"I've sent for Lemuel," Sophronia told her. "He should be here soon." She turned on Amelia, her expression foreboding. "If I were you, I would *not* bring up your absurd theory to him. Spare yourself the embarrassment." Marching across the room, she waited by Fanny's bed. "Bring your medicine bag over here, Amelia. If I have to, I'll hold her down while you dose her."

Chapter Eighteen

Hank drew the buggy into the shade and, hat in hand, waited for Amelia. Eventually, Sigrid brought him a glass of lemonade and said she had no idea how long the doctor might be.

Cowhands passed by, going about their duties. Some acknowledged him with a tug of a hat brim. Others ignored him completely. He couldn't imagine what it would take to run such a huge spread. Compared to Harroway House, the Ellenberg place was little more than a log hovel—yet love made up for its lack of amenities.

Hank was debating climbing into the buggy to take a nap in the shade when he noticed two riders approaching through the entry gate at the end of the long drive. One was dressed as a hired hand, the other wore a dark suit and a black, low-crowned hat. A gold watch fob caught the sunlight, as did his shiny plum-colored satin vest beneath his open jacket.

As the man drew closer, his looks and dress reminded Hank of some of the riverboat gamblers he'd seen in Saint Louis. The regal way the rider in black sat his horse, the curt nod he gave Hank as he rode up, dismounted and absently tossed his reins to the hired hand marked him as the man in charge. Hank figured him as none other than Lemuel Harroway.

A womanizer, Joe Ellenberg had said. Did Amelia know?

Hank watched the arrogant way Lemuel Harroway strode toward him and had to remind himself to keep an open mind before he passed judgment.

Harroway introduced himself and offered his hand.

Hank shook it. "I'm Hank Larson." Thinking of Amelia's concern for the Harroways' privacy, he merely said, "I drove Miss Hawthorne over from the Ellenberg place where she was visiting."

"And exactly who are you, Mr. Larson? What is your connection to Miss Hawthorne?"

"I'm a friend. I'm also sheriff of Glory." Let him chew on that, Hank thought.

"I didn't know Glory had a sheriff."

"Up until a month or so ago, there wasn't one. Now I'm it. There has been a rash of holdups and robberies in the area. Miss Hawthorne accompanied me out to the Ellenbergs to see about their newborn while I asked them to be on the lookout for a couple of desperados who hail from around here."

"You don't say?" Lemuel surveyed his property and the men working in the corrals. If he was at all concerned, he didn't show it. "Who is it, exactly, we should be watching out for?"

Hank hesitated, hoping the information wouldn't cost Amelia.

"Evan Hawthorne and Silas Jones."

"Miss Hawthorne's brother?"

"Yes, unfortunately."

"I'm not familiar with the other man." Lemuel glanced toward the house, looking impatient to head inside.

"He's a hired hand. He's worked at ranches in the area. Ellenberg fired him a couple of summers back."

"My foreman would know better than I who is on our payroll. I'll be sure to tell him. Silas Jones, you say? And Evan Hawthorne?"

"That's right."

"Thank you for the information. Now, if you'll excuse me?" He took a few steps in the direction of the house and suddenly stopped. "Is there a reason you're out here cooling your heels when you could be inside out of the heat?"

Hank shrugged. "There was an emergency. Your maid brought out some lemonade."

"Come inside. No sense simmering in the heat."

Hank almost declined, but decided he might not ever get another chance to see the inside of Harroway House so he caught up with Lemuel and, together, they went inside.

The home was elegant and extravagant at the same time. No expense had been spared on the carpentry, the wood floors, the ceiling medallions, the wall fabric or the carpeting. Hank stopped in the entry hall and took it all in. Lemuel was just telling him to make himself comfortable in the front parlor when both men were drawn to the sight of Amelia coming down the wide, gently curving staircase.

She seemed lost in thought, but when she realized they were waiting in the entry hall, her frown was replaced with an absentminded smile. Hank knew she was concerned about Lemuel's sister.

"How is she?" Lemuel had already handed his hat to Sigrid, who appeared out of nowhere to take both their hats.

Hank was embarrassed to hand over his mauled bowler. He gave Sigrid an apologetic shrug when he caught her staring at it.

Amelia was saying, "I've sedated her with a

bit of laudanum. She's calmer now. Hopefully she'll sleep for a while. After that, we'll see if we can get her to eat something and keep it down."

Hank noticed Lemuel's arrogance was gone. He was genuinely concerned for his sister's welfare and, much to Hank's relief, the man was cordial and solicitous to Amelia.

Lemuel took her arm and led her into the front parlor.

"Sophronia will be right down." Amelia moved away from Lemuel and went to stand beside Hank near the settee.

Hank's heart swelled with pride when she made it obvious they were more than mere acquaintances.

"Please, have a seat," Lemuel said. "I'll ring for beverages." He walked over to a long embroidered bellpull near the double doors and gave it a tug. Hank and Amelia sat on the settee.

Just then a striking dark-eyed woman with raven hair pulled back into a severe knot walked into the room. Her emerald gown complemented her flawless ivory skin. She seemed as aloof as her husband. When she noticed Hank, she bridled and gave him a once-over.

"Who are you?" she said cooly. Her gaze drifted to Amelia and back to Hank.

"This is Mr. Larson, sheriff of Glory," Lemuel told her. "He accompanied Miss Hawthorne. How is Fanny?" Lemuel wanted to know.

Sophronia shot a look at Hank before she said anything.

"If you'd like me to leave—" he offered.

"Not at all," Lemuel said, surprising Hank and obviously Amelia, too.

Sophronia looked aghast. "But, Lemuel—"

"He's a friend of Amelia's. And the sheriff of Glory."

"But—"

Lemuel dismissed his wife. "Amelia? What's happening to my sister that is so dire I've been called home from Austin?"

Hank admired Amelia's calm.

"Apparently, she's been overwrought for the past few days. I was called out last week and she was distressed, but manageable. She spoke of hearing voices—"

"Nothing new," Lemuel interrupted.

"No. Not at all. She mentioned a shadow man, someone who visits her room at night."

"Obviously just another of her hysterical hallucinations." Lemuel dismissed the notion with a shrug.

Hank could tell Amelia wanted to say more, but then Sophronia cut in.

"Amelia is of the opinion that Fanny might be—" Sophronia glanced at Hank and stopped. "I really don't think this is a discussion we need carry on in public."

Before Lemuel could protest, Hank was on his

271

feet. "I agree, Mrs. Harroway. This conversation is of a private nature. I'll be happy to wait outside." He turned to Amelia and bowed. "Whenever you're ready, Amelia."

She nodded almost absently and he took his leave.

Twenty minutes later, she met him beside the buggy.

"I'm sorry, Hank."

"I'm sorry for you. What an obnoxious woman."

"She's not always that rude, but there is a hardness there. She married Lemuel in good faith and since their marriage, he spends most of his time in Austin while she's left here to manage his sister and the ranch."

"Still, I hate that you have to deal with her. Is the sister going to be all right?"

A sadness crept back into Amelia's eyes. "I doubt it. She's been this way for years. Most of the time her illness can be managed, but once she gets out of control, it takes days, sometimes weeks, before she settles again."

He noticed she didn't have her bag with her. "Do you need to stay a bit longer?"

"I came out to tell you I'm going to spend the night. When Fanny wakes up, I'd like to encourage her to try to eat. I've some ginger compound that might help with her nausea."

"On top of everything else, she's ill?"

"She claims to be. It's very odd. I wish—"

"Wish what, Amelia?"

"I wish I was at liberty to talk to someone about it."

"It's that troubling?"

"It is if something beyond Fanny's control is happening to her. Perhaps Brand—"

He could tell she was musing aloud, trying to work things out in her mind. He wished she felt she could turn to him for help, but he couldn't blame her.

"McCormick is not only wise and level-headed, but he's a preacher. Who better to advise you?"

"You're right. I'll talk to Brand if it comes to that. Mr. Harroway will have someone drive me back to town tomorrow."

"You're certain you need to stay on?"

"I am," she said. "I want to. I hate to ask, but could you possibly stop by the house and feed Sweet Pickle?"

Hank took her hand. She'd looked so content with the Ellenbergs, so at peace. Now, she had not only her brother to worry about, but she'd taken on the Harroways' troubles, as well.

"Of course. I'll see you when you return to Glory." He glanced up at the house, wishing he could kiss her goodbye, knowing his very proper Miss Amelia Hawthorne would be mortified at the very idea.

The afternoon passed quickly as Amelia sat at Fanny's bedside, watching the troubled young woman sleep. She was given the guest room beside Fanny's for convenience. The rooms shared a connecting door. She borrowed a nightgown from Sophronia and the family Bible from Fanny's room. It was old, the leather bindings nearly worn through, and dusty from sitting ignored on one of Fanny's crowded shelves.

Amelia locked Fanny in, took the Bible into her room and lit a lamp on the bedside table. She changed into the borrowed nightdress, her thoughts as jumbled as buttons in a button jar when she finally slipped into bed.

She kept picturing Hank with the Ellenbergs, the easy way he chatted with all of them. The regard he had for Joe and his family. She was glad he was getting to know folks in and around Glory and she wondered if he'd actually be able to make a success of his newspaper. Right now it certainly didn't seem as if he spent much time at it. Then again, as he said, there wasn't much news to report. She was certainly thankful that he wasn't devoting more space to the Perkins Gang.

But if the paper failed, would he have to leave town and move on to greener pastures?

She found herself thinking of how solicitous he'd been after seeing her stricken by the sight of the new Wanted poster. She even found herself wishing he could have kissed her goodbye this afternoon. The way he'd lingered, the way he'd held her hand made her certain that he'd wanted to as much as she'd wished he could have.

She turned to the pages of the Bible as she always did when in need of consolation and answers, hope and comfort.

She had no idea how long she read before she suddenly awoke with a start and discovered she'd been dozing.

She thought she heard the floor creak, but she couldn't tell if the sound came from Fanny's room or in the hallway. If Fanny was awake, perhaps she was hungry. Amelia decided to wait and see if she heard her charge stirring before she got up.

No one goes in or out of this room without my knowledge—only Sigrid and Lemuel.

Sigrid. And Lemuel.

Sophronia had been so insistent. Amelia knew without a doubt the woman was vigilant when it came to locking Fanny into her room, for truth be told, Sophronia was more than a little afraid of Fanny.

There were bars on the windows, but if Fanny had discovered a way to escape then she'd been clever enough to know to return to her room before dawn. She may have been able to sneak out of her room for illicit trysts with a cowhand. If Fanny was pregnant, and if she had not been sneaking out, then someone had been sneaking in. That *someone* had to have stolen a key somehow.

Or it's Lemuel.

Amelia would not, could not seriously consider such an abomination.

She pressed her hands over her eyes. Exhausted, she was about to reach for the candle and blow it out when she definitely heard a floorboard creak. The sound came from Fanny's room.

She threw back the sheet and slipped out of bed and nearly fell on her face when she tripped over the hem of Sophronia's nightgown. Amelia scooped up the extra fabric in one hand and headed for the connecting door, careful not to make a sound.

She'd left the key in the door. All she had to do was turn it and walk in.

She pressed her ear to the wooden panel and listened. Was that someone whispering on the other side?

Her courage nearly failed her. Did she *truly* want to discover what was on the other side of the door?

Don't be ridiculous, she told herself.

Lord, fill me with the courage you gave Daniel in the lion's den and give me the wisdom of Solomon so I'll know how to best help poor Fanny.

Her hands shook as she twisted the key and the lock clicked open. Slowly, slowly, she turned the doorknob and pulled the door open.

"Is that you?" Fanny's hoarse whisper scratched the air as it crossed the room.

"It's me, Fanny. It's Amelia."

Amelia lifted the candle higher, but darkness burrowed into the corners of the large room. She paused just over the threshold of the connecting door, listened intently. The only sound was that of Fanny's agitated breathing.

"Is that *you?*" Fanny repeated. Under the effect of the laudanum, she sounded groggy.

Amelia hurried to the bedside, set the candle down. Fanny's eyes were open. She stared up at Amelia for a moment and then, disappointment evident in her tone, she mumbled, "Oh. It's only you, Amelia."

Fanny's eyelids fluttered closed. Amelia took hold of her wrist. Her pulse was slow. Fanny's breathing settled and she fell into deep slumber. Satisfied Fanny was alone and safe, Amelia gazed around the room. She walked to the window, paused to stare out over the stables and barn in the near distance. Nothing moved. Nothing appeared out of the ordinary.

She went back into her own room, locking Fanny's door behind her. Before she climbed into bed, she knelt and said a prayer of thanks-giving, prayed for Evan, for Hank, for everyone she remembered in her nightly prayers. She prayed for Fanny's healing. Tonight she even prayed for Sophronia. She prayed for Lemuel.

Then she blew out the candle and climbed back into bed.

By afternoon of the next day, Amelia was back in Glory, knocking at Reverend McCormick's front door. Charity ushered her in and almost immediately there was another caller at the door. Charity excused herself and left Amelia stand-ing in the parlor as she hurried to answer it.

Amelia recognized Hank's voice the moment he said hello and her heart filled with joy.

I'm beginning to realize how very much I need you in my life, Amelia.

Charity led him into the parlor.

"You're back," Hank said as he walked into the room. He sounded relieved rather than surprised to find her here. "I recognized the Harroway buggy as it passed by. I stopped by your house, but you weren't there so I came by here on the off chance that you'd visit Brand first." He lowered his voice and took a step closer. "Are you all right?"

"I'm perfectly fine." She turned to Charity. "I came to see Brand, if he has time to spare," Amelia said.

"He's in his study. I'll tell him you're here," Charity said before she hurried down the hall.

"I missed you," Hank said softly when they were alone.

"I was only gone one night." She wondered if it were a sin to feel so joyful when there was so much sorrow in the world.

"I sleep better knowing you're safely tucked in your own bed."

She wished she could control the blush that crept up her cheeks. It burned all the way to her hairline.

"You look tired," he added.

"It was exhausting, but Fanny finally seemed a bit better when I left."

"I had no doubt that you'd help her."

"I wasn't certain." Her mind began to wander down the worry trail until Charity reappeared in the doorway.

"Brand will see you now," she told Amelia. Then to Hank she offered, "Would you care for some tea or coffee?"

"No thank you. I'll be heading back to work now that I've found Amelia."

As Amelia followed Charity down the hall, her heart may have been heavy, but a smile kept teasing the corners of her mouth.

"Please, have a seat, Amelia," Reverend McCormick offered. "I take it this isn't a social call?"

She sat on the leather chair opposite his wide mahogany desk. His office was compact yet organized, nothing like Hank's disorderly piles and crammed bookcases. Neat stacks of papers and books nearly covered Brand's desk. He folded his hands in the empty space in the center and waited for her to take the lead.

"I don't even know where or how to begin, but I need your advice," she said.

"I can't imagine this being an easy time for you."

"This is not about Evan," she said. "The fact is, I've had some troubling thoughts in regard to a patient. Although I'm not a physician in the true sense of the word, folks around here trust me to keep their confidence—just as my father would have done."

He nodded. "I understand completely."

"I'm sorely wrestling with something that is so very troubling that I must talk to someone about it. Since you lend an ear to folks during troubled times and keep their confidence, I hope you will keep mine, now."

"Of course, Amelia. You know that I will." He leaned back in his chair.

Just then a mockingbird landed on the window-sill and trilled a few notes of its summer song. Amelia took its appearance as a sign of God's blessing and was reassured she was doing the right thing.

"If I suspected that a terrible sin was being perpetrated on an innocent victim—and yet I have no proof—am I obligated to tell someone? If my suspicions are invalid, if this person is completely innocent, then I would have slandered him. He would be completely ruined if anyone were to find out—and for no reason other than some hysterical musing on my part."

The reverend sat for a moment in contemplative silence. The fact that his steady gaze never wavered was comforting.

"Amelia, you have never been the hysterical type. In fact, you are one of the most even-tempered females I've ever known. How great is this 'terrible sin'?"

She looked down at her clenched hands where they rested in her lap. "One of the worst," she whispered. "Enough to ruin at least three lives."

"You have no proof whatsoever?"

She shook her head. She would have no proof until she was sure Fanny was definitely in a delicate condition. Even then nothing would be completely clear unless Fanny confessed all.

"In a week or two, I'll know more. But even then I won't be absolutely certain that I know the whole story."

"You must weigh all the consequences and decide what to do. If you need my help, don't hesitate to come to me."

"I will definitely come to you first. Thank you for seeing me, Reverend."

"You know you're welcome anytime."

Amelia collected her reticule and rose, ready to take her leave. The preacher was watching her closely.

"Are you sure this isn't about Evan? He hasn't been back, has he?"

Afraid she'd led him to believe she was talking about Evan, hiding him, or that she even knew where he was, she said, "No, not at all. I haven't seen him. Thank you again for your time, Reverend."

She left the office and made her way alone down the short hallway, thankful that at least one of her problems had nothing whatsoever to do with her brother.

Chapter Nineteen

Three days later, Hank was in the Gazette office working with Ricardo Hernandez, the fourteen-year-old son of Laura Foster's cook. Not only did Ricardo deliver papers for him, but Hank had apprenticed the youth, teaching him to work the hand press.

Ricardo took to printing like a duck to water.

He was methodical and thorough and the look of pride on the boy's face when his two-page edition of the *Glory Gazette* came off the press was worth the extra time it had taken Hank to train him.

The headline stood out in boldface type: All Quiet In Glory No Further Robbery Attempts. For Amelia's sake, Hank wanted to downplay the fact that the Perkins Gang had escalated their attacks on other establishments around the county. As he reread the headline, Oz Caldwell's words came back to haunt him.

I hope you'll do the right thing, Larson, if and when Hawthorne shows up again.

"I hope so, too," Hank mumbled to himself.

"*Señor?*" Ricardo looked up from where he was stacking neatly folded pages.

"Just thinking out loud," Hank told him.

"*Pardon?*"

"*Nada.* Nothing." Hank's Spanish was rudimentary at best. He crossed the room, speaking slowly and distinctly. Adding hand gestures, he instructed Ricardo to finish folding and stacking the papers and then to clean the press.

When the new bell he'd installed over the front door rang, Hank looked up and saw Brand McCormick walk in. He appreciated the minister's easygoing manner and the fact that the preacher never pushed or prodded him about his lack of faith.

"Howdy, Reverend."

"I hope this isn't bad timing." Brand walked over to the stack of papers and glanced down at the headline.

"Have one," Hank offered.

"I'll wait for it to arrive on the front porch. I like to read it over my coffee in the morning."

"You must not have more than one cup. There's not much to read."

"It's a far cry from no paper at all, believe me. We're all appreciative of what you're doing, Hank. A newspaper puts our little town on the map, so to speak." Brand settled on a corner of Hank's desk. "You've done a good thing."

"Thank you, Reverend." From the way Brand hesitated to go on, Hank began to suspect this wasn't just a social call.

"You've been spending a lot of time with Amelia." As usual, the preacher wasn't a man to waste words.

"I have." He frowned, wondering what Brand was getting at.

He'd called on Amelia just yesterday and they had taken a stroll around the square together. She seemed fine—as fine as could be with her brother wanted all over Texas. "Is something wrong?"

"Are you growing to care for her?"

Hank took a deep breath, shoved his fingers through his hair. A glance across the room assured him Ricardo was fine on his own. He moved closer to Brand, rested an elbow on a bookcase haphazardly stuffed with papers and books he'd shoved in at random. The entire office was filling up with paper, both blank and printed. There were volumes of books that he'd shipped from his personal library in Saint Joe as well as journals stuffed with his own musings.

"When my wife died, I never thought I'd be attracted to another woman again. Especially someone like Amelia." He pictured Tricia—ethereal, blond, genteel. "Tricia was not nearly as independent minded as Amelia. I can't imagine her ever fending for herself the way Amelia has had to do. My wife was stunningly beautiful. She wasn't conceited in the least, but she was aware of her beauty. Amelia is lovely, but has no idea. She's selfless and modest, attuned to nature—"

"It sounds as if you're falling in love, Hank."

Hank shrugged in admittance, finding it hard to believe himself.

"I came to Texas to start a paper and write a novel. I never thought I'd fall in love again. Not in a million years. Certainly not this soon."

"Sometimes God has plans for us other than the ones we have for ourselves," Brand said.

When Hank didn't respond, the reverend watched him closely. "Amelia is a God-fearing woman, Hank. Do you believe in God?"

"I never was much of a believer. After I lost Tricia and the baby, I swore I never would be."

"You realize her faith in God plays a sizable role in Amelia's life."

"I would never ask her to give up her faith."

"I didn't think you would. I just hope that you'll keep your heart open to one day accepting the Lord into your life, too, Hank. It's not all that impossible, for as you've seen, you never know what's down the road. Here you are in Glory, acting as sheriff and discovering He may have brought love into your life again. For all you know, He just might come knocking at your heart Himself."

"*Señor*?"

Hank looked over and found Ricardo waiting patiently beside the Hoe press with a rag. Hank turned back to Brand. "I can't make you any promises, Reverend," he said.

"Just keep your heart open. God will do the rest." Brand pushed away from the desk and headed for the door. The bell tinkled when Brand opened the door. He paused on the threshold. "Folks in this town care deeply for Amelia, Hank. No one wants to see her hurt."

"You're not the first person to tell me that. Hurting Amelia is the last thing I'd ever want to do."

When Mick Robinson, the blacksmith, ran into

trouble extracting an impacted tooth, he sent for Amelia. She rummaged through a drawer in the back of the apothecary cabinet and grabbed both her dental chisel and a tooth key and tossed them into her bag. She climbed on a step stool and reached for a bottle of Magnetic Tooth Cordial and Pain Killer she'd concocted from one of Dr. Chase's recipes.

As soon as she walked into the shady interior of the huge barn on Main Street, she saw Denton Fairchild, the bartender, seated on an upended barrel with a rag tied around his head. His right cheek was so swollen he looked like a greedy squirrel. Sweat had broken out on his bald pate. His skin was nearly as white as the bandage.

"Thanks for comin', Amelia." Mick wiped his meaty fists on the front of his smithy's apron. "Never was a tooth I couldn't yank until now."

Denton moaned and rolled his eyes. When Amelia took a step in his direction, he whimpered and drew back.

"Let me just have a look, Mr. Fairchild," she said. "I promise not to touch your tooth."

Of the belief that men made much worse patients than women, Amelia spoke to him as patiently as if he were a child as she unwound the bandage. "Can you open your mouth?" The swelling was enormous.

" 'ink tho," he mumbled. He opened his mouth slightly.

"Could you pull your cheek out with your finger so I might peek inside?" She knew that he'd be less likely to yelp if he did it himself.

He complied. Amelia saw enough to recognize a fractured molar.

"I'll have that out in no time," she promised.

He shook his head and started mumbling protests while she opened the bottle of Magnetic Tooth Cordial. She poured a dab onto a wad of lint. As she reached toward his head, he jerked back.

"Sit still, Mr. Fairchild. I'm going to apply this mixture to the outside of your cheek first. A slight numbing effect will occur and that'll allow me to dab some inside on your tooth. In few minutes, you won't feel that terrible pain anymore. Won't that be wonderful? While the cordial is working, I'll take out your tooth. How does that sound?"

" 'errible."

"You'll be suffering until that tooth is out. The nerve is exposed."

Denton moaned but held steady. Amelia swabbed his cheek with the cordial—a blend of laudanum, chloroform, gum camphor, oil of cloves, sulphuric ether and oil of lavender.

The bartender began to relax almost immediately. Soon he permitted her to swab the offending molar. After allowing the cordial to work a few moments longer, she discreetly slipped the chisel and tooth key out of her bag and nodded to Mick.

The smithy slipped up behind Denton and placed his hands on the man's shoulders to keep him steady on the barrel. The bartender's eyes widened.

Amelia located the broken molar. She nodded to Mick and then as fast as she could, tried to slip the hook of the extractor as far into the area between the tooth and gum as she could. Then she quickly began to turn the crank. At first the man felt nothing. Then he gurgled a yelp and struggled to lunge off the barrel, but Mick shoved him back down.

Amelia kept cranking, gritting her own teeth until Denton's tooth made a distinctive sound like that of a cork coming out of a bottle. Both halves of the tooth popped out of his mouth.

Amelia tidied up her things and then took a small vial out of her bag. "Here's some clove oil." She handed it to Denton and said, "If you need anything stronger for the pain, don't hesitate to stop by my house."

Mick handed Amelia a newly minted silver dollar.

"Thanks for helping out, Amelia. Denton was squealin' like a piglet and I didn't know what to do for love nor money. Sorry I took you away from whatever you were doin'."

She was about to tell him that she was merely

watering her garden, but just then a great commotion started at the far end of town. Evidently, the ruckus was headed their way.

Amelia and the others ran up to the corner of Main Street. Stores emptied and shopkeepers followed customers out onto the street. A band of riders was headed toward the center of town.

Amelia's blood ran cold when she recognized Sheriff Oswald Caldwell in the lead. Behind him, on a second horse, a man was slumped over his saddle. His hat brim hid his face and features. Amelia caught her breath and waited, afraid Caldwell had captured Evan and was parading him through Glory, forcing her brother to face his shame.

The man moved. When Amelia saw that he was of heavier build and older than Evan, her breath came out in a rush. As she watched, Harrison Barker and a few of the others ran out to where Caldwell had reined in and dismounted. Someone reached up for the wounded man whose wrists were bound and pulled him down off his horse.

He appeared to be the same man who held up the Cutters' bank a month ago. The man collapsed on the ground at Caldwell and his posse's feet. Harrison started yelling for someone to go find Amelia just as she began to run toward the fallen outlaw.

Hank was in the doorway of the *Gazette* office telling Brand goodbye when they heard the commotion and turned to see what was going on. Seconds later, someone was shouting Amelia's name and Hank saw her racing down the street from the direction of the livery stable.

He and the preacher headed down Main toward the growing crowd. Hank recognized Oz Caldwell, standing head and shoulders above his deputies. Everyone was milling around near the corner. Hank could hear the preacher's heavy footsteps pounding along behind him.

As he drew near the circle of onlookers, Harrison Barker ran up to him.

"The Perkins Gang broke Harvey Ruggles out of county jail. Sheriff Caldwell is mad as a hornet. He and his men shot Ruggles during the escape and the other four left him behind. The posse tracked the rest of them back this way. Almost into Glory!" Harrison's voice went up an octave on his last sentence. Sweat beaded his upper lip.

Hank pushed his way through the crowd encircling Amelia, Caldwell and the wounded outlaw, hoping the man on the ground wasn't Evan Hawthorne.

Amelia was kneeling alongside the wounded man, pressing his bloody, wadded shirt against a shoulder wound. Her expression was one of conern, but her composure assured Hank the man wasn't her brother.

"It's a clean shoulder wound," she told Caldwell, looking up. The sheriff towered over her but she didn't cower. "Bullet went right through. He should be all right."

"Good," Caldwell spit out. "I want him fit enough to hang."

Hank saw Amelia blanch. She turned her attention to the outlaw again. Hank realized Caldwell had spotted him when he said, 'Larson, round up your posse and let's get going before the trail gets cold."

"Posse? I don't have a posse."

Caldwell spun around pointing to men in the crowd. "You, you and you," he ordered, "saddle up. You're riding with us."

No one dared refuse. Not even Charlie Scout, who'd been lounging on the walk outside the mercantile that morning. Caldwell had chosen him first.

Hank hurried back to his office to collect his borrowed gun and saddle his horse. By the time he rode back to the corner, the wounded outlaw was sitting up in the dusty street, leaning against the boardwalk. Amelia was carefully repacking her medical bag, winding a strip of linen bandage.

She paused and looked up, scanned the gathering of men on horseback until their eyes met. Hers were bright with unshed tears, her forehead creased with worry. She rose to her feet, ignored the dust on her skirt. Earlier she'd shoved off her straw hat. Now it dangled from her neck, rested against her shoulders.

More than anything he wanted to dismount, to hold her, convince her that everything would be fine. He wanted to ease her worry, but he knew realistically, there was nothing he could do to assure her brother's safety. Nothing at all save what he'd already promised her.

Ignoring the crowd, her shoulders straight and proud, she walked over to where he sat his horse. She paused beside his stirrup. As if there were only the two of them in the world, she held his eyes with her gaze as she tried to smile. Her courage wavered, her chin quivered. She didn't let one single tear fall.

"There were five men in the Perkins Gang. Four of them are at large. One is Evan." Her brother's name came out in a whisper. "He is as tall as you, Hank. He's lanky. He's got dark hair and blue eyes. And he's only nineteen."

He leaned down so that only she could hear. "I'll do everything I can to keep him safe, Amelia. I promise."

She gently placed her palm on his knee. "I know you will. I trust you. Just be careful," she whispered.

Without thinking, he leaned close, cupped the back of her head in his hand and kissed her ght then and there in front of the whole town.

Caldwell shouted, "Let's ride!"

Both posses headed down the street after him. Hank turned his horse around, rode a few steps way and glanced back. Amelia was watching im, flanked by Brand McCormick and his sister. Brand's voice carried over the sound of hoof-eats.

"Let us bow our heads and pray."

Chapter Twenty

T rail Dust and Guns.
Guns and Dust.
Of Men and Guns.

Titles for his novels came to mind as Hank rode alongside Oz Caldwell.

Charlie Scout had taken the lead. The Indian picked up the trail not far from Glory and now, miles later, the posse was still pounding across the open plain tracking the outlaws.

Hank's writer's mind had slipped outside himself as they pushed on. His thoughts echoed in his head, keeping time with the sound of hoofbeats around him.

Remember this. Remember it all. Remember the taste of dust, the anxiety, the sweat, the smell of horses and leather, the weight of the holster, the feel of the rawhide cord anchoring it to my thigh. Remember. Remember so you can write it all down.

They thundered to a halt when Charlie Scout reined in. Caldwell talked to the smaller man for a moment, then he shouted, "Looks like the gang split up. One fella rode off in that direction. You, you and you—" he pointed again "—go that way. The rest of you, that includes you, too, Larson, follow me."

Hank gladly let the seasoned lawman command the search. He was more than thankful when he realized none of the outlaws was headed in the direction of the Ellenberg ranch. Hank reckoned Joe and his cowhands could defend his family, but they had survived enough over the years.

As they drew near Harroway House, they heard the distinct pop of gunshots in the distance. Unintelligible shouts warned them to approach with caution. Hank grudgingly admired Caldwell's skill with the men. His no-nonsense commands left the unseasoned posse with little time to waver. They dismounted a good distance from the house and fanned out.

"Watch and learn, Larson," Oz told him as they headed for the house. Hank followed him, gun drawn, as they darted from tree to tree. They crouched behind a wagon, and then a water tank.

As a bullet whizzed close to Hank's head, he

silently assured himself that anything he learned today was *not* going to be repeated except, perhaps, as a scene in his novel.

One of Caldwell's men had made his way around to the house and brought back the Harroway foreman.

"Talk," Oswald commanded. "What's going on?"

The shaken foreman, Wayne Morgan, had a hard time getting anything out after another shot flew over their heads and they all ducked. He rubbed his hand over his eyes, took a deep breath.

"I was here with a skeleton crew when three men rode in firing guns and shouting. We dove for cover. Before we knew what was happening, one of my men was badly wounded and the gunmen stormed the house. They've got us covered from most of the second-floor windows."

From where they crouched behind the water tower, Hank saw rifles jutting out of an upstairs window. He thought of Sophronia, wondered if her cool, unruffled exterior was helping her keep a level head. Though he'd never laid eyes on Fanny, he figured she had to be frantic and confused. Then he remembered the maid.

"I was out here last week with Amelia. There are three women in there," Hank told Caldwell.

"Miss Hawthorne was *here* last week? *That's* quite a coincidence." Caldwell's eyes narrowed.

Hank realized how suspicious Amelia's recent

visit to Harroway House must sound now that the Perkins Gang had also showed up here at the ranch. Doubt tapped at the edges of his heart until he remembered Amelia standing in the middle of Main Street with her hand on his knee. He pictured her flawless green eyes, the trust mirrored in them. He still tasted their kiss. He refused to believe she had anything to do with this. Not Amelia.

"She was here to treat Miss Harroway, a long-time patient of hers." He tried to sound as if he hadn't been pestered by the same suspicion he saw in Caldwell's expression.

The foreman spoke up. "There are only two women inside. The maid ran out the back door a couple of minutes ago."

"Where is she?" Caldwell wanted to know. "Maybe she can tell us what's going on."

It took a few more harrowing minutes for Hank, Oz and Morgan to make their way to the back of the barn where two more gunman inside had rifles trained on the outbuildings.

"If we could get someone onto that second-floor balcony," Caldwell muttered, "we might be able to take out the man watching the front of the house."

They found the maid shivering with terror in the shadows behind the barn. She was sitting on a milking stool someone had brought her, her face buried in her hands.

"Sigrid," Hank said, taking a knee beside her. "Sigrid, we need your help."

Her shoulders shuddered. She pulled her hands away from her face and turned teary blue eyes his way. Her face was drained of color, except for two bright red splotches on her cheeks.

"My help?"

"What happened?"

"I don't rightly know, sir. I vas dustin' the bookshelf in da library ven I heared poundin' and shootin'. I ran an hid behind a fern stand. It sounded like a whole herd of men vent runnin' up the back stairs. I heared Mrs. Harroway screamin' 'Get out! Get out!' "

"Did you hear Miss Fanny?" Hank prodded.

"No, I didn't hear her at all."

"How'd they get in?" Oz was studying the back of the house.

"Dey valked in. De doors are unlocked durin' the daytime," Sigrid said.

"What about Lemuel Harroway?" Hank asked.

"He went back to Austin," the foreman said. "One of my men is wounded. He's in a bad way. He won't make it without help."

Hank noticed Caldwell didn't seem all that concerned. "If he dies, that'll just make it easier to tie knots in the nooses," he said. "The Perkins brothers and their friends are going to swing for murder." He studied the foreman for a second, then turned to Hank. "Send somebody after Miss Hawthorne."

"Absolutely not." Hank refused to contemplate Amelia here. It was far too dangerous. Besides, by all accounts, her brother might very well be in the house holding two women hostage.

"Is she the only one does any doctorin' around these parts?" Sheriff Caldwell asked Morgan, ignoring Hank.

"She is." The man nodded. "One time one of the men was gored by a bull and Miss Amelia—"

"Send somebody to town after her," Caldwell said, cutting him off. "Tell her to get out here on the double."

"Leave her out of this, Caldwell." Hank had a hard time not going for Oz Caldwell's throat. "I don't want her anywhere near here. She could be killed."

"Yeah, and she might be safer than any of us. Maybe she's in this deeper than you know. She might be able to talk that fool brother of hers out." Oz turned to the foreman. "Go on. Get somebody moving."

The man darted from behind the barn, zigzagging across the open yard. Shots rang out and then silence. Hank held his breath until he saw the foreman talking frantically to one of the men. A few minutes later, a lone rider cleared the barn and stable area, headed for town. Again, shots were fired, but the wrangler was soon out of range.

Hank and Caldwell peered around the corner. Each time shots were fired, he noticed the bars on one of the windows upstairs. A rifle barrel rested on the sill.

"That's the sister's room," he told Caldwell, pointing out the barred windows.

"Why the jail bars?"

"She's got nervous troubles." It was all Hank would and could say.

"Nervous, eh? She's plum *loco* from the looks of those bars."

If she wasn't before, she probably is now, Hank thought.

Just then, without warning, Caldwell stuck his head around the corner of the barn and shouted, "You! In the house! I'm Sheriff Oswald Caldwell and I've got a posse of men staked out around the perimeter of the outbuildings. If you don't surrender, you're not going to make it out alive—"

"You expect them to simply walk out?" Hank asked.

"This has gone on long enough. They're already dead men."

Hank knew Caldwell would show the men no mercy. If Evan Hawthorne was inside and if he was going to get any kind of a hearing, it was up to Hank to make certain.

For Amelia's sake.

Suddenly a shout came from upstairs. "Hey, Caldwell!" It was a man's voice, rough, loud enough to carry across the yard. "We got Harroway's wife in here. You get word to him that if he wants to see her alive, we want twenty thousand dollars."

Caldwell got to his feet, cupped his hands around his mouth and bellowed back, "He's in Austin."

"Get word to him that the Perkins brothers want the money pronto, or he'll never see his wife and sister alive again. We're not going anywhere."

Caldwell mumbled, "I'll flush 'em out or die trying. The maid and the foreman said there are two men in there. The other must have high-tailed it the other way. Still, we ought to keep an eye out for them." Oswald hunkered down against the wall of the barn. "Might as well sit it out," Caldwell suggested. "Looks like we're going to be here for a while."

Afternoon intensified the summer heat until it shimmered in waves above the dry ground. Flies pestered the animals as well as the men in the barnyard. Sweltering in his wool suit, Hank stripped off his jacket and vest and was down to his shirtsleeves. His cotton shirt stuck to him like a damp washrag. Now and again he'd take ff his hat and wipe his brow on his forearm. He'd rolled up his sleeves an hour ago.

He kept scanning the road hoping that Amelia refused to come back with the messenger, but he knew better. She wouldn't turn down a call for help, nor would she miss an opportunity to try to talk sense into her brother.

Suddenly a woman's scream rent the air. It came out of nowhere and sent a chill whipping down Hank's spine. Caldwell, dozing against the wall of the barn, awoke with a start. Sigrid, still sniffling in the shade, let out a squeal.

"That's Miss Fanny," she cried. The scream went on and on until it abruptly stopped.

Hank chanced a look around the corner of the barn. Rifle barrels were still trained at the yard. There was a flurry of movement behind the curtains in one of the upstairs windows and then he saw what appeared to be a young woman with hair nearly as short as a man's climb out of a window near the end of the second story.

On hands and knees, she awkwardly scrambled along the sloped roof that covered the veranda below. The window opened behind her and a man's head and shoulders appeared. A volley of gunfire from the ranch hands on the ground rang out.

The man in the second-story window pitched out headfirst, tumbled down the roof past the young woman and hit the ground.

The woman on the roof began to pull her hair, screaming in fits and bursts. Below the roofline, the outlaw lay on the ground unmoving, his arms and legs twisted at impossible angles.

"I'm putting an end to this madness," Caldwell mumbled. He began to shout orders to his men, demanded Morgan show himself. The foreman came running out of the barn.

Caldwell barked orders. "Pile a wagon with barrels, bales of hay, whatever else you can get your hands on. We're gonna get behind it and get as close to that house as possible. Hopefully it'll look like enough of a threat to draw some of them farther out to where we can get a clear shot at them."

"Trojan horse," Hank said.

Caldwell stared at him. "We're not using a horse. They'd probably shoot its legs out from under it."

"What about the girl on the roof?" Hank asked.

"She's lucky she hasn't been killed yet."

They waited while Morgan and his men loaded the wagon.

Hank stared at the rifle barrels in the upstairs windows.

"If there are men behind two of those three guns, then nobody's watching the front of the house anymore," he reasoned.

The seasoned sheriff squinted up at the second floor of the mansion. "You may be right. One down, two to go." He drew his gun, leaned out and fired at one of the windows. The rifle barrel jumped as someone returned fire.

Fanny screamed and inched perilously close to the edge of the roof.

"You're going to make her fall," Hank warned.

Caldwell didn't acknowledge that he'd heard. If he did, he didn't care. He took aim and shot at the second gun barrel. The rifle didn't move. Fire was returned from the first gun, but not the one Oz fired at.

"The other man must be watching the front of the house," Hank said.

"Slip around front. Tell the men out there to fire at anything that moves, anything that doesn't move, anything that looks like it *might* move. I don't care if you bust up every window in the place."

Hank took a deep breath, thought about the dead man sprawled out on the ground.

"Afraid, Larson?"

"Not really. Just biding my time."

"We don't have that luxury," Caldwell reminded him. "That woman looks as if she might leap off the roof any minute. It's about time we settled this, don't you think?"

Hank nodded. He wondered if it was too much to hope that Evan Hawthorne was the one who rode off alone when the Perkins Gang split up a few miles back.

"I'll watch your back," Caldwell promised.

Hank held his breath and started running.

The McCormicks refused to let Amelia go home after Hank and the others rode out of town. With Harvey Ruggles bandaged and securely tied up again in Harrison Barker's back room, the town settled down to wait for word. Folks went back to their daily routines as much as they could after such a dramatic turn of events, at least until a cowhand from the Harroway ranch came riding into town asking after Amelia. He was quickly ushered to Foster's Boardinghouse where Amelia and Charity were taking tea with Laura.

Laura admitted the cowhand as far as the entry hall. The three women crowded around him.

"I'm to bring you out to Harroway House," he told Amelia after introducing himself. She noticed the cowhand stared at Laura Foster far longer than was polite.

"Is it Fanny? Where's Isaac?" Amelia wanted to know.

"Miss Fanny is trapped in the house. Isaac's been shot pretty bad."

"What happened?" Charity cried.

"Three men stormed in, shootin' up the place. Then a posse from hereabouts rode in on their trail. The outlaws are holed up in the house."

"Has anyone else been hurt?" Amelia glanced around the room, forgetting where she left her bag. Laura ran to the settee, grabbed the bag and hurried back.

"One of the outlaws is dead," the cowhand said.

Amelia's blood ran cold. Her hands started to shake uncontrollably. She could barely breathe.

Three men. Three men stormed in, shootin' up the place. Then a posse from hereabouts rode in on their trail. The outlaws are holed up in the house. One of them is dead.

Ruggles had been rearrested. There were four men left at large. Evan might very well be one of those men.

Then again, he might not.

Dear Lord, please, please, don't let Evan be there. Let him have come to his senses. Let him walk the path of righteousness from here on. Don't let him be dead.

"You absolutely cannot go out there, Amelia," Laura protested.

"I'm needed there. I have to go."

"Then I'll go with you," Laura volunteered.

Amelia shook her head. She could tell Laura's offer was sincere. She didn't look the least afraid of riding into danger whereas Charity was as white as a sheet, her hands trembling.

"I'll be fine alone, thank you. You've guests to attend to." Amelia turned to the cowhand. "I'm ready when you are."

They hurried to Amelia's house. The cowhand tossed a saddle on Sweet Pickle and Amelia followed the man back to Harroway House with her heart in her throat. She wished someone other than Oswald Caldwell was in charge. He was not a kind man. Nor a forgiving one.

Hank is there, she reminded herself. Hank with his strong yet gentle way.

Hank who had kissed her right in the middle of town in front of everyone.

Hank who had promised to help Evan. Promised to keep her wayward brother safe.

The young cowhand reined in a distance from the house. Silence surrounded them. "Wait here, ma'am. I'm gonna ride ahead a bit and see what's going on. When I left, it weren't so quiet." He skirted the front of the house, keeping well out of gunshot range.

Sweet Pickle pawed the ground as Amelia waited for the cowboy's return. When he came back for her, he motioned for her to hurry.

"Looks like we missed all the fireworks, ma'am. But they need you more than ever."

Her heart was hammering double time as they rode around to the barnyard. Men seemed to be swarming all over the house. Staring up at the second story, she noticed not a single window had survived.

Most of the men were gathered around the back veranda. A rifle lay on the roof amid more glass shards. What appeared to be a trail of blood led to the edge of the roof.

307

A woman's body lay on the ground near the back door. Not far away, a man's body had been tightly bound in a blanket. His head was covered, the blanket securely tied with rope.

Amelia's breath caught. She stared at his boots.

They weren't Evan's. And they weren't Hank's.

She saw neither her brother nor Hank among the knot of men gathered around the fallen woman. All she could hope was that they were together somewhere, that Evan had surrendered and Hank was talking sense into him.

She slid out of the saddle, untied her medical bag and ran across the few yards that separated her from the others.

" 'Bout time you got here." It was Oz Caldwell. The man towered over the others, dwarfing them with both his size and his pomposity.

She paid him no mind as she focused on the woman on the ground. Fanny lay sprawled on her back, her eyes wide open, staring at the sky. She was so still, so very pale, that for a moment Amelia thought she was dead. Then she blinked.

Unmindful of the others, Amelia knelt beside Fanny and took her hand. She tried to forget that one of the outlaws was laid out not fifty feet away.

"I'm here, Fanny. You'll be fine now." Fanny's fingers and arm were limp.

"What happened?" Amelia glanced around at

the men. Still no sign of Hank. She recognized Patrick O'Toole, the town butcher. He'd been ordered by Caldwell to join the posse.

"What happened, Patrick?"

The man's voice shook. "She crawled out the window, tried to escape. Nearly made it, too, but in the end she got winged in the back and fell off the roof." He glanced up at the overhanging veranda roof. Amelia followed his gaze, saw the bloodstain again.

"Oh, Fanny," she whispered. "Can you hear me?"

She pinched Fanny's thigh, her waist, her upper arm. There was no reaction whatsoever. Fanny was paralyzed.

"I can hear you." Fanny's voice was so weak Amelia had to lower her ear almost to Fanny's lips to hear. "He said he loved me, Amelia. He said he wanted to marry me. I let him . . . I let him love me. No one ever loved me the way he did. I let him in the house at night. No one knew. I showed him how to get in and out of the house—the way I did sometimes. . . . I'm sly as a fox, you know? I stole one of Sophronia's keys and gave it to him."

Her words were thready, breathless, fading.

"Who did you give a key to, Fanny?"

"My shadow man." A haunting smile lifted the corners of her pale lips. "He only comes out to me at night. Except for today." Fanny's smile

309

faded. "He wasn't nice anymore. He wanted to hurt Sophronia. To steal Lemuel's money. He called me . . . a spoiled brat."

She tried to take a deep breath but couldn't. Her lips slowly turned the color of pale violets. A trickle of blood seeped from the corner of her mouth.

"Shh, rest, Fanny," Amelia told her. "Don't try to talk."

There was nothing to do for Fanny. Her body was broken. She was lying in a puddle of blood. Her spirit was leaving her. The Lord would take her soon. He would enfold Fanny in His loving embrace and for the first time, Fanny's troubled mind would be at peace.

But Fanny refused to rest. Her eyes darted back and forth, searching for someone among the men gathered there.

"Sophronia?" Fanny whispered. "Where is she?"

Amelia turned to Caldwell. "Where is Mrs. Harroway? What happened to her?"

"She's in the front parlor, ranting about all the broken windows. A lot of thanks we get for saving her hide."

"Send for her," she told him. "Quickly!"

Oswald didn't move, but he sent one of his men after Sophronia.

"Where is Mr. Larson?" Amelia asked him.

"In the barn, tending to business." The answer

was brusque, his stare cool. His hint of a smile chilled her.

Amelia couldn't bring herself to ask *what* business Hank was tending to. Not as poor Fanny lay dying.

"He shot me," Fanny whispered hoarsely, her tone one of disbelief. "He shot me in the back and then they killed him." Fanny's eyes widened. "He . . . he didn't love me at all." Her eyes widened. She stared into the sky. Amelia leaned closer.

"God will keep you now, Fanny. You'll be safe and loved and cherished."

With her very last breath Fanny whispered, "Evan didn't love me at all."

Chapter Twenty-One

E van.
Evan is responsible for this. For Fanny's death.

Evan had relations with Fanny. Innocent, confused Fanny. She let him into her room, her bed, and Evan and the Perkinses laid their evil scheme.

Shame coursed through Amelia. Shame and disbelief. How could Evan, the little boy she'd raised, the child who'd trustingly held her hand, listened as she read him stories, dried his tears, made him laugh—how could the child she'd cherished become the man who had used Fanny, shot her, sent her tumbling to her death?

How, Lord? How?

Where is he now? Where is Evan? And Hank. Dear Lord, where is Hank?

Shaking so hard she could barely move, Amelia reached out and gently closed Fanny's eyes.

Somehow, she rose to her feet, amazed that she could stand. The men had gathered around her. Hardworking, hard-driving men, their faces were creased by the weather and the sun. Cowhands who worked for Lemuel stood shoulder to shoulder with men from Glory and Comanche. Their expressions were grave as they stared down at Fanny. A few had unshed tears in their eyes.

Amelia's heart faltered when she looked around and didn't see Hank anywhere.

Oh, dear Lord. Please let him be safe.

Just then Sophronia came out of the back door and crossed the porch. Her long black hair hung wild and free, cascading past her waist. Gone was the haughty Spanish don's daughter. Disheveled, unkempt, Sophronia was a far cry from the woman Amelia knew. Her blouse was spattered with blood and dirt. Some of the pearl buttons on her torn bodice were missing.

Sophronia took one look at Fanny's body before her gaze cut to Amelia.

"Get away from her," Sophronia ordered. "When Lemuel finds out your brother was part of this he . . . he'll ruin you."

Amelia tried to move but couldn't. She could barely breathe. She glanced around at the men, at Sophronia. The woman stood protectively over Fanny and commanded the men to carry her sister-in-law's body inside. She sent someone to fetch Lemuel in Austin.

She may not have looked like a don's daughter just then, but Sophronia could still issue commands.

Movement near the barn drew Amelia's attention. Her breath caught when she recognized Hank. His sleeves were rolled up to his elbows. His shirt was stained with blood and mud—but he was alive. As he walked slowly into the sunlight from the shadow of the barn, she noticed he was leading a horse behind him—a horse that she knew all too well. Evan's horse.

She recognized the saddle their father had given Evan on his thirteenth birthday—a man's saddle, with his initials tooled in the leather. He was trussed up like an animal beneath a canvas tarp with a thick cord around it. Someone had slung his shroud-wrapped body over his saddle, head and heels down.

Amelia opened her mouth but she couldn't speak.

Mercifully, her world went black.

Hank flipped the reins around the top of the corral fence and ran, but couldn't reach Amelia before she hit the ground. He sank to the dust and pulled her into his arms, held her as gently as one would a babe. He smoothed her hair back, traced her cheek with his fingertips.

It pained him to know that from this day forward, she'd no longer be known for all the good she'd done. She'd no longer be thought of as Amelia Hawthorne, apothecary and healer, but as the sister of the outlaw Evan Hawthorne.

He'd asked someone to come and find him as soon as she arrived. He'd hoped to spare her this, to tell her as gently as he could that Evan was gone. He wanted to be the one to explain, to prepare her before she was subjected to seeing her brother's body like this.

But no one came to let him know that she had arrived. Now it was too late. He tightened his hold, clasped her to his heart. Rocking back and forth, he whispered her name. A moment passed, then another before her eyelashes fluttered. She smiled up at him, until she suddenly remembered. An expression of horror crossed her face.

"Evan—"

"He's dead, Amelia." Hank would sooner cut out his tongue than have to tell her the rest. She closed her eyes and let her tears flow. They streamed down her cheeks, plopped onto the bodice of her gown.

Hank shifted, helped her sit. They sat in the dirt facing each other, unaware of anything or anyone else. Finally he took a deep breath and began.

"The Perkins brothers took Fanny and Mrs. Harroway hostage. There was a gunfight."

"I know," she whispered. "Fanny's dead, Hank."

He glanced over at the house. Fanny's body had been taken inside. Caldwell's men were hefting one of the Perkinses' bodies to the back of a horse, tying it down for the trip back to Comanche. Only the two Perkins brothers and Evan Hawthorne had attacked the ranch. Silas Jones was still at large. For Amelia's sake, Hank wished it could have been Evan who had disappeared, wished the young man had finally come to his senses.

"Help me up," Amelia said softly.

He helped her stand, refusing to let go of her hand.

"I want to see Evan." She turned toward her brother's horse.

"Not now, Amelia. Wait until we take him back to town. Until he's laid out properly."

"I want to see my brother." She started toward the horse.

"Wait," he commanded. His harsh tone stopped her in her tracks. "Please. Come with me first," he begged.

He walked her over to a pump near a windmill. A metal cup dangled from the handle. He pumped a cupful of water, offered it to her, but she refused. He lifted it to his lips, drained it. Hung the cup again.

"Let me tell you what happened," he said, wishing the ground would open up and swallow him whole. He *needed* to tell her what happened.

"I'm sure you did everything you could." Her voice was barely audible.

"Amelia, I killed Evan. I'm the one who shot him."

She looked startled. "What?"

"I killed your brother."

"No." She shook her head in denial. A fleeting smile touched her lips. "No, Hank. Not you. You couldn't kill anyone. Besides, you *promised* me you'd watch out for Evan. That you'd protect him." She actually reached out and brushed his hair back, then tried to straighten his collar.

Her trust in him, her denial, broke his heart.

"I'm sorry, Amelia," he whispered. "The younger Perkins brother was dead. I was covering the front of the house with Charlie Scout when Evan came running out. He was holding Mrs. Harroway at gunpoint. He threatened to kill her if anyone came any closer. She was struggling, fighting like a wildcat, trying to break his hold.

"I called out to him, told him to let her go. To surrender. But he charged out. Charlie Scout fired over his head, thinking Evan would bolt, but he didn't. He fired back and hit Charlie in the arm. Then he raised his gun to Mrs. Harroway's head. I had no time to think. I fired."

He didn't think he could actually hit the side of a barn under pressure. It was a miracle that he had killed Evan and not Sophronia Harroway. The shot could have gone wide, but somehow Sophronia lunged to the side and he'd put a bullet right into Evan's heart.

"It was a clean shot, Amelia. He was dead in an instant." No consolation, he thought. None at all.

She stared at him as if he were speaking in a language incomprehensible to her. Then, without a word, without warning, she started walking toward Evan's horse.

"Amelia, wait!"

She stopped in her tracks, slowly turned. The look on her face broke his heart.

"And if I don't? Will you shoot me, too?"

If she intended to wound, she had hit the mark. Hank opened his mouth, closed it again. What could he say? He'd promised to do what he could to protect her brother, but he'd killed him instead.

The distance between Hank and Evan's horse was the longest journey Amelia had ever had to make. Afraid she would faint again, she faltered and took a deep breath. She forced herself to continue to breathe. Finally, she was beside Evan's body. She thought she'd wanted to see him, but Hank was right. Better to wait. She hadn't the courage to fold back the canvas shroud. To see him draped over his saddle, his body treated with as much respect as a deer carcass, wounded her to her very soul.

I'll do everything I can to keep him safe.

He'd sealed his promise with a kiss right there in the middle of Main Street in front of everyone.

She thought Hank was different. She had thought that because he was well-educated, because he was well-mannered and well-spoken, that he was a caring man. A man of his word. Obviously, he was no better than Oswald Caldwell. No better than the rest of them.

She was surprisingly calm as she laid her hand on the shroud. She closed her eyes, tried to summon the words of a prayer.

"Dear Lord . . ."

For the first time in her life, she couldn't find words to say to Him.

Why bother? He isn't there.

Surely if there was a God in heaven, He would have heard her pleas. He would not, could not, have taken Evan this way.

"Evan is all I had," she whispered. "And You've taken him."

She stood beside her brother's horse, beside Evan, as the hot Texas sun beat down upon them. She didn't know how long she stood there. All she knew was that she couldn't move. She couldn't leave his side. Her heart was as empty as her mind was void of words to say and thoughts to think. As empty as her soul.

Finally, after a while, her tears dried. She let her hand fall away from Evan's body and slowly turned. Hank was still there beside her. She didn't meet his eyes. Couldn't meet his eyes.

She gazed around the yard. Harroway's men were busy cleaning up broken glass, tending to the house, the livestock. Oswald Caldwell was nowhere to be seen. He'd taken his posse and ridden off.

Charlie Scout sat on the edge of the veranda, clutching his wounded right arm with his left hand. He stared woefully in her direction. She noticed someone had set her medical bag beside him.

Sigrid came through the back door and hurried across the yard.

She hovered uncertainly at Amelia's elbow. "I

got some tea ready for you, Doctor. Come vit me."

Disjointed thoughts floated through Amelia's mind. She pictured Sophronia's grand silver tea service. She thought of the jumble of things always strewn about Fanny's room. She remembered today's summons to the ranch. She turned to Sigrid.

"Where is Isaac? I was told he was wounded."

Sigrid's eyes filled with tears. "He's dead, Doctor."

Isaac is gone, too.

Isaac, the old cowpuncher who'd never done anything to hurt anyone. He'd been loyal to the Harroways, first the father and then the son, for the last thirty years of his life. He'd told Amelia more than once how lucky he was that Lemuel had kept him on, how lucky he was to live out his days on the ranch tending to things the younger men wouldn't or didn't have time to do.

Now he was gone.

"I'll see to Charlie Scout," she told Sigrid. "And then I'm going home."

"Vat about da tea?"

"No . . . no thank you. Maybe just a glass of water." She doubted she'd be able to taste anything but sorrow for a long time to come.

Somehow she survived the trip home. She'd insisted on riding back to Glory alone, but after she'd patched up Charlie Scout's wound, he'd trailed her all the way—no doubt at Hank's insistence. No one else paid her any mind. Thankfully Hank hadn't insisted on accompanying her himself.

She made arrangements with Max Bratton, the undertaker, before she went home. Once there, she somehow found the strength to walk into Evan's room, open the armoire. She chose a shirt with a fine blue and burgundy stripe on a field of white, along with his only suit. It was three years old. No doubt the sleeves were too short, but there was nothing she could do about that. No one was going to see her brother laid out anyway.

Not if she had anything to say about it.

Later, she argued with Max Bratton and refused to hold a viewing. Folks would demand it, he told her. No one, she insisted, *no one* was going to gawk at Evan—which was also what she told the traveling photographer who was crass enough to knock at the door offering her a goodly sum of money for the opportunity to photograph Evan's body. The man had already taken pictures of the Perkins brothers. She was adamant about not putting Evan on display merely to satisfy the curious.

She made certain Evan was laid out properly, that his hair was combed and his suit pressed by her own hand. The last time she would see her brother was the day the undertaker nailed his coffin shut. Every blow to every nail pierced her heart.

Brand and Charity were the first to come calling late that afternoon. They begged her to move in with them for the time being. She refused. She also refused a church service for Evan's funeral, which shocked them both. She didn't care anymore. God had turned His back on the Hawthornes. She didn't need Him anymore.

She finally agreed to let Brand speak at the grave site, just so they would stop badgering her. When the McCormicks finally went home, they left behind a crock of ham and scalloped potatoes. The food went untouched. Neighbors came and went.

She didn't answer the door.

Hank came morning and night. He was the easiest and hardest to ignore.

The heat became unbearable before a summer lightning storm hit. Two long and tedious days of rain and waiting passed before the funeral. Amelia locked herself inside, pulled down the shades and refused to answer the door. Not until nightfall did she slip outside to feed and water Sweet Pickle.

When the rain let up, the heat returned with a vengeance. Her gardens became parched and dry.

Soon they would be as dead as Evan.

The morning of the burial, she dressed carefully, donning the one formal black gown she owned. The lace cuffs and collar were a bit worn, but she couldn't care less. She walked out the front door, head high, her face shaded by a black veil draped over the wide brim of an equally black hat that had been her mother's.

She'd heard folks knock, heard their footsteps as they crossed the porch. She walked past the covered dishes they left, ignoring them just as she ignored a copy of the *Glory Gazette* near the front door.

How cruel of Hank, she thought, to deliver a newspaper that most likely contained the story of the assault on the Harroway ranch. And yet how telling. Had he included *all* the sordid details of Evan's death? Had he reported that *he* had killed her brother?

On her way to the cemetery she was certain she could feel the neighbors watching her through cracks between their curtains. With a start, she recognized the Ellenberg wagon as it came rumbling up the street. She hadn't thought of her friends since Evan's death. Hadn't even remembered they existed.

Joe and Hattie sat high atop the seat. Rebekah rode in back with the children. They pulled up alongside Amelia. She was tempted to keep walking as if she hadn't seen them, but Joe quickly dismounted and helped Hattie climb down from the high buckboard seat. They flanked Amelia before she could walk away.

"Oh, Amelia. We just heard the terrible news yesterday," Hattie said.

"We came to escort you to the burial." Hat in hand, Joe shifted uncomfortably.

She wanted to run. To hide. To deny what was happening. Seeing them like this, hearing their words of sympathy made this all too real. Their kindness brought her too close to letting go, to giving in to tears.

"I'm sorry, but . . ."

Joe would hear none of it. "We're not letting you go through this alone."

She hadn't the strength to argue. The sooner she reached Evan's grave site, the sooner this would all be over.

By the time Hank walked through the gate in the iron fence that surrounded the small cemetery behind the church, Brand had already begun the eulogy. Hank let his gaze roam over the small knot of people gathered near the open grave. Evan's casket had already been lowered inside.

The sky was the color of Texas bluebonnets and perfectly clear except for an occasional cumulus cloud drifting by. Hank was thankful Joe and Hattie were beside Amelia like bookends near the yawning grave.

Her heavy black gown was two sizes too large. Through a thin black veil, her skin looked as pale as a lily. She appeared not to be listening while the preacher described her brother as a young man who took the wrong path and had paid the ultimate price for his sin. Instead, Amelia stared toward the wide, empty horizon where heat waves shimmered above the parched earth. She seemed completely unaware of what was going on around her.

The preacher's words drifted to Hank on the close, humid air.

"In times like this we often ask ourselves, 'Why?' Above all we must remember what Christ said. 'Do not let your hearts be troubled.'

"Today our hearts are troubled as we remember Evan Hawthorne. We cannot help but ask ourselves, 'What happened? Why did Evan choose to turn to a life of sin?'

"It's not for us to know the answers in this lifetime. It's not for us to cast blame, or to blame ourselves. For now, we must rely on our faith. We must put our trust in the Lord and remember not to let our hearts be troubled. Never forget—the Lord comforts His people and will have compassion on His afflicted ones."

Though he was there to see Amelia, to try to speak to her in the hope that she'd one day be able to forgive him, Hank had never expected to be at all moved by Brand McCormick's prayer.

Yet the preacher's words lifted the heavy weight of guilt upon his soul and he was inexplicably comforted.

When Brand finished, Amelia didn't move, so Hattie picked up a handful of soil and let it sift down into the open grave. Mary Margaret and Timothy Cutter, Harrison Barker and his mother, and Mick Robinson were there. So was Charity McCormick. Each of them tossed a handful of soil into Evan's grave and then slowly walked toward the gate.

Hank waited until Joe and Hattie escorted Amelia across the barren ground. Rebekah and the children had taken shelter beneath the shade of the only tree in the cemetery.

Harrison Barker approached Amelia first. Hank was near enough to hear Harrison say, "I'm sorry about Evan, Amelia. Truly I am."

The man seemed at a loss for words for a few seconds, then he added, "Mrs. Washington wanted me to tell you that she'd like you to drop by and tend to little Abel as soon as you're up to it. He's had some kind of croup and she's worried—"

"I'm sorry. I can't help anyone right now." Amelia's expression was void of any feeling what-soever. There was no anger, not a hint of warmth, either. Her voice sounded as if it were coming from the depths of a hollow cavern. She walked away and left Harrison staring after her.

Hank moved quickly to block the cemetery gate just as Amelia reached it. He nodded stiffly to Joe and then Hattie.

"May I have a word with Amelia alone?" he requested.

Joe did not look on him unkindly. In fact, the sympathy in the man's eyes was more than evident. Still, Joe hesitated for a moment and asked her, "Amelia?"

She turned toward Hank and refused to meet his eyes. Her gaze fell somewhere in the vicinity of his collar. He thought for a moment she was going to speak, but then she turned away and left him there without a word. Hattie quickly caught up, linked her arm through Amelia's, and together they headed for an old buckboard not far away. Joe mumbled that he was sorry and went to collect his wife and children.

Crestfallen, Hank was powerless to do anything but let Amelia walk away.

As Joe and Rebekah reached the gate, Joe paused. He shifted his son to his shoulder. Hank noticed how much the little boy had grown in just a few weeks.

"Give her time, Larson," Joe advised. "She needs to work through her grief."

"She'll never forgive me," Hank said. "I'll never forgive myself."

"You did what you had to do," Joe said. Then a look passed between Joe and Rebekah, a look

Hank could not decipher. Joe smiled warmly at his wife and she gazed into his eyes with complete trust.

"With time, God heals all wounds. Believe me, my family knows that's true." Joe bade Rebekah return to the wagon without him.

"We'll come into town to visit, make sure she's all right," Joe assured him.

"Will you let me know how she's doing?" Hank asked.

"Of course." Joe extended his hand. "Just remember what I said. In time, God heals all wounds."

Before Hank had left Missouri, he was convinced his own grief would never heal—and then he met Amelia.

God led me to her. God brought me here.
God?

The direction of his thoughts shocked him. Was he giving credence to the God he'd never believed in before?

Has God truly led me here, to Amelia? If so, how could He have wanted this for us? Why was it necessary for me to take her brother's life?

Now his greatest challenge was no longer grief, but carrying the terrible burden of guilt. He thought of the times she'd made him smile, made him think, made him feel and open up his heart again. She'd brought him back to life.

328

Now he was the one responsible for her sorrow. It was his fault that she was all alone in the world.

Perhaps if he went to Brand McCormick and asked his counsel. Perhaps if he turned to the preacher for answers.

Absently, he thanked Joe. The rancher left to join his family. Hank made certain Amelia climbed into the Ellenberg wagon before he went to look for Brand.

Chapter Twenty-Two

A week later, Amelia was still inside with the shades pulled low when Mary Margaret Cutter came knocking at the door. Eventually she started pounding, refusing to take a hint and leave. Amelia finally cracked open the door.

"Please, Mary Margaret. I'm not in the mood for a visit." She tried to close it again.

Mary Margaret shoved her foot in the way.

"Frankly, Amelia dear, I don't care," the banker's wife told her. "You have the contents of covered dishes rotting out here on the porch. Why, it's shameful. Most of them are past putrid. Mice wouldn't even touch this food. Open the door, dear, and I'll bring the dishes in and wash them for you. Then I'll *think* about leaving."

Amelia was aware of the dishes lined up along the edge of the porch. Obviously, it hadn't mattered to folks that she wasn't eating the consolation food they brought over. What mattered was that they'd done something to make *themselves* feel better about helping her in a time of need.

"Open up, Amelia, and let me bring these things in. Let me in or I'll yell for help and everyone within shouting distance will come a-running."

Amelia backed down and Mary Margaret breezed in. She went to the pump out back, toted water in and started heating it. Watching her bustle around the kitchen made Amelia's head ache. She'd taken to dousing herself with a few drops of laudanum at night to make herself sleep. Lately she'd begun taking it in the daytime, as well.

Now, while her head was pounding, all she could think about was having a few more drops of laudanum and going back to bed.

She watched Mary Margaret work up a sweat dumping out and scrubbing the food encrusted on other people's dishes. The older woman's vigor would have amazed her if she'd been in a better frame of mind. Mary Margaret turned around at one point and said, "You need a bath, Amelia. I'll fill your tub for you but I'm not scrubbing you down."

More of a force than Amelia had ever reckoned, Mary Margaret stayed until she'd had a bath and was dressed in a clean nightgown. The woman wouldn't leave until Amelia gave her word that she'd raise the shades and get on with life.

"People need you, Amelia. People miss you," Mary Margaret told her.

Amelia promised she'd be all right.

The promise was a lie.

Once Mary Margaret Cutter was out of the house, Amelia drew the shades again and went back to bed.

If He was ever really there, God has deserted me.

Why shouldn't I turn my back on the towns-folk? What do I owe them? What do I owe any-one? Certainly not loyalty. If God Himself can turn His back on me, then turnabout is fair play.

She no longer prayed. She saw no reason to do so. For the next three weeks, days and nights became one.

On her way out to feed Sweet Pickle early one evening, she noticed the dried flowers and plants in her garden. She thought about salvaging what she could before she lost a full season's worth of precious herbs she needed for her compounds.

Then she asked herself why.

Why should I care?

The way she saw it now, she'd served the Lord, served the town, served Evan and her father all her life. For *what?*

Worst of all, she'd been fool enough to fall in love with Hank Larson.

Where had any of it gotten her?

She went back inside and locked the door.

She had no idea how many more days had passed until the outside world finally intruded again.

"Amelia, open up!"

Hank. Would the man ever give up? Even through a laudanum-induced haze she recognized his voice every time he'd come calling. She'd been able to ignore him, but today he was pounding on her door so hard that the sound rattled around in her brain.

"Amelia!"

She tried covering her head with her pillow but to no avail. Finally she grabbed a wool shawl off a nearby chair and dragged herself through the front parlor. She jerked the door open, not because she wanted to see or talk to him, but to end the pounding.

Even in her drugged state, she recognized the shocked expression in his eyes.

"Let me in," he demanded. "I've got something for you."

She tried to slam the door on Hank. but her movements were sluggish and inept. He braced his forearm against the door and shoved it open.

"Go away," she mumbled. "I don't want to see you. Please, leave."

She thought he was about to give up, but before she knew what was happening, he grabbed her by the wrist, tugged her out onto the porch and planted himself in front of the door.

"What are you doing?" she demanded.

"It's not seemly for me to come in, so you have to come out."

"I'm not dressed."

"You're covered from your neck to your toes." He looked her up and down.

With both hands, she pulled the edges of her shawl together over her nightgown and blinked against the brilliant sunshine. She'd forgotten it was summer. Forgotten about everything except the one thing she didn't want to remember—Evan's death.

When Amelia answered the door, Hank tried to hide his shock but failed miserably. It was amazing how much she'd changed in so little time. If they'd both been walking down Main Street, he might have passed her by without even recognizing her.

Her skin was sallow. Her usually bright green eyes were clouded, devoid of their usual sparkle. Her auburn hair was knotted and lank around her face and thin shoulders.

It was all he could do to keep from taking her in his arms and carrying her away from this house where she'd buried herself as surely as she'd buried her brother.

His mind raced as he ticked through his options. The Ellenbergs would take her in. So would the McCormicks. Or the Cutters. Hattie would likely help her the most. Hattie had suffered more shock and grief than anyone he'd known. Surely that God-fearing woman could help Amelia come to her senses.

"I need to go back inside," she whispered.

He barely heard her. Her throat sounded rough from lack of use. She stood there compliant, staring at her bare toes as they peeked out from beneath the flounce of her nightgown.

"You need to hear me out," he said.

"I don't want to talk to you."

"I don't care. I brought you something." He reached into his pocket. Felt the smooth, cool metal and wrapped his hand around it.

"Here's your father's watch."

She didn't say a word, merely looked at the gold timepiece lying in his palm.

"Take it," he urged.

"Where . . . where did you find it?" she whispered. She reached for the watch, took it in her hand and stared at it.

"A rancher brought it in to the newspaper office when he saw your father's name engraved inside. Said he bought it from a drifter. After he read the stories in the paper about the Perkins Gang, he felt sure someone in the family might want it back."

Hank didn't add that he'd paid the rancher what the man had given for the timepiece. He didn't tell her that he had memorized the inscription inside the watch cover.

To my dear husband, Esra Hawthorne, on our wedding day, from your loving bride, Camilla.

A long, awkward silence hung between them before Hank said, "Amelia, there's nothing I can do or say to change what's happened. I didn't intend to kill your brother. I *had* to in order to protect Sophronia Harroway. I know if you were thinking clearly, you'd understand."

"I asked you to help him." She stared down at the watch, refusing to look at him.

"I would have, had he not been holding a gun to a woman's head!"

He thought she couldn't get any paler but she blanched at his words. Instantly furious at himself for losing his temper, he was afraid she was going to pass out. He grabbed her upper arms. She shook him off with more force than he thought someone in her state could muster.

He took a deep breath. He'd come here to see

what, if anything, he could do to help. No one had seen her for days, not since Mary Margaret Cutter barged her way in.

No one had been successful at getting her to answer the door. Brand McCormick and his sister had called, but Amelia ignored them, even when they'd knelt and prayed on the front porch. Finally, after the rancher brought him the watch, Hank had the opening he needed.

"Everyone is worried about you," he told her.

"Tell them not to worry. Quote me in your paper."

"I can understand why you hate me, but not your friends and neighbors. They care about you. They need you. And you need them."

She tugged the shawl tighter and glanced over his shoulder at the door behind him. He wasn't about to budge.

"I'm not in the mood to help anyone," she said.

"Then use this time to help yourself." He'd mourned Tricia and the baby. He missed them and always would, but not like this. He'd been angry. He'd lashed out at friends and family and finally left Saint Joe and some of his painful memories behind. But he hadn't been self-destructive.

Frustrated, at a loss for words, he took off his hat and raked his hand through his hair.

"I've been meeting with Reverend McCormick," he admitted, hoping it would help. "A couple of nights a week, in fact." Hank shrugged and leaned back against the door frame, folded his arms across his chest. "Three weeks ago, if anyone would have asked me if I thought I'd ever believe in the power of knowing the Lord, I'd have laughed in his face."

He could tell he had her attention when she whipped her gaze up from her toes and met his eyes. Brand McCormick had counseled him with John's words from the Bible.

Whoever lives by the truth comes into the light, so that it may be seen plainly that what he has done has been done through God.

"I've struggled, Amelia. I've wrestled with my guilt night and day."

"Am I supposed to feel sorry for you, Hank?"

He shook his head. "I don't want your pity. I want your understanding. You are a woman of faith, Amelia. You know better than I, that if you turn your heart to the Lord, you'll find the comfort you need. Trust in Him to help you heal."

"How dare *you* preach to me, Hank? You who never set foot in a church *before*."

"I don't mean to preach. I want to help. I took your brother's life. Don't make me responsible for taking your faith, Amelia."

"What do you care?"

He took her hands in his, forced her to look him in the eye.

"I care because I love you."

She tried to pull her hands from his grasp, but he held on tight.

"I love you, Amelia. So do the people in this town. We love you and we're all worried about you. God has finally helped me realize I can't do this alone anymore. I've turned to the only One who can help me. I don't know any other way to help you than to beg you to look deep within yourself, remember who you are, remember to turn to 'the One who comforts His people and will have compassion on His afflicted ones.' "

This time when she tried to pull away, he let her go. There were unshed tears gleaming in her eyes. He watched her waver, thought she would finally give in to her pain. Instead, she held her head high, her shoulders straight, and stubbornly dashed away her tears with the backs of her hands.

He knew it was too much to hope that she'd tell him she forgave him. That she still loved him.

But he never expected her to say, "If you've said your piece, then I'd kindly thank you to get off of my porch and leave me alone."

Amelia walked inside before Hank was off the porch. She shut the door and stood in the dim light with her father's watch clutched in her hand.

Her reticule was hanging on a hook on the hall tree. Unfortunately, she caught a glimpse of herself in its oval mirror before she dropped the watch inside. Deep shadows filled the hollows beneath her eyes. Her hair was matted and lank, her mouth drawn into a hard line.

She reached out and touched the glass surface. When the woman in the mirror pressed her finger-tips to Amelia's, she knew it was but a reflection of herself. No, not of myself, she corrected, but what I've become since Evan's death.

I killed Evan. I'm the one who shot him.

I killed your brother.

Hank's words pierced her heart. Reason seeped away. Anger erupted, as fast and furious as the tornadoes that ripped through Texas during storm season. She covered her ears, rushed through the house, flung open Evan's bedroom door. She hadn't been in his room since she'd chosen his burial clothing. In just a few short weeks, the closed space had grown musty.

The few possessions he hadn't taken with him were lined up on his chest of drawers: his shaving mug, a set of cuff buttons, a pair of suspenders he never wore. With a sweep of her arm, she shoved everything off the top of the bureau but felt no satisfaction as they clattered to the ground.

One by one, she opened the drawers, grabbed handfuls of clothes and threw them every which way. She ran to the bed, tore off the spread and the sheets, balled them up, stomped on them.

She pushed over a small bedside table. A glass lamp fell to the floor, shattered.

The sound of breaking glass rent a hole in the haze of her fury as successfully as a slap. Gulping in air, she looked around at the chaos and found herself wondering what had happened. Who could have done such a thing?

Then she slowly crumpled to her knees atop the pile of bedding.

She was as insane as Fanny.

Leaning her head back against the mattress, she closed her eyes.

And saw Hank's face.

I care because I love you.

So do the people in this town.

If he cared so much, if he indeed loved her, how could he have killed her brother? And now he had turned to the Reverend McCormick for counseling, turned to the Lord, searching for a way to ease his guilt.

Before Evan died, she would have been overjoyed with Hank's newfound faith. She would have considered it a blessing. Recalling the day he'd driven her out to the Ellenberg ranch, she remembered he'd said, "I don't want to hear *anything* about God."

Her rusty laughter echoed in the empty room.

How ironic. Hank has turned to God and I have turned away.

I love you, Amelia.

She put her hands over her ears and tried to forget all the years she'd offered up her hope and dreams in useless prayer. All the years she'd asked for guidance and trusted that God was there, watching over her, listening to her, guiding her hands and her heart.

She couldn't trust God any more than she could trust Hank.

Sitting there on the floor, leaning against the bed, she fell into a natural sleep for the first time in days. When she finally stirred, she thought she heard her father's voice.

Get up and dry those tears, Amelia.

She struggled to her knees, looked around Evan's room. She didn't recall wreaking such havoc, and yet the proof was all around her.

I'm going crazy, she thought. I'm as crazy as Fanny.

Insanity terrified her more than anything. She pushed herself to her feet, refusing to go on like this. Not another day. Not another hour.

She kept a shotgun behind the pantry door—unless Evan had stolen that, too. She went into the pantry. The shotgun was still there.

There wasn't a breath of air inside the house or out. She was hot and sweaty and tired of being exhausted. Sick of feeling nothing. She drew in a deep breath, lost it on a sigh. The scent of cinnamon and spices in the pantry awakened her senses. There was a bundle of dried lavender hanging from the ceiling. The aroma soothed her, quieted her.

She reached for one of the lavender-scented soaps she'd made last Christmas, pulled off the twine, carefully unwrapped the brown paper. Inhaling the heady scent, she closed her eyes and imagined soaking in a tub of cool, clear water.

She glanced down at the shotgun. It wasn't going anywhere.

She decided that before she did anything rash, she would bathe.

Chapter Twenty-Three

Nearly a week later, Hank was alone in the newspaper office, wondering just how long he was going to be able to keep putting out a paper before he had to find another source of income. He'd spent most of his savings on the building, figuring it was better to own than to rent. The Cutters held a mortgage for the balance, with interest. He could always walk away and let them take the building, but he'd be penniless.

Too soon to worry, he told himself. Best to hold on to the dream for at least a few more weeks.

He decided to take a suggestion Brand made at last Sunday's service and turn his problems over to God. Though it wasn't a habit, he figured he might as well turn to his newfound faith. If there ever was a time of need, this was it.

Ricardo was out delivering the latest issue of the *Glory Gazette* to the community and Hank had finally cleared enough space on his desk to prop his feet up on the corner and read his mail. There wasn't much, so he took his time.

Feeling unsettled, he glanced out the front window. To the naked eye, everything appeared perfectly normal on Main Street. Maybe it was just his heart that was off-kilter. Since Amelia had turned him away, nothing in his world seemed right anymore. Glory was a town with a sheriff who couldn't wait to step down and a healer who no longer wanted to heal anyone.

The new Bible that Reverend McCormick had presented to him at his baptism sat atop everything else on the desk. Hank was beginning to find solace in the words written there. He enjoyed the writing, the pageant of characters that filled the pages, the details and richness of the words, the sojourn back to ancient times and foreign lands with exotic names like Mareshah, Hebron, Ashkelon, Bethlehem—names that conjured up wanderlust in him.

Remembering the letter in his hand, he read the first couple of lines and then sat up a bit straighter. He turned the single page toward the front window so that the light hit it just right. He wanted to be sure he hadn't misread.

Dear Mr. Larson,

I obtained a copy of your newspaper through a traveling photographer recently in your area. If it has not already been filled, I am writing to you to express my sincere interest in applying for the position of sheriff of Glory.

I come from a long line of lawmen. Two of my brothers are Texas Rangers. My father was a sheriff, so I know what's expected.

I'm a crack shot, a hard worker, and most people tend to get along with me just fine. If you need letters of recommendation, you are welcome to contact the references I've listed below.

There followed a list of names and addresses. The letter was signed,

Yours truly, Madison James

Hank dropped his feet to the floor, rummaged through his desk drawers until he found a clean sheet of vellum. His inkwell was buried beneath a pile of newsprint. He had to sharpen the nib of his fountain pen before he could begin, but he had a response to Madison James in record time. If he hurried, he'd be able to get the letter out on the next mail packet.

With any luck at all, the prospect for the new sheriff would be on his way to Glory within the next two weeks. The *only* prospect for the new sheriff. Unless Madison James was blind or had two heads, the job was his.

He took a half-dozen steps down the boardwalk when gunfire erupted inside the Silver Slipper Saloon.

Horses up and down Main Street reared back in fear and tugged at their reins. A man with a wagonload of seed bags struggled to get his team under control.

Hank noticed men running out of the saloon, hightailing it to safety. A woman on the street grabbed her child's hand and ducked between two buildings. Within seconds there was no one visible—except him.

He ran back to the newspaper office to get the gun he kept tucked inside his desk drawer. The gun Harrison had just now chided him about not wearing.

"You are a lawman," the storekeeper had reminded him. "You might not have a badge yet, but you should wear your gun."

"The Perkins boys are dead," Hank reminded him. "Besides, nothing ever happens here, remember?"

Hank grabbed the holster and gun and ran to the door. Sporadic shots rang out. A ricochet bullet pinged off a metal lamp cover down the street. The garishly painted front window of the saloon was shot out and glass exploded everywhere.

He hadn't used his gun since the day of the shootout at Harroway House and hoped he'd never have to use it again. He made certain it was loaded, strapped on the holster, and ran out the door.

Amelia raised the shades in Evan's room first. She hadn't been inside since the day she'd torn it apart. Since then, she'd slowly begun to put her life back together. That was five, maybe six days ago, now. She wasn't certain. She'd lost track of time.

The afternoon she'd contemplated ending it all, she'd soaked in a tub of cold water instead, inhaled the scent of lavender, sipped some fragrant rose hip tea and decided she could at least live another day.

After that it was another and another, one day at a time. Now here she was, ready to clean up the mess she'd made, ready to clear out her brother's room.

She washed all the bedding and hung it on the clothesline. She swept up the broken glass. She neatly folded and stacked Evan's clothes, then

346

carried them out to the back porch until she could bring herself to deliver them to the Rocking e. Rebekah Ellenberg would see to it that they were given to the local Indian agent.

She remade the bed and scrubbed the floors until they shone. She washed the windows with vinegar and water.

Tomorrow she would wash the lace curtains in boiling water and hang them out to dry. She climbed on a chair and was reaching up to take them down off the rods when she heard the sound of agitated voices out front. She leaned out of the open window and saw a crowd of at least a dozen people running up the street.

There were mostly men, but one or two bonnets bobbed and skirt hems flashed amid them. She was headed to the front room to see what might be happening when someone shouted her name and began pounding on her front door.

"Amelia! Open up! You gotta help!" It was Harrison Barker and he sounded frantic.

She dried her hands on her apron and quickened her steps. It had been almost a month since she'd opened her door willingly, days since anyone had even bothered to call.

No one had been there since she'd sent Hank away.

A glance in the hall tree mirror assured her there was no help for her appearance. At least she was no longer existing in her nightgown and she'd brushed and braided her hair. Her hand fluttered to her throat. Her top button was neatly fastened at her throat.

"Amelia! Help!"

She opened the door and faced what amounted to sheer chaos.

Six men supported a wooden plank between them, three on each side. The board served as a makeshift stretcher for a wounded, bleeding man. They carried him in feet first.

"Wait a minute!" She tried to stop them, but they were already headed for the kitchen.

The men huddled around her table, shoving and pushing the unconscious man off the board. She bounced on her toes, trying to see over their shoulders and finally she succeeded in shoving two of them far enough apart to squeeze between them.

She gasped and clung to the edge of the table to steady herself.

Hank Larson was stretched out unconscious. His right arm hung limply over the side of the table. The front of his white shirt was covered with a spreading crimson stain. There was a hole in the thigh of his trousers. It, too, was seeping blood, but not as fiercely as his chest wound.

She pulled off her apron, balled it up and shoved it at Mick, the smithy.

"Press this against his chest," she ordered. "Lean on it to stop the bleeding."

"He's leaking like a stuck pig." Mick pressed down so hard Amelia feared the huge man might break Hank's ribs.

"Not that hard." She shoved him away and placed her hands over the apron. Everything around her slowed to the thready tempo of Hank's weakened heartbeat. The men's voices faded away as she stared down at Hank. Oddly, she noticed his lashes were surprisingly lush for a man. His face was smooth shaven. His lips—

She forced herself to concentrate.

"What happened?" She was afraid to lift the apron and look at the wound, yet she needed to determine the extent of his injuries.

The blacksmith explained, "Silas Jones rode through town and walked into the Silver Slipper. He was wearing a disguise, but the ranch hands from the Rocking e were in town and one of them recognized him. He told the barkeep to send for Larson. Jones musta figured out they were on to him and when somebody tried to stop him from walking out, he drew his gun and started shooting. He had a roomful of patrons penned in."

A cowhand Amelia didn't recognize interrupted.

"A couple men was winged, but nothing this bad. The sheriff musta heard the gunshots because he came busting through the door. He surprised Silas. Hit 'im, too, but Silas got off two shots after he hit the ground and Sheriff Larson went down. After that, just about ever' man in the place jumped up and filled Silas with lead."

"That's the last of the Perkins Gang," someone said.

Amelia looked up, realized her front room was jammed with people.

She turned to Harrison. "Get everyone out of here, please."

"So, are you going to help him?"

Her hands were shaking. So were her knees, truth be told. She'd refused to nurse anyone since she returned from Harroway House and the condemnation in Harrison's tone was more than evident.

Shortly after Evan's death, folks continually knocked at her door and she'd refused to answer. Eventually, word must have gotten out that she was no longer doctoring, for folks stopped coming to fetch her.

Now they wanted her to save the man who had killed her brother.

If I still believed in God, I'd think He was playing a cruel joke.

Carefully avoiding Hank's face, her gaze drifted to the cuffs of his white shirt. There were ink stains beneath the bloodstains. Ink stains on his fingers, too. She thought of those first few times she'd seen him, talked to him.

I'm a writer, not a lawman.

He'd come to Glory following a dream. Moved to Texas to leave behind all his dark memories and start over. Now this place had brought him down.

There's no surgeon nearby? No real *doctor?*

He'd asked her that once, doubted her capabilities.

God led me to you, Amelia.

She looked around at the faces in the crowd, friends, neighbors, strangers she hadn't met. They were all looking to her for help, looking to her to save Hank.

"I'll see what I can do," she told them, "but I can't promise you anything."

Judging by the amount of blood on Hank's shirt, the table, the apron, and now her hands, he wasn't long for this world anyway.

Harrison cleared the room and left. Amelia noticed only Laura Foster remained. Dressed in another of her fine gowns, her curly blond hair was piled high into a cascade of perfectly coiled ringlets. A thick strand of pearls lay against her throat.

The lovely widow refused to leave. She volunteered her services, rolled up her sleeves, covered her gown with an apron she'd grabbed off a hook inside the pantry. She stoked the fire in the stove to boil water. She did it without being asked.

Amelia stared at Hank. She'd never treated anyone without praying first, never picked up an instrument or stitched a wound closed, never even swabbed a cut with tincture without calling on God for His blessings and His guidance.

I refuse to believe in a God who doesn't play fair.

Sophronia's words came to her. Amelia hadn't understood them that day. She did now. She understood them all too well.

She refused to become a hypocrite. She wasn't about to pray if she couldn't find it in her heart to believe.

She'd never felt so utterly lost or alone as she did in that moment.

Coldly, clinically, she began to inspect the bullet wound between Hank's shoulder and lung.

"It's bad, isn't it?" Laura moved to her side and stared down at the wound.

"It's bad. It could be worse. At least there's no air bubbling up out of the hole. The bullet missed the lung." Amelia glanced up at Laura, met the widow's blue eyes. "You aren't squeamish, I see."

"Where I come from, I couldn't afford to be," Laura said.

Amelia had always figured Laura Foster for a wealthy, pampered city gal who'd inherited or married well or both. She'd assumed the boardinghouse in Glory was merely a diversion for a woman with too much time and money on her hands, a woman content to take in boarders and play hostess until the right man came along. With Laura's beauty, Amelia had thought that wouldn't take long, but if the rumors were true, Laura had turned down countless proposals since she moved to town.

Amelia bound the hole in Hank's leg, needing to focus on the bullet wound in his chest. She couldn't allow herself to think of the man beneath her hands as Hank Larson. She couldn't think of him as anything but torn flesh and blood. She couldn't dwell on the fact that the bullet had come so close to his heart, or that he had killed her brother, or that he was the man who had professed to love her. Right now, he was a patient, nothing more.

She swabbed the purpled flesh around the chest wound and instructed Laura to act as another set of hands. The widow found Amelia's medical bag, opened it up and spread out her instruments, bandages, needles and catgut thread along the dry sink.

"Hold his shoulders down while I probe for the bullet," Amelia instructed.

She glanced at Hank's face just before she gingerly inserted her finger in the wound, afraid he might struggle against the pain.

"Hang on," she told Laura.

Laura did as she was told and also watched

Amelia's every move. "How did you come to be a doctor?"

"I'm not a doctor. I have no degree."

"A healer, then."

"My father was a doctor. I worked alongside him during the war."

"You couldn't have been very old."

"I was fourteen when I started. I grew up fast. Wounds from a Minié ball are terribly ugly. They smash and crush bone, tear away intestines."

"There's nothing you haven't seen, I'll bet." Laura sounded sympathetic.

"Pyemia is the worst. Pus in the blood. Thousands died from surgical fever after treatment."

"How long were you a war nurse?"

"Almost four years. We moved all over the South, came through Tennessee, Kentucky, Arkansas."

Laura shook her head in disbelief. "What was your father thinking, dragging his children around during the war? Exposing you to that kind of carnage?"

Amelia swabbed the wound again and pondered the question. What *had* her father been thinking? It was one thing to act selflessly to help others, but had it been wise to haul his children around from battlefield to battlefield like camp followers? Would Evan have grown up differently if he hadn't been raised in the shadow of battlefields and temporary hospital wards full of suffering and death?

"He felt it was his duty."

"How could you stand it?"

Amelia looked up at Laura again. "I put my faith in God back then."

"You don't now?"

Amelia paused. "Not anymore." She'd never seen Laura at church. Never seen the woman at any of the church socials, except for the masquerade party. "Do you?"

A thoughtful expression crossed Laura's face. "No."

Amelia closed her eyes, probed Hank's wound with the tip of her finger, quickly came in contact with the bullet. He moaned. She remained steady. He didn't move or awaken. She glanced up at Laura.

"Pass me those long-handled tweezers, please."

Laura moved quickly and efficiently, handed the tweezers to Amelia then pressed down on Hank's shoulders again.

Amelia wiped her brow on her shoulder. This was another moment when she would have prayed. Instead, she forged on without it. Within a second or two, she slowly extracted the bullet from Hank's flesh.

"Excellent work," Laura said as Amelia laid the bullet aside. "He's sure lost a lot of blood. You think he'll make it?"

Amelia was afraid to be too optimistic. "Now

the worries will be tetanus, fever, at the worst, gangrene." Hank could die in countless painful ways.

The truth hit her hard. Amelia's head began to swim.

"Are you all right?" Laura grabbed her by the elbow.

Amelia shook off the momentary wave of panic and reminded herself she felt nothing anymore. She reminded herself she didn't care. Especially about Hank.

Amelia ripped his pant leg open and inspected his leg wound. The bullet hadn't broken the bone and was easily removed. As she stitched him up, Laura volunteered to make a pot of tea.

"He's a mess," Laura commented once Amelia was through and washing her hands and arms of his blood. "Let's cut off his clothes and I'll bathe him."

Amelia's face caught fire. "I . . . could you?"

Laura shrugged. "It won't bother me in the least, but I reckon it would be hard on you. You're sweet on him."

"No, I'm not."

"It's no secret he kissed you right in the middle of Main Street."

"That was before he killed my brother."

Laura was pouring water into two coffee mugs. Her hands stilled, the kettle suspended over the second cup. "Sometimes we do things we don't want to do, things we know aren't right but we have to do them."

"Not all of us do."

"You telling me you never had to make a choice and wound up doing something that went against everything you believed in?" Laura set down the kettle and waited for Amelia to answer.

Amelia began washing off her instruments and placing them back in the case. There was no way she could tell Laura Foster that, yes, she'd finally done something that went against everything she ever believed in—she'd turned her back on God.

The unanswered question hung between them. Thankfully, Laura didn't press the issue. Amelia was glad the woman respected her silence. Soon they stood over Hank again. Together they cut off his ruined shirt. While Amelia put her equipment away, Laura swabbed the blood off Hank's upper body.

"You realize folks are still waiting for word out on your front porch?"

"What?" Amelia blinked, looked around the kitchen as if coming to herself.

"People are camped out on your front porch, waiting for word. Go get some of the men to help move him to the bedroom."

"What?"

"You still speak English, don't you?" Laura

planted her hands on her hips. "You plan on leaving this man right here in the middle of your kitchen table? Or will you be moving him to the bedroom?"

"I can't . . . he can't stay *here*."

"He's unconscious, Amelia. I think your chastity is perfectly safe for the time being."

"It's not that—"

"What is it then?"

"It's simply impossible."

"I'll stay the night. I'll go back to the boarding-house and gather a few things for myself then stay until you find someone else. Is there any-one who could help out and stay with you while he's bedridden?"

The first and only name that came to mind was Hattie Ellenberg.

"I suppose Hattie wouldn't mind."

"Fine. You want to go out and tell everyone the sheriff is all right for now, or should I?"

Amelia walked back over to the table and pressed the palm of her hand to Hank's forehead. Despite everything that had gone between them, despite what he'd done, she was loath to leave his side. At least not now.

"I'll stay here. You let them know how he's doing and then ask Harrison, Mick and a couple others to help us move him. I . . . I have a spare room."

Evan's room.

The bedding was clean and aired. She'd polished the windows, buffed the floor. As if she were preparing the place for a welcome guest.

Little had she known the man responsible for Evan's death would be sleeping in her brother's bed tonight.

Laura and Harrison had managed to get Hank into one of Harrison's nightshirts and the men carried him to bed. Exhausted, Amelia spent the night dozing in a chair beside the bed.

Hank never stirred. It hadn't worried her at first, but the longer he remained unconscious, the more her concern grew. She continually felt his forehead for signs of fever. She checked his head for bumps and bruises, thinking he may have suffered a blow, too, but found nothing.

Sometime before dawn, she slipped into a deep sleep and when Laura finally woke her and handed her a welcome cup of fresh coffee, Amelia had a crick in her neck. She rubbed the back of her neck, rolled her head around.

Laura reached down and smoothed the covers over Hank's chest.

"He's still alive, at least," she said.

Amelia sipped the coffee and looked down at Hank. He appeared to be sleeping peacefully. "He's never gained consciousness, though. That has me worried."

"He's healing," Laura told her. "Let him sleep."

Amelia felt every joint creak as she got to her feet and thanked Laura for her help. "You'd better get back to your guests," she told the other woman. "I can't thank you enough for your help."

Laura nodded. "Glad to be of service. I have a feeling you wouldn't yell for help even if you were on fire in the middle of Main Street."

Amelia smiled for the first time in a long time. "Probably not."

"You're as stubborn as I am. I spotted that in you the first time we met."

They walked through the house. Laura paused by the front door, glanced in the mirror and tucked one stray curl into place. Somehow she'd managed to sleep all night without disturbing her intricate hairstyle. Amelia was amazed.

"I'm going to send Ricardo over with some food so you won't have to cook. You need to put a little meat back on your bones."

"Thank you, but that's not necessary, really." Amelia couldn't remember the last time she'd eaten.

"I know it. I'm sending it anyway. I'll make certain someone goes to the Rocking e to fetch your friend Hattie."

"You know the Ellenbergs?" Amelia wondered.

"I do. I was there when Joe proposed to Rebekah, but that's a story for another time. You take care, Amelia. I'll be back to check on you in a couple of days."

"I'll look forward to seeing you," Amelia said.

As Laura stepped out the front door and crossed the porch, Amelia realized that for the first time in a long while, she was looking forward to tomorrow.

Chapter Twenty-Four

Hattie arrived without fuss or fanfare and moved in to help spell Amelia.

Between them, they were able to give Hank Larson round-the-clock care. Amelia wasn't certain she would be up to the task of nursing Hank back to health alone any more than she was willing to have him in her house without someone else present. The Hawthorne name had been sullied enough.

She was thankful for Hattie's speedy arrival, and her willingness to help with everything.

"I can stay as long as you need me," Hattie told her.

"My father always said that good nursing was as necessary as doctoring for the patient's recovery. I thank you kindly, Hattie, for helping."

When the woman took off her bonnet and hung it on the hall tree, Amelia saw the angry scar above Hattie's forehead. It was a visible

361

reminder of how close Hattie had come to losing her life. Most of the time, Amelia completely forgot it was there. Today she also noticed that Hattie had not only brought along her quiet determination, but her Bible.

Amelia fell silent as Hattie carried the Bible into the sickroom and set it on Hank's bedside table.

Hours slipped into days and still Hank failed to regain consciousness. Sometime during the second night, he grew feverish. While Hattie took over giving him fever baths with cold water and brisk rubs, Amelia administered a mixture of snakeroot and valerian, which she tried to spoon into him every couple of hours.

He fought the spoon, fought her hands, but thankfully he was too weak to struggle very hard. She managed to get some of the liquid down. Soon she and Hattie settled into a routine.

Hattie spent nights on a pallet on the floor in Hank's room while Amelia tossed and turned in her own bed. She nursed Hank during the day and left the house long enough to feed and water Sweet Pickle. Hattie took care of laundering the linens. True to her word, Laura sent over enough food to feed an army so they didn't have to worry about cooking or going after supplies.

Harrison called for a report to the community. Amelia had to tell him there was no news.

Hank was alive, but his condition hadn't changed. He was battling fever and was still unconscious.

She bade Harrison goodbye after his latest visit and walked into Hank's room only to find Hattie deep in prayer. She was on her knees at Hank's bedside, her hands folded, her head bowed.

". . . watch over him, dear Lord, give him the strength to survive to serve You again. Heal his wounds, strengthen his resolve. He has turned his life over to You, O Lord. Now give him back his health so that he may spread word of Your loving blessings and—" Hattie paused, looked up. "Come in, Amelia. Come pray with me." She raised her hand, invited Amelia to the bedside.

Amelia couldn't move. "I can't," she whispered.

"Can't? Or won't?" Hattie got slowly to her feet and crossed the room. After a glance at Hank, she ushered Amelia into the kitchen and left the bedroom door cracked open so that they could hear if he made the slightest sound.

"Would you like some tea or coffee?" Amelia asked her. "Or how about lemonade? Laura sent some over—" She paused when she saw the way Hattie was looking at her and raised her hand. "Whatever it is you are about to say, Hattie, please don't."

"I don't need anything right now, thank you."

Hattie sat down heavily at the table. "I see all the hurt and pain inside you. It doesn't have to be, Amelia."

Amelia went completely still. "What are you saying?"

Hattie shook her head. "I saw it in Joe, when he was in his teenage years . . . and after the Comanche raid when his pa and Mellie were killed. He turned hard, indifferent. I see that same loss, that same anger in your eyes, Amelia. I saw it when you looked at my Bible and I saw it a minute ago when I asked you to pray with me."

"Hattie—"

"Don't turn away from God when you need Him most."

"God turned His back on me. On Evan. I don't need Him any more than He needs me."

Hattie covered her cheeks with her hands and stared at Amelia over her fingertips.

"Oh, dear," Hattie whispered.

"Yes. Oh, dear."

"A trial of our faith builds strength, Amelia. You are being tested, that's all. Don't give in."

"It's too late, Hattie."

"James said, 'Let him ask in faith, nothing wavering. He that wavereth is like a wave of the sea driven with the wind and tossed.' "

Amelia argued. "I believed all my life. I was certain God was there, that He was watching over us, that my spirit was nurtured by knowing and serving Him. I never asked for anything other than help in healing those who came to me in need. I asked Him to help my brother turn away from a path of destruction. He refused."

Hattie sighed. For her it was all so clear. So simple.

"God works for the good of those who love Him, those who have been called according to His purpose, Amelia. *His* purpose. Not ours. We can't even guess what He has in store for us. Everything that comes to us through Him—the riches, the sorrows, the joy, the difficulties, the loss, He gives us for our greater good. For our *spiritual* good."

"Are you saying He took Evan for *my own good?*" Amelia laughed, but there was no humor in the sound. Only bitterness.

"He took my Orson. He took my only daughter when she was still a child, an innocent who'd never done anything but brighten our lives and warm our hearts. He brought our enemies down upon us when we were vulnerable against them and He left me alive to live the rest of my life scarred in body and heart."

"Yet you don't hate Him."

"Because I believe, Amelia. I have faith that He is teaching me, guiding me, loving me enough to mold me and make me worthy of Him with each and every passing day. Think about it,

Amelia. Had the Lord not taken Orson and Mellie, Joe would have most likely left the ranch the way Evan left. He'd have gone out seeking a new life on his own and wound up in terrible straits. Instead, his guilt kept him here, seeing to me. If he hadn't been around, he'd have never met Rebekah. If I'd never suffered at the hands of the Comanche, I would have never been asked to take Rebekah in. The army came to me, knowing I was the only one who might be able to help her. Think of what Joe's and my life would be like without Rebekah and the children. Think what Joe would be now if God hadn't brought them together."

Hattie brushed her skirt over her knees. "We have been called according to His purpose," she repeated. "I'm not asking you to believe when you can't. I'm just asking you to think about what faith really means. Yours has been tested in a terrible way. You have suffered a great loss, but this is the time to embrace God, to take comfort in His holy word. To go to Him in prayer. This is no time to turn away."

With that said, Hattie stood up, got herself a glass of water. Amelia remained silent, thoughtful. And ashamed.

Hattie had survived unspeakable acts committed on her person. She'd endured losses she never usually spoke of—and yet her faith remained unwavering.

"I'm going out to tend to your garden," Hattie told her. "It's been sorely neglected. It's about gone, but with some watering and a little care, it might just be saved to thrive again. I'm thinking maybe you need some time alone to think. Just give a holler if you need me."

Amelia sank into an empty chair and watched Hattie walk out the back door.

Hank was trapped in a world of heat and cold and searing pain.

He fought to open his eyes, to swim to the surface of consciousness, to break through the fog that imprisoned him. Sights and sounds beyond his ability to reason haunted him while he existed in a netherworld. He thought on occasion he heard Amelia's voice, knew that was impossible. She hated him now. He'd handed her his heart on a platter and she'd sent him away. She would never, ever forgive him for killing Evan.

Images whirled through his mind like bits and pieces of a shattered dream. He was outside Harroway House, his gun drawn and trained on the front door when it flew open. Sophronia Harroway screamed a moment before she was shoved outside. A bead of sweat trickled from beneath Hank's hatband, stung his right eye. He swiped it with the back of his wrist. Aimed again.

A tall, thin young man had one arm wrapped

around Sophronia's throat and was shoving her ahead of him as they exited the house.

"Shoot and I'll kill her," he shouted.

Sophronia kicked and spit and screamed like a banshee. Beside Hank, the Tonkawa scout moved, crouched down, aimed his carbine rifle.

"Hold your fire," Hank said.

At the very same moment, the scout pulled the trigger.

Evan shot back. Sophronia screamed. Evan turned the gun on her, held it against her temple.

"Stop!" Hank reacted without hesitation and watched in disbelief as the young man fell. Spattered with her captor's blood, Sophronia ran screaming into the yard, hair flying, her torn clothing flapping around her.

Now Hank was on fire. Surely he was burning in hell for what he'd done.

Amelia's brother.

Memory came to him in fragments of thought. The man he'd killed was Amelia's brother.

He tried to call for help, but his dry tongue felt too big for his mouth. He couldn't wrap it around words. His chest ached. His leg throbbed ceaselessly.

Let me die, he thought. Let me go.

Suddenly Tricia was there. He saw her holding a babe in her arms. A babe that looked like Little Orson Ellenberg. She was smiling, waving to him. He tried to reach her, but his feet were leaden. He tried to call her name, but his tongue got in the way again. She turned around without hearing him. Turned and walked away.

Amelia was still sitting in the kitchen when she heard Hank moan. She jumped up, pushed the door open and found him thrashing around in a state of delirium.

Hattie had left clean towels and a basin of water on the floor beside the bed. Amelia soaked a towel and wrung it out, then swabbed Hank's forehead, his cheeks, his neck.

Over the past few days she'd memorized every line on his face, the laugh lines that bracketed his mouth, the squint lines at the corners of his eyes. She'd shaved his beard stubble when it grew out overnight, kept his skin smooth shaven the way he did. She was still amazed by his lashes.

He whispered something that sounded like *fish. Fish?* Then Amelia realized he was saying Tricia. His wife's name. She took hold of both his hands, turned them over, pressed the wet compress against his wrists. For the first time in forever, raw emotion coursed through her. Fear.

Hank was dying.

She'd seen it all too often. Sometimes folks cried the name of those gone before them just before they passed on.

"Tricia." The sound was not even a whisper, barely a hush of breath.

Amelia squeezed his hands, refused to let him go. "Hank," she said too harshly, but it didn't matter now. Nothing mattered but saving him. "Hank, if you can hear me, open your eyes."

He didn't move. Again, the hushed sound escaped him. "Tricia."

Amelia steeled herself for him to draw his last breath, to shudder, to leave her. He began to thrash, tried to avoid her touch with more strength than she thought he could muster. She tried to calm him, shushed him even, but he continued to moan and toss and turn. His head shifted from side to side on his pillow.

Suddenly, he was no longer burning up.

Though his eyes were still closed, he unerringly found Amelia's wrist when she laid her hand on his forehead again. He clung to her, held on tight. His eyes opened and he stared into hers, but she knew he was out of his head when he said, "Don't worry. I'll take care of your brother, Amelia. I promise."

Spent, he closed his eyes without ever really seeing her.

Shaking, she reached for the blankets at the foot of the bed and drew them over him with her free hand. Then, because he wouldn't let go, she lowered herself to the chair at his bedside and let him cling to her hand.

Not until he fell into a peaceful slumber was she able to tuck her fear away.

Unfortunately, there was nothing inside her to take its place.

The next afternoon, Reverend McCormick and Charity showed up at the door. Hattie welcomed them inside and Amelia found them all congregated in the front room.

"Look who has come to pay a call." Hattie acted as if conditions had not been strained between the reverend and Amelia since Evan's burial.

Amelia nodded in greeting, but she hung back in the doorway.

"We've come to see how Hank is fairing." Brand's concern was evident. "We've been in Austin for a meeting of ministers from the surrounding counties."

Amelia couldn't help but notice Brand was watching her closely. "Reverend?" she said.

"I hoped we could visit with Hank. Just for a while."

"He's . . . he's never regained consciousness," Amelia admitted. "He's had a raging fever, but it has tapered off."

"With your permission, I'd still like to sit with him a while. To pray. Charity, too."

"May I join you?" Hattie asked.

"Of course." Brand nodded. "I know better than to try to keep you away. Besides, when many pray together, miracles often happen." He turned to Amelia. "Will you be joining us?"

There was such a look of hope, of expectation in his eyes, that Amelia turned away. If they were waiting for a miracle in this house, it would be a long wait.

"I think not. I'll fix you all some lemonade instead." She headed for the kitchen.

Brand immediately handed his Bible to Charity. "I'd like to speak with you alone if I may," he said to Amelia.

"I thought you were—"

"Hank's not going anywhere, obviously. Let's talk." His tone was firm and insistent.

Amelia refused to meet Hattie's eyes. Had the woman put Brand up to this? she wondered. He followed her into the kitchen where she turned away from his thoughtful stare. She began to take glasses out of the cupboard and set them on the dry sink.

"Amelia, please," he said softly. "Sit down."

She sighed, turned and pulled out a chair at the table. He sat across from her and leaned back. He was silent for so long she found herself fidgeting nervously. She smoothed her hands over the worn fabric of the tablecloth.

"I have things to do, Reverend."

"You really can't see it, can you?" He stared at her in a kind of amazement. There was incredible sadness in his eyes.

"See what?"

"The darkness you're living in. The bitterness flourishing in your heart and soul."

"If I wanted to hear a sermon, I'd go to church on Sundays."

His usual smile was gone. His tone hardened.

"You're a healer, Amelia. A nurturer. You have a God-given gift that has always stood you in good stead. You've spent your life being selfless, tending to others, caring and supporting everyone around you with good works and by living an exemplary life. Until now.

"But now, just as you tended others, just as you toiled in your garden to grow the medicinal herbs and flowers that help sustain life, you have turned to nurturing bitterness and sorrow. You're drowning in it and you aren't even aware of how it has taken over, like a suffocating weed. This darkness has cut you off from everyone and everything you loved, including the Lord."

She was shocked at the severity of his tone.

"The Bible says, 'Harden not your hearts.' It's time to let this grief and anger go, Amelia. Time to fix your eyes upon the Lord. He is the only one who can help you now, but you must let Him in. Open your heart and let Him ease your pain. Offer it up to Him in the form of prayer. Start by forgiving Hank. He was protecting Sophronia. Doing his sworn duty. Forgive him. Then forgive yourself. God will help you find the strength to forgive."

"He's not there. He's *not* listening."

"He is there, Amelia. He's never left your side." The preacher sighed, shook his head. "He will never desert you, no matter how long or how hard you deny Him."

They sat in silence in the overly warm kitchen. The back door was wide open. So were all the windows, but not a breath of air leaked in. They needed rain. There was no breeze blowing across the plains today. Only the shimmering heat, the dust, the dry air. That was the trouble with living on the edge of the land. There was either too much rain or not enough. Too much wind or not a whisper of breeze. Too much heat, too much cold. There were only extremes.

She realized the same could be said of faith. You either believed or you didn't. There was no middle ground.

She heard the chair legs scrape across the floor and she looked up. Brand was standing, carefully replacing his chair.

"Think about what I've said, Amelia. You have a choice to make before it's too late. You have to decide whether to let darkness triumph or to let the Light back into your life."

With that, he walked away. She watched him return to the front room to collect Hattie and Charity. She heard the three of them enter the room beside the kitchen. Brand's voice was clear and strong as he began to pray.

Amelia rose without making a sound, slipped out the back and onto the porch hoping to escape the sound of their voices lifted in prayer. Their words chased her through the open bedroom window.

Never had she felt like such an outcast. Never had she felt so isolated and alone. Never so hopeless.

He's never left your side. He will never desert you.

She leaned back against the rough wall of the house and closed her eyes. Was Brand right? *Had* she been cultivating bitterness by shutting herself off? She'd worn her anger and sorrow like a shield in a battle against life and she was losing that battle, losing her spirit.

Brand's strong, steady voice drifted outside on the still, close air. His words filled her, touched a vibrant chord in her that had been silent far too long. Its power was overwhelming.

"I was sick and ye visited me," Brand prayed. "Lord, visit our brother Hank, help him in his time of need. Guide him with Your hand. Heal him with Your love. The prayer of faith shall save the sick, and the Lord shall raise him up and if he has committed sins, they shall be forgiven him. Confess your faults to one another and pray for one another, that ye may be healed."

That ye may be healed.

That ye may be healed.

Blinded by tears she hadn't known were there, Amelia staggered off the back porch, found her footing and ran across the yard, escaping into the dark interior of the barn.

She didn't know how long she crouched in the back of Sweet Pickle's empty stall with her arms clasped around her legs, her forehead resting on her knees. At first she couldn't stem the flow of tears and eventually gave up trying. Finally, exhausted and broken, she stretched out on the straw and slept with her cheek cradled in the crook of her arm.

She slept until Hattie gently touched her shoulder and called her back.

"Amelia? Wake up, honey."

She rolled over, wiped her swollen eyes and blinked. "I must have fallen asleep."

"You gave me quite a start. I didn't know where you were."

Amelia looked toward the open barn door. "Have they gone?"

"Some time ago." Hattie reached out, smoothed back Amelia's hair and pulled out strands of straw. "You look a sight."

"I'm afraid, Hattie."

"What are you afeard of?"

"Myself. Of what I've become. I've lost my way and don't seem to know how to get back to where I was."

Hattie sat beside her. "Oh, I'm sure you do know. You've known all along."

Amelia swallowed. Nodded. "Will you help me? Will you pray with me, Hattie? I'm afraid to pray for Hank. I prayed for Evan and he's gone. I've turned a blind eye and a deaf ear to God. I don't deserve to ask His forgiveness. I don't—"

"Hush now," Hattie took her hand and got to her knees. Amelia pulled herself up until she was kneeling, too.

"I don't know what to say."

"Say what's in your heart. Talk to God the way you talk to me." Hattie bowed her head.

A dove flew into the rafters of the barn and settled with a handful of others in the hayloft above them.

Amelia took a deep breath and began, her voice shaking. "Lord, I'm sorry. I'm sorry for turning away from You, for giving up my faith in You and Your goodness." She paused, thought for a moment before she went on.

"Hattie says that we don't know what You plan for us, or what our true purpose is here on earth. We have to trust that You give us hardships for our own good. I thought I had enough faith to go on, but after Evan died, I felt You betrayed me. I've been bitter and content to wallow in my grief. I've turned my back on everything and everyone who needed me. Now I'm alone and adrift without You. I don't know where to turn or what to do. I can't exist on my own with this hole in my heart anymore.

"Jesus said if we have faith, even as small as a grain of mustard seed, that nothing is impossible. I'm good at growing seeds, Lord. I'm good at healing. Help me to grow my faith again. Heal me so that I can heal others."

She didn't know what else to say. She looked to Hattie for guidance.

Hattie nodded, squeezed Amelia's hand and said, "Amen."

"Amen," Amelia whispered.

Suddenly, above their heads, there was a flutter of wings and the doves in the hayloft flew out the door and into the sunlight.

Chapter Twenty-Five

The next morning, for the first time in over a month, Amelia left the house.

She went out early, before too many folks were out and about. Her first stop was Foster's Boardinghouse where she returned a stack of Laura's tins and dishes and tarried over the cup of hot coffee that Laura offered.

When she walked into Harrison Barker's mercantile, she was pleased to note she was his only customer. There wasn't much she needed other than some dry beans and a bit of flour. He was surprised to see her and didn't hide it as he rushed around the counter.

"How is the sheriff?" Harrison asked.

"He's mending." She tried to sound confident. Hoped it was true.

"I hope he's anxious to get back to work. Everybody misses the *Gazette*."

"Actually," she said, lowering her voice because a cowhand had just ambled in, "he hasn't regained consciousness yet."

"Really?"

"He's not awake yet." She might just as well have posted a sign outside the store. Word would spread like wildfire. "His body needs the rest."

"Has he got the fever? That'll kill a man faster 'n anything," Harrison told her.

"It seems to be under control now." That much was true. His fever had dropped the day after his delirium. Now he slept on and on, instilling her with a helplessness she couldn't ignore even now that she was away from the house.

She quickly asked after his mother and discovered Mrs. Barker had gone to New Orleans to visit her sister. As soon as she could, Amelia said goodbye to Harrison, anxious to hurry back home.

The minute she walked through the gate, Hattie came running out to greet her.

"He's awake." Hattie's face was wreathed in smiles. "Hank's awake."

Momentarily stunned, Amelia could only gape.

He's awake.

Once comprehension struck, she went weak in the knees. An overwhelming sense of relief came over her, as if she'd been holding her breath since they'd carried Hank's broken and bleeding body into the house and now she could finally breathe again.

Hattie waited on the porch, her excitement mirrored in her smile. "I walked in to check on him and he was lying there with his eyes open, trying to figure out where he was. When I told him he was at your place, he just nodded and closed his eyes again."

Somehow Amelia made it inside. She paused outside the sickroom door, rested her hand on the knob, turned it before she lost her nerve and stepped inside.

She thought he was asleep until his eyes slowly opened and he gave her a weak half smile.

"Miss Peep." His voice was barely audible, rusty from disuse and fever.

"Mr. Larson."

"I see you somehow pulled me through."

She nodded, approached the bed. Now that he was awake, she felt awkward being alone with him until she heard Hattie bustling around behind her, picking up an armload of towels, collecting washrags and bustling out through the door that led to the kitchen.

"I hope . . ." He began to speak, paused, cleared his throat.

She rushed to his bedside before she realized she had even moved and poured him a glass of water from the pitcher on his bedside table. Just as she'd done so many times when he was unconscious, she slipped her hand beneath his head and raised it. Touching him was second nature to her now—at least it seemed so before he was awake and aware. With his eyes on her, she was suddenly embarrassed and uncomfortable.

When he was settled, he thanked her and then added, "I hope I wasn't too much trouble."

"Not really."

"Thank you, Amelia," he said again.

She looked down at her hands, unable to find words to say.

"I know this is hard on you . . . having me here."

"Hattie has been a great help."

"You look tired."

She turned her attention to the window beside his bed, anything rather than look at him. "Are you hungry?"

"Maybe."

"I'll make you some soup broth. Nothing heavy yet."

He frowned. "Exactly how long have I been here?"

"A bit over two weeks."

"No."

"Yes." She clasped and unclasped her hands. "I'd best go make that broth."

"Amelia, wait." She'd started out of the room but she halted, slowly turned.

"I'm sorry," he said softly. "I'm sorry you did this, that you had to do this, knowing how you feel about me—"

How could he know what she was feeling when she wasn't certain herself?

"Don't mention it. It was nothing."

Hank knew she'd done far from nothing. Even in his weakened state, he could see these past few weeks had taken a toll on her. She was too thin. Violet shadows stained the delicate skin beneath her eyes.

"If you'll send for Harrison and Brand, I'm sure they'll move me back to my place." He couldn't lift his own head off the pillow but he figured with help, he could clear out and leave her be.

"You're not fit to care for yourself," she said.

"I'll manage."

"Don't be ridiculous."

"I shouldn't be here—in your home."

"Hattie will stay on to help as long as you're here."

"You don't need me around as a constant reminder of—of what happened to your brother."

When she failed to respond, he tried to sit up. His head spun. Pain shot up his leg. He hadn't enough strength to lift his head. His shoulder was tightly bound. He reached down, felt another bandage on his thigh.

"Jones must have done a good job of filling me full of lead."

"Your shoulder wound is the worst. Your leg is healing nicely. Half an inch to the left and your artery would have been severed. And if gangrene had set in—"

Her words drifted away. She didn't have to say more. He knew the slightest infection could mean death.

"I have you to thank for my life, Amelia."

She refused to look at him. He knew how hard it must have been for her to care for him all this time, to have him there, to remember Evan's death each and every time she laid eyes on him. She'd held his very life in her hands—and she'd saved him.

Though the idea that she'd suffered plagued him, the knowledge that she'd saved his life ignited new hope for them.

"It would be best if you try to sleep," she said

quietly. The sound of her voice soothed him like a healing balm.

"It sounds like I've had enough sleep for a while." He managed a smile until he tried to lift his head again and winced. "Doesn't look like I'll be getting the *Gazette* out anytime soon."

"I think not."

He could tell she was highly uncomfortable. She'd made excuses to leave, but was too polite to simply walk out.

"Maybe I do feel like a nap," he admitted grudgingly, wishing there was a reason for her to sit in the chair beside the bed. Just looking at her made him feel better. "You go on and do whatever you need to do."

"I'll send Hattie in to check on you in a little while."

"Don't worry about me." He tried to move again and winced. "I'm not going anywhere."

Two days later he was still lying flat on his back, embarrassed now that he was conscious of just how much care he actually required. He reckoned Hattie's grandson, little Orson, didn't take this much looking after.

Hattie fretted like a mother hen while Amelia stood by, silent and watchful. He was beginning to think Amelia delighted in forcing her ill-tasting potions and tonics down him, insisting he drink every last drop of the foul-smelling teas and broths she concocted.

Rather than stare at the ceiling and four walls, he asked Hattie to keep his mind occupied by telling him the story of her early years as a new bride on the Texas frontier. Her stories were colorfully told, alive with detail and passion. Time passed quickly as she described how she and Orson constructed their first dwelling with little more than rocks and lumber from the dismantled wagon that carried them to Texas.

She spoke in such detail that he could easily picture the images of a younger Hattie and a man who looked a lot like Joe, battling the elements and the Comanche. She told of isolation and the endless struggle to make a home out of nothing but a pile of split logs and a living out of a few head of cattle.

Even with the pleasant distraction, he found himself waiting anxiously for Amelia to walk into the room. He constantly listened for her footsteps in the kitchen, aware of the click of her heels against the floor, the rustle of her skirt.

Most of all he found himself hoping for a smile when she looked at him. He prayed one day he would see a light in her eyes again.

One afternoon, while Hattie was out hanging linens on the clothesline, Amelia appeared without warning to see if he needed anything.

"More than anything," he said, "I'd love to sit up and see the world from another point of view."

She looked about to deny him, then said, "I'll help you sit up, but most likely your head's going to spin." She walked over and slipped her arms beneath his, counted to three and pulled him to a sitting position. He moved like dead weight with no more strength than a newly hatched duckling. She was right—he closed his eyes when the room started to whirl.

She made a production of fluffing pillows and stacking them just so. She pressed her palm against his forehead and then along his jawline —obviously blind to what her touch was doing to him. This closeness, this gentle touching, seemed an old habit to her. Little did she realize that each time she leaned over him, he caught his breath and closed his eyes as an intense longing to kiss her was nearly his undoing.

Thankfully, she never lingered longer than a few seconds. Her expression told him quite clearly that caring for him was a tedious chore— one she had undertaken because no one else was qualified.

"Have you heard Hattie's story?" He found safe ground in a new topic.

"Some. Not so much the early years. I know all about the Comanche raid. I nursed her afterward."

"She didn't dwell on it, but I imagined it was far worse than she let on."

"Only a woman could understand how bad it

386

was. They . . . did unspeakable things, then tried to scalp her. Left her for dead."

"She believes it's by God's grace that she survived. She credits Him for saving her, and Joe, and for bringing Rebekah into their lives."

Amelia looked down at her folded hands. "That's what she believes."

"What about you, Amelia?"

She remained silent, unaware that her emotions were flitting across her perfect features—confusion being the most identifiable.

"Have you found your way back to God?" he asked.

She drew herself up, straightened her spine.

"I don't see as what I believe or *don't* believe is any of your concern, Mr. Larson."

"I would think that since you've seen most all of me by now, I ought to have some right to know what you're thinking about just about anything. Faith seems a pretty safe topic."

Her face turned beet-red. She jumped up, obviously intent on leaving. He wound up struggling to find a way to keep her there.

"I know I don't have the right to ask any favors—"

"No, you don't."

At least he'd succeeded in getting her to stay.

"I'm afraid I'll forget some of Hattie's details if I don't write them down," he began. "I need pens, ink and paper. If you could find the time to go to my office and collect some things for me, I'd be truly grateful." He glanced down at the striped nightshirt he was wearing and hoped it wasn't one of her brother's.

As if she'd read his mind she said, "That's Harrison's nightshirt."

"If you could bring one of my own, then. A change of clothes would be nice, too."

She was blushing to beat the band. "I'll consider it. When I have a spare minute."

"I'd truly appreciate it, Miss Peep."

She turned her back and walked out without another word.

The next morning, Amelia let herself into Hank's office.

A hint of lye still lingered in the air but now the scents of ink, machine oil, stacks of paper and the must of old books tainted the long narrow space.

It was odd being here without him, moving about in the place where he worked, staring at the papers and articles on his desk. A rancher walked past the window, drawing her attention to the wide glass. She found herself thinking about the day she'd literally fallen into Hank's arms.

He'd caught her gently, yet there was nothing unmanly about him. His hold had been strong, confident.

Pleasant.

No time for this, she thought. No time to stop moving. No time to think, to feel. Not when it was too easy to find herself longing for the strength of his arms, the warmth of his touch. Not when it was all too easy to face the terrifying fact that she had grown used to having him in her home, used to worrying about him day and night. She looked forward to sparring with him, watching him smile each time she walked into his room.

His room.

What would happen when he moved out? In the small quiet hours of the night when she heard him snoring peacefully in the room next to hers, she often found herself contemplating what their lives might be like if she could bring herself to forgive—

She shook off the thought and headed upstairs in search of his clothes. It was one thing to have Hank lolling around in Harrison Barker's nightshirt when he was unconscious, but quite another now that he was awake.

The sooner Hank Larson was up and dressed and able to move around, the sooner she could send him on his way and get on with her life.

Upstairs, Hank's private quarters were more Spartan than her own. A narrow iron bed covered with a faded, handmade quilt was shoved up against the far wall. An upended crate served as a bedside table. It held a single oil lamp and a stack of books. A threadbare upholstered chair in the corner oozed stuffing. More books were piled on the floor beside it. A small chest of drawers held his personal things.

Here, mirrored in his surroundings, was the stark loneliness of his life. Of course, he had his books and his work. When the office was open he had the companionship of newly made acquaintances and friends. But whenever he was at home, when his workday was through and darkness gathered, he was as alone as she.

No one knows what God has in store for us.

Had God led Hank to Glory, to her, because they were two lost souls in need of each other?

The silence in the empty room magnified the sound of her confusion. She quickly collected a couple of neatly folded shirts and a pair of trousers and turned to head downstairs. Back at his desk, she noticed a new Bible near a stack of correspondence. It should have been the first thing she'd seen when she walked into the office, but somehow she'd missed it entirely.

She paused, ran her fingertip across the new leather cover, traced the embossed letters, then opened and read the words inscribed inside.

To Hank Larson

From your friend and pastor,

Reverend Brand McCormick, Glory, Texas, 1874

After a moment's hesitation, she lay the Bible atop the things she'd collected.

By the time she returned home, she'd filled a small fruit crate with Hank's things.

Back at the house, she found him awake, sitting up against the stack of pillows Hattie had planted behind him.

She set the box beside him on the bed, taking care not to bump his bad leg. "Here are the things you asked for."

He stared at the box a moment, recognized his clothes.

"How did you get in?"

She opened the reticule dangling at her wrist, found his key and handed it over.

"This was in your coat pocket the night the men carried you in. That coat, by the way, did not survive the gunfight." She looked away as she added, "Nor did your trousers."

When she met his gaze again, she tried to ignore the jolt initiated by his smile.

"I brought you some street clothes."

"I doubt I have the strength to dress myself." He let the words linger between them.

"I'll send for Harrison as soon as you feel you're up to it. It's about time you tried walking, too."

"You're the doc."

He smiled directly up into her eyes and her heart tripped over itself. She watched as he reached reverently for his Bible, drew it out of the box and rested it on his lap. "Brand gave me this the day I was baptized."

She didn't tell him she had read the inscription.

"I thought you might want it." She'd surprised herself by choosing to bring it to him when she'd taken no comfort in the holy words for so long. She watched him thumb the pages, let the book open of its own accord.

Hank scanned the page and then began to read, " 'If you seek him—' "

" 'He will be found by you,' " Amelia finished for him.

He looked amazed. She shrugged. "I know the Bible inside and out," she told him, wishing that in itself made faith that much easier.

"When I was struggling, Brand told me not to make understanding so hard. He told me to simply open my heart and let God in. Why don't you give it a try, Amelia?"

She looked around the small room. The white cotton curtains were fresh and clean, teased by a warm breeze blowing in from the west. Though Hank's presence filled the room, as would the memories of his stay here, she still thought of it as Evan's room and always would.

"When Evan died, my heart crumbled," she whispered.

"When Tricia died, I was convinced mine had

turned to stone. Then I came here, met you. Fell in love again. When I lost you, I surrendered my heart to God."

She sighed. "It's not that easy."

"Don't you think I know that better than anyone, Amelia?"

He raised his hand and she thought for a moment he was going to reach for hers. Her breath caught, her pulse quickened.

"Hattie's out back hanging the laundry," she blurted. "I'll send her to fetch Harrison when you feel like getting dressed."

"I don't think I'm up to a visit from Harrison today." He paused, thoughtful for a moment. "Are you—have you been seeing other patients again?"

She shrugged. "No, but I suppose it's time."

It was past time, she realized. She'd distanced herself so completely that folks had stopped asking for help. It was time she thought about doctoring again, that or decide how she intended to put food on the table from now on.

"I hate to be a burden. Now you have two of us underfoot," he said.

"I enjoy having Hattie here." She stopped short when she realized that truth be told, she enjoyed having him here, too. "I know she misses Joe and Rebekah and the babies." She stopped, unable to trust what she might say anymore.

He tried to straighten, taking care not to dislodge the box and send his things toppling to the floor.

"Why don't you send for Harrison tomorrow? No reason he and some of the others couldn't move me back to my place."

The image of him lying abed in that stark, lonely room above the newspaper office bothered her more than it should have.

"You need a bit more care before you're on your own."

He was smiling that smile again. The one that warmed her to the toes. The one that almost made her believe in love and loving, that God had brought them together for a reason. Hank was smiling the smile that just might mend her broken heart.

"Then I guess I'll just have stay here as long as I'm under doctor's orders."

"I just don't want you undoing all my hard work." She smoothed the front of her skirt as she stood. "I'll leave you to your writing until the noon meal is ready."

"Thank you for collecting my things for me." He began to take pen and ink out of the box.

"I gathered up a pile of letters that were on your desk, too. Just in case there was anything that you need to attend to."

He looked mighty pleased as she excused herself and went to find Hattie.

As she stood on the back porch and stared at

the white linens flapping on the line, she thought about what she'd done. Hank wasn't on his feet yet, but he certainly didn't require full-time nursing. Had she ordered him to stay because he needed time to heal, or because she wasn't ready to let him go?

Chapter Twenty-Six

T wo days later, Amelia was in the kitchen cleaning up the breakfast dishes.

She pulled a plate out of the soapy water and just then a chill ran down her spine. She felt as if someone was watching her. Her hands immediately stilled in the dishwater. Slowly, she looked over her shoulder and there, leaning against the doorjamb, was Hank. He had donned one of his clean white shirts, suspenders and trousers, but he was barefooted. Apparently, he hadn't been able to manage shoes and socks.

He smiled a lopsided smile at her when she looked up from his bare toes.

"Couldn't quite get the socks on by myself." He took a step toward the kitchen table and immediately began to weave on his feet.

She flew to his side, slipped her arm around his waist and helped him limp to the table.

"I guess dressing and walking are too much for one day," he decided.

She could tell he was fighting to keep his tone light, but his breathing was shallow.

"What hurts?" she wanted to know.

"What doesn't?"

She relaxed a bit once she had him on a chair. "Sit a minute and catch your breath."

"Don't worry," he told her. "I don't even know if I can hobble back to bed."

She went to dry her hands.

"That coffee sure smells good," he commented.

She hadn't yet given him anything stronger than chamomile tea.

"I guess one cup won't hurt you." She filled a mug.

He took a sip and sighed with pleasure.

"Thank you for this." He took another sip. "And thanks for catching me a minute ago. I'd never get over the embarrassment of ending up on your kitchen floor in a heap."

She found herself smiling again, remembering the way they'd collided on the day they met. Her smile faded when she remembered the robbery.

"I guess we all need someone to catch us when we fall," she said softly, thinking aloud.

"Who catches you, Amelia? Who do you lean on?"

She met his gaze. His never wavered.

"I'd like it to be me," he said. "When I have

the strength that is. I'd like it to be me you lean on."

"Hank . . . I—"

"I still love you, Amelia."

"Don't—"

"Don't love you? Or don't say it?"

"Both. Please."

"It's too late for me to stop loving you. I've tried, believe me. I tried when you sent me away. Not seeing you, not being near you, only made me want you more."

"Hank, I—"

He cut her off. "I know you haven't forgiven me. I couldn't forgive myself for what happened, not until I turned my life over to God. If He can forgive us, then why can't we forgive ourselves? Why can't we forgive each other?"

Shaken to the quick, she leaned against the dry sink, still watching him. He set his coffee cup down and stared back intently.

"I tried to save Evan, Amelia," he began.

"I know that now," she said.

"You do?"

She nodded. "You spoke of it when you were delirious. And I know you well enough to know you did all you could, given the circumstances. When it happened, my grief was so bottomless that I wasn't thinking clearly. All I could think of was Evan. He was my responsibility and I failed him."

"*Can* you forgive me?"

She took a deep breath. Let it go.

"Yes," she whispered. Relief washed over her when she realized she wasn't just saying what he wanted to hear, what he needed to hear. She'd said it because it was true. "Yes, I think so."

Somehow over the past few weeks she'd come to accept the fact that Hank did what he had to do in order to save Sophronia. He'd been forced to make a split-second decision and her brother had ended up dead.

Evan was in the wrong that day. Wrong in his actions, wrong when he chose to put Fanny and her sister-in-law in harm's way.

"You were just doing your job. You had to make a choice and you did the right thing." She dropped her focus to where she'd knotted her hands at her waist. "I forgive you," she whispered.

She heard the chair legs scrape against the floor and looked up. Hank was on his feet, bracing himself with both hands against the table.

"Sit down, Hank." She was afraid he was going to fall before she could get to him but when she made it to his side, he shook his head and held her at arm's length.

"I want to stand on my own feet for this."

"Hank—" She was more concerned that he was going to black out than intent on what he was saying.

"Marry me, Amelia."

"Please, sit *down*." Her mouth went dry when she realized what he had said.

"Marry me. Please." He took both of her hands in his, wavered and hung on so tight she winced.

"Sorry." He loosened his hold a bit. "Will you be my wife?"

"No." She was shaking like a leaf. She'd put him through misery. She didn't deserve him.

"I'm going to keep asking until you say yes."

"You're delirious."

"Not anymore. I'm in love with you. I want you to be my wife."

"I want you to let go of my hands and sit down before you fall down."

Hank sat just as Hattie came in the back door. She set down an empty bucket and planted her hands on her hips.

"Hank Larson, 'cept for the pallor of your skin, you look a far sight better than you did yesterday. Just look at you, all dressed and sittin' at the table."

All Amelia could do was stare at Hank.

Dear Lord, don't let him say anything about proposing.

Dear Lord.

Thankfully, Hank merely smiled and said, "Thank you kindly, Hattie. I'm feeling much better, even if I'm not too steady on my feet just yet. It won't be long."

Amelia turned and dipped her hands into the now tepid dishwater.

Who knew it would be a proposal of marriage that would inspire a spontaneous prayer?

Nearly another week passed during which Hank had a setback after trying to walk too soon. Frustrated at his own weakness, he was learning the hard way that each time he pushed himself to write late into the night or he dragged himself out of bed and tried walking alone, he would suffer for his efforts.

Today, as he sat on the front porch, safely tucked into an upholstered chair Amelia and Hattie had wrestled outside for him, he reminded himself that even though he was anxious to be restored to good health, he wasn't looking forward to leaving Amelia's.

Just about every day lately, Brand McCormick had stopped by for a visit, but today, Hank's thoughts kept drifting to Amelia. If only she'd accept his proposal—

He'd given up asking.

"Are you all right, Hank?" Brand's voice drew him out of his reverie.

Hank smiled. "Better every day. How could I not feel better with two women fussing over me all the time?" He stared down the street at the houses scattered here and there on either side. "Despite the bullet holes in me, I think I'm more content than I have been in years and I have you to thank for it, Reverend."

"I think Amelia is the one you should thank," Brand said.

"Of course. She saved my life, but it was you who helped me find my way." Hank shrugged. "I guess I didn't know I was so lost until I was found, eh?"

"We never do. It's God who guides us home."

They sat in amiable silence for a few minutes. A dragonfly flitted around the geraniums bordering the front porch. Amelia's garden was no longer thriving as it had in the spring, but it was no longer as neglected as after Evan's death.

With Hattie's help, the herb garden had nearly recovered and a healthy morning glory trailed the trellis beside the porch.

Hank suddenly remembered the letter he'd tucked in the chair beside him. He pulled it out and handed it to Brand.

"Would you mind posting this for me?"

"Of course not." Brand tucked the letter inside the jacket he'd slipped off and hung over the porch railing.

"Before the shooting, I received a letter from an applicant for sheriff. I'd forgotten all about it until I found it inside a box of things Amelia brought from my place. I've written back asking him to come to Glory. I'm assuming that, with the town's approval, he can take over right away."

"Is he qualified?"

"He says he's from a family of lawmen and is supposedly a crack shot." Hank couldn't resist a laugh. "Of course, nothing ever happens around here."

McCormick laughed with him. "I hope it works out. Soon enough you'll be on your feet and able to publish the *Gazette* again. Everyone sure misses getting a paper."

"I'll be doing *something,* that's for certain, but I'm not so sure I'll be putting out the news."

Brand frowned and hooked his elbow over his knee. "You intend on staying in Glory?"

"You said once that God led me here. He might have, but unless He leads me to a way to make a living I'm going to have to move on."

"Aside from the fact that you were forced to become sheriff, shot at and nearly killed—you enjoy it here, don't you?"

"I do, believe me."

"Surely once you're on your feet you'll be able to make of go of things."

Hank paused, lowered his voice. "It's not just the *Gazette.* I don't know if I can live in the same town with Amelia and not . . ." He didn't know how to go on. "I've asked her to marry me."

"You have? That's wonderful."

"But she won't have me." Hank thought about it for a second and added, "I don't much blame her."

"She can't forgive you. Is that it?"

Hank shook his head no. "She says she can, and has. That in itself is a miracle as far as I'm concerned. But I don't have much to offer anymore. Not only am I barely limping around, but I've got so many stitches and scars on me, I look like a rag doll.

"And I'm about out of all my savings. I don't have a way to get out another edition of the *Gazette* anytime soon and without advertisement money, I'm going to be forced to sell the printing press and give the building back to the bank."

He thought of the day he had made the decision to buy the printing press and leave Saint Joseph. It had been exhilarating and terrifying at a time when he thought he'd never feel anything but sorrow again. And what a thrill it had been to see the first issue of the *Gazette* come off the press.

The dream of owning his own newspaper had faded in the light of harsh reality. The only dreams he'd dreamed lately included Amelia, but a week of her adamant refusals to his proposals had finally convinced him to give up.

"Amelia isn't the kind of woman who judges a man by the size of his bankroll," Brand said.

Hank had a feeling that was true, but Amelia deserved a man who could bring something to a marriage. "That may be true, but there's too much muddy water under the bridge. Besides, a man can only ask so many times."

Chapter Twenty-Seven

I *'ve asked her to marry me.*
A man can only ask so many times.

She hadn't meant to eavesdrop. Amelia was innocently dusting and straightening the vials and jars on her apothecary shelves, paying no attention to the men at all as their conversation drifted through the open window. Not until the topic became Hank's marriage proposals did she realize they were talking about her.

Her first reaction was to leave the room. Natural curiosity compelled her to stay. Then she heard Hank tell Brand he was in dire straits.

Then she heard him confess that he had finally accepted the fact that she was serious in her refusals. He was finally convinced that she was never going to change her mind and marry him.

Amelia set down her dust rag and escaped through the house, all the way back to Evan's room because it was farthest away from the men on the porch.

The room was neat as a pin, though there were ink-stained fingerprints along the top hem of the sheet. If she couldn't scrub them out, they'd serve as a constant reminder of the man who'd recovered in this room. Hank's writing implements were neatly lined up in the apple crate, his mail all sorted and stacked.

She sank down heavily on the end of the bed and felt the mattress sag beneath her weight. She sat there with her hands folded in her lap, staring down at them. They were work worn, tanned by exposure to the sun. Not the hands of a lady, that was certain.

Her thoughts drifted back to what Hank had just said. She *had* persistently refused his proposals, but certainly not because of the reasons he'd given Brand. He might not be able to walk on his own yet, but once he healed, she expected him to get around just fine.

And how in the world would she have any idea that he was nearly broke? Or that he'd gambled everything he owned on the newspaper? What made him think that his financial status would matter to her in the least?

Admittedly, she hadn't been acting like herself since Evan died, but she would never be the kind of woman who would marry a man for worldly gain.

She thought of all the weeks Hank had been laid up and unable to solicit for advertisements or ferret out news stories.

She won't have me.

Oh, Hank. You deserve so much more. Someone prettier. Someone young enough to give you lots of babies—not a plain, old, left-at-the-altar spinster like me.

Marry me, Amelia.

She pressed her hands to her cheeks, wondered if the preacher had taken his leave yet. Was it safe to return to the front room and finish her task?

Help him. You have to help him.

The notion slammed into her out of the silence.

She'd stitched him up, doctored and nursed him for weeks now. She'd found the strength, with God's help, to forgive him. Hadn't she done enough? How could she help him now? She couldn't lend him any money. She didn't have two bits to rub together most of the time.

She didn't know how or where to begin to save the *Gazette*. She wasn't a gifted businesswoman, obviously. If she was, she wouldn't be living hand to mouth.

She sat in silence a few moments longer thinking about her lack of business savvy and suddenly thought of Laura Foster. Laura earned a far cry more than a dozen eggs, a side of ham or a host of bartered donations. She'd made a success of her boardinghouse right from the beginning.

Getting to her feet, Amelia paused for a moment before the oval mirror above Evan's old dresser. She tucked a strand of contrary hair back into her long braid and studied her reflection.

Maybe she wasn't as fancy a woman as Hank deserved, but she had been comely enough to attract his eye in the first place. He was fond enough of her to offer marriage—not once but a good half-dozen times over the past few days.

She might not be as young as some men preferred a new bride to be, but she was educated and she had a profession—albeit without a diploma to prove it.

She might not be rich, but she'd always put food on the table and paid the taxes. That had to count for something.

She closed her eyes and whispered, "Lord, I know I don't deserve to ask You for anything after what I've done, but I need Your help and guidance. I'm not asking for myself. I'm asking You to show me a way to help Hank. Amen."

Amelia opened her eyes and shrugged at the woman in the mirror. "I've got to at least try." The whispered pledge became a promise.

She found Hattie in the kitchen and asked her to fix some lemonade for the men on the porch. Then she grabbed her straw hat and plopped it on her head.

"I'll be back shortly, Hattie," she said. "If you need me, I'll be at Mrs. Foster's."

She'd been closeted in the front parlor at Foster's Boardinghouse for a good thirty minutes and now Amelia watched as Laura Foster looked over two duplicate lists lying in the middle of the butler's table in front of the settee.

"It might seem like an awful lot to accomplish in a short time, but with help, we can do it." Laura's confidence was astounding.

Amelia took the list Laura handed her.

"It does appear daunting," she agreed. "But I'm afraid I can only stall Mr. Larson for another week. After that he'll be well enough and more than anxious to move back to his own place. We have to have everything finished before he moves out."

Amelia couldn't help but notice the dimple that appeared in Laura's cheek whenever the woman smiled.

"Isn't there a little something you could slip into his food?" Laura asked. "Some herb that would set him back a bit without doing great harm?"

"Why, Mrs. Foster!" Amelia pretended shock.

"Call me Laura, please. I'm just teasing you, of course."

"I suppose I'd better get back." Amelia slipped the strings of her reticule over her wrist.

"And I've got to plan this week's menus," Laura admitted. Then she added, "I'll have Rodrigo round up Ricardo. I think he's out hunting. That boy's been moping around ever since Mr. Larson was wounded."

Amelia folded her list and tucked it inside the reticule as Laura walked her to the door. "Thank you so much for all your help, Laura. I wouldn't even attempt this without you."

"You could manage, I'm sure. Drop by day after tomorrow and we'll chat again."

Amelia wasn't halfway down Main Street when Jenson Addler reined his horse in beside her.

"Miss Amelia? You doctorin' again? Please say it's so." The weathered cattleman shoved his hat to the back of his head, revealing a forehead that was ten shades paler than his sunburned face. The man was in his early forties and had ten children. She'd delivered six of them.

Amelia shaded her eyes as she tipped her head to look up at him.

"I guess I am, Mr. Addler. What's wrong?"

"Oh, it ain't me, ma'am." He blushed and shook his head as if the notion of her doctorin' *him* was plum loco. "It's Justin, our youngest. He's busted his arm and my wife wants you to set it proper like."

She could have said no, could have extended her self-imposed exile and isolation a bit longer, but the heartache and darkness that had caused her to turn a blind eye to her fellow man had receded. As soon as she realized there was no way she could refuse Addler's plea, she felt as if a heavy weight had been lifted from her heart.

Amelia smiled, feeling lighter than she had in weeks.

"Follow me home, Mr. Addler. I'll collect my bag and ride out to the ranch with you."

● ● ●

Once word was out that Amelia was treating folks again there was a steady stream of patients at the door. It was almost as if they'd saved up every ache and pain until she was willing to see them.

More often than not that week, she was forced to leave Hank in Hattie's capable hands. It wasn't long before he turned cantankerous whenever Amelia said she was going to pay a call on one of her patients.

On Sunday morning, she announced that she and Hattie planned to leave him home alone for two hours while they both attend Sunday service. It was the first time she'd been to church since Evan died. Hank looked surprised at first, but then he smiled.

"I'm pleased to hear it," he told her. They had him situated in a comfortable chair, his writing implements and papers close beside him.

"I don't want you walking around on your own. All you need to do is fall and bust your noggin open. Will you promise me you'll stay put right here in the front room?"

She settled her Sunday hat on her head. He raised his hand and wiggled his hand to the right until she straightened it.

"You're always complaining that there's too much noise to work around here," she reminded him. "This will give you some time alone."

"Well, there has been a lot of commotion ever

since you started dispensing cure-alls again. Folks are always knocking on the door."

"I thought you *wanted* me to join the living."

"I wanted you all to myself. I wanted you to say you'll marry me, but it doesn't appear I'm going to get my way," he mumbled.

She turned on her heel and hurried out the door to catch up with Hattie.

The congregation was just as surprised to see her walk in as Hank had been by her announcement. Her cheeks flamed red-hot as she made her way up the aisle to her usual seat near the front. Hattie scooted in beside her.

It felt good to sing hymns along with friends and neighbors. As they sat through Brand's sermon, Amelia fought to calm her nerves. How had Hattie borne public humiliation after the Comanche attack? How had the woman suffered the stares and whispers? The speculation? The condemnation? How had she lived through it all and gone on?

Thinking of the challenges Hattie had faced, thinking of the scar beneath Hattie's bonnet, Amelia promised herself she'd do well to show half as much courage.

She began to listen to the words of Brand's sermon. It was as if he had chosen the topic just for her, as if he was speaking to her heart when he read from Colossians, "'Put on therefore, as the elect of God, holy and beloved, bowels of mercies, kindness, humbleness of mind, meekness, long suffering; Forbearing one another, and forgiving one another, if a man have a quarrel against any: even as Christ forgave you, so also do ye.'

"In other words, bear with each other. Have compassion for one another. Forgive one another as Christ and His Father forgive you." He closed the Bible on the lectern, looked out over the crowd and paused. Then his gaze met Amelia's.

"Before you leave today," he announced to the congregation, "one of our members has asked to address the gathering."

Amelia's heart began to pound so hard that it nearly drowned out Brand's introduction.

"Amelia, please come forward."

She felt as if her head was stuffed with cotton.

"I don't . . ." In her moment of panic, she turned to Hattie and grabbed her hand. "I can't do this."

"You *can* do this. Get on up there."

"What if I faint?"

"Just remember, you're a fighter, not a fainter."

Amelia took a deep breath and pushed herself up off the pew. When she reached the lectern, Brand gave her an encouraging smile and stepped aside.

She took a deep breath and remembered what Hattie just said.

You're a fighter, not a fainter.

She decided it would be best to get right to the heart of the matter and not dillydally. "I'm here to apologize to all of you." She let her gaze slowly drift over each and every face, slowly, which helped her to remember them as individuals and not a mass of strangers packed together staring up at her. She looked into the faces of women whose children she'd delivered. She saw those children tucked into the pews beside them, some of them a decade old now. There were men she'd treated, too. Not as many as she would have liked, but times were slowly changing. Perhaps the day would come when it made no difference at all that she was a woman in a man's profession.

"Many of you offered help and sent condolences after my brother died, but I turned away from you. I refused your kindness and your sympathy. I turned away from God, too. But thanks to Reverend McCormick and Hattie Ellenberg, who were patient and strong willed when I needed it most—and above all, thanks to God—I have found my way through the darkness and back to the light and the living again."

A murmur passed through the crowd.

"For that, I'm here to ask your forgiveness."

"You got it, Miss Amelia." It was the butcher who shouted from the back row. Titters of nervous laughter filled the church. When she saw many heads nod in agreement, the vision of all those familiar faces wavered as tears filled her eyes.

"Thank you," she said softly. "Thank you all so very much." Then she took a deep breath and added, "Now I must ask you all for the help you offered me before."

Chapter Twenty-Eight

O n the very next Friday at noon, Hank was dressed, packed and ready to move back to the newspaper building—but Amelia wasn't at home to bid him farewell.

She'd hurried off somewhere before dawn. Not only was she still gone, but Joe had arrived an hour earlier to pick up Hattie. The woman had been all packed and excited to be going home at long last.

"I'll never be able to thank you enough for what you've done for me, Hattie," Hank told her, not surprised when she protested.

"It weren't much," she said. "I just pitched in to help out Amelia." Then she winked, "That and chaperone."

Now it was his turn to be embarrassed. He had noticed her hovering in doorways and treading the hall with a heavy foot lately. How many times, he wondered, had she overheard him propose to Amelia? How many times had she heard Amelia turn him down?

"I thought she'd be here to say goodbye." He knew he sounded like a petulant child, but at this point he didn't much care.

Hattie shrugged. "I'm sure Amelia will stop by your office and see how you're fairing. She's good about following up with patients."

Just a patient was all he'd ever be to her now.

He glanced out the window and saw Rebekah and the children in the back of the wagon. They waved to him from the street as Joe headed up the front walk.

Hattie gave him a hug and wished him well. Joe pumped his hand and told him not to be a stranger. He couldn't tell them he might be leaving soon.

He tried to pass the next solitary hour writing, but the relentless tick-tick-tick of the clock on a shelf behind Amelia's dispensary counter kept interrupting his thoughts.

Each time he heard someone ride past the house, he would put down his pen and wait, hoping it was Amelia. Finally at five minutes to twelve, Harrison Barker arrived earlier than planned, ready to load Hank into his buggy and drive him home.

When the storekeeper walked through the front door, he handed Hank a shiny hickory cane.

"What's this?" Hank tested its weight and

strength before he slowly rose and tried it for support.

"Ordered it special for you," Harrison told him.

"Well, thank you, Harrison. That was mighty thoughtful."

"No problem at all. I added it onto your account."

"Well, thanks for thinking of me, at least." He hoped he could settle his account when it came time to leave.

"Hey," Harrison said, changing the subject, "rumor has it you found a new sheriff."

"Someone inquired. I've invited him to come to town. All I have to say is that even if no one approves of the man, he's taking over."

"We've all gotten a little bit tired of hearing you gripe about the job. What are you gonna do with all that time on your hands?"

He would have time on his hands now, that was certain. More idle time than he'd ever bargained for. Even if he could afford to stay, if he could afford to pay Ricardo to help run the press and deliver copies of the *Gazette* around town, advertisements would still have to be solicited and stories written.

There was no hope of finishing his novel, sending it off to a publisher and making money off it anytime soon.

Harrison helped him outside, down the stairs

and into the buggy before he ran back for Hank's things and loaded them up.

Harrison jumped up onto the buggy seat and took the reins into his hands. "Ready?"

Hank scanned the street in both directions. Main Street was ominously quiet. Even more so than usual. If Amelia was rushing back to say goodbye, he would be able to see her.

"Is that everything?" Harrison asked.

"Everything but Amelia."

"Sure, let's go."

Hank sat on the high-sprung seat beside Harrison and payed little attention as the man guided the buggy along Main Street. It wasn't until they were pulled up in front of Foster's Boardinghouse that he realized they'd driven two blocks past his building.

The first thing Hank noticed was an abundance of extra rigs and horses parked on the street around the establishment.

"What are we doing here?" Hank asked.

"Mrs. Foster's organized a little gathering and invited me to stop by. When I told her I was picking you up, she said to bring you along."

"I'm really not in the mood, Harrison. How about you drive me back to my place and come back alone?"

"I hate to disappoint her. Besides, she said you might pick up something newsworthy."

"It'll be a while before I'm ready to work on another edition." If ever, he thought.

Harrison climbed down from the buggy seat without a care in the world for Hank's request. "Come on. I'll help you down. Hand me your cane so I'll have it ready."

"I really don't want to do this." What Hank wanted was to get back to his own place and sulk.

"I know you don't, but do it for Mrs. Foster. You really don't want to hurt her feelings, do you?"

Hank thought of the young, vivacious blond widow who never seemed to have an unkind word to say about anyone.

"I'm really not up to it."

"All you have to do is walk in and say hello. You might get a front-page story out of it."

Hank didn't have the heart to tell him that more than likely he'd be shutting down the *Gazette* sooner rather than later. He sighed heavily, making certain Harrison heard. When he realized he was being ignored, he gave up, handed over the cane and struggled out of the buggy.

"Five minutes," he told Harrison.

"Ten at the most, if you're not comfortable," Harrison agreed.

They walked up the front porch steps, no little feat for Hank at this point. Harrison used the door knocker. It was a few seconds before any-one answered. It was Laura Foster herself who ushered them in.

Hank thought the house awfully quiet for a gathering of any size.

"Everyone is out back." She led them past the staircase and down a long central hall. They walked beyond the communal dining room where she served guests their meals, then out onto a covered veranda that bordered the entire house.

The first thing Hank noticed was that the back-yard and carriage house drive was filled with people. This was no *small* gathering, as Harrison had made it out to be.

Inwardly, Hank groaned when he imagined making small talk with half the town. Trestle tables covered with fancy linens and place set-tings were set up beneath canvas awnings that provided shade from the relentless sun.

As soon as Laura opened the back door, everyone in the yard fell silent. Harrison followed her across the porch, and then Hank stepped out-side. He paused at the edge of the porch, cane in hand, and was contemplating how to negotiate the steps when someone started singing, "For He's A Jolly Good Fellow," and everyone fol-lowed suit.

It was a second or two before Hank realized he was the object of attention. Momentarily stunned, he scanned the crowd. Hattie, Joe,

Rebekah and the children were there. Timothy and Mary Margaret Cutter, too. The Reverend McCormick was front and center. At a table on the other side of the yard sat Charity. The McCormick children suddenly appeared from beneath one of the tables, paused for a second to stare before they dashed off toward the outhouse at the back of the property. Familiar faces of ranchers and merchants, townsfolk and home-steaders made up the crowd.

Everyone he knew was there.

Everyone but Amelia.

Laura Foster was waiting for him at the bottom of the porch steps looking as pleased as punch.

"What's going on?" he asked her.

Harrison made certain Hank cleared the steps without mishap.

"Aren't they here yet?" Harrison whispered to Laura.

Her gaze flitted over the crowd. "They're sorting things out in the carriage house."

"Excuse me," Hank tried again. "What is all this?"

"Let's get you seated before you fall down." She took Hank by the arm and led him over to a chair at a nearby table. Brand was already there.

"Anything I can do to help?" the preacher asked her.

Hank couldn't help but notice the way McCormick smiled at the comely widow.

He's smitten. Hank silently wished his friend better luck in love than his own.

"Would you mind bringing Mr. Larson a glass of lemonade, Reverend?" Laura blushed a lovely shade of peach. She looked more than relieved when Brand hurried away to do her bidding.

"Are you comfortable?" she asked Hank.

"I would be if I knew what was going on."

"Folks wanted to express their appreciation for you risking your life to rid Glory of the Perkins Gang and for taking on a job you never wanted in the first place."

"I didn't—" He was embarrassed beyond measure. "I don't deserve—"

She cut him off with a wave of her hand and leaned close enough so that only he could hear. "Don't be modest, Mr. Larson. Folks need a hero as much as they need to feel useful and generous. Don't take that away from them."

He certainly wasn't hero material, he knew that much, but Laura's plea kept him from protesting. He suddenly realized that any public salute for his taking on the Perkins Gang explained perfectly well why Amelia wasn't present.

Just then, Brand returned with a tall glass of lemonade and handed it to him.

"They're ready," the minister told Laura.

She nodded, beaming with excitement. She clapped her hands until she had everyone's attention.

"Everybody take a seat. Gents, let the ladies and children sit first. Anyone who doesn't find a place at a table can sit on the benches around the edges of the crowd. First things first, I'm going to turn things over to Reverend McCormick."

Laura was as poised at addressing the crowd as anyone Hank had ever seen. Her voice was well modulated and carried a sense of command. There was nothing shy or retiring about her and, indeed, with her fair skin and curly blond hair, her angelic beauty was unheralded.

Brand stepped up to take over. "I'll make this short and sweet. After all, it's not one of my sermons."

Laughter rippled through the crowd and everyone quickly settled down.

Brand turned to Hank.

"Hank Larson is a man of few words in life, but many words on paper. He stepped into a job he didn't want and he's done it as well as anyone here could ask. He set aside his own needs and wants and put himself in harm's way more than once while doing his duty. He's a living example of what folks should strive to be—an everyday man who goes a step further than he has to for the benefit of all. He's proved to be more than an asset to this community. He's proved to be a good friend.

"The cornerstone of our community is the faith we have in God, in each other, and in this land we've all come to love. But our faith is often tested in life, and Hank here has proved he can stand up to the test."

Hank was already so stunned that he didn't really comprehend what the minister was leading to when Brand said, "Hank, we owe you our thanks. We tried to come up with a way to show our gratitude that we hope will help the most."

Before Hank could even begin to thank Brand for his kind words, to thank everyone for gathering in celebration, there was a commotion near the carriage house that drew his gaze as well as everyone else's.

The carriage house's double doors opened wide enough for Amelia to step out into the sunlight. When he saw her, everyone around them faded away.

She was wearing her pink and yellow calico gown. Her hair was unbound, but flowing free around her shoulders. The simple style allowed her natural curl to spring to life. The sun picked up rust highlights and set them ablaze.

The minute Amelia stepped out into the sunlight, her eyes met his. Her gaze never wavered as she crossed the yard.

It wasn't until she drew near that he noticed she held what appeared to be a folded newspaper and then he noticed Ricardo trailing behind her. The youth was toting a tall stack of papers that he began to distribute to the guests.

"For you." Amelia handed him the pages.

"What's this?" He couldn't quite believe what he saw.

"It's the latest edition of the *Glory Gazette*."

He stared at the banner, then into her eyes. They were bright with excitement.

"How?"

"Everyone helped."

"Look it over," Reverend McCormick encouraged. Hank had forgotten Brand was still standing nearby. He'd forgotten everything and everyone but Amelia. Now he was holding his newspaper in his hands and he'd had nothing to do with publishing this "Special Commemorative Edition" of the *Gazette*.

"Sit beside me," he urged, relieved when she slipped into the empty chair next to him without protest. Brand, Laura and Harrison took their own seats at the head table. A glance around the crowded tables assured Hank that for the time being he was not the center of attention. Everyone was content scanning the pages of the newly printed *Gazette*. Some were reading aloud.

"Where did all these stories come from?" Hank scanned the headlines. Many brought a smile to his face, others elicited outright laughter.

Farley Temple Grows Texas's Biggest Turnip

Bankers to Celebrate 50 Years of Marriage

Church Sewing Circle to Auction Quilt

New Line of Seed at the Mercantile

Little Mellie Ellenberg Rolls Over

Charlie Scout's "Necklace of Gold Teeth"

Some stories were short, others quite lengthy.

"We held a contest," Amelia explained. "Harrison and Brand helped put the word out that anyone could enter. They dropped their entries off at the mercantile. Then Laura, Brand and I chose the ones we thought would be the most interesting. There were so many that we couldn't put them all in this edition and have it ready by today, so we saved them and thought you could use some for the next issue."

His gaze kept drifting back to Charlie Scout's "Necklace of Gold Teeth" and wondered if the story went into any detail about where those gold fillings might have originated.

Page two was mostly filled with recipes submitted by readers—something he'd never thought of doing, but he liked the idea. There were recipes for everything from dumplings to squirrel pie and one for liver pudding.

Amelia was reading over his shoulder. "There was a real dustup at the mercantile when the recipes were handed in. Some of the men proclaimed their wives' entries were the best and deserve to be printed first."

Hank chuckled.

"You should have been there," Harrison added, rolling his eyes. "It wasn't funny. I feared for my life."

Knowing he didn't have to continually search for Amelia among the crowd, Hank relaxed and studied the paper. The stories were humorous, touching and unique. He was moved by the effort everyone had put into them.

It wasn't until he turned to what usually amounted to one small page of advertisements and a lot of filler that he was truly astounded by everyone's generosity.

There were not only the usual business ads from his original sponsors, Laura Foster, Mick and the Cutters, but nearly everyone in Glory and the immediate outlying area had paid for a small advertisement or an announcement of some kind.

There were birthday and anniversary congratulations, birth announcements, commemorative memorials and lost and found notices. Others had bought two lines of copy simply to wish him a speedy recovery and salute the *Gazette*.

Hank wanted to read every line of every page, but there would be time for that later. He carefully folded the paper. When he gazed around at the gathering, his vision wavered and he had to duck his head to compose himself.

"Are you all right?" Amelia was so close her breath was a warm hush against his ear. "If you're feeling poorly, I'll have Harrison take you home. The worst thing you can do is wear yourself out."

He succeeded in blinking his vision clear before he turned to her.

"Thank you," he said softly, indicating the paper in his hand. "Thank you for this. For saving my life, too."

"The good Lord saved your life, Hank. I just patched you up."

A stray breeze came across the land, ruffled the pages, teased her curls.

"How did you do it all?"

She shrugged as if it was nothing and yet it was everything.

He thought of all the people who had sought her out for medical care lately. He'd watched her measure out powders and potions, patch up cuts, race off with her medical bag in tow whenever a harried caller came by begging for help.

"*When* did you do this?" he wondered aloud.

"I read the entries at night. After you were asleep. I had lots of help. No one wanted to see the *Gazette* fail—"

He recalled discussing his financial woes with Brand during one of his visits—but he never intended for the whole town to find out he didn't have the funds to go on.

Now he knew how and when this latest issue of the *Gazette* came about, or at least he thought he did, but he still wanted to hear from Amelia why she had taken it upon herself to help him.

His heart stumbled. He couldn't keep himself

from reaching out, cupping her cheek. He stopped short of rubbing his thumb across her lips.

"*Why,* Amelia?" He dropped his hand to where hers lay knotted together in her lap. He covered them with his own. "Why did you do all of this?"

"No one wanted you to leave Glory," she said softly.

"*Why,* Amelia?"

"Because they like having you around."

"That's not what I meant and I think you know it."

She dropped her gaze and whispered, "Ask me again, Hank."

"Why did you do this?"

She closed her eyes. "Not that. Ask me to *marry you* again."

He leaned close enough to kiss her. Her eyes flew open and he suddenly remembered he'd already kissed her in front of the whole town once. That hadn't stopped him the day he rode off with a posse, but today she might be handing over her heart into his safekeeping. He wouldn't embarrass her again for anything.

"Will you marry me, Amelia? Will you be my wife?" he whispered.

Her smile grew wide and bright as the clear Texas sky.

"How about today?" He thought it a grand idea. "Everyone we know is here. There's a preacher sitting right next to you." Hank squeezed her hands and then turned to their friends and neighbors gathered around. It wasn't until that very moment he realized all eyes had been watching them. Not only that, but everyone within hearing distance had been hanging on every word.

Brand McCormick jumped to his feet. "I couldn't help but overhear you two. I think last-minute nuptials can certainly be arranged, Hank." He turned to Laura. "Mrs. Foster, do you have a Bible in the house?"

Timothy Cutter, seated nearby, bellowed to his wife, "Why did he jump up like that? Did he say he saw a mouse?"

Mary Margaret yelled back, "Not a mouse. He wants to know if there's a Bible in the house! They're finally getting hitched."

Laura Foster was suddenly on her feet, too. "Hold it right there, all of you!"

Hank glanced at Amelia, captivated by the astonishment on her face. He followed her gaze and couldn't help but notice the way the lovely widow held the preacher's undivided attention before Laura turned to Hank.

"Hank Larson, this is *your* surprise party—not Miss Hawthorne's wedding day. She deserves a celebration worthy of her and I for one intend to see that she gets it."

"But—" Hank began to protest.

Amelia did, too. "I don't want—"

Laura cut them both off. "I don't care *what*

either of you wants. One more week. That's how long it took us to pull off a newspaper edition, so I can certainly organize a *very* sumptuous wedding in a week." That said, she drew a lace-edged hankie from her bodice and patted her perfectly smooth brow before she turned to Brand.

"I'm sure you agree, *don't* you, Reverend McCormick?" Laura prodded.

Hank was astounded when she winked at the man. For the first time since Hank met Brand McCormick, the preacher was rendered speechless.

Chapter Twenty-Nine

A week later, Amelia moved through her wedding day as if in a dream.

True to her word, Laura took charge of everything—from Amelia's gown—one of her own designs that she had made up for Amelia as a gift—to the luncheon to be held in the boarding-house dining room—to the guest list.

When Amelia asked Laura to stand up for her, the always composed, confident woman had burst into tears and claimed it would be her great honor. Now, closeted upstairs in Laura's sumptuous private quarters, Amelia couldn't help but stare at her own reflection in the mirror as Laura fussed with the ribbons and flowers she'd woven in Amelia's hair.

"Absolutely perfect," Laura declared as she stepped back and surveyed her handiwork. "Even if I do say so myself."

The peach-striped silk gown was a confection of bound ruffles, cuffs and trim. A low-placed bustle cascaded into a train held in place with stiff bows of a darker peach. Fanciful puffed sleeves showed Amelia's bare arms. She wasn't certain she could even take a step in the low-heeled silk slippers Laura insisted *must* be worn with the gown.

"I really don't know what to say." Amelia's eyes filled with tears as she smiled at Laura. "You've been so gracious, so generous."

"My pleasure, believe me. I haven't had this much fun in a long, long while. Just say thank-you and try not to trip on the stairs." Laura motioned for her to turn. "I'll make sure that train stays behind you. We'd better get downstairs or they'll start without us."

Laughter bubbled up inside Amelia and escaped. She'd found herself growing more and more lighthearted all week and relished the joy that spread through her.

"Are you ready?" Laura paused with her hand on the doorknob.

"More than." Amelia nodded. She took a step

and then suddenly stopped. "Did you give my gift for Hank to Harrison?"

"Oh, my word! I did give it to him, but I forgot to give you the box he gave to me."

She rushed over to her vanity, frantically moved crystal bottles of toilet water and perfume. Jewelry rattled as she shoved it out of the way. "Here it is." She hurried back to Amelia and handed her a long, midnight-blue box. "From Hank to you."

Amelia took the box. "What has he done?"

She knew that the *Gazette* was no longer threatened, but it would be a long hard road back and he was scraping to get by.

"Open it," Laura urged.

Amelia slowly lifted the lid to reveal a lovely strand of pearls.

"They're stunning," Laura cried. Then she said, "Look, there's a note tucked into the lid."

"Can you take them out? My hands are shaking." Amelia handed her the box and Laura removed the small piece of paper carefully folded and tucked into the lid before she lifted out the pearls.

Amelia opened the note and recognized Hank's handwriting.

My darling Amelia,

These were my grandmother's. Now they are yours.

She carefully refolded the note and tucked it

into her bodice. Laura slipped the pearls around her throat and fastened them. Amelia turned to the mirror once more and traced the ivory pearls with her fingertips. Cool when Laura first put them on her, they were warming to her skin.

Thank You, Lord. For this day. For this love that You have brought me.

Laura was waiting by the door. "Time to go, Amelia."

Amelia took a deep breath, lifted the hem of her wedding gown and started the journey downstairs to her groom.

Hank was pleased that Amelia had insisted on a short guest list and that Laura agreed.

Brand McCormick, Bible in hand, waited beside the bay window ready to officiate. Charity, along with Hattie, Joe and Rebekah Ellenberg were all in attendance, as was Harrison Barker, who would stand up for Hank.

The two of them were fidgeting nervously near Brand when Amelia appeared in the open doorway. A hush fell as one and then another and another guest noticed her.

Hank's breath caught in his throat the moment he saw her. She was a vision in silk the color of a soft new sunset. When he saw his grandmother's pearls around her throat, he was thrilled that he had something of value to give her—something other than his heart. She was more precious than any gem. She deserved to be pampered and protected and he intended to love and watch over her for as long as he lived.

He couldn't tear his eyes away as she hesitated in the doorway. He watched her hand go to her throat and her fingers toy with the pearls as she smiled just for him.

Harrison had presented him with a small packet from Amelia just before he was to take his place before the preacher. He pushed back his new black suit coat, reached for the vest pocket beneath to make certain she noticed the gold watch fob and chain dangling from his pocket. He slipped her father's gold watch out far enough for her to see.

Amelia was not only willing to give him her hand in marriage, her heart and her love, but her most valuable worldly possession.

As they stared into each other's eyes, time stopped for both of them.

But not for everyone else. Laura gave Amelia the slightest nudge and Amelia crossed the room. Hank noted there wasn't a dry eye in the house as she took his hand and joined him before Brand.

Laura took her place at Amelia's side. Hank assumed Harrison was still next to him. He only had eyes for Amelia.

Brand opened the Bible, but didn't look away from them as he began the ceremony.

"We are gathered here today to join this man and this woman in the holy bonds of matrimony. Personally, I don't know when I've been happier to officiate at a wedding. If anyone deserves happiness, it's Hank and Amelia. They deserve the love they have found in each other for they have, from the very day they met, been tested. Now they stand before the Lord and this circle of friends to make their vows to one another.

"Hank, not long ago I swore you in as sheriff of Glory. The Bible says, 'If a man vow a vow unto the Lord, or swear an oath to bind his soul with a bond; he shall not break his word, he shall do according to all that proceedeth out of his mouth.' Hank kept that vow, though it brought him trials and tribulation. Though it nearly killed him. I have no doubt that he will keep the vows he makes today and they will bring him nothing but joy."

Brand looked at Amelia.

"Amelia, the path you have walked since the day you met Hank has not been easy. The Bible tells us, 'The Lord will not cast off forever: But though He cause grief, yet will He have compassion according to the multitude of His mercies. He does not afflict willingly nor grieve the children of men.'

"The Lord has brought you grief, but He has brought you great joy, as well. He has taken away and He has given. He has brought you love and He has given you the strength to renew your faith. There is a time for sorrow and a time to laugh. Today is a day of great joy. And now, Amelia and Hank, it's time to speak your vows."

Hank repeated his without hesitation.

Amelia's words came out in the barest of whispers, but her eyes shone with love and happiness as she looked up at Hank and said, "I do."

The reverend pronounced them man and wife.

"Congratulations to you both," Brand said. "Hank, you may kiss your bride."

Hank took him at his word, drew Amelia into his arms and kissed her.

And kissed her.

He kissed her until Brand finally cleared his throat and then tapped Hank on the shoulder.

"Better save some of that for the honeymoon," the pastor advised.

Joe Ellenberg hooted and clapped.

Amelia covered her flushed cheeks with her hands and closed her eyes. Hank pulled her close and whispered in her ear.

"I vowed to love, honor, cherish and obey. I did not promise *not* to kiss you in public."

Amelia's cheeks caught fire as she gazed around the room at all the friends she loved so dearly and who loved her in return. When she looked into Hank's eyes again, she was smiling.

"All right, everybody." Laura clapped her hands. "Let's give the lovebirds a minute alone, shall we? There's a spread waiting to be served in the dining room."

Hank slipped his arm around Amelia's shoulder and turned to Reverend McCormick to thank him for his kind words and a wonderful ceremony. He caught Brand staring after the lovely Mrs. Foster as she shooed everyone out.

"I think the pastor might be sweet on Laura," Hank whispered in Amelia's ear.

She laughed and leaned closer. "And perhaps vice versa?"

"Now that would be interesting." Hank gazed around a room teeming with expertly crafted furnishings, silver candelabra, gilt-framed paintings, cut-crystal vases, cabbage rose wallpaper, velvet curtains and porcelain figurines. "Can you imagine Sam and Janie running loose in here?"

"Oh, poor Laura."

As soon as everyone cleared the room, Amelia surrendered to Hank's embrace.

"We're alone now," she whispered.

"Why, Mrs. Larson, how kind of you to point that out—although I'd already noticed."

As Hank lowered his head to kiss her again, Amelia couldn't help but smile even as she held him off with both hands.

"I really think we should discuss kissing in public when we get home," she said.

"Practice makes perfect." He kissed her long and thoroughly. When he raised his head again, he said, "I'm so thankful I found you, Amelia."

"Brand was right when he said the path we've walked together has been hard, but we can never forget, it's the Lord who brought us to each other. My faith was tried, yours was found, but we're still together and we have our love. We owe Him our thanks."

"We'll be thanking Him together daily, Amelia, for the blessing of our love and all the good yet to come."

"Amen," she said softly, still not fully believing that they would be returning to her house together, that she would no longer be living there alone, but sharing all the hours of her life with this man she'd vowed to love, honor and obey. This man she cherished.

Just when she thought he was going to take her hand and lead her into the dining room, Hank drew her into his arms. His warm breath teased her ear and sent a chill down her spine when he whispered, "Get ready, wife. I'm about to kiss you again."

QUESTIONS FOR DISCUSSION

1. When Amelia avoided telling Hank that she might have seen a second robber outside the bank, was her evasion of the truth the same as a lie? Have you ever kept silent just to avoid telling a lie? Was your silence as hurtful to someone as lying?

2. Dr. Esra Hawthorne devoted four years to treating the wounded on both sides during the War Between the States. Do you think Evan would have grown up any differently had Esra provided a stable home life for his children rather than moving them from one battlefield hospital to another?

3. The townsfolk more or less talked Hank into becoming sheriff. Have you ever been talked into a position you later regretted? Looking back, how could you have avoided the situation? Did it turn out for the better or worse?

4. Was Amelia right to go to Brand with her suspicions about Lemuel? Was she right to wait for proof, or did her hesitance put Fanny at greater risk? What do you think you would do in the same circumstance?

5. Hank vowed to uphold the law. He also made a promise to Amelia to help her brother. Have you ever made a promise that you couldn't keep? How did you feel when you let someone down?

6. When her spirit was broken, Amelia remembered Sophronia's words and refused to "believe in a God who doesn't play fair." How can we be certain that God does "play fair"? How do you hold on to your faith when all appears lost?

7. In what ways were Hattie and Amelia alike? Even though Hattie suffered great loss and hardship, her faith never faltered. Why not?

8. Amelia told Hank that she knew the Bible inside and out, which should have made her faith that much easier to hold on to. Do you agree? Does knowing the Bible inside and out prove one's faith is steadfast?

9. Brand advised Hank to open his heart and let God in. Do you think that finding one's faith is that simple? Why or why not?

10. Given what Hank had to do, if you were Amelia, could you have found it in your heart to forgive him? Could you forgive him enough to marry him?